PRAISE FOR

my keen knife

"A bloody and dark retelling of *Macbeth* with an unforgettable heroine, *My Keen Knife* is a tightly plotted debut that will make you laugh, make you cry, make you scream, and make you demand the second book immediately. Lady Adelina is the villainous heroine of my dreams."

—**KAMILAH COLE**, Lodestar Award finalist and best-selling author of the Divine Traitors duology

"Davis serves revenge dressed in gorgeous prose and rich world-building. *My Keen Knife* is the definition of supporting women's wrongs, and it's so beautiful you won't mind the blood it leaves behind. A must-read for anyone who loves manipulative queens who will do anything to get what they want."

—**T. R. MOORE**, author of *The Gods Must Burn*

"If Adelina is wicked, then I want nothing to do with good. This riveting *Macbeth* retelling offers something to both bardolators and those less familiar with the source material. I was swept away by the lush Portugal-inspired setting, twisty plot, and morally-grey heroine who will steal your heart while holding a knife to your throat."

—**S. HATI**, author of *And the Sky Bled*

"A vividly written historical reckoning featuring a sharp cast of characters that interrogates the macabre and sublime all at once."

—**YEJIN SUH**, author of *The Last Soldier of Nava*

"Wickedly good and as sharp as a blade, Davis's prose cuts through Shakespeare's original text and creates something wholly new and devilishly divine. Legacy, betrayal, and an undying desire to fulfill one's destiny culminate to form a unique retelling of a beloved and bloody classic. *My Keen Knife* will slice through the deepest parts of your soul and ask the ultimate question: Are we human or are we monster?"

—**TEAGAN OLIVIA KING**, author of
Spit Back the Bones and *Bitterbloom*

"*My Keen Knife* is an addictive, fast-paced read with treacherous twists and turns. Adelina is a delightfully conniving heroine, who manipulates everyone expertly, including the reader. Lovers of fantasy will devour the rich and darkly magical setting."

—**R. A. BASU**, author of *To Bargain with Mortals*

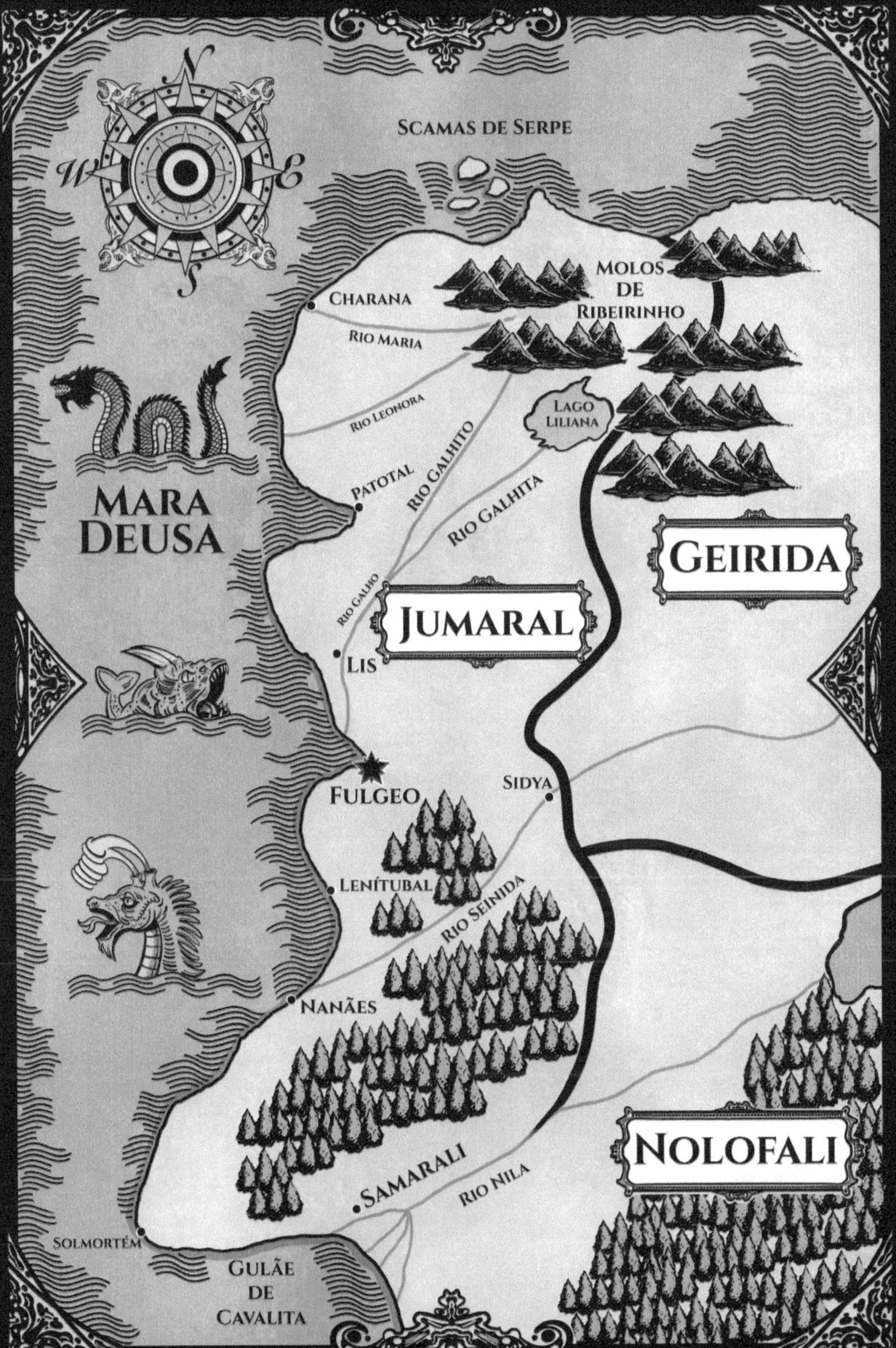
N
W
E
S
SCAMAS DE SERPE
MOLOS
DE
RIBEIRINHO
CHARANA
RIO MARIA
RIO LEONORA
LAGO
LILIANA
MARA
DEUSA
PATOTAL
RIO GALHITO
RIO GALHITA
GEIRIDA
RIO GALHO
JUMARAL
LIS
FULGEO
SIDYA
LENÍTUBAL
RIO SEINIDA
NANÃES
NOLOFALI
SAMARALI
RIO NILA
SOLMORTÉM
GULÃE
DE
CAVALITA

my keen knife

Ana Davis

KEYLIGHT
BOOKS
AN IMPRINT
OF TURNER
PUBLISHING

KEYLIGHT BOOKS
AN IMPRINT OF TURNER PUBLISHING COMPANY
Nashville, Tennessee
www.turnerpublishing.com

My Keen Knife

Cover design by M. S. Corley
Book design by Ashlyn Inman

Library of Congress Cataloging-in-Publication Data
Names: Davis, Ana, 2002- author | Shakespeare, William, 1564-1616. Macbeth
Title: My keen knife / by Ana Davis.
Description: First edition. | Nashville: Keylight Books, 2025. | Audience term: Teenagers | Audience: Ages 12-15 | Audience: Grades 7-9
Identifiers: LCCN 2024059289 (print) | LCCN 2024059290 (ebook) |
ISBN 9798887980874 hardcover | ISBN 9798887980881 paperback | ISBN 9798887980898 epub
Subjects: CYAC: Prophecies—Fiction | Fate and fatalism—Fiction | Kings, queens, rulers, etc.—Fiction | Fantasy | LCGFT: Fantasy fiction | Novels
Classification: LCC PZ7.1.D3535 My 2025 (print) | LCC PZ7.1.D3535 (ebook)
LC record available at https://lccn.loc.gov/2024059289
LC ebook record available at https://lccn.loc.gov/2024059290

Printed in the United States of America

Para os meus pais—
lembrem-se que isto é uma obra de ficção <3

For my parents—
remember this is a work of fiction <3

Come, thick night,
And pall thee in the dunnest smoke of hell,
That my keen knife see not the wound it makes,
Nor heaven peep through the blanket of the dark,
To cry "Hold, hold!"

—William Shakespeare, *Macbeth*, Act I Scene V

ACT I:

SO FOUL AND
FAIR A DAY

CHAPTER 1

ADELINA

Lady Adelina Maria Malves Ducança of Lis did not consider herself to be a murderous person, but she was a rational one. It was for this very reason she had hidden a dagger in the folds of her dressing gown before creeping down the empty corridors of the Manor of Lis.

The moon outside was bright, and the stars shone like pinpricks. They cast odd shadows across the tableaus of old white and blue tiles set into the walls, each portraying a different scene from the goddess Ostrea's defeat of the sea demons.

May Our Lady accept me, Adelina silently prayed.

She averted her eyes from the iconography, only to jump at her own reflection in a dark window. Her dressing gown, with its glowing white silk, made her appear like a ghost haunting the halls.

For a moment, Adelina paused, staring at the glassy reflection of herself and hoping a different specter might show itself.

Simão? she thought. *Mano?* It was what she had called him when she was little—they were *mano* and *mana*, brother and sister.

But her brother remained a vacant presence existing only in her own mind.

There was an idea in ethical philosophy she had learned in one of those long sessions tucked away from the world, with nothing but a tutor and her books: *A rational being acts in pursuit of their goals.* If the goal was to become a dancer, a rational being practiced dance. If the goal was to write epic poetry, they picked up a pen.

If the goal was to be queen, they learned the proper way to wield a knife.

Adelina tightened her grip on the dagger and pressed onward.

This was the only way to save her own life, to avoid Ostrea striking her down, like She had done to Simão.

Adelina pressed herself against a wall painted with red roses and breathed deeply. She willed her mind to ignore the memory of blood mingling with seawater, of death mingling with earth. Her grip on the dagger tightened against the ghostly sting of her palm, now healed, which she had slashed open on a rock when she had fallen earlier that night.

It was Simão's fault they had been at that wretched beach in the first place. He had been acting odd for weeks, running around the city with his personal servant, like he was searching for something. There were a few times she had watched him from her window, pacing around the outer walls of the Castle of Lis beside their manor house for hours. He had refused to tell Adelina anything, no matter how much she had questioned and bargained.

That is, until tonight, when he had brought her to the beach to finally divulge whatever secrets he had been keeping.

But Adelina never learned her brother's secrets.

He had lost his evidence. Simão had stood there, searching his pockets with wild eyes, fear lacing every word when he had asked her, *Did you see it fall? The medallion? With Santa Belinha and the wyvern? Did you see it?*

Then, before he could tell her why it was so important, they were interrupted by the witches uttering their foul prophecy. It was what Adelina had never wanted to hear—the fate Ostrea had set for her, defiled by Adelina's own knowledge of it.

All hail, Malves, that shall wear crowns hereafter!

The three witches on the beach had appeared from the waves themselves, and Simão had only just called out to deny the prophecy, pushing Adelina behind him, when he had gone still. Far too still.

Adelina had reached out for him, her own mind spinning with horror at the witches' words. She was wishing she had never heard them at all when he crumpled to the ground. Adelina had half caught him, and they both fell. Black blood already poured from his every orifice—eyes, nose, mouth, ears—all sticky and hot under her frantic touch while she tried to hold him together. Simão had gurgled out his final words: *Not here....*

Adelina had screamed for the witches, for Ostrea's mercy, for anyone to help, but the three women remained inscrutable beneath their hoods. Her panicked mind scrambled while she had sat gasping on that beach, covered in her brother's blood and with his stiffening body splayed out across her lap. Then she had understood.

By denying the prophecy, Simão had denied Ostrea and the fate She had created for him. The goddess had struck him down. If Adelina did nothing, she could be next.

"What do I do?" she had screamed—once again addressing anyone who would listen. "Please, Ostrea, I do not deny you! Please!" Her desperation had transformed into fury as another question went unanswered. She clutched her brother's body against her chest and raged at the witches. "How could you? How—"

"Seek your fate," said a witch.

"Fight for it as a fish struggles from its net," added another.

"Embrace the sacrifice of a scale or a fin along the way," said the third.

"Or face damnation," they spoke together.

And then they had gone, as quickly as they had come. By wind or wave, Adelina had no idea.

Adelina had screamed again, cursing. She had tried not to look at her brother's still face, at his black eyes and stained skin. Adelina wiped her hands on her dress, desperately wishing the blood to be washed from her palms. She had closed her eyes, willing herself to focus. Everything in her, everything she had ever been taught, told her to never listen to a witch.

But while she had racked her mind for what to do—shuddering as story after story of terrible deaths resulting from a prophecy's curse flashed across her vision, including her own ancestors in the

Second Great Wave—she realized the witches were right. People died from denying their prophecies, denying the fates Ostrea created for them.

So, all Adelina needed to do was the opposite: fight tooth and nail for her fate.

It hadn't been the first time Adelina had pictured herself as queen, sitting on her uncle's throne, having the power to save her failing country.

Simão had made the mistake of denying such a fate.

But Adelina was not cowardly or weak.

She was rational.

All hail, Malves, that shall wear crowns hereafter!

Now that Simão was dead, Adelina was the last Malves. Ostrea meant her to be Queen of Jumaral, and Adelina was prepared to honor the goddess by fighting for it through whatever means necessary.

The witches would not win.

Adelina pushed herself off the wall in the hallway leading to her parents' bedroom, swallowing her dread. Now that her brother was gone, there were three people she would have to dispose of to honor her fate: her uncle, Dom Aristides, King of Jumaral; her cousin, Crown Prince Calixto; and her father, Infante Benigno, Duke of Lis.

Her parents' bedroom was at the end of a long corridor. The door's brass handle glinted in the silver light of the moon.

I can do this, she told herself. The accelerating beat of her heart spurred her forward. *I can because I have to.*

Her fingers closed around the cold metal of the handle. She took a shaky breath.

I can because I will.

The door creaked on its hinges, and Adelina slipped inside. She froze, dagger behind her back, when the shape of her mother stirred at the noise.

A few moments later, the duchess of Lis was back to a fitful sleep. Adelina closed the door behind her, letting it click quietly with the turning of the lock.

The room was bright, much too bright.

The duke liked to go to bed early and wake up with the sunrise, so the curtains were almost always opened by the duchess when she came to join her husband at night. The moonlight clearly illuminated each piece of velvet furniture and the small statues adorning the mantle over the empty fireplace—Our Lady Ostrea and Her many saints. Hanging over the bed was a large wooden carving of Ostrea summoning the First Great Wave, which had drowned the coastal cities hundreds of years ago. The golden body of the goddess glowed in the light.

Stars, Adelina wished, *hide your fires.*

But Adelina could make out every breath her parents took, each one nearing the last, deep and steady, without the knowledge that their son's corpse was currently floating in the Rio Galho. She thought of their last dinner together just hours earlier.

They had spoken about Simão's upcoming twentieth birthday, the friends he would be inviting from his travels abroad. The dinner had ended with their father laughing so hard he almost choked on the spindly bones of his cod. Their mother had clapped him on the back while Simão and Adelina cackled into their own fish, which the cook had—as usual—made far too salty.

Adelina shuddered and looked at her parents' sleeping forms. Darkness gathered at the edges, as though the night had descended into her mind.

She made herself creep closer.

I don't want to see! her mind screamed. Something told her that if she looked upon her father's face before she plunged the dagger into his heart, she wouldn't be able to commit the act, much less move on to her mother. She wasn't even sure if she had to kill her mother, but leaving her alive seemed a sure way to get caught.

And there would be one less person to challenge Adelina for the crown.

It was the only way to achieve Adelina's fate. For Ostrea.

It was better to get rid of her mother.

That was the rational thing to do.

The moonlight fell directly on her father's face, and all Adelina could hear was his voice. "Sweet dreams, my *couraninha.*"

My heart.

Each pinprick of starlight illuminated the hand slowly emerging from behind her back. Her racing heartbeat echoed one thought: *I will be queen. Or I will be killed.*

She raised the dagger in front of her, grasping the handle with two hands to keep it from shaking. The light glinted off the blade and shone on the eyes of Ostrea.

Our Lady, Adelina prayed, staring down at her father's calm face. *Deem me worthy.*

It was necessary.

It was right.

She choked down another sob.

It was wicked, but it had to be done.

Then something caught her eye.

A tiny glint of gold shone in the reflection of her dagger's blade, and Adelina's attention drifted toward it.

A small coin hidden beneath a pile of her father's papers winked from the bedside table. She lowered the dagger to her side and lifted the coin to her eye. It was attached to a chain and held the face of a saint imprinted in the metal. It was the soft outline of Santa Belinha. Tiny roses curled around the edges of the neat circle, and thorns reached out to connect it to a larger circlet. The other side had the coiled form of a wyvern.

Adelina's breath, moments ago wild and unsettled, suddenly stilled.

She gazed again at the sleeping forms of her parents and frowned. They looked so innocent, so devoid of the authority that graced them as the closest living relatives of the king of Jumaral.

But they had this medallion.

Her brother's *lost* medallion.

She remembered his paranoia when he realized the medallion was gone—the panic that had overtaken him even before the witches had arrived with their sacrilegious curse. He had collapsed after denying the prophecy.

But there must have been a reason he had denied it, a purpose behind rejecting the power Ostrea had envisioned for a Malves child.

Adelina willed her mind to focus, to work this out like she would solve a mathematics equation or break down a linguistic puzzle.

She remembered his panic, his insistence they speak away from the manor, away from their family. The medallion had been his evidence, the source of whatever doubts he held, and now here it was. Effectively, the murder weapon. In her parents' bedroom.

Adelina stared at her parents. All thoughts of over-salted codfish and laughter were overshadowed by the lessons they had taught her, the logic that had kept the House of Ducança reigning over Jumaral for hundreds of years: *Ostrea requires loyalty. Without Ostrea, there is no House of Ducança. Without us, there is no Jumaral.*

Adelina returned the necklace to where it had been tucked away amidst her father's papers, slipped the dagger into the folds of her dressing gown, and quietly let herself out of the room. She marched back down the corridors, past the tile portraits and the rosy wallpaper, grateful for the moonlight. Her vision filled with new plans.

Once again, she dared to envision her fate coming to fruition: the crown on her head, her future as the head of the country and not just a frilly figurehead on the sidelines, the power she would hold...

Adelina didn't yet understand what had happened to Simão or why he had rejected that future for himself, but fighting for her fate would reveal it to her. She would make sure of it.

The first step would be to determine what secrets Simão had wanted to share that night. She would discover the importance of the medallion and unearth what had been deemed so dangerous for Jumaral if Simão were ever to speak it out loud. Adelina would uncover the roles of her parents and the rest of her family and then find a way to get rid of them when the time was right.

And, through it all, Adelina would make herself a queen.

CHAPTER 2

SEBA

One Week Later

Seba wished the club owner smelled nicer. It would be so much easier to scare the man out of his fortunes if Seba wasn't so focused on the stale stench of smoke, drink, and bodily discharge bringing unwelcome images floating from the depths of his memory.

He adjusted the cloth mask tied around his nose and mouth, praying to Her Ladyship the disguise might have a broader purpose than covering up some of his best features.

"Hey, Skipper," Jas snapped, drawing Seba back to the task at hand. Jas, sinister in his own mask and low hood, sat crouched in front of the drunken lump of Heitor Alves.

Alves was tied to the chair in front of his own desk, eyes wide and bloodshot. They flicked between Jas and Seba.

Seba's arm had dropped in his distraction. He raised the pistol so it was once again aimed straight at the quivering forehead of the club owner. Alves flinched, hands clenching and unclenching around the dark wooden armrests of the chair.

"It's not *Skipper*," Seba corrected through clenched teeth. "We agreed that I am *Captain*."

"Same thing."

"The details are in the connotation," Seba argued. "I'll just start calling you *the Bell*, then, shall I?"

"That's different. A knell is a specific type of bell. It announces death." Jas placed a gloved hand on Alves's arm, making the other man jerk as far away as he could within his binds. "And I am about to teach Senhor Alves here all about death."

Seba huffed, his arm already aching from being held up for so long. He would need to build some muscle if they were going to continue this kind of work. And—*by Our Lady*—how heavy would this thing be when the gun was loaded?

Seba adjusted his grip, silently willing Jas to speed things up. He didn't need his arm to hurt while he simultaneously fought off the grimy memories of childhood drifting around him. It was impossible to tell if he had been here before or if these types of places were all so similar that it didn't matter.

What he did know was that the safe was close, hidden behind a golden-framed painting of the cliffs of Solmortém. Seba itched to grab Alves by the lapels and push the barrel of the revolver against his head until the man turned the lock to all the right numbers and made cash spill from the wall. But Jas's strategy was better.

A conversation between the Knell and a bartender had led them straight into Alves's office to wait for him. Another word and that same bartender had gone home, or perhaps to a church—far away from anyone he could warn, giving Jas and Seba plenty of time to figure out the painting on hinges. Two words from beneath the hood of the Knell's cloak and a stumbling Alves, unsteady from a night of revelry, was all too glad to quietly take a seat in front of his own desk. The red-faced man had even steadied his arms long enough to be tied down.

And now he seemed just about to burst.

"I already told you that your sister isn't happy," Jas hissed in that low, skin-crawling voice, like something slimy that had crawled out of a pit.

"My sister...my sister is dead. You couldn't know what she... what she thinks," Alves protested.

Jas tilted his head, leaning forward so the cloak would brush the skin on Alves's bare hands. "I speak to the dead. They whisper things to me. Things that make them mad, things that fill them with vengeance. If I were sold off by my brother to pay his gambling debts, I'd be pretty mad. Wouldn't you?"

Alves said nothing. He stared into what he could see of Jas's face, as if looking for the trick.

"Ask me something," Jas said. "Something only she would know."

When Alves remained silent, Seba made a show of cocking the revolver. "Ask," he said, doing his best to channel all the intimidating energy he had. He suppressed a smile when Alves shuddered. Intimidating people didn't smile at their own intimidation.

"I...I was seventeen, and she was eight." The man's eyes roved anywhere but the gun. "I broke something...something of our mother's. I blamed it on her."

"A soup tureen," Jas said. "Hand-painted by your grandmother. Green with pink flowers."

The noise that came out of Alves might have been a sob. Seba adjusted his grip again, hoping whatever it was meant they were almost to the point of opening the safe. This smell was going to haunt his nightmares.

"Now you know I'm telling the truth," Jas continued, "and you know I have a special little connection to the ones who hate you most. So." He leaned both his hands on Alves's arms so their faces were less than a foot apart.

Seba could only imagine the ungodly odor emanating from that man's mouth. *May Our Lady bless Jasibin Guan and help his nose to heal from its trauma.*

"Why don't you tell me the code to your safe, and I can make sure they all stay where they're supposed to."

Alves took several deep breaths, and Seba cursed the man for every moment his arm was still in the air.

"If it's money you want, I can get you money. There's a coven of witches in the east hills outside of Lis. Rua da Vieira. Bounties have gone up since the marquis of Lis died. Lord Simão. They say a witch killed him. Fifteen hundred *rejas*, and there's talk of it rising. You'll get a good deal if you turn them in to the city guard."

Seba had seen the new wanted posters going up with the raised bounty, but he had only noted them as further proof that he, Jas, and their guardian, Hala, needed to get out of the city as soon as possible. The threat of bounty hunters had dogged Seba's existence since he had moved in with Jas and Hala when he was six years old. The draw of potential reward from becoming one of them had always been overshadowed by the risks of getting in between bounty hunters and their money—or worse, of getting discovered for illegal magic use themselves.

Besides, Jas had always been resistant to capturing witches for the crime of simply existing, which Seba couldn't necessarily argue with, even if he did have reservations about exactly what threat that existence could pose. There were stories of witches killing people with a snap of their fingers, cursing people by sharing prophecies of the future Ostrea had created for them. It was a world Seba and Jas hadn't been willing to get involved in.

But this was different.

This was a quiet way to obtain quick business and get out before anyone even knew to chase them. And Alves had said *coven*, hadn't he? So three, all worth 1500 *rejas*. It would certainly be a start to their funds and possibly set them up for future bounties. This could be their way out of Lis. Maybe out of Jumaral entirely.

"Knell," Seba said.

Jas stared hard at him before turning back to Alves. The bound man flinched. Jas was digging his gloved fingers into the man's arms.

"You try to shrug off the consequences of selling people by selling *more* people, Alves. What are you hiding in that safe? More than 4500 *rejas*? Something intimate?"

Alves shook his head, although it might have just been nervous twitching. Seba couldn't tell. His pulse was now thrumming from Jas's words.

"Not people," the man forced out. "Witches. Thieves of Ostrea's holy gifts. Their prophecies damn us, and their potions conjure evil forces."

"The code, Alves." Jas's next words were barely a whisper, though they sent chills down Seba's back. "Or I think your sister might very well like to see you again."

The man's mouth opened, but no sound came out.

"Louder."

"Twen...twenty-six, thirty-eight, t-ten."

Seba tucked the revolver into his jacket pocket and joined Jas at the chair, where they retied Alves's hands behind his back. He kept a hold of Alves, who was almost a head shorter than him, while Jas swung the Solmortém painting to the side. It revealed a sizable iron safe inlaid in the wall, a silver combination lock at its center.

Seba positioned Alves just behind Jas so he would be in the line of fire of any traps he might have set up. Jas raised a gloved hand and carefully spun the lock to each number.

The door opened, and Seba was blinded.

Thick, black, sulfurous smoke erupted from the safe, billowing over all of them. Seba instinctively lurched back to cover his face. His mind turned to the myriad alchemical explosions he had witnessed throughout childhood—all varying in toxicity and magic.

Alves grabbed at his arm, pulling him downward. They wrestled for a few moments in the darkness. Seba tried to retreat from the scene, protecting his nose with one hand, but the backs of his legs hit the edge of the desk. He tried to catch his balance. A sharp twist of his wrist took the gun from his hand.

"I'll shoot!" Alves yelled through the dissipating smoke. "Don't move."

Seba clutched his wrist, sure it would soon be adorned with a bracelet of bruises. *At least it wasn't the face*, he thought. *Always be thankful it's not the face.* He ducked under the desk as a precaution.

"Too late, Alves," came Jas's voice.

Seba could now make out the shadow of the cloak still standing by the safe above him.

"I'll shoot!" Alves said again.

Seba couldn't suppress the laugh coming out of him. "Then do it."

The figure of Alves became clearer. He was raising the gun in Jas's direction, a desperate edge to his rocking movements. Somehow, his wrists were unbound, which probably meant Seba needed to work on his knot-tying capabilities.

But Heitor Alves did not seem like he was going to shoot. His eyes were fixed on something Jas held in one hand—a small wooden box he must have removed from the safe.

Jas held it up so Alves could get a better look. "This is what you didn't want me to see? Your sister's telling me it's her jewelry. Were you going to sell that off too?"

"Put it back." Alves's voice shook with emotion, though his hand remained still.

"I'll make you a deal," Jas said. "Shoot me. If I die, you can have it back and know that all your sins are forgiven. If I live, well...then at least you know what's coming."

There was barely time for a breath before Alves pulled the trigger, the revolver's barrel aimed directly at Jas's heart. The click of an empty chamber echoed through the office. Alves glanced down at his hand then fired again. Again. Again. Each time, he found the chamber empty. The Knell remained standing, holding the damning evidence.

The man let out a desperate scream and threw the revolver to the side. Alves charged at Jas, and Seba stuck out a leg from his refuge. Alves hit the floor with a loud bang. He didn't get up, seeming to resign himself to whatever waited for him.

"Fate can be a funny thing, huh, Alves?" Seba emerged from his place under the table. "Best not to run from it."

Eagerly, Seba nudged past Jas to where the last wisps of smoke were drifting away, mixing with the rest of the room's stench. Inside the safe were a few documents and barely enough coins to pay for a cut of pig. The heading of one of the top documents caught his eye: "Notice of Asset Seizure."

Alves was broke. Something inside Seba that had been coiled up with hope loosened and fell away, all potential disappearing into a universe that never paid its debts. At least not to him.

Seba was yanked from his thoughts by a gasp from behind him. He whirled around, expecting guards, rifles, at least several grenades. All he found was Jas bent over in pain. The box fell to the ground with a clatter. The contents spilled just beside Alves's head. The man wailed.

"Knell?"

Jas didn't respond. It wasn't easy to tell with the mask and cloak, but he appeared to be staring at his hands. His breathing was hard, and he was trembling.

At their feet was a simple collection of rings and necklaces, many of them rusted and cloudy. Still, they might fetch a pretty price somewhere.

"A witch," Alves whispered hoarsely, his voice muffled by the floor. "That's what you are. And that's why you'll be punished in death when you meet Ostrea at the gates. Not me."

A bold statement coming from a man who uses alchemy to booby-trap his safes, thought Seba.

"You are mistaken," Jas replied. "Witches must knock to be admitted at the gates of death. I am welcomed home."

Then a bang sounded through the office, and this time, it was exactly what Seba had expected.

"Well, shit," he muttered when the office filled with bat-wielding thugs. He hoped there were no grenades.

CHAPTER 3

ADELINA

Adelina made herself cry during the funeral. It would have looked suspicious if she hadn't. But what she felt when she watched her brother's coffin paraded across the courtyard of the Cathedral of Lis, Jumaral's flag draped across the wood in loud red and blue behind a green wyvern, wasn't sadness.

She sat next to her father, whose arm was around her. He pulled her close, his grip viselike while he watched the procession of the late Lord Simão Luís Malves Ducança, Marquis of Lis. On his other side, Adelina's mother wailed, a grief so palpable it made the air difficult to breathe through. It was a terrible sound—one Adelina had never imagined coming from her normally stoic mother.

All the while, Adelina shook with rage.

If she was right about her parents' involvement in their son's death, then their tears and their cries and their desperation were all an act. A convincing act, but an evil one just the same.

She almost felt guilty when she joined them in their charade, forcing hot tears to pass down her cheeks, tasting salt on her trembling lips. But her act was different.

Our Lady Ostrea has a plan for me, and I'm fighting for both of us, Simão.

More cries echoed across the courtyard. A current of Signs of the Sea—the passing of the right hand from the left to the right shoulder—ran in parallel to Simão's coffin. The sobs drifted up, perhaps caught by the breeze and taken all the way to the ocean, where Ostrea would hear. Adelina wondered how Ostrea would judge her brother and whether the prayers to preserve his soul in the Beyond would be heeded.

The actual burial would take place later that evening. It would be a smaller ceremony, just Simão's immediate family, who would say goodbye to him as his body disappeared into the tomb, along with his secrets. Adelina didn't want to think about that moment, and she didn't have to. There was plenty to hold her focus in the present moment.

Adelina observed everyone in the courtyard with blurry eyes. Her attention caught on someone directly across from her. Many people were looking at Adelina and her family—among the mourners were several eager photographers and reporters who had made it their mission to capture the royals at their lowest—but this attention was different.

The high priestess of Lis, who had just minutes ago stepped down from the podium where she had eulogized Simão and led the prayer for his safe journey to Ostrea's judgment, stared at Adelina with curious eyes. A mild frown turned down the corners of her lips, less like grief and more like calculation.

Adelina glanced away quickly, not wanting to appear startled. She had attended church services led by the high priestess since the woman had first assumed the position nearly ten years ago. She had moved to Jumaral from Huojen as a pilgrim of Ostrea and quickly rose through the ranks of the city's religious elite. Perhaps she was staring because she could read the rage beneath Adelina's superficial grief.

Or maybe the high priestess knew about Adelina's curse, her defiled fate. To be high priestess meant having a better understanding of Ostrea than most people. Some had even become saints, prophets of Ostrea who could communicate Her bidding. Of course, there were also those who pretended to be prophets but were just witches, thieves of Her power who did their best to undermine the Royal House of Ducança.

The high priestess could have heard of Adelina's curse from Ostrea Herself.

The thought shook her.

Adelina needed to get her plan in motion. Quickly.

The funeral's reception was held in the ballroom of a bureaucratic building just one street down the hill from the Cathedral of Lis. It was where the Council of Lis met every week, headed by Adelina's parents, the duke and duchess of Lis. The usual meeting room provided an excellent view of the old stone castle crowning the city, as well as the top floor of the Manor of Lis below the castle's gated entrance.

Though the castle had been rendered dangerously fragile by the Second Great Wave fifty years before, it remained a solid touchstone of the city. No one had gone in it since the Wave, and the family of the duke and duchess of Lis had long taken residence in the manor at its side. But still, the outside of the castle was often decorated to reflect the city.

Today it was draped in black banners, with two flags hanging from the highest turret: the wyvern crest of the country of Jumaral and the city of Lis's red rose against blue.

Adelina had already observed the decorations from her bedroom window that morning when she woke up from one of the lightest sleeps of her life. Her stomach had clenched when she took them in. Memories of her aunt and cousin's deaths ten years prior pushed to the forefront of her mind.

The clothes that had been laid out for her for Simão's funeral were disturbingly similar to the castle's decoration. A heavy black gown, a black lace veil, and two brooches: a wyvern to claim her as a member of the House of Ducança and a red rose to identify her as the new marquise of Lis, heir to the Duchy of Lis.

She straightened her second brooch now. The witches' curse echoed at the back of her head when she looked for Isaque. They were where she had expected, standing along the wall behind the tables laden with fruit, cuts of meat, and sweet pastries.

Isaque Silveira wore the simple black suit of the servants, even though they hadn't been employed by the House of Ducança for a week. Their slim face appeared hollowed out, even from this distance. Isaque had been the first one to alert the household that Simão was not in his bed. It was only in the early hours of the next morning that Simão's body had been found, and by the time Adelina was woken up and alerted, Isaque had been dismissed, and Adelina had lost her chance of speaking to them. Now, Adelina watched them lean down to listen to a blond girl whose eyes were red from crying.

Dalila.

Adelina started toward the pair but was swiftly stopped by a figure with an emerald-green sash cutting across the chest of his crisp black suit. She scowled at her cousin, and he offered a resigned grimace in response.

"Calixto," she said by way of greeting. "You're in my way."

Calixto glanced around before tipping his drink in her direction. "A prince is never in the way. You are simply in the wrong place." His breath already stank of alcohol.

Adelina remembered a time when she, her cousin, and her brother had all been close. They were so near one another in age it only seemed natural the younger members of the House of Ducança had grown up as playmates, despite the fact Calixto lived in the capital, Fulgeo, while Adelina and Simão had always lived in northern Lis. That was before Calixto's brother, Manuel, had died and left Calixto as heir to the throne. It was also before Simão and then Calixto had turned eighteen, and they had become serious and intense.

Adelina had always wondered what did it, if she too would change the moment the clock struck midnight on her eighteenth birthday, or if she was already serious enough for adulthood as a royal.

Now Adelina looked at Calixto's carefully parted curls and cold dark eyes, the way his constant infuriating smirk gave way to a single dimple on his right cheek, and all she could see were the numerous ways he was becoming his father.

Adelina's uncle, Dom Aristides, was a fair king. He was just and strong and as loyal to Ostrea and Jumaral as it was possible to be. But he was cold.

"You're right. I don't know what possessed me to enter any room that you're in. Please accept my apologies," she deadpanned, trying to move around him.

He stepped in her path again. "What are you doing?"

"Mourning my brother. What are *you* doing?"

"Wondering why you look like you're marching into battle."

Adelina scoffed, keeping her voice low. "I'm off to speak to my friends. Shame you don't recognize the look."

Calixto looked over his shoulder to where Isaque and Dalila were still whispering. "Shame you don't recognize that those people are not your friends."

His expression shifted almost imperceptibly, but Adelina recognized the change from teasing to business. He leaned forward, his words barely audible over the memories of Simão being exchanged around them.

"It's family before all else. Now more than ever. Which is why I'll be staying in Lis for a while, instead of returning with the king to Fulgeo. To watch over my dear cousin."

She kept her expression blank, aware of all the eyes around them, all the people who would be curious about what the crown prince of Jumaral and the new marquise of Lis might be discussing so intensely.

"I thought it was *Jumaral* before all else," she murmured.

The corner of Calixto's lips quirked. The dimple appeared, and a manic spark entered his eyes. "Aren't they the same thing?"

She held his gaze for a moment before sidestepping him. This time, the prince did nothing to stop her. From the corner of her eye, she watched him take a swig of his drink and then disappear into the crowd.

Isaque and Dalila were only a few paces away the second time Adelina was impeded by royalty. Princess Iraida of Dumatsya wasted no time on formalities before wrapping Adelina in a bone-crushing hug, made significantly less comforting by the amount of jewelry and gemstones Iraida had inlaid on her voluminous dress of deep purple—the Dumatsyan mourning color.

"Adelina, I'm so sorry," she said in Dumatsyan. Her whisper was uncomfortably hot against Adelina's ear.

Behind Iraida, her brother, Prince Demyan, looked like he was barely holding back on enveloping them both in what was promised to be an equally unpleasant hug, given the amount of medals pinned all down his front. Adelina extricated herself from Iraida as soon as she was able and took a step back from the siblings.

"Thank you for coming," Adelina said in Dumatsyan. Her tongue twisted easily into the slopes and falls of the other language. "I know Simão would appreciate it, Ostrea bless his soul."

"We both wanted to race here as soon as we heard," said Demyan. "It's awful, for someone so young, but most of all for Simão. Is it true they think a witch did it? We saw the wanted posters with the raised bounties, looking for the killer. Is it really wise for Jumaral to increase its attacks, create more ill will between magic users and the royal family? In Dumatsya, we—"

"Criminals must be punished, should they not?" said Adelina, acutely aware of Simão's true killers socializing amongst the nobility behind her. "Our Lady Ostrea makes no mistakes."

Demyan grimaced. "Well, I hope your goddess does lend guidance to the situation, just as I hope our Northern Saints will extend their grace in this tragedy."

Iraida nodded solemnly.

This was the first time Adelina had ever interacted with the siblings without Simão at her side. It was Simão who had studied with the prince and princess at the university in Dumatsya's capital city, Abilya. He had lobbied his parents hard for the opportunity, and Adelina had done the same years after him—hoping to study mathematics and practice her languages in Nolofali—but had been unequivocally denied.

To Demyan and Iraida, Adelina had always just been their friend's younger sister.

So, what does that make me now?

The grief took the breath out of her. She forced herself to inhale and exhale.

Adelina smiled. "In Jumaral, we have a saying: *Those who do not die when they are young, die when they are old.* It is Ostrea's plan, after all. Please excuse me." She stepped past them.

"Wait. Adelina, please, wait."

She sighed, forcing herself to not let her growing frustration show. "Yes?"

The siblings exchanged a look, and Adelina had to fight not to roll her eyes. The two of them were ridiculous, dripping in Dumatsyan jewels and purple fabric against Jumaral's simple black and lace. Here they were, speaking about Dumatsyan Northern Saints in the country of Ostrea.

Finally, Iraida stepped forward. "Simão sent me a telegram a few weeks ago, saying he had something to discuss. That there was something *both* of you would want to discuss with *both* of us."

Adelina's stomach flipped. "He didn't provide any other details?"

Iraida shook her head.

"We thought we should ask you," said Demyan. "Perhaps if we were able to meet at some other time, you could tell us—"

"I don't know what he was talking about. Please, excuse me." She didn't wait to hear if they did. Her mind raced. Adelina crossed the final distance to Isaque, rounding the dessert table and purposefully avoiding several people who tried to reach out and share their condolences.

"You haven't seen her?" Dalila was whispering.

"No, not since that morning," replied Isaque.

"That's not like Luísa. You don't think—" Dalila noticed Adelina first. Her blue eyes widened before she sank into a curtsey, followed swiftly by Isaque.

"Is there anything I can get for you, Adelina?" Dalila's brows tilted downward with worry and pity. She had been like that all week—overly attentive and teary, only leaving Adelina's side when Adelina specifically requested her to.

Luckily, there were several tasks she had been able to set Dalila to over the past week, including using her connections around the city to find those three witches from the beach.

"I just wanted to speak to Isaque," Adelina said. "Perhaps alone?"

Isaque's gray eyes grew larger, and they exchanged a look with Dalila.

"Of course," said Dalila. "Let me know if you need anything." She left them to straighten the rows of cream tarts at the end of the table.

"Do you know anything about a medallion?" Adelina asked the moment Dalila was out of earshot.

Isaque's eyes, impossibly, went wider. They wiped a hand across their nose and crossed their arms. "I—What medallion?"

"Santa Belinha on one side, a wyvern on the other. Simão wanted to tell me something about it before he died. What do you know about it?"

"I...um, I don't really..." They glanced around, long curls brushing back and forth against their shoulders. Their cheeks became rosier by the second.

"What do you know?" Adelina shifted slightly so Isaque was stuck between her body and the wall.

They tried to take a step back and stumbled, finally stilling. Isaque stared at some point over Adelina's shoulder.

"N-nothing. I don't know anything."

Adelina almost rolled her eyes. Her instinct was just to keep pressing harder, asserting her power over them until they bent to her will. But she had also known Isaque since she was six years old, and her rank was no longer intimidating to them.

She sniffed loudly, allowing hot tears to gather and fall down her cheeks. "Please, Isaque. Simão is g-gone now, and I just know I'll never be able to rest until I find out what he wanted to tell me. You're the only one who can help me."

Isaque inhaled and exhaled deeply, bracing themself. "I'm sorry, Adelina, but I can't help you."

"W-why not?" she cried, making a show of wiping her gloved hands across her cheeks. "I've just felt awful for a week, like I can't breathe, and I know that you feel awful t-too." Her words grew louder, and a few other servants glanced their way.

Isaque still hadn't looked at her, but their eyes were filling with tears. "Please, Adelina," they whispered.

"You don't think Simão would have trusted me?"

"Of course he would, but...I think it might be dangerous to talk about, and I don't even really know anything anyway."

"Then why would it be dangerous?"

Isaque finally did look down, though not at Adelina's face. They focused on the brooches pinned over her heart. Their lips trembled.

"Was it something illegal?"

"I don't want to get anyone in trouble."

"Simão is dead."

"Other people."

"*Who*, Isaque? Please. If you tell me, I can stop people from getting in trouble. I'm the marquise of Lis, remember?"

It took three more heartbeats for Isaque to break, sending a prayer to Ostrea before beginning a whispered story. They clenched their arms tighter across their chest.

Isaque didn't know where Simão had gotten the medallion, only that he had been obsessed with it. After spending months sneaking out to ask antiquers, historians, and townspeople about any ideas regarding the medallion's owner, Isaque had finally asked if Simão thought the owner might be dead.

"To get him to stop looking?" Adelina asked.

"No, because I...I know someone who can sort of..." They closed their eyes and tilted their head up, probably sending another prayer to Ostrea. "Speak to dead people."

Adelina waited for them to elaborate, but they didn't. "A witch?"

Isaque shushed her and looked around frantically, but Dalila was the only one close enough to hear. "*No*. No, he's not—Well, actually, I don't know *what* he is, but he's not that. He just has some sort of connection to the dead, so there was a time where he was doing spirit reading sort of things. I took Simão to see him, but I wasn't at the meeting. Simão never told me what he said."

"Who is he?"

"I can't—"

Adelina forced another tear to fall, and Isaque sighed.

"He calls himself the Knell. He's been making a bit of a name for himself in the lower town."

Adelina's heart was going to beat out of her chest. Simão had gone to not just some kind of witch, but one with a criminal moniker?

She had had enough of witches. The crime of stealing power from Ostrea was high enough to her, without adding in whatever would make someone's name known in the lower town.

But she needed this. Adelina needed to know what this *Knell* had said about the medallion and use it to figure out what Simão had wanted to tell her. Something so important he had preemptively scheduled a meeting with the prince and princess of Dumatsya.

So, she would have to speak to this new witch. The thought made her dizzy.

What if the Knell curses me too?

Adelina would just need insurance. That was all. A way to control him and make sure he would be loyal to her and not share their meeting with any unwanted parties.

"Adelina, are you—" Isaque's voice sounded slippery in her ears.

"I'll need his real name. You know it, don't you?"

They pressed their lips together. Tears still fell down their narrow cheeks.

"Isaque, if I'm going to figure this out for Simão, I need all of the details. Please."

Their eyes lingered once again on Adelina's brooches. "I can't say it. Not here."

The words were a punch to Adelina's gut. The repetition of Simão's last words.

Her breaths came too fast.

Her hands suddenly felt grimy and bloody underneath her gloves.

She was going to vomit down her dress.

"Tell Dalila the details by tonight," she whispered. Then, as calmly as she could, Adelina walked purposefully toward the wide double doors on the other side of the ballroom.

People called her name and touched her shoulders, offering condolences she accepted with tight grimaces. But she did not stop, with bile working its way up her throat.

It wasn't until she had finally escaped into the quieter hallway, fresh air from the open windows cooling her sweaty face, that she realized who she had subconsciously been hoping to speak to about everything that had just happened: Simão.

But Simão was dead.

And Adelina was alone to deal with murderers and curses and witches and secrets.

Her mind was stuck in an idiotic loop: *Simão is dead. I need to talk to Simão about it. Simão is dead. I need to talk to Simão about it....*

The tears were real now, streaming down her face. Her breath became choked gasps. Adelina put a hand over her mouth, trying to quiet herself. She strode along the hall and down a wide carpeted staircase to find a place to pull herself together.

"Adelina?"

She recognized the voice. Adelina stopped at the bottom of the steps. She wiped the tears and snot from her face while Dalila's footsteps caught up with her.

She turned just as Dalila reached the ground floor.

"Dalila, please return to the ballroom." Adelina's voice was disgustingly muffled and nasal through her tears.

Dalila stayed where she was, examining Adelina's face as though trying to diagnose the source of Adelina's distress. She had been raised to become Adelina's maid, and much of the formality between them had been lost through the experience of growing up together, just as it had been between Isaque and Simão.

Her presence was just another reminder to Adelina of what she had lost last week.

She made herself breathe steadily through her nose to prevent the next flood of tears. Could she allow herself just this one person to confide in, at least partially? Just one person to tell how scared she was of her curse and her family and everything that was to come?

Footsteps sounded above. Adelina recognized the crisp, booming tone of her uncle, the king, and then the responding softer voice of her own father.

They couldn't see her like this.

Adelina grabbed Dalila by the arm and hurried down the hall, entering the first door on her left. It was a wide meeting room with a long rectangular table at its center and woven images of the sea and various saints hanging from all the walls. On the far side of the room was an armoire, and Adelina wasted no time in turning the key in its lock and shoving Dalila inside before her.

Dalila gave no protest. They squeezed in among the few musty-smelling jackets and scarves left over from some past meeting. Adelina shut the door behind them, enclosing the pair in stuffy darkness. The only light came from the slim crack where the doors didn't fully latch.

They had hidden just in time. A group of people entered the room immediately after them. The girls shuffled further back, making the wood creak beneath their feet. Adelina grabbed Dalila's arm again, forcing her to still.

"Must we speak about this now, Lady Rodrigues?" came the voice of Adelina's father.

"If we are to avoid another attack, then yes, Your Grace." Adelina vaguely recognized the brisk voice of Lady Rodrigues, who, as Chancellor of Lis, ranked highest in the Council of Lis under Adelina's family. "We must discuss this before his majesty, Dom Aristides, departs for Fulgeo."

There was the scrape of a heavy wooden chair against stone.

"I don't believe there is reason to worry, Lady Rodrigues," said the king, and Adelina pictured him sitting at the center of the table—the position usually reserved for his brother. "The circumstances that led to the murder of Lord Simão will not be repeated. The people of Jumaral are enraged by the death of the marquis, and any empathy that those witches have garnered over the years will be gone within the week."

Dalila trembled beside her. Adelina herself was barely containing her urge to scream. Snot flowed freely from her nose, but she couldn't risk moving to wipe it or sniffing to staunch it. Adelina could only listen while her family twisted their story of her brother's death into a tale of political advantage.

"I'm afraid that may not be the case, Your Majesty," said Lady Rodrigues. She sounded steady, though even Adelina's own father was sometimes uncomfortable with disagreeing with the king. "Outside of state-organized events, the people of Lis and wider Jumaral seem unimpacted by the death of Lord Simão. I've been in touch with your cabinet members in the capital, and it appears that many citizens outside of Lis were unaware of the marquis's existence and his place in the royal family. Even many citizens within Lis had never seen an image of the marquis until his official portrait appeared in the papers to announce his death."

"Lady Rodrigues, are you saying that no one cared about my son's death?" asked Adelina's mother. Her voice took on a flat tone, which meant Infanta Rosália was seething.

"Your Grace, I only mean that Lord Simão's death has highlighted ongoing trends we have seen in the citizenry's opinion of the royal family. We are now in the fifty-third year since the Second Great Wave, which we were only able to recover from with Dona Maria's and now Dom Aristides's investments in modern industry. As more of Jumaral's rural citizens move to cities or have connections with those who live in cities, literacy and scientific understanding are growing. It is a trend that we expected, as it has previously been studied in most of our industrialized neighbors. Jumaralians are finding other things to believe in than Ostrea and are, therefore, becoming disillusioned by the traditions of the monarchy."

Adelina would have recognized Prince Calixto's scoff anywhere. "Do the people not understand that Ostrea Herself granted our family this position? That she trusted our lineage with the protection of Jumaral? Our family is the only reason Jumaral hasn't been dragged into the resource wars bursting across the continent. Do the people *want* Jumaral to be taken for its coast? Do they *want* Ostrea to punish us all with a Third Great Wave?"

"What do you suggest, Lady Rodrigues?" asked the king. Though his voice was soft, it posed a danger to Lady Rodrigues, depending on her following words.

"The Council has discussed measures to remind the people of Our Lady Ostrea's wisdom by placing the royal family in a more prominent position, particularly starting with the new marquise of Lis, Lady Adelina."

Dalila sniffed behind Adelina, as if she were about to sneeze. Adelina put her hand over Dalila's nose and leaned forward so she wouldn't miss a word.

"We feel it is important to increase Lady Adelina's visibility through attending events around the city, making herself available to journalists, and perhaps even finding a suitor to promote more interest in her life."

Adelina's mind fogged over while she listened to the ensuing discussion and the too-fast agreement from her parents to a media scheme centering Adelina to keep the monarchy alive. The meeting finished a few minutes later, with plans to find a suitable person for the role: someone the regular people of Jumaral would respond to, someone who would be willing to follow the rules of the monarchy, someone who could put on an act.

They vacated the room, and Adelina was left reeling in an armoire with her maid. The thought of that "someone," whoever they were, disgusted her.

"Adelina?" Dalila whispered, when Adelina made no move to let them out of the armoire. "Are you—"

"When I'm at the burial, tell Isaque to give you the information I requested." Adelina wiped her face and stepped out into the bright light of the room.

This changed nothing. She had a curse to break, secrets to uncover, a goddess to convince, and now a lead to help her do all of that.

It was time to speak to the Knell.

CHAPTER 4

JAS

ala's tonic burned while it traveled down Jas's throat and sat, simmering, in his stomach. He tried not to flinch but couldn't help gagging as he emptied the cup with a final gulp.

"Better?" Hala asked. She took the cup from his hands and threw it with a clatter into a cauldron-like pot she had long used as an increasingly rusty sink.

"Loads." Jas's voice came out as a low wheeze. He blinked tears from his eyes.

"Now we just need to get a salve for your eye, and with any luck, no one will be able to tell that you, *ahem*, tripped, was it?" She raised a brow.

He sat at Hala's cluttered worktable in the laboratory behind her shop, the Silver Salamander Apothecary. Around him was a barely restrained explosion of scales, alembics, and crucibles clustered around a cast-iron furnace. A table was almost invisible under the piles of open books topping and surrounding it.

A bookcase was cluttered with writing utensils, stacks of old notebooks, rolled-up papers, an entire shelf of broken glass and clay pots, and the occasional empty teacup and saucer. Though the sun had almost fully risen outside, the small windows had been covered with old sheets and blankets, and the entire room had a gloomy, flickering yellow tinge to it from the one gas lamp and the dozen stubby candles placed precariously around the space. The strange mixture of scents—chemicals, rusty metal, and warm spices—made his already pounding head feel like it was about to start leaking from his ears.

Perhaps that would be better.

Jas clenched his fists in his lap, glad Hala had her back turned to him while she rummaged amongst her shelves for salve ingredients.

The voice in his mind had been there long enough that its occasional interjections shouldn't have been a surprise to him, but now its sound was accompanied by a piercing shock through the back of his head, like a spark of lightning.

The pain had started a week ago, sometimes randomly but most acutely when Jas actively used his powers, like when he had touched the jewelry in Alves's safe earlier that morning. His head had exploded with the sister's screams, and for a full minute, he had thought he was about to pass out.

Leaving Seba to fend for himself, said the voice. *Be stronger.*

Jas waited for the pain to pass. It was hard to ignore the voice when it was so often right. It understood the way Jas owed Seba in a way nobody else did, not even Hala. Only the voice knew how much Jas hid from Seba, how cruel every interaction truly was.

In the time he had been unfocused, Hala had found her ingredients and was pounding them into a paste with a stone mortar and pestle.

"Why were you two even out in the middle of the night?" she asked, looking over her shoulder to observe him. Her dark eyes pierced his. The low glow of the candle glimmered over the few strands of gray hair just beginning to highlight her long brown hair.

"Collecting ingredients. Like you asked us to."

Her eyes narrowed. "You brought me a single tomato."

"You said best attained at dawn."

"No, I said best *harvested* at dawn. It doesn't count if you get it from Senhora Gabriela at the market."

Jas shrugged, feigning confusion. It was the first thing he and Seba had seen on their way back from the club, and Senhora

Gabriela was usually willing to part with her ugliest tomato of the week just before the market opened.

Hala often sent Jas and Seba out to pick up ingredients from sellers, either for her apothecary shop or for the illegal alchemical operations she conducted in her laboratory, which would draw unwanted attention from the bounty hunters if they were detected. The latter were only to be collected from a specific network of magic users and traders, many of them immigrants who hadn't grown up with the Jumaralian prejudice against magic.

There were always rules to alchemical ingredients, where every characteristic served a purpose. A single discrepancy in color or the moment of harvesting could be the difference between turning gold to water or just having a murky, poisonous soup. Sometimes, Hala asked for Jas's and Seba's help in concocting her potions, and both had spent countless hours presiding over simmering sludge or taking tiny sips of new mixtures while Hala took notes.

Then there were other times where she would block them from the laboratory, keeping her thoughts to her ancient notebooks and whatever project she had deemed so secret. Jas and Seba had often tried to guess what she was working on—immortality, endless riches, perhaps a single food that could provide all the nutrition a person could need—but she never divulged a clue.

Hala joined him at the table with the bowl, and he once again tried not to flinch while she dabbed it, more forcefully than necessary, onto his blossoming black eye.

"Seba doesn't have a black eye," she noted quietly.

Jas said nothing.

"If I were to guess which one of you would be coming home with a black eye in the early hours of the morning, it wouldn't have been you."

Hala met his eyes carefully then, and she was close enough for Jas to notice she had already gotten a smudge of ash across the dark brown skin of her jaw. It was not an unfamiliar look. Hala had been Jas's guardian since he was an infant and Seba's guardian since he was six.

Jas was long used to that calculating stare, which meant Hala had detected a lie. He also understood why she sometimes had to be strict with them about whatever trouble they got into around Lis— the same reason why he could never tell her about the Knell and the way he was using the powers she had always told him to keep secret. Drawing attention to Hala's work or Jas's powers would be deadly for them all.

Jas would not be able to bear the look of her disappointment if she found out how reckless they were being. But he also wished she could read his mind and put a stop to all of it.

Seba had been closest to the door in Alves's office, and the bruisers had gone for him first, but Jas had jumped in front of him. He had blocked each blow, taking the hits in his arms, in his sides, even his face, blocking Seba's body—which had dropped into a fetal position—with his own. Jas had grasped at any semblance of a spirit from any of their attackers amidst the pain in his body and mind. It was only when he remembered the bruisers were under Alves's command that he was able to get them out.

"*Alves*," he had growled. "Your sister wants you to hear a story..."

And then, while he had bled and dodged, he began twisting the dark tale being whispered in his ear by the spirit of the little girl whose brother had damned her. The story slithered into Alves's subconscious no matter how hard the man pressed his hands to his own ears and screamed.

He had finally called off his goons. Jas and Seba had been allowed to pass, with Jas swaying on his feet and bleeding profusely into that horrible black cloak.

It's the least you can do, said the voice.

The door to the laboratory swung open then. Both Hala and Jas turned to see Seba, hair wild and exhaustion graying his skin. His eyes locked with Jas's. Seba hadn't slept a moment in the hours they had been back.

"You look like you've developed a terrible disease," Seba said, taking in the salve under Jas's eye.

"And you look like you're not ready for work," Hala retorted.

Seba glanced down, as if only now realizing he was wearing stained pajamas and thick woolen socks.

"A state that will soon change," Seba promised.

"It had better change in the next ten minutes." She passed Seba to go to the front of the shop, letting the door swing shut behind her.

As soon as they were alone, Seba threw himself into the seat Hala had just occupied. "So, when do we try again?"

Jas pushed down the urge to groan. Exhaustion and pain weighed him down on his stool. "Can't we take a few nights off?"

"Absolutely not. You've seen the new posters. Bounties are up, and it's only a matter of time before you or Hala get caught. We just have to find a goon who's more careful with his money than Alves."

When Jas still appeared unconvinced, Seba wrapped an arm around his shoulder. His hazel eyes glittered hungrily. Jas winced.

"Dream with me...No bounty hunters, no sewage smell, and no bad memories. And all it will take is a trip to a nice club with a bigger safe and less security."

It's the least you can do, the voice hissed in Jas's head again.

As much as Jas hated putting the fear of Ostrea into people, even those who deserved it, he knew Seba's drive to collect funds came from a place of terror. If anyone caught on to Hala's alchemy or Jas's power to communicate with the dead, Seba would be in just as much trouble as them.

"Fine," said Jas, already dreading the amount of pain his head was going to be in later. "We'll go tonight."

The smell of fresh soil wafted over them while they dashed up the cobbled streets lined with stucco houses that were once white but had gone gray, their orange terra-cotta roofs a dulled brown.

"Do you think we lost them?" Seba gasped over the pounding of their feet.

They sprinted up one of the narrow streets on the outskirts of the city.

"I hope so." Jas thanked the adrenaline coursing through his veins for allowing him to speak at all. He skirted around a bush of hydrangeas hanging over a low stone wall.

"I think...that if we didn't...they deserve to catch us." Seba's arms swung wildly at his sides.

If Jas wasn't careful, he might have been bludgeoned by a rogue fist.

Seba practically crashed into a wall, and he clutched at it to stay upright. A dog barked from behind one of the gates. Its long, white teeth glowed in the moonlight. Jas and Seba dragged themselves past before anyone could think to look outside. They didn't need anyone alerting the bruisers of where they had been.

Running for his life from yet another gambling den was the last place Jas wanted to be, but it had seemed the simplest way of building up the funds Seba wanted.

That you owe *him*, the voice corrected.

Jas had no argument. More than anything, he wanted to be in his warm bed, belly full of one of Hala's barely edible soups. But if there was anything he could give Seba, it was his responsibility to do it.

"Say," Seba began after a few minutes of silent walking to catch their breaths. "Aren't these the east hills?"

A guilty, growing knot pounded in Jas's gut. He knew what Seba was thinking. Even here, at the outskirts of the city, the notices featuring the new witch bounty were posted at the gates to a few houses. "Yes."

"And isn't this where Heitor Alves said that coven of witches lives? On Rua da Vieira?"

"It is, but we are *not* going to be bounty hunters. We've already escaped one violent death tonight."

You should tell him to run away from you to avoid another.

"Of course not." Seba gasped, as though Jas had proposed something preposterous. "I was just thinking that we could maybe check in on them. We know Heitor Alves is after them, don't we? So, isn't it the responsible thing to do that we go and warn them?"

Jas looked sidelong at Seba. He had never been a good liar, and Jas recognized the greed in his darting eyes and fingers fluttering at his sides. While Jas watched, he even licked his lips.

It wasn't that Jas believed Seba harbored any ill will toward witches as a population, not when Seba had been living with Jas's powers and Hala's alchemy since he was six. But Seba still carried fears of their power from the stories he had heard from his mother when he was young.

Jumaralian children were told from birth about witches and their dangers, the myth that a witch's prophecy could damn a person in the eyes of Ostrea. Jas only knew those stories because of Seba, but his own understanding had always been tempered by Hala's view that Jumaralian superstition was nothing more than fear and prejudice.

Still, Jas wasn't sure any amount of Hala's logic would stop Seba if there was money to be made. Their pockets were no heavier than they had been that morning.

And Seba was right that, if they had a chance to warn the witches, they should take it. Jas knew better than most that the persecution of witches was wholly unfair. It was not their fault they had been born as natural catalysts to the magic existing all around. Nor was it wrong for Hala and other alchemists to use plants, organs, and metals to command magic for themselves.

There was a narrative around the country of Jumaral that witches and alchemists were thieves of Ostrea's power, but magic was just a tool, not some all-powerful, limitless source of power. In fact, based on what he had picked up from Hala's study of the subject, magic was quite limited.

The use of magic by witches relied on ideas of balance and connection. Performing any spell took something from the user as payment. It was why so many witches only used magic as part of a coven—the cost would be split amongst them. Some solely used potions, which further split the cost amongst the ingredients. To cast magic on another person required physical touch or a sample of blood. Even replications of magic, like Hala's alchemy, took time and energy. One of Hala's experiments could span anywhere from ten seconds to ten years. It was no cure-all.

"Fine, we'll check on them," Jas said.

Seba whooped. Jas shushed him and looked around to make sure no one had heard.

"Which way?" Seba whispered, swinging his entire body between the two tracks of a fork in the road.

One way led them back down the hill, the street lined with rose bushes and laundry lines. The other path was up, the houses becoming sparser and the land dissolving into skinny pine trees reaching to the stars.

"That way," Jas said. Alves had said the witches were in the hills, and Jas doubted they would be in the more densely occupied part of the town.

"I'm glad the moon is so bright tonight." They continued their march into the trees, and Seba gave an exaggerated shudder. "Or this might be creepy."

Jas glanced up, taking in the bright full moon and the night sky speckled with stars. They weren't always visible in the city, but he had to agree he was glad to see them now. Even just half an hour's walk from the main city, there were no street lamps to be seen, and anyone who might have lit a candle inside the houses was resting before a day of work beginning at dawn. Since they hadn't anticipated exiting the main city limits tonight, Seba and Jas had also not brought any of their own lamps to see by.

They walked for several more minutes, navigating the winding dirt road between the trees with a mixture of sight and feel, until there were no more houses left.

"You know..." Seba continued up the hill with Jas following reluctantly. "I always thought we wouldn't be good bounty hunters because the other bounty hunters would swat us like flies and we would die. But there is another obstacle I might have disregarded, which is that we don't actually know what a house belonging to witches looks like."

"Maybe there will be a giant cauldron next to the clothesline," Jas quipped, "or a talking cat flying through the chimney."

A sudden shriek made Jas jump. Seba's body knocked them both to the ground. Dust flew into Jas's mouth, and his elbows stung from the impact, but he twisted around to see what had caused the commotion.

His heart pounded in his chest. His eyes fell on three shadowy forms stepping out from the tree line, as though slithering out of the night itself.

Seba scooted himself slightly behind Jas, an arm raised to cover his own head. Jas moved to join him, crawling backward as quickly as he could to get away from whatever attackers these could be.

Three women stood over them, wearing cloaks on top of deep green and gold robes, which could have been pulled from an old storybook about the time before the First Great Wave. The woman closest to him was the oldest, her back crooked and hunched, though she still couldn't have been much more than thirty. To her right was a slightly younger woman, perhaps in her twenties. On the left was a girl around Jas's and Seba's age or a few years younger—somewhere in her teens.

None seemed to wear the expression of a murderer. They were all looking at Jas and Seba with benign interest. Still, Jas felt blindly behind him, trying to grip the revolver in the pocket of Seba's jacket. Empty chamber or not, it was the only weapon they had.

"Who are you?" Seba's voice came from behind Jas's ear, low and trembling.

The women gave no indication they had heard him, at least not that Jas could see. He was about to repeat Seba's question when the oldest woman spoke.

"All hail, Sebastião! Hail to thee, Marquis of Lis!"

Seba stilled against him.

"All hail, Sebastião! Hail to thee, Duke of Lis!" said the middle woman.

Jas fumbled with new fervor. His fingers finally closed around the handle of the gun.

"All hail, Sebastião," proclaimed the youngest, "that shall be king hereafter!"

Seba still hadn't moved, and Jas had no idea what to do.

These were witches.

This was a prophecy.

All the nightmares and fears of Jumaral came to Jas unbidden, thrust forward by the voice and his own memories. If a person heard their own fate, they were cursed. Ostrea's plan for them was defiled. Their life could be over.

No. Those stories were just used to create hatred against witches. The small part of Jas still thinking rationally knew the real harm of hearing a prophecy was how a person reacted to it.

His heart had not stopped pounding since he had first hit the ground, but now there was a new desperation to it. Each beat was a reminder he wasn't doing anything to protect Seba from having to face that reaction.

You and your demonic abilities got him here. Get him out.

"How do you know him?" Jas asked hoarsely.

"Hail!" the oldest woman said, and the two others repeated the cry. "Lesser than Sebastião and greater."

"Not so happy, yet much happier," added the middle.

"Thou shalt get kings, though thou be none," said the youngest. "So all hail, Sebastião and Jasibin!"

The other women each repeated her last words, and then there was silence once more. Jas's hand had gone slack on the revolver.

Thou shalt get kings.

"Is this real? Are you—" Seba yelled, making Jas jump. "You're lying. I'm not any kind of royalty, and the marquis of Lis just died. But he was replaced by his sister, wasn't he? So how would I become any of those things? This can't be a real prophecy!"

The oldest woman's lips twisted slightly, a mocking smile thick with knowledge.

And then the women were gone.

Seba jumped to his feet. The revolver caught on Jas's still limp hand and clattered to the dirt. Jas swept it up when he rose, keeping a firm grip on it as he joined Seba in searching the tree line for the women.

"No, no, no, no, no. By Our Lady, no," Seba muttered. "Where did they go? They can't just say that, ruin my life like that, and then..." Seba cursed loudly into the empty woods, running his hands through his hair.

A chill settled over Jas's body. He wrapped his arms tightly around his shuddering torso, still clutching the revolver in one hand. The wind had blown a cover of clouds into the sky, blocking out some of the stars.

"We should go," he said, and for once, Seba made no remark.

They hurried down the hill, both casting occasional glances over their shoulders. As much as Jas knew it was just the shock of the encounter getting to him, he couldn't help but think each snap of a twig, rustle of a leaf, or slight shift in the darkness was someone else preparing to jump out.

"What even is a *marquis*?" Seba asked when they were almost to the outer town, closer to houses and less likely to be jumped.

Jas searched his mind. "The child of a duke, I think."

"Oh."

They were silent for a few moments, both trying to calculate how on earth Seba, the orphaned ward of an illegal alchemist, would ever become a marquis. They came to the same conclusion.

"It's impossible. I'm doomed, then. I'm going to be killed by a witches' curse." Seba's voice broke on the last word.

"No. Seba, you know all those things about witches stealing magic from Ostrea aren't real. Hala's always said they're just lies to keep the monarchy in power." Jas glanced at Seba, who was still muttering curses under his breath. Worry clenched Jas's heart.

It was true that people who said they had heard prophecies often went mad or died horrible deaths, but Hala had always taught them there was a rational explanation for everything. It wasn't a prophecy, whether real or not, which killed people; it was the paranoia, greed, and recklessness.

"Just put it out of your mind, Seba. Don't—"

But for the second time in fifteen minutes, their walk was interrupted by a shriek from Seba.

Jas expected the three women to appear from the trees again, but this time, there was only one figure behind Seba. They were shorter than him, barely coming up to Seba's chin, but that didn't stop them from being able to press a knife to his throat. The blade reflected the light of the shining moon like a star fallen to earth.

"By Our Lady, these woods are dangerous," Seba muttered.

Get him out of this, little Knell.

All Jas could see of the person holding the knife was the glow of dark eyes from the light of the blade. Everything else was in the shadow of the hat they wore on their head or hidden behind Seba's body.

"I have a gun," he warned.

"It isn't loaded," the figure replied. It was a girl's voice, sharp, cold, and completely certain in her claim.

Had she been following them? Was she another prophesying witch?

"And what if it is?"

Seba's eyes were wide. He was forcing himself to keep his mouth shut.

"You still wouldn't shoot," the figure said.

"Why?"

Jas flinched when the girl adjusted her grip on Seba, making him bend back further to avoid the blade of the knife against his throat.

"Because it would be more trouble than it's worth. But feel free to try it. I do love proving people wrong."

Get him out.

Jas tried to focus his mind, pulling at any of the ghosts that might have clung to this girl. He almost gasped at the number of spirits existing just beyond his reach, watching her from afar, but none stepped forward to speak.

"And I love egg custard croissants, but we can't always get what we want in the middle of the woods in the dead of night, so either explain or let me go," Seba blurted.

Jas tensed when the girl once again tightened her grip.

"I'm talking to the Knell," she hissed. "Not you."

It took a moment for Jas to realize she had used his moniker. He felt vulnerable without the Knell's usual mask, which he had stuffed in his pocket as soon as they had lost sight of the bruisers chasing them out of the gambling den.

"Then tell me. Why shouldn't I shoot?" Jas finally asked.

The girl adjusted the angle of the blade slightly so more of the light hit her features. Jas took an instinctive step away from her. It was a face he knew, one he had seen across every newspaper in Lis over the past week, often half covered in black veils and shawls while she attended vigil after vigil for the dead marquis.

"I'd hate to see the kind of trouble there would be if you shot the marquise of Lis," said Lady Adelina Maria Malves Ducança.

CHAPTER 5

SEBA

It took a moment before the full impact of the girl's words hit him. When it did, it was like he had fallen off the highest turret of the Castle of Lis and found himself unharmed.

Sure, the marquise of Lis was holding a knife to his throat in the middle of the night, far away from anyone who could hear him scream. But on the other hand, *the marquise of Lis was holding a knife to his throat, right after a bunch of witches had scared him shitless and told him he would be marquis of Lis* and *the duke of Lis* and *the king of Jumaral.*

Despite what Jas had said, Seba was not willing to shrug off this prophecy like it didn't matter. Like it wouldn't *kill* him if he didn't honor Ostrea's will and chase it. If the first eighteen years of his life were any indication, he did not have that kind of luck.

The danger of curses was ingrained in every Jumaralian child from the story of the Second Great Wave, when the ruling members of the House of Ducança had all been wiped out after Dom Francisco failed to fight for a fate told to him in a witches' prophecy. Of the heirs to the throne, the Second Great Wave had left only Princess Maria alive, who then became queen.

Seba's knowledge of the royal family tree could not have been described as robust, but the girl holding a knife to his throat was probably related to that queen from fifty years ago. Whoever her family was, her interest was clearly an opportunity to make sure this curse didn't destroy his future.

Relief coursed through him, steadying his heartbeat despite the blade that would slice his neck if he or the marquise so much as sneezed.

Jas didn't seem to be having the same thoughts. Far from relief, he looked like he had just been condemned. Seba supposed he had, since Jas, too, had received a prophecy. Jas had always been quite pale, but now he was positively translucent, and the contrast with his black hair and clothes was not helping. It was only then that Seba realized what it meant for the marquise to know about the Knell.

All his thinking reversed.

The marquise was not their savior; she was the one who would finally do what Seba had always feared by reporting the Knell.

Jas was going to die. *Seba* was going to die. And probably Hala too.

They were damned, after all.

The marquise shifted against Seba's back, which was arched awkwardly to account for their height difference and the nearly unavoidable blade at his throat. He inhaled a lungful of her rose perfume.

She pushed him away from her. The cool press of the knife disappeared with a faint sting. A hand on his arm steadied Seba when he stumbled. It was Jas, but Jas wasn't looking at him. He was staring at the marquise as though she could jump forward and bite them at any moment.

The forest grew darker as more clouds drifted in, but the marquise was still visible. The only thing the papers had not truly captured were her eyes, which bore into him with such intensity that he felt like he was staring into twin solar flares.

Seba had half a mind to grab Jas and run.

"I have a proposition." The marquise lifted her chin when she spoke, like she was speaking to an audience of more than just Seba and Jas.

The smallest bit of hope flipped his stomach.

"I'm sorry," Seba said. "But could we just...review the last few minutes? If possible?" Jas elbowed him in the ribs. "My lady, or, um...marquise-lady. Please."

Her dark brows rose. "What exactly would you like to review, Senhor Pinheiro?"

"Like, how you know us, or why you were hanging around the woods in the middle of the night? Or if you're involved with the witches that just told us—"

Jas elbowed him again.

"Um, or, I don't know. Why you decided you needed to hold me at knifepoint?"

For a moment, the marquise just stared at him, and when she did reply, it was like she was reading a script.

"I know you because I've been watching you, I'm in the woods in the middle of the night because you are, I'm not involved with the witches, and the knife was for me to test something." She tilted her head, reminding Seba strongly of a cat. "Any more questions?"

Possibly more than I had before, yes, he thought. Aloud, he just asked, "What's the proposition?"

"I'd like to hire both of you."

"To do what?" Jas asked.

"Different jobs. The Knell performed a service for my brother, Lord Simão, several weeks ago, and I need to know what it was."

Jas said nothing, but from the unsteady breath he released, he and Seba were both thinking the same thing.

Several weeks ago, even before the bounty rose, they had decided to use Jas's skills for something Seba had coined "spirit consulting." Seba had thought they would make a fortune from having people hire Jas to read the possessions of dead people. In a harrowing turn of events, it quickly became clear that it was difficult to run an illegal magical business through word-of-mouth when everyone in the country was too scared to admit they had even looked at anything close to witchiness.

They'd had only two clients over several months. One of them had been Isaque Silveira, mostly just because Isaque had already been at the apothecary when Seba and Jas had decided to try to run such a business, but the other had never given a name. The person might have worn a mask when the Knell met them, though Seba hadn't been allowed in the room. But if that stranger had been the marquis of Lis, it could only bring trouble.

"Jas isn't the Knell," Seba said. He ran a hand through his hair. "He doesn't—I mean, he can't—"

"Don't lie to me," said Lady Adelina.

Seba's mouth clamped shut.

"Why do you want to know?" Jas asked.

Seba shot him an annoyed look.

"Because it's important to me. And it doesn't seem important to you, so I don't think you'll have an issue telling me."

"If I tell you, will you leave us alone?"

There were several awkward seconds of the marquise staring Jas down, assuring Seba their paths would end tonight. Then Jas's eyes flickered to Seba, and he seemed to make a decision.

"What was the artifact?"

"A medallion. Santa Belinha on one side and a wyvern on the other."

Only because he was standing so close to him did Seba notice the nervous shift of Jas's weight.

"It belonged to a woman who died in her sleep ten years ago. She didn't know how it happened or who did it—just that she woke up beyond death's gate with her neck slashed open."

The marquise blinked. "That's it? There's nothing else?"

"And...she knew the king, Dom Aristides. She didn't say, but it was implied that they were...intimate. She was pregnant."

Lady Adelina's chin lifted again, though now it seemed like she was inflating herself with an inhale of chilly night air.

"Is that the end of the job, my lady?"

"No. It's not enough. But you can speak to the dead, so you should be able to contact him to get the full story."

"I can't force him to do anything, my lady," Jas protested.

"I'm sure we'll be able to convince him. He'll want to tell me what happened to him."

"Wasn't he killed by witches?"

She paused. "It seems that way."

"And *my* job?" Seba asked.

Now that it was clear he and Jas weren't going to be immediately murdered, he hoped to turn the conversation away from awkward recollections of the dead and back onto the very real opportunity to fight this curse. And then there was the additional monetary benefit of doing a job for the marquise of Lis.

If he and Jas didn't take advantage of any opportunity they could, it would be them or Hala being hunted, which would destroy his future, whether or not he was able to deal with this curse. The marquise was like an encantada out of legend—the guard and purveyor of all the riches fate would bring him.

"I need a love interest," she said.

Seba's breath stopped. "Excuse me?"

"I need a love interest."

He searched her face for some sign she was joking.

All hail, Sebastião! Hail to thee, Marquis of Lis!

All hail, Sebastião! Hail to thee, Duke of Lis!

All hail, Sebastião, that shall be king hereafter!

It was a more perfect opportunity than he could imagine, but he also didn't think his heart would be able to take many more flips between terror and relief.

"I take back what I said before," he muttered. "By Our Lady, these woods are amazing."

"Why do you need a love interest?" Jas asked. "And why is this so secretive, if you're looking into what happened to your brother?"

"Because I am going to be queen, and my family doesn't know that yet," she said, as if it were the most natural explanation in the world. "My uncle's government wants me to create a romantic narrative for media attention, but I think it could be a useful distraction from my own endeavors as well. I need someone that will fill a seat and look pretty, not one with any sort of desire to lead. Preferably, this will all happen before I turn eighteen in two months, since people in my family tend to get increased attention when they turn eighteen—something I'd rather avoid during this particular process."

"You're not the heir," Jas said.

"I'm third in line," she replied coldly. "Sometimes, the line of succession needs adjusting."

"And now is one of those times?"

"Jas," Seba grumbled, elbowing him. "Can't you see the marquise is offering us a fine opportunity?"

"How exactly are you planning on adjusting the line of succession?" Jas asked.

Seba rolled his eyes.

"Methods that will become clear with time."

There was a pause in which the two of them just stared at each other.

"Do those methods involve murder?"

"*Jas,*" Seba hissed.

"No murder," she said easily. "A queen must keep her hands clean. But if you'd prefer not to help, I'm sure the bounty hunters would be glad to know where the Knell sleeps. Now." Her dark eyes flicked between the two of them. "Do we have a deal?"

Seba's heart pounded, and his mind returned to its usual nightmare—bounty hunters crashing through the apothecary, dragging Jas, Hala, and Seba from their rooms while they burned all of Hala's work to the ground and took away the only home, the only family, Seba had known since his mother died.

His first time meeting Jas had been in the tiny apartment they'd had before the Silver Salamander Apothecary. Seba had clung to Hala's hand and the edges of her skirt. She had seemed so tall and old to him then, even though she had been only a few years older than he was now. The apartment had been small and cluttered with things he didn't recognize, and the whole thing smelled like smoke and rusty metal.

Seba had been about to start wailing again, distraught this strange woman, the only one who had volunteered to take him in, had brought him to such a foul-smelling place. But then he had seen the boy.

He was Huojenese, like so many of Seba's neighbors had been, and he was wearing ratty clothes, just like Seba. He had black hair and a pointed face, and he was sitting so still Seba thought he must have been a statue. Seba had never been as unmoving as that. The boy stared at Seba with wide eyes and a blank expression, saying nothing.

"Seba," Hala had said.

Even her Almaric accent sent a familiar warmth through Seba. He remembered the sweet, syrupy pastries of the neighbors in the apartment above him.

"Meet Jas. He is your new friend."

It had been weeks before Jas smiled at Seba and months before he said his first words in Seba's presence, but Seba had never minded. He talked and smiled and had enough energy for them both. They chased cats through the streets and did somersaults through the park. The boys learned alchemy and medicine as Hala's tiny assistants, though they hadn't known it at the time.

The streets of Lis were their playground, Hala's tiny apartment their home, and Seba even came to look forward to the smell because it meant he was safe. It was only when he got older, after they had moved to the apothecary and Seba had realized what Hala's odd little experiments really were, that he understood the indisputable truth of his existence.

Something about this city or maybe this country, perhaps even the entire world, didn't want Seba to be safe. The prophecy curse was just the latest example.

But here was an opportunity to *make* himself safe. And to secure Jas and Hala with him. The marquise clearly needed them. He wondered how much.

"This job," said Seba, "does it pay?"

The marquise raised her dark brows, and Seba felt an odd thrill. He might have surprised her.

"With more than the life of the Knell, you mean?"

"Think of it as an addendum. You say nothing, we say nothing, we do your weird jobs, and what happens after?"

Jas's gaze was focused on him, but Seba only had eyes for the marquise of Lis. This was his chance to get everything he had always wanted. He would go along with the marquise's plan, become all the things the witches had said, and prove his loyalty to Ostrea. His curse would be broken.

But, after all of that, Seba had no desire to remain any kind of marquis or duke or king or anything else. He wanted to be free.

"Once I become queen, I don't care what you do. In fact, it would be best if you stayed away," said Adelina.

"Would you pay us to? Let's say, 100,000 *rejas* a year for us to leave you all alone and powerful in Jumaral?"

Lady Adelina paused, her eyes narrowing. She was a fascinating person to look at, Seba thought. Her expression remained completely inscrutable, but he sensed the gears in her head moving at impossible speeds.

Finally, she lifted her chin. "It's a deal. Shall we discuss step one?"

CHAPTER 6

ADELINA

The carriage trundled down the narrow streets of Lis, along the same route Adelina had taken early that morning on foot. Business owners and pedestrians ducked out of the way. Colorful aprons and headscarves dotted the edges of Adelina's vision.

"You look tired, *couraninha*," said her father, peering at her from the other side of the carriage.

"So do you," she replied.

Her parents sat side by side, carrying a sort of wary disposition that makeup and coffee had not been able to resolve. Adelina's mother *tsked* at the retort, but her father's lips twitched into a good-natured smile. It crinkled the skin around his dark eyes.

"Hopefully, this motorcar demonstration will give all of us a burst of energy."

The carriage swayed when they turned onto the wider streets of the main shopping district. The faint sounds of the weekend market floated toward them. Shopkeepers hawked wares ranging from hand-painted plates to secondhand shoes to a full crate of ducks, while customers haggled eagerly over the smallest button on a child-size dress.

Adelina and Simão used to sneak out of the house in clothing borrowed from the servants to see all the animals and eat croissants in a café around the corner. It had been on one of those outings he had first suggested they sneak to the beach. Though now, those same streets and shops were dotted with wanted posters for Simão's killer.

"Sit up, Adelina." Her mother's voice snapped her mind back into focus. "If the people see you acting like a worm, they'll start treating you like one."

From his seat beside her, Calixto leaned so close their shoulders touched. He muttered, "I hear it's mating season for worms."

"Be quiet," she hissed back, though she didn't miss the look her parents exchanged.

She knew what was coming before her father even cleared his throat.

"Adelina," he began, adopting the tone he usually saved for official meetings. "Before we present ourselves to the public, there's a decision you should be made aware of. The Council of Lis, as well as researchers in Fulgeo, have reported rising levels of apathy by the people towards the House of Ducança."

"And you want me to fix it," finished Adelina.

The duke's jaw ticked. "Not fix it, exactly. Just—"

The duchess interjected. Her cool eyes fixed appraisingly on Adelina. "You are to do your duty as the new marquise of Lis."

Adelina made a show of considering the statement. "And what exactly does this duty entail?"

She let them explain—her father uncomfortable and withdrawn, her mother with about as much emotion as if she were ordering lunch rather than demanding her only daughter make a media campaign out of courtship. Calixto said nothing, but she could sense his careful observance of her every move and reaction.

"Why doesn't Calixto do it?" she asked when they were done explaining, only a few streets away from their final destination.

"Because I'm busy. And because I'm currently here in Lis, so it wouldn't make much sense for me to take up a suitor and then drop them as soon as I return to Fulgeo."

Adelina bit back her retort that living in the capital city hadn't stopped him before. Every time Calixto spoke, he acted like he was the most knowledgeable and important person in the world. It had grated on her nerves since childhood, though it had only gotten worse since he became the crown prince.

"Rosália," began Adelina's father. "If Adelina does not want—"

Her mother held up a hand. "We all do what we must for Jumaral, and this has been decided by your role as the marquise of Lis. Your job is to make sure the people care about you—*both* of you—so that one day Prince Calixto can rule. Not very far from now, we could all be dead, and it will be down to the two of you to keep the House of Ducança alive, thus keeping Jumaral alive. That will mean fulfilling your duties and providing Jumaral with heirs who will do the same. Understand?"

Adelina nodded tightly, ignoring the haughty look Calixto sent her way. It wasn't uncommon for her parents to apply the "when I'm dead" argument, but now the words scraped at her thoughts. She didn't understand how her mother and her father could sit there and talk about death and legacy and the children of the family outliving them, when she was fairly certain their son had just died because of them. And then there was the fact their daughter had just tried to kill *them* too.

That she still might.

But Adelina had time. The plan was more complicated now, but it was smarter. And maybe it would end without her having to bloody her hands, just like she had promised the Knell. There was a way out of this without killing the people sitting before her.

It was by the Rio Galho that they finally stopped, exiting with waves and rehearsed smiles aimed at a small crowd of city dwellers. Photographers stood the closest, their accordion cameras stuck on tripods in front of them. They were held back by ropes tied between old eucalyptus trees, leaving a clear space of grass surrounding a large black motorcar. The engineer, Eva Vilar, lingered nervously beside it.

There was excited movement at their arrival. Usually, the royal family only made public appearances for large events like the annual Festival of Dom Sebastião, which celebrated the legendary king of Jumaral.

Adelina took the elbow Calixto offered her, and they followed her parents to greet Eva and marvel at her feat of engineering. While Eva explained the many parts of the vehicle she had designed, Adelina searched the thin crowd of onlookers.

Sebastião Pinheiro was exactly where she had told him to be: as close as possible to Dalila, who hovered amidst the line of trees at the river's edge. Purple shadows had set into Seba's skin from lack of sleep, and his dark hair stood completely on end, but there was a sort of kinetic energy in his movements—a buoyancy making him look like he could run to the moon and back in that moment.

Beside him, Jasibin Guan looked less lively and even a little gray. From exhaustion or dread, Adelina couldn't tell.

"So," Calixto murmured while Eva Vilar gave the duke and duchess a detailed demonstration on the uses of the steering wheel. "What do you think of this engineer? Contender?"

"We're here to witness her genius, not goggle at her."

"I didn't say anything about goggling." She sensed his annoying grin without looking at him. "Are you goggling?"

"You are the one with romance on your mind."

"Romance is the only thing on anyone's mind."

There was a slight edge to his voice that hadn't been there before, and it made Adelina wonder if the conversation in the carriage had bothered him as well. Maybe he wasn't being pushed into a media campaign, but his older brother, Manuel, was dead too. Both of their older siblings had left them with titles and thrones they were never meant to fill. His father, Dom Aristides, was certainly not a comforting figure, and Calixto probably received some version of Adelina's mother's speech every day—it was all about utility, in their family.

Stop it. Calixto would never see the seat he was currently meant to inherit. Adelina was going to be queen. It was *her* fate, and Adelina was not in the practice of denying it.

"One moment. I have to speak to Dalila." Calixto gave her a questioning look, to which she only said, "It's about ladies' things," to get him to graciously drop her arm.

Adelina smiled at the people crowded on either side of the clearing she passed to stand beside her maid at the water's edge. One of the large eucalyptus trees towered over them, and Dalila was giving it many wide-eyed looks.

"Is everything ready?" Adelina whispered, careful to keep up her pleasant smile.

Her mother cast her a pointed glare from the other side of the motorcar.

"It is," Dalila replied, brushing a wisp of blond hair from her reddening cheeks. "Are you sure about this, Adelina?"

Adelina glanced to where Seba was unashamedly staring at her. She would have to teach him about the concept of discretion if this was going to continue. And the only way it could, the *only* way her parents would possibly let an apothecary's ward be one-half of the media scheme to save the House of Ducança, was if he forced his way in.

"I'm sure." Adelina brushed a finger by her brow, a signal to Seba that wouldn't have been noteworthy to anyone else. "Thank you, Dalila."

"Of course, my lady."

A moment later, there was a resounding crack over Adelina's head, a scream from the surrounding crowd, and a shove at her side. The breath was smacked out of Adelina's lungs by the surface of the Rio Galho.

CHAPTER 7

SEBA

It was possible Seba had miscalculated.

Shouts erupted around him as the marquise of Lis went crashing into the Rio Galho. Water swallowed Adelina and her dress so fast that Seba could barely process the fact that—by Our Lady—she wasn't coming back up.

He whirled around to look for Jas in the crowd. Guards and photographers surged forward, some already jumping in. Jas was gesturing furiously at the water.

The message was clear, but Seba still wrinkled his nose before jumping into the murky depths of the Rio Galho. The cold hit him instantly, but his mind was so focused on his own vague understanding of a city river's relationship to the sewage system that he didn't care.

Others were crashing around him, splashing his face in a soup of limbs. But the others hadn't noticed exactly where the marquise had gone under, and it was impossible to see her through the opaque water.

Remembering the curse on his fate and the promise of enough riches for a lifetime, Seba screwed his eyes and mouth shut as tightly as he could and dove beneath the surface.

For what felt like too long, the space around him rippled with other searchers. He couldn't tell what could be a sign of Adelina and what was simply another guard. Then, just as his lungs were starting to strain, his hand closed on what had to be an embroidered hem. He pulled it toward himself. No one dressed like this would willingly jump into a river.

She was heavy and limp, but just for a second; when his arms wrapped around her torso, she fought him. Half-heartedly and with no strength, but still there.

By Our Lady, Seba thought. He kicked them both to the surface, struggling with her weight and his own lack of oxygen. *Just let someone help you.*

Breaking the surface was like emerging into another world. Sound filled Seba's ears. People screamed and gasped at the marquise's return. His own hair flopped over his eyes, and camera flashes obscured the rest of what he could see. The sudden addition of gravity and stillness made Adelina even heavier than she had been before. Her head lolled back onto his shoulder, their cheeks touching. Her skin was freezing.

Seba tried not to show his relief too clearly when several guards took her from him, but he couldn't stop himself from lying flat on the hot stone ground for a few seconds after he had climbed from the river. He caught his breath and attempted to avoid contemplating where he had just been.

The money, he thought instead. *The curse and the money.*

He was vaguely aware of the small group gathering around Adelina, just a few feet from him. Adelina's maid, Dalila, was bent over her unconscious form, along with two guards and the duke of Lis. Prince Calixto and the duchess of Lis were both yelling at other guards, their hands gesticulating wildly.

Still coughing, Seba pushed himself to his knees, using every ounce of strength he possessed. He searched the crowd for Jas. Most of the journalists and photographers were still focused on Adelina—a cheer went around as she coughed up water—but some had their lenses pointing at Seba. He straightened and ran a hand through his hair, hoping there wouldn't be too many images of him face down on the ground, like a drowned rat.

It took him a few moments to spot Jas, who was sitting with his back against a tree, appearing shaky and pale. Even from this distance, the sheen of sweat on Jas's forehead caught the sun.

Had Jas been that worried about him and Adelina? He and Seba had spent the entire morning arguing about the plan, about Adelina.

It's a bad idea, Jas had repeated a million times.

It's a lucrative *idea*, Seba had returned just as many, knowing there was no way to convince Jas of the curse's danger.

While Seba had his mother's stories, Jas relied on Hala's skepticism for his own explanations of the world. In over a decade of holidays and festivals, Seba had heard enough of Hala's "logic" against Jumaralian religion, which Jas repeated without question, and trying to change either of their minds would be useless at best and devastatingly frustrating at worst.

"Thank you."

Seba jumped. He turned his attention to the duke of Lis standing beside him. Seba scrambled to his feet and quickly attempted to straighten his shirt, though it was plastered to his skin and had turned an odd greenish-brown color.

"Of-of course." Seba's voice was hoarse. He took the hand the duke extended to him, feeling slightly awed the duke would even deign to touch him in his current state.

But then he remembered that this was one of the men he was helping Adelina to usurp. The awe left him.

The duke said nothing else, just turned and followed the train of people now ushering Adelina back into the carriage she had come in. The moment she was gone, the crowd turned to Seba. Shawls were being passed forward to help him dry off, photos were being taken, and reporters were asking for his name.

Seba couldn't help but grin. He shook hands with people, answered questions from the reporters, and accepted the shawls and pastries and whatever else people handed to him. By the time the crowd started to thin, he had almost forgotten why he was there.

The last person to approach him was Eva Vilar. He hadn't paid much attention to her or her motorcar before his sojourn into the river, but now that she was close, there was something oddly familiar about her thick black curls; her dark skin; and the long, thin scar stretching along the right side of her jaw. She wasn't much older than him, probably in her mid-twenties, but she approached him with such surety he thought he might be in trouble.

"Sebastião Pinheiro, you said?"

"Um, yes?"

Her gaze softened. The corner of her mouth lifted slightly. "I knew your mother."

Seba's heart thudded, and all thoughts disappeared.

He realized he was smiling. Seba hadn't been able to talk about his mother in years, not since Hala had taken him in. "You did?"

Eva glanced toward the retreating journalists, as though afraid of being overheard, but everyone around them had already moved on to the business of the day. She leaned in and whispered, "Just be careful. You know, with your name out there. A lot of people don't remember her as fondly as I do."

"Wait, what do you—?"

But she was already walking away, toward her motorcar, with only a wave back at him.

It was then that Jas appeared beside him. "*You threw the marquise of Lis into a river?*"

"No," Seba corrected, trying to shake the interaction with Eva from his head. He tightened the shawl someone had passed him around his shoulders. "I *saved* the marquise of Lis from a river... after I saved her from a falling branch."

Jas gave him a look that suggested Seba had just murdered a kitten. Seba threw a soaked arm around Jas's shoulders, but Jas shoved him away with a wrinkled nose.

"What do we tell Hala?" Seba asked.

They strode down another cobbled street of shops. People cast him odd looks when he passed in his sopping clothes and decorative shawl. Half of him felt quite smug about it, knowing his appearance would make sense to them once the papers came out in the morning. The other half, the one still fixated on the words of Eva Vilar, needed to keep looking over his shoulder.

He wished she had stayed longer or that Jas hadn't shown up when he had. Sometimes, it felt like his mother, Teodora Pinheiro, existed only in his memory. He had cried a lot when Hala had first taken him in after his mother's death, and she had always told him the same thing: *It doesn't help to miss what's already gone.* So he had never spoken about Teodora with Hala, and he rarely mentioned her to Jas either.

It was surreal to hear Eva had known her. Maybe more bizarre to picture his mother associated with danger, when all he had focused on for twelve years were her stories and her warm hands, her hugs and her laugh while she taught him to swim and bought him his yearly birthday croissants.

"We tell Hala as much of the truth as we can," Jas said.

When the little bell above the apothecary door rang to announce their entrance, Hala was with a customer. Her hair was in a messy bun at the back of her head, and she wore a shabby leather apron over her dress. She spared them a glance across the shoulder of the woman she was assisting—then did a double take. Her large brown eyes grew wide, taking in Seba's state with some mix of annoyance and confusion.

She returned her attention to the customer, smiling warmly. Hala pushed a jar of tea leaves across the counter and wished her a blessed rest of her day. Upon catching sight of Seba, the customer pursed her lips, as though she had just come into contact with something rotten, and hurried from the shop.

Hala's friendly demeanor dropped. "What in the many cages of the Gods, Seba?" she whispered. "Did you fall into a fountain again?"

Seba bristled. "I was *eight*. And provoked."

"Then what did you do?" She emerged from behind the counter and crossed her arms. Her lips curled slightly when she neared. "And where did you get that shawl?"

"We stopped at a motorcar showing by the river," Jas explained. Hala's expression only grew more confused while she took in the rest of the story.

Seba admired the fine craftsmanship of the embroidered shawl now soaked through.

She looked at Seba as though she had never seen him before. "You saved her?"

"Yes." Seba grinned.

"On purpose?"

"Hala!"

She threw up her hands. "I'm sorry. It's just a bit hard to picture."

Seba scowled, but Hala and Jas laughed.

"Yes, yes, it's all very funny. Now, if you'll excuse me, I think I'll go wash myself of whatever filth I *heroically* and *purposefully* dived into to save *a marquise.*"

He adjusted the shawl and moved toward the stairs. Hala's gloved hand closed around his arm.

"Wait," she said, squinting at him. Her grin faded slightly. "What's that? On your neck?"

Simply a slight wound from where my future wife, the marquise I just saved, held me at knifepoint in the middle of the woods last night. His heartbeat leapt into his throat, as though determined to draw even more attention to the inexplicable cut at his neck.

"Shaving," Jas cut in before Seba could release whatever wheezing sound he had been about to produce. "Seba thought he had developed neck hairs."

Seba nodded. "I'm a growing boy, Hala."

Her eyes darted between the two of them suspiciously. This close, with the light streaming through the windows, they shone the amber color of tea.

"You're eighteen," she finally snapped at Seba. "And we should put something on it so that it doesn't get infected by whatever's in that river. Jas, watch the counter."

Jas shot Seba a warning look.

Seba followed Hala through the beaded curtain behind the counter separating the shop from her laboratory. His impression of Hala's laboratory had always been that there were ten times the amount of things there should have been. Upon entering, he barely avoided tripping on three stacks of books and a large jar with something disturbingly fleshy inside.

A bright green fire burned in the furnace—a sign Hala was in the midst of another reincarnation experiment. Seba had stopped believing they would ever work, ever since Hala had failed to bring back the elderly striped cat he and Jas had taken off the street when they were nine. If not even little Stripey could return, it didn't make sense to hold out for anyone else. Maybe that was why Hala had been so intent on six-year-old Seba not missing his dead mother.

He lowered himself onto a stool at the table, cringing at the press of wet trousers against his skin. Hala rummaged around as though blind, searching for antiseptic amongst jars of cat tongues and frog toes.

"I find it interesting," she said. Hala shifted aside something that looked suspiciously like a mini human heart.

"Find what interesting?" Seba's voice broke. He cleared his throat.

Hala took a seat at the stool beside him, a bottle of clear liquid in one hand and a cloth in the other.

"Yesterday morning, I treated Jas after it looked like he had been beaten to a pulp." She flipped the bottle upside down against the cloth, letting it soak some of the liquid. "Today, you show up with a cut across your neck after allegedly diving into the Rio Galho to save the marquise of Lis."

"Allegedly?" Seba repeated. Then, "By Our Lady, Hala," when she dabbed the cloth against his neck.

"Stings, does it?" Her eyes glinted.

"*Burns*, actually."

She smiled mischievously, reminding him of the jokes he and Jas had continuously tried to play on her as children and how she had always been one step ahead.

"Good," she said. "Now that you are reminded of the level of control I have over your well-being, is there anything you want to tell me?"

Seba momentarily forgot the burning sensation. His hand flew to his hair, and the heat spread to his cheeks.

"No." Even he wouldn't have said his voice was exactly trust-instilling. It didn't help that he did *want* to tell her, and he probably would have, if he didn't think she would try to shut it down.

Seba assumed she was about to press, but after a few seconds, she just sighed.

"Well, whatever you two are involved with, just...be careful."

She finished dabbing at his wound and rose to return the jar to its chaotic origins. Seba watched her, annoyance curling in his stomach.

Of course, he knew the dangers. Of course, he knew who—*what*—Hala and Jas were. It was why he spent every night trying to make cash. So he, Jas, and Hala could buy their way out of this city, which had done nothing but take from them. It was Hala who always said she couldn't leave Lis, which of course meant Jas didn't want to leave either.

And now here Seba was, taking a risk, yet again, for all of them. Jas didn't believe they were in any danger from the curse, and Hala would laugh him out of the room if he told her about it. Seba was the only one who *did* understand all the dangers threatening their family.

"When you wash up, use the water in that bucket there." Hala nodded her head at a basin half filled with clear water. "I made it this morning from some jewelry one of the ladies in the upper town used to pay."

Seba frowned, his frustration ready to overspill. "Hala, have you ever thought of—oh, I don't know—keeping the payment people give you instead of using it as an experiment?"

She shrugged. "It gets more use this way. If I turn gold into water enough times, there might be a day when I can do the reverse. But the potion also used up our last rat intestine, so if you hear any scuttling over the next few days, maybe put that razor to use. Now, get out of here. I have work to do."

Seba scowled, marching back into the front of the shop and then up the stairs to the room he and Jas shared.

Down below, tucked away in her laboratory, Hala was surely turning to her stack of aging notebooks and the secret project she never spoke to Jas and Seba about. It was just one more piece of evidence that could get them all killed.

Hopefully, this plan with Adelina would offer them all a chance at escape before that happened.

CHAPTER 8

JAS

Jas's withdrawal from sleep was slow, like his unconscious was a gooey and sticky place that didn't want to let him go. It took him far too long to realize he was no longer beneath the murky water with the ghostly blue corpses of Seba, Lady Adelina, and Lord Simão. His entire body had radiated pain while their voices beckoned him to join them—to drown.

Then came the jingle of the downstairs bell.

Jas sat straight up in bed, blinking against the sunlight just starting to bleed through the window. His head swam, and pain shot down his spine. His body had not yet recovered from his close encounter with Simão at the river the day before.

It worried him—the way the pain lingered longer than it ever had—but there was no time to think about that now. Seba was still fast asleep, his mouth gaping open and half his body hanging limply off the side of his mattress. His deep breathing almost covered the sounds from below, but Jas could distinguish the rise and fall of Hala's voice. It was the tone she used with customers, higher-pitched and cheerier than the way she usually spoke, but surely, she wouldn't allow customers in this early.

The voice that replied was lower, clipped and precise. Jas's heart leapt to his throat.

"Seba." Jas jumped up, frantically trying to get his bed in order

and push the piles of dirty clothes into the wardrobe. He simultaneously used his foot to nudge Seba awake. "*Seba.*"

"What?" Seba moaned, his eyes still closed.

"Lady Adelina's here."

For a moment, Seba didn't react. Then, like Jas, he leapt into
action. Unlike Jas, he maintained a low stream of curses while
promptly pulling on a pair of socks.

"I have ugly feet," he said in response to Jas's questioning look.

They had barely a few more seconds to get themselves in order
before the sound of approaching footsteps echoed up the stairs.
Pain shot through the back of Jas's skull when the voice reminded
him, *She won't be happy with yesterday's events.*

He and Seba stood awkwardly between their beds. The door
creaked open to reveal Hala, a dressing gown over her threadbare
nightdress and her hair in a long braid down her back. Her eyes
scoured over them and the room. From this angle, it was clear she
was on edge, but when her inspection was complete and she stepped
back to reveal the marquise of Lis, she was all smiles.

"You have a visitor."

Lady Adelina stepped forward, wearing a light blue gown and
clutching a flowered hat in her hand. Though he had now met her
several times over the last day, it was odd to see her here—appearing so formal in the bedroom he and Seba shared. Her eyes met
Jas's, and he knew what he was supposed to do.

"Lady Adelina, what an honor to have you here. I'm Jas, Seba's
brother."

Lady Adelina smiled. Satisfaction glinted in her eye while he
kept up the act for Hala.

"It's a pleasure to meet you, Jas. I was hoping I might speak to
you both about some plans my parents have to thank you, Seba, for
your heroics yesterday. Privately, if that would be fine."

Hala looked between the three of them, and Jas almost thought
she might say no.

*She wouldn't want the marquise of Lis messing with her little
experiments*, said the voice.

But Hala acquiesced only a moment later, giving a tiny bow of her head to the marquise before returning downstairs. Lady Adelina waited until Hala's steps had faded completely before closing the bedroom door. When she turned, her expression had lost any semblance of pleasantry.

"You'll need to be careful with her."

"Hala?" asked Seba.

"If the plan is going to work, everyone must be convinced of our innocence. That includes your guardian."

It was uncomfortable to hear her speak so casually about Hala. The Knell wasn't in danger from the bounty hunters, as long as he was useful to her, but Hala would not be so lucky if Adelina found out about her alchemy.

"Speaking of the plan," the marquise continued. She sat daintily on the edge of Jas's bed. "Shall we discuss your little bit of improvisation, Senhor Pinheiro?"

Seba ran a hand through his hair. "It wasn't improvisation," he explained. "It was an accident."

"It wasn't part of the plan."

"You wanted me to save you, right? Throw myself into the public eye? I did that."

"I am *paying* you to follow the plan that I laid out," she snapped. "You didn't do that."

Seba sat forcefully on his own bed so he was facing the marquise. "I saved your life."

"You threw me into a river."

"Yes, and then I saved you."

"Voices," Jas reminded them. Hala was still downstairs.

Lady Adelina pressed her lips together. Her chest rose and fell with steady breaths. "You need to be more careful."

"You were yelling too."

"I *meant* with the plans."

Seba made a large show of rolling his eyes. "I am caref—"

"Your face is as readable as a book. The farther you stray from the plan, the more you'll have to hide, and the more everyone will be able to tell that something strange is going on."

"My face is *not* a book."

Jas raised a brow, and Seba shot him his fiercest glare. Both remembered the hundreds of times Seba had been the reason that Hala caught them in their childhood antics.

"It *is*," said Adelina, "and you have to find a way to fix it because you're meeting my parents tonight. Both of you."

"What?"

Seba's jaw dropped in horror, and Jas couldn't help feeling a similar emotion storm through him. As someone with the inexplicable power to communicate with the dead in a country that sent bounty hunters after anyone even remotely associated with magic, meeting the duke and duchess of Lis was perhaps the last thing Jas wanted to do.

But you'll do it for Seba.

The voice was never wrong.

But Jas still wasn't sure following along with Adelina's plans was really the best way to keep Seba safe. Seba hadn't mentioned the prophecy since meeting Adelina, but Jas had a feeling he hadn't been fully convinced by Jas's argument about prophecy curses being a myth. If all went according to Adelina's plan, Seba's prophecy would likely be fulfilled, and Jas was scared of what Seba might do to get there if he truly believed he would be damned if he didn't.

"There's a plan to set me up with a suitor, and it appears we've succeeded in getting you chosen. The city already knows you and was part of how we met, you have connections to the market class, you're relatively attractive, and you don't seem particularly cunning or even intelligent, based on the actions everyone witnessed yesterday. You're perfect." As she said it, the corners of Adelina's mouth twitched, and Jas wondered if she was enjoying the perfect display of Seba's emotions while he was simultaneously lauded and insulted. "Of course, they need insurance, which is where you come in, Jas."

"Why do they want me?"

"Well, they don't know about you yet, but they did say they'll offer employment in the household to a family member of Senhor Pinheiro. As further reward."

"How does that make me insurance?"

"Because if Seba acts out, you'll be within gun range." She gave him a cold smile that sent chills down his spine, and he couldn't tell if she was joking. "And having an excuse to be in the manor will give you more opportunities to speak to my brother. That's what you need, isn't it? Something that belonged to him, places he visited?"

Jas shrugged. He despised explaining his powers, hated thinking about them. "Really anything or anyone he had a connection to helps, but even that's not enough all of the time. I can't go to the Beyond myself. He needs to come to me, and I can't force him."

"Did you speak to him at the Rio Galho, then? That's where they pulled his body from."

The lingering pain surged at the memory, and Jas flinched. He didn't want to experience it again, but even more than that, he didn't want to find the answers Lady Adelina was looking for. The entire city of Lis knew witches were likely responsible—the new signs plastered around Lis made it clear enough—and Jas couldn't blame them for wanting to strike against the royal family.

"What are you going to do when you find the...the killer?"

Adelina shrugged. "I'm sure I'll think of a punishment to fit the crime of murdering the king's nephew. I can be very creative. Did you speak to him or not?"

Jas hesitated. No one knew what happened to witches after they were caught, only that they ended up dead. He did not want to put any of them at Lady Adelina's mercy.

So you'll leave Seba to her mercy instead?

"No," Jas replied. "I just...felt him. He was near but not interested in talking to me."

It felt like an understatement for the burning that had spread through Jas's body, the crashing wave of dizziness that had sent him collapsing into a tree, the still-present throb at the back of his skull. But—though Lord Simão had made it known he was there—he had communicated nothing Jas could make out.

"Well, then we try again," said the marquise, straightening her clothes as she stood. "You'll receive an invitation to the manor later today. Be prompt and wear something clean." Then she left as quickly as she had arrived.

It was only about an hour past dawn, but there was no prospect of Jas going back to sleep after that. He had thought Seba would, but if the lack of snores were anything to go by, they were both wide awake in their beds, even though they had crawled back under their blankets while the sun rose.

Jas's magic was broken. It wasn't something he had told Seba, not something he would soon divulge to the marquise. It wasn't even something he had wanted to admit to himself. But it was true. The pain he had felt at the mere presence of Lord Simão, the shock of the ever-present voice in his head—none of it was normal.

When have you ever been normal? Maybe the world is simply catching up with you.

Maybe. But that didn't change Jas's fear that perhaps his death wouldn't come at the hands of bounty hunters, the House of Ducança, or even the witches he might be forced to turn in as culprits behind the murder of the marquis of Lis.

If he didn't figure out what was happening to him and learn how to control it so he could complete Lady Adelina's plan, it would be his own magic killing him from the inside.

CHAPTER 9

SEBA

Seba didn't know what Jas's problem was. The opportunities Adelina was presenting them with were not ones that came about every day. And yet, Jas could do nothing but moan about how dangerous it was, how Adelina wasn't trustworthy, and how she was much too flippant about the potential of any of them being either the perpetrators or victims of murder.

Jas had always been annoying in that way—too stuck on moral philosophizing to recognize when he was being handed something good. Even that time Hala had attempted to bring their cat, Stripey, back to life had been met with questions such as, "But what if he doesn't *want* to be brought back to life?" and "But what about all the other cats?" Eventually, Hala had just sent Jas out of the room, while Seba had been left to watch the experiment fail.

Most weeks, Seba and Jas performed any number of tasks for Hala—stocking shelves, cleaning beakers, testing weird ointments and potions, managing the books, and very occasionally doing some light dissection of whatever rodent she had found in the alley behind the shop. Today was meant to be an ingredient collection day when Seba and Jas would wander around the city, eating croissants from their favorite bakery before making the rounds at the markets. They would visit some suppliers at their homes, workshops, or even just at mysterious drop sites, if the contraband was too exciting.

Seba liked ingredient collection days because they were an excuse to eat and use up some of the excess energy that always seemed prepared to burst out of him, but it turned out they were only fun when they were with Jas.

The sun beat down on him when he left the last market before making his way to the apartments down the narrow street further in the city. He had a heavy bag looped around his shoulder, weighed down with odd herbs and dried meats, and sweat trickled down his back. Seba cursed Jas under his breath. Jas had given him no excuse for skipping out on the day—just that he was busy, which Seba didn't believe. It wasn't as though Jas knew anyone Seba didn't.

Seba had still gotten his croissants—which he had enjoyed for free because the bakery owner recognized him as the marquise's savior from the front page of the newspapers that morning—but now they sat dully in his stomach. He hauled himself down side streets, stepping around piles of dog shit and ducking under clotheslines.

There weren't many people out around these streets, as most worked closer to the city center. It was good for ensuring few people saw him coming and going on these errands, but it also made him feel completely exposed.

This was so much better with Jas.

He returned to cursing Jas's name under his breath as he turned down a particularly narrow alley. Seba had walked only a few steps when a pounding came from behind him.

Before he could turn to see what was coming, he was thrown against a wall. The breath was expelled from his lungs, and the force of the impact shuddered from his back through every bone in his body. The bag fell from his shoulder, thumping at the feet of the man who currently had Seba's jacket lapels in his fists.

He looked to be in his thirties, gray scattered amongst the stubble of his jaw. The man reeked of cigar smoke and alcohol.

"Afternoon," Seba wheezed, painfully aware this sort of situation was becoming a pattern for him.

"You the Pinheiro boy?" the man growled.

Seba looked up and down the alley, praying to Ostrea someone would appear to help him.

When he didn't answer, the man slammed him into the wall again.

"Maybe," Seba whispered, unable to do much more than shape his lips around shallow gasps. The man pressed him harder into the wall, and prickles of stone dug into the back of Seba's head. "Yes."

"You have something for my boss."

"What? No, I don't."

"Debts have to be paid, Pinheiro. Your mother owed a lot of people a lot of money."

The words sent shivers down Seba's spine. He remembered Eva's words from the river, *Just be careful. You know, with your name out there. A lot of people don't remember her as fondly as I do.*

"I don't have any money," he hissed through clenched teeth. "And I don't know who your boss is."

"You've never heard of Heitor Alves?"

Seba cursed.

"That's right, boy. Teodora Pinheiro owed Senhor Alves 300,000 *rejas*, and that's on you now. Get it to him by the festival, or the next time I see you, we'll see if we can get your head *through* that wall."

With that, he let Seba go, flashing a grin while he primly wiped the dust from Seba's shoulders.

"May Ostrea bless you," he called over his shoulder, striding casually out of sight.

For a moment, all Seba could do was stand there, staring at the place the man had disappeared. Then everything hit him all at once, like he was still being slammed against a wall. He coughed, sliding down to sit amongst the spilled ingredients.

Seba didn't know how long he sat there, head between his knees, heart pounding and breaths too short. He became fixated on one of the sprigs of herbs now spread across stone, the way the little green leaf fluttered slightly in the breeze. It looked so odd, so verdant, against the gray of musty rock.

He needed to move. It wasn't safe here. Maybe it wasn't safe anywhere. His mental map of Lis felt blurred and disjointed. He only knew it would take way too long to get home.

Maybe it was because his mother was on his mind, but the only thought clear to him was that he used to live somewhere around here. The last home Seba remembered was a spare room in the deepest, most cluttered part of Lis, where the smell of sewage covered the spray of the distant sea and the produce of the city markets.

But that was unhelpful. It wasn't like he had a home to return *to* anymore. Unless...*I knew your mother.*

Before he could truly consider where he was going, Seba gathered up his ingredients, tucked the bag safely under his arm, and scrambled to his feet. He had no idea where to find Eva Vilar, but if she had known his mother, then it wasn't a horrific assumption that she might be around here.

He half ran through the streets of Lis, unable to stop panic from gripping him. *Three hundred thousand* rejas. If he'd had that kind of money, he, Jas, and Hala would have fled Lis a long time ago. As it stood, he probably had twenty? Maybe thirty? Even if he asked Hala and Jas, their savings altogether probably didn't come out to more than a few hundred.

All the dread he'd pushed down since realizing Adelina didn't plan to immediately have them killed resurfaced tenfold. It had been too easy. The curse would stop him somehow. Here was his cosmic punishment for hearing what no mortal was supposed to—an obstacle to force him to fight for what Ostrea had already planned for him or face death.

After a few minutes, he made it to his old street. It was just past lunchtime at this point, and many people sat on their front steps with cigarettes and tiny cups of coffee, loudly gossiping. A group of small children chased a stray dog up the street.

Not seeing any sign saying, "EVA VILAR THIS WAY," Seba turned to the first person he noticed and asked where she lived. He had expected to have to ask for a long time, but it seemed Eva was a local celebrity. The woman gave him directions to the garage Eva owned a few streets over. It felt strange looking at all the faces he passed, knowing he might have recognized them when he was younger. He might have been one of those kids chasing the dog, growing up in the center of everyone's afternoon gossip session.

Seba wondered what his life would have been like at this point if his mother had remained alive and if he had stayed here. She would have had time to pay her debts, even to rats like Heitor Alves. Seba didn't know what business she'd had with him and doubted he wanted to.

He would probably have become some kind of farm laborer, or maybe he would have worked at one of the factories cropping up around Lis. Seba would likely have been illiterate, as his mother and most of the adults in Lis were. Hala had been the one to teach him, and his first books had been gory alchemical textbooks that carried no resemblance to the fairy tales and legends his mother had filled his mind with.

Eva's garage was open when he came to it, panting and sweaty. A large metal door slid to the side, revealing what looked like the skeleton of a motorcar. Piles of gears, tools, and things Seba couldn't begin to understand were neatly gathered around it and hanging from the walls. The smells of oil, gasoline, and metal overtook him, even before he entered, but Seba wasted no time darting inside and pressing his back against the wall so no one looking in would be able to see him. He let the bag fall from his shoulder and ran a hand through his hair, fighting to catch his breath.

Seba didn't have to wait long for Eva to appear. She emerged just moments later from behind a curtain cutting off part of the room, with a steering wheel in her hands. Eva froze when she saw him. Her face only briefly showed her surprise before melting into something like resignation.

"What are you doing here?" she said.

"What a pleasant surprise for me too," Seba replied with mock enthusiasm.

Eva set down the steering wheel and dusted her hands on her trousers. "Look, if you came to ask me about your mother—"

"You'll happily tell me everything you know?"

"I don't really *know* anything."

Some of Seba's panic sparked in his stomach. "Then why would you say anything?"

She shrugged. Her shoulders almost reached the edges of the

shawl she had wrapped around her hair. "I just know that there are rumors. I was too young to know any details. Now, why do you look like that?"

"*What* rumors?" As much as he wanted to scream about being jumped by one of Alves's goons and about his newfound money problems, Seba wanted this answer more.

"I don't really—"

"Obviously, you do know, or you wouldn't have come up to me and warned me to be careful. Right?"

Eva pursed her lips. She seemed to consider him for a moment. Then, she opened the curtain behind her and gestured him through. "I don't know a lot."

Seba kept a wary eye on her as he walked past the curtain, finding a narrow spiral staircase. It creaked while he climbed it, and Eva's footsteps were just as clear behind him. If someone did come looking for him, at least he would probably hear them coming.

The door at the top of the stairs opened to a neat apartment. Its airiness was in stark contrast to the workshop downstairs and even the streets outside. Seba took a seat at the dainty table beside the old but starkly clean stove.

Eva locked the door behind her. "Cookies?" she offered.

Seba tried to keep his frown. "Please."

She went about preparing a coffee for each of them and setting out a tin of assorted cookies. Seba took three.

"So?" he said, after swallowing his first bite. "Anything you want to tell me?" *Particularly about why my mother would owe 300,000 rejas to Heitor Alves and if she somehow left that amount lying around anywhere*, he thought.

"How much do you remember about Teodora?"

Everything, he wanted to say. Except it wasn't true. His mother had died when he was six years old—disappeared for a week and then turned up in their house as a corpse. Of course, he remembered moments, but even those were broken up and confusing. Stories, hugs, smiles, and those more puzzling moments of hushed voices and odd trips in the night.

"Enough," he said instead. He remembered what Adelina had said about being able to read lies on his face like a book.

Eva gave a slow nod. The scar on her jaw caught the light. Seba's eyes fixated on the way it framed her jaw, almost like she was a drawing.

"She owed a lot of people a *lot* of money. When she died, I remember people were worried about you. What they'd do to you."

Seba's fists clenched involuntarily, crushing the cookie in his hand. His head echoed with the snap of breaking bones.

"It was lucky that you'd disappeared by the time anyone came looking."

"But why did she borrow?"

Eva furrowed her brows and looked at some place over his head, clearly trying to remember something. "I don't know. Lots of people struggle in Lis."

"And so, the people that came looking for her...they just...let it go? Lost the money?"

"I guess so?"

"You *guess* so?"

"I was twelve," she snapped. "And no one really likes to talk about what happened to Teodora, so it's not like I could ask around."

"Why don't people like talking about her?"

"Not *her*, I don't think. Just her death." Eva tapped a nail against her cup, and the sound crawled up Seba's spine. "It was...odd. It feels strange to talk about, can't you tell?"

Seba didn't reply, but he absolutely could. The air felt off, like the rules of the universe were slightly disjointed.

He clenched his fists tighter, trying to get the image of his mother's corpse out of his head. Sprawled as he had found it, with her head to the side, her mouth open, and her arms spread like she could be flying if her shoulder wasn't making a strange angle with her neck. Her eyes—usually the exact same hazel as his own—black as night.

"What about it?" he asked, his voice strained.

"Something about the suddenness, I think. It wasn't normal. The theories that came about were...unique, to say the least. I remember the high priestess of Lis visiting, though I guess she wouldn't have been high priestess at the time. She was rambling about encantadas and magical corruptions of Ostrea. The usual."

"Do encantadas really exist?"

They were creatures out of legend—people trapped to guard some treasure, waiting to grant a wish to the ones who released them. But, unlike witches and their prophecies, to Seba's knowledge, encantadas weren't just appearing in the hills of Lis anymore.

Encantada stories were mostly from times before the First Great Wave, fodder for religious fanatics. Seba had always assumed they were just mythical extractions of something real, like how the wyvern symbol of Jumaral was probably inspired by the little lizards found around the entire country.

"Was my mother killed, then? By the people she owed money to?"

Eva's next words were careful. "Considering how upset they all were when she was no longer around to pay her debts, I doubt it. But someone else probably knows. And they'll want to talk to you too."

"You're saying I need to be careful of who I'm around?" He thought about Jas's worries about Adelina, his warnings.

"Maybe." Eva gave him a knowing look. "I guess just don't assume that everyone has your best interests in mind. Even the most powerful among us can be washed away."

"By Ostrea?"

She shrugged. "Or whatever else you believe in."

Seba stayed to finish his coffee, chatting with Eva about life since they had last seen each other, which apparently had been twelve years ago. If he'd had any way of contacting Jas, he would have told him to meet him so he wouldn't have to walk home alone, but that wasn't possible.

He visited well past his welcome, by the amount of times Eva mentioned how much work she had to do, but he only left when it became clear staying much longer would make him late for his appointment with Adelina. There were more people around than there would have been if he had tried to go home right after the incident, but he still ran the whole way back to the Silver Salamander Apothecary.

If he was going to ask the marquise of Lis for 300,000 *rejas*, he needed to make a good impression.

CHAPTER 10

JAS

Jas had left their bedroom that morning just as Seba was waking up. He had only muttered a quick, vague excuse before hurrying down the stairs, and he was almost out the door when Hala had stopped him in his tracks.

"Anything you'd like to share before you go?" She had been standing behind the counter with her arms crossed, watching him with an almost bored expression. Her box of rusty jewelry, which she accepted from customers, had been half emptied on the counter, waiting to be sorted into their experimental uses.

"I don't—She just came to meet Seba," he had said. Whatever he thought about the marquise of Lis and her plan, telling Hala anything about it would not be in Hala's best interest.

Because Hala has been so concerned for your safety, with all her forbidden experiments?

"She didn't say anything about—"

"No, not even anything about the apothecary." That part was true. Lady Adelina had said nothing about Hala, except to refer to her as the guardian of Jas and Seba. As far as Jas knew, she didn't realize Hala was an alchemist, and he would keep it that way.

"I was going to ask," Hala had continued softly, "if the marquise had said anything about *you*."

"Oh."

The skin around Hala's eyes had creased. "A letter came this morning. She's invited both of you to the manor. I know Seba will want to maintain this connection with her, but you need to remember your position. You know what she and that family are. You can't trust them. If she or anyone else in that house suspects you at all, it won't take a word before you're in chains."

And before Hala is in chains too. And Seba.

"It will be fine, Hala."

He was going to fix his magic, he was going to perform the job for Lady Adelina and get Seba his crown, and he was going to stop anyone from finding out about Hala's alchemy.

Jas was going to make it fine.

The city of Lis was full of ghosts. It was mostly because it was full of people—people with big emotions and hearts stretching to the farthest reaches of those they did and didn't know. It was a city of talking and shouting and laughing and crying, churches chiseled from human hands and imagination, air smelling of fresh bread, pastries, fish, and flowers.

The ghosts fed on the attention the people of Lis gave with their whole souls, calling for their loved ones, shouting their greetings, insults, and cries of emotion with the rest. But Jas was the only one who could hear them.

Recently, though, the ghosts of Lis had become nearly unbearable. Their voices scraped through Jas's brain like nails, sending shooting pain through his body. He was never going to last through dinner with some of the highest members of the House of Ducança.

It was a relief when he left the crowded streets of the main city and started working his way up the hills. The day's heat was just starting to emerge, and he wiped sweat from his brow while he made his way up the winding dirt street. Jas and Seba had never actually made it to the witches' house on the night they had been looking, and he wasn't sure if he would be able to find them this time either. Maybe they would find *him* again.

Lesser than Sebastião and greater.

Not so happy, yet much happier.

Thou shalt get kings, though thou be none.

Jas hadn't had much time to dwell on the words, not when the prophecy had been so quickly followed by the appearance of the marquise of Lis. Some of the pain lessened with his distance from the main city, and he allowed himself to consider them for the first time.

Each statement was in complete contradiction to the other, and there was something odd about the way his prophecy had been so connected to Seba's—as if they were being put in opposition to each other.

Like that's different from before?

Jas bristled, and not just because of the shock the voice sent through his brain. He and Seba had never been foes, and they never would be.

Jas just needed to take the advice he had given Seba and put it out of his mind. Whether it came true or not, it wasn't up to Jas.

It was then that he came upon the house.

It looked just like all the others—orange roof over once-white walls, an overgrown vegetable garden, and a bright blue door. There was nothing particular about it at all, except for the feeling it gave him. There was magic in this house, and it nagged at him just as clearly as if someone had pulled on his sleeve. He and Seba must not have come this way because there was no way Jas could have missed this.

That same feeling from the other night descended on him—the wrongness of the quiet. Was it the magic or just his own fear? Jas had been so preoccupied with his pain that he had forgotten to be anxious about the fact he was paying a visit to witches. He couldn't help looking over his shoulder, but there was no one there. Even the next closest house was barely visible through the narrow trees.

Another shock sparked through his brain, a nudge from the voice in his head.

Jas squared his shoulders, straightened his clothes, and walked up to the front door. He knocked only once before the door swung open. He recognized the girl standing there, slightly taller than Jas, straight black hair hanging loosely to her waist, freckles smattered across her nose, a knowing smile on her face, like she had been expecting him. She had been the youngest of the three witches that night... *Thou shalt get kings, though thou be none.*

"Jasibin Guan," she said.

It was the normalcy of her voice that struck him. He had expected the throaty, raspy call of the earth he had heard that night.

"Jas," he corrected, not knowing how to respond.

The girl's grin widened, and she stepped aside to let him in.

He didn't know what he thought he would find—maybe a whole house like Hala's laboratory? Cauldrons, black cats, and more clothes like they had been wearing that night? Weapons to ward off bounty hunters?

But if any of those types of things were in the small house, they were not in the room Jas saw. Instead, their normal kitchen was light and airy from the open windows. There was a rickety table against one wall, with dirty dishes piled at one end. Charred logs lay shriveled in the open fireplace, and what looked like a crocheted image of a flower hung framed over the mantle.

What caught Jas's attention the most was the small silver icon of Ostrea and Her Great Wave hanging above the doorway to the next room. Jas couldn't say he had ever described himself as faithful to Jumaral's Lady of the Seas—maybe because he had been born in Huojen, on nearly the other side of the continent, and raised by Hala, who had spent most of her life in Almard—and he didn't believe in the idea witches had stolen their magic from Her, but he was still surprised by the presence of this blatant sign of faith. Witches in Jumaral had spent centuries being told the Jumaralian ocean goddess hated them, ever since the First Great Wave, but it seemed that hadn't stopped these witches from worshiping Her.

Why so interested? You are not a witch, little Knell.

He flinched.

"Sit," said the girl, snapping Jas out of his thoughts.

He accepted a seat at the small table. The chair creaked slightly beneath him. Without asking if he wanted any, the girl started rummaging around in the kitchen cupboards, preparing four cups of coffee.

"What's your name?" Jas asked.

"Ágata." She set one of the cups in front of him and placed the others around the table. Ágata turned back and put a fifth, empty cup on the counter.

Jas eyed the empty cup, but Ágata offered no explanation before joining him at the table. She said nothing but watched him like he was the most interesting thing she had seen in a long time.

"Um, are the others here as well?" Jas asked.

As if responding to his words, the front door swung open, and the two other witches from that night stepped into the room, carrying baskets of leafy green herbs and wearing floral aprons over their skirts. One, the younger of the two, was pale and slim, her eyes brightening when she saw Jas. The other had a slight hunch to her back. Her skin was sun-worn and creased, and she, too, seemed to sharpen when she noticed Jas at the table.

"Jasibin Guan," said the women in unison, just as Ágata had greeted him.

His cheeks heated. "Jas," he said again.

"Just as you said, Hermínia," Ágata noted to the oldest woman.

"Now only Gilda's warning left to discover." Hermínia looked at the other woman.

See? You were a warning too.

Jas was sure he didn't flinch that time, and yet all three pairs of eyes turned on him. Interest flooded each of their gazes. He was starting to think he should leave. This was dangerous.

More dangerous than what you're doing tonight? More dangerous than Seba's daily life, thanks to you?

Though his hands shook, he made himself sip at the bitter shot of coffee while the older women set down their baskets and joined him and Ágata at the table. He steeled himself to begin his questions—both about his powers and why the witches had targeted Seba and Jas for the prophecy.

But Hermínia spoke first. "You hear those passed, don't you, boy?"

There was no use hiding it. "I always have." It felt wrong to admit without the protection of the Knell cloak and mask. "But recently it's felt...wrong."

You've always been wrong.

He had expected to have to explain more, but the three witches exchanged looks at his words.

"What is it?" he asked. His heart thudded in his throat.

"Magic has been unruly," said Gilda.

"Since his death," added Hermínia.

"The death of the marquis of Lis," clarified Ágata.

Jas thought back, trying to pinpoint when he had first started feeling the pain of his magic. He remembered the morning after the marquis of Lis died, just over a week ago. The feeling of the city's mourning the second he woke up.

Jas had thought the ache in his bones had been down to the collective grief all around him, but maybe that had been the start. It wasn't until a few nights later, when he had been with Seba in yet another gambler's den, that he had felt that burning for the first time, the same he experienced days after in the office of Heitor Alves.

"But what happened to it? The magic?"

The other two looked at Hermínia, and it was the oldest witch who set down her cup and answered him.

"There is magic in every breath, every life, and every death. Magic is all around, but only a few can harness it."

Jas knew all this already. Those who could harness magic by themselves were witches. Those who couldn't but looked for other ways to wield it were alchemists—like Hala.

And you are neither—an abomination all your own.

Hermínia continued. "Because magic is built into this world, magic will become unruly when the rules of the world start to break down. It started on the night of the death of the marquis of Lis. When it will end is up to you."

"Up to me? So, I can fix it?"

"And break it. You. And Sebastião Pinheiro. And Adelina Malves Ducança."

Jas's hand jerked, his coffee spilling across the table. Hermínia's words and the responding spark from the voice were too much for his body to contain. He jumped up from his seat, apologizing while the witches sat there serenely. None of them made a move to stop the spread of coffee. Jas grabbed a dish towel from the counter to clean up his mess.

Are you really surprised, little Knell? Surprised that the world will crack beneath your fingers?

Could there actually be some outside force that had brought himself, Seba, and Lady Adelina together that night?

"What can I do?" Jas did not take his eyes off the towel now soaked in coffee. His voice shook. "How do I stop that from happening?"

It was Ágata who responded. "Simply wait for the cycle to end."

"No, I'll—" *Fix it*, he wanted to finish.

"It's too late now," said Gilda.

"It has always been too late," added Hermínia.

He made himself look at them, once again forcing away the fears of Jumaral, the feeling he was cursed. "If magic is unruly, that must mean you're struggling too, right? So, if you can help me stop this, then I can help all of you."

Did he imagine the pity creasing their expressions?

"You will help witches in your time, but not like this. We feel the change in magic like a fish feels a change in tide," explained Hermínia. "But you are made of the water itself. And if you need an example of what this magic can do, look to the castles."

"Wha—?"

But Jas couldn't finish expressing his panic.

Gilda rose abruptly, and her own cup clattered to its saucer. She looked to the window, her focus completely on the view outside. Gilda moved slowly to stand beside the door, as if in a trance. Her fingers tapped against each other at her sides.

"It's here. My warning."

The other two witches stood and joined her. The same slow grace came over their movements. Jas followed cautiously and peered over Gilda's shoulder.

For almost a full minute, there was nothing but the subtle sway of grass and leaves in the wind, the faint twittering of birds flying above. What was her "warning"? Bounty hunters?

The thud of hooves came first, and the hair rose on the back of his neck. Ágata went to prepare the fifth cup, which had sat empty, waiting for the expected visitor.

Jas's stomach flipped when the rider crested the hill. Lady Adelina Maria Malves Ducança was sitting astride a horse as black as shadow, galloping toward them.

"By the pricking of my thumbs." Gilda's voice had returned to that low crawl Jas remembered—like her words were rising from the earth itself. "Something wicked this way comes."

Panic gripped Jas. He must have led Lady Adelina straight to them. "Is she here to capture you?"

All three women were perfectly serene, none of them matching his own terror.

"Her majesty is here to fulfill an agreement," said Gilda.

"But"—Jas watched Lady Adelina dismount and lead her horse to be tied at the gate—"you said 'something wicked'—"

"Adelina Malves has a role to play, just as you do, Jasibin Guan," said Hermínia.

Jas thought his heart might explode from his chest. Lady Adelina had already begun marching up the path, and every step she took only made it clearer Jas could *not* be there when she entered. She would discover his powers weren't working, or she would think he was hiding secrets, decide to investigate, and find out about Hala or the prophecy. Either way, she would surely decide the costs of employing the Knell outweighed the benefits.

As if reading his thoughts, Ágata said, "There's always the back window."

With no other option, Jas shoved open the window by the kitchen table and scrambled through it. A knock sounded at the door. His foot caught on the ledge in his haste, and he landed hard across a row of leafy strawberry plants.

Lady Adelina's footsteps entered the room he had just flung himself from. Jas spit dirt from his mouth and pressed his back against the wall, regretting the squashed plants he had left in his wake. He listened to the marquise order for the window to be shut and the curtains to be drawn.

Someone doesn't want to be overheard, said the voice.

Did she suspect those witches of being the ones who had killed her brother? Or was she using them to find the ones who had?

Jas carefully rose, just enough to glimpse snatches of the scene inside through the lacy curtains. Though he couldn't hear much, he watched Lady Adelina spread maps and papers across the table where the coffee-soaked dishrag still lay. Lady Adelina's shoulders remained tense while she pointed things out. Her lips pinched, and her jaw clenched whenever she wasn't speaking.

The witches, for their part, carried expressions of mixed intrigue, concern, and—maybe he imagined it—triumph.

Jas didn't know what to make of it, but he knew it wasn't something he was supposed to see. He waited until Lady Adelina left. The sun had already begun its downward descent before he scrambled down the hill himself, realizing he was going to be late to meet Seba.

This connection between the witches and the marquise of Lis made no sense. They were meant to be fighting on opposite sides—with Lady Adelina part of the government giving out money for the capture of witches.

She made a deal with you, *didn't she, little Knell?*

The voice was right. Lady Adelina must have seen some utility in whatever agreement she had made with Hermínia, Gilda, and Ágata. Their lives were in the hands of the marquise of Lis just as much as his own, which left the question of what the witches had agreed to give her in return.

CHAPTER 11

SEBA

Jas wasn't back yet. They had to leave for the Manor of Lis in five minutes, and *Jas* hadn't returned. Between the two of them, Jas had never been the late one, and Seba didn't really know what to do with the fact that he was now.

He frowned at himself in the small mirror above the sink, trying for the millionth time to get his hair to at least all go in one direction. It felt uncomfortable to be dressed like this in the little bathroom at the apothecary, the door open so he had a full view of the tiny hall and Hala's cramped bedroom across it.

Seba was wearing a suit that didn't belong to him, and it was loose and tight in all the wrong places. Hala had put word out to her network of fellow immigrants living in Lis and, in an hour, had a man from Geirida at the door with two suits—barely worn since he had decided to move to the continent's western coast ten years prior.

Seba fiddled with the collar, which was far too stiff against his neck. He didn't like that this suit had been to more countries than he had.

It was then that the bell over the apothecary door jingled, and seconds later, Jas hurtled through the open door of the bathroom. He smelled horrible and was covered in sweat, dirt, and a few crushed leaves, like he had been rolling around in someone's garden.

"Sorry!" he said before Seba could even tell him off. Jas was already unbuttoning his shirt with one hand and wetting a washcloth in Hala's bucket of alchemically changed water with the other.

Seba wrinkled his nose and stepped back. "What have you been *doing*?"

"Errands." Jas ran the washcloth over his face and chest, creating tracks of clean skin through the grime. Without his shirt, Jas's scars were on full display, mapped around his chest and knotting around his heart.

Seba used to be obsessed with Jas's scars. Hala had said they came from the attack on his village in Huojen when he was a baby, the one that had killed his family and sent his neighbors fleeing with an orphaned Jas across the border to Almard. All Seba had to show from his childhood were two hands of crooked fingers that ached when the weather got cold. Jas's scars made his chest look like an artistic map. Seba's hands just seemed like they had been put together wrong.

"What errands could possibly be more important than our meeting tonight?"

"Just lost track of time," Jas muttered.

Seba handed him the borrowed clothes.

"Well, while you were off on your *errands*, I was getting jumped in an alley."

Jas, in the middle of putting on his trousers, barely managed to catch himself on the edge of the counter to avoid tumbling to the floor. "What?"

Seba told the full story, including his conversation with Eva, while Jas fumbled his way through getting dressed. His face drained of blood with Seba's every word. He couldn't protest fast enough when Seba explained his plan to ask Adelina for the money.

"We'll find another way. We don't need to continue this plan, if that's what—"

"No, it's not just..." Seba pursed his lips, annoyed they had somehow returned once again to Jas's resistance toward Adelina's plan. "The witches said that this is my destiny."

Jas finished his tie. "Then maybe it will come to pass anyway.

Maybe we could just stay home tonight, and we find another way to
make 300,000 *rejas*."

"By Our *Lady*, Jas. We're going." Seba rolled his eyes, still pulling at his collar, and led the way from the room.

The Manor of Lis sat in the shadow of the Castle of Lis, crowning the
hill around which the whole city was organized. Seba and Jas had
come to know the city of Lis very well during their visits to and sub-
sequent flights from the shabbiest of gambling dens. But the upper
town—literally higher due to its position on the hill—was an area
Seba had almost never had cause to explore.

By the time his legs were starting to burn from the upward
march, they had reached the arch marking the beginning of the
royal grounds. The property hosted the city guard headquarters,
the Manor of Lis, and the Castle of Lis. Seba had never expected the
manor to look quite so large. The walls were painted a crisp white,
with curling iron fixtures webbing the gates and windows like spi-
ders' legs.

Just when they passed the iron gate at the edge of the manor's
garden, Jas lurched to the side. His shoulder bumped Seba's. He
had gone completely white, sweat shining on his forehead and his
upper lip.

"Jas?" Seba righted the other boy.

He darted his gaze between Jas and the front door of the manor.
Concern lanced through him when Jas didn't answer, but battling it
was the knowledge that this meeting could not go wrong.

"Pull it together, Knell." Seba whispered the last word, but it
was the moniker that seemed to make Jas come back to himself.

Jas shook his head, straightening so he was no longer being
supported by Seba.

They both turned when the front door opened. The blond maid
from the river appeared in the doorway.

"Are you all right?" she asked as they got closer, her blue eyes
fixed on Jas.

"He's fine." Though Seba kept himself carefully positioned so he would be able to catch his brother should he fall again.

"Of course. Welcome, Senhor Pinheiro and Senhor Guan, isn't it?"

"That's us." Seba brought his focus back around to give her a winning grin. It felt fake, given the amount of stress coursing through him, and he wondered if he was truly as readable as Adelina said.

"Please, come in." The maid stepped back to let them in.

They entered a great vaulted hall filled with paintings of people Seba assumed had been past regal leaders of Lis and Jumaral. Some held a spooky resemblance to Adelina in the cool brown eyes and carefully relaxed mouth.

"The duke and duchess of Lis and the marquise of Lis are just finishing their preparation. I'll escort you to the drawing room to await them."

They were led down a hallway lined with more paintings, mostly landscapes of the Jumaralian countryside. The old floors, padded with thick blue carpet, creaked and groaned beneath them. There were few others around, though at some point Seba caught a flash of someone darting out of sight at the end of the hall.

The brief glimpse of them had been familiar, and Seba realized it had been Isaque Silveira.

Heat rose to Seba's cheeks. He'd seen Isaque only once since everything had fallen apart between them, and it had been a strained interaction of Isaque requesting a "spirit consultation" for a friend, who Seba now knew had been Lord Simão. It had been ten minutes of Seba desperately trying to forget the times running around Lis with Isaque, Jas, and Isaque's older sister, Luísa. And then there was that last night. With just Seba and Isaque.

But Isaque had been the servant of Lord Simão, who was dead. Just as Seba was wondering what Isaque would still be doing here, Jas almost went crashing into the wall, and Seba had to steady him again.

The maid looked back with concern. She motioned for them to enter a room at the end of the hall. It was almost stiflingly warm and soft, full of tufted chairs and dark wood. The dark blue color of Lis's coat of arms was present in almost every piece of furniture, and a low fire burned in the grate.

Seba guided Jas to one of the couches, but his anxiety only grew as Jas fell into it as limply as a corpse, appearing barely conscious.

"Their Graces and Lady Adelina should arrive soon. I'll get you both some water." The maid cast one more worried glance at Jas before leaving them alone in the room.

"Are you okay?" Seba hissed the second her footsteps began to fade.

Jas didn't answer. He just leaned forward and put his head in his hands.

"Are you going to throw up? Because literally any other time in our lives would be more ideal."

"It's just loud."

Seba paused, listening to the crackle of the fire. Somewhere in the house, there were footsteps and low voices, but the people were not speaking nearly loud enough for him to make out their words.

"Like...ghosts?"

Jas didn't respond, which Seba took as confirmation.

"Is the former marquis of Lis in there?"

It wasn't uncommon for Jas to become lost in the world of the dead. Normally, he just became quiet and withdrawn rather than sick. Seba looked around the room for some way to distract him. He eyed the framed painting across from them. It was a map of Jumaral with intricate images of sea monsters off the coast, diving amongst the dipping blue lines of the ocean.

Seba traced those lines with his eyes. What would it have been like to take a ship and swim amongst them himself? Maybe even go beyond them to some other place, where there weren't so many reminders of the world that had been stolen from him?

He stood to get a better look just as the door opened. Jas shot to his feet at the entrance of the marquise of Lis, and Seba was just glad the other boy didn't topple over.

Adelina wore a long sapphire evening dress. It exposed her collarbone and hugged her waist before flowing down over her hips to the floor. She inspected them with narrowed eyes.

"Good. You're clean."

Seba frowned, trying to pull Adelina's attention toward him rather than Jas for a few more moments. "Is this supposed to be a real map or a fantasy creature map?" he asked, noting the sea monsters.

"Both. It's one of the maps Dom Sebastião had made by the scholars at Solmortém while he was king. It was meant to be used by Jumaralian explorers to conquer the unknown world, which included the real and fantastical. The monsters are supposedly based on the demons that Dom Sebastião defeated."

Seba flushed with pride at the mention of his namesake. "I thought people in Dom Sebastião's age believed Solmortém was the end of the world. Why would they make maps to go beyond it if they thought they would fall off the edge or be eaten by demons?"

"Hubris. Dom Sebastião defeated the demons once with the help of Ostrea's Great Wave. They believed they could do it again."

"But the Second Great Wave—" Jas started.

"—destroyed the capital fifty years ago," Adelina finished. "Which was taken to be Ostrea's message that there were demons within the walls, so to speak. The monarchy's been scrambling ever since."

"Which is why your parents want me?" Seba asked.

"Part of it. There's a lot of talk about avoiding a Third Great Wave. The Second killed my great-grandfather and his first two children, so my grandmother became queen. People viewed it as her divine right, proof that she was chosen by Ostrea. Everyone outside of the government she chose immediately lost all legitimacy."

"That's rough."

"But a convenient story for the ones who took over," Adelina added.

Seba cleared his throat for the speech he had spent hours preparing. "So...it sounds like I'm an important part of the plan."

His words sent a frost over the room.

"Really?" said Adelina. "Because what I take from that story is that there are very few irreplaceable people."

"Well—" He sensed Jas's eyes on him, probably willing him to shut up. "I've thought about it, and I don't think the deal is quite sweet enough on my side."

"The life of the Knell isn't enough to sway you? Not the promise of a crown and total freedom after you have it?"

"Seba," Jas murmured.

Seba ignored him. His cheeks heated in anger at the implication that he didn't care about Jas's life.

"I want payment upfront."

Adelina raised a brow, looking unimpressed. "No payment until the job is done."

"Fine." Seba ran a hand through his hair. "No payment until Jas's job is done. The second he makes contact with your brother, you get me 300,000 *rejas*."

"*Seba*," Jas hissed again. "I don't know if—"

"No. Payment when I'm queen. That's the deal."

"Really?" There was something emboldening about making this deal here, under this roof, in this room, when fate was in his favor if he only chose to fight for it. "Because my thought is that you have a lot more to lose in the next ten minutes than I do."

Footsteps silenced all of them. The door opened, revealing Infante Benigno, Duke of Lis, and Infanta Rosália, Duchess of Lis. Seba focused on greeting the duke and duchess while Adelina glared daggers at him from behind their backs.

After the initial pleasantries, Seba turned to Jas. "This is my brother, Jasibin Guan."

He was almost scared to see what state Jas was in at this point but was glad when Jas was able to go through the proper greetings once the initial confusion of the statement had passed.

While they both had black hair, that was where the similarities ended. Seba's skin was slightly darker and had a warmer tone than Jas's. His eyes were hazel, where Jas's were so dark they sometimes looked black. Seba had also always been a bit thicker than Jas, even though they were around the same height. That, in combination with the different last names and the general lack of shared personality traits, often made people tilt their heads curiously when Seba and Jas called each other brothers.

It was just the closest label the boys had to explain to the outside world what they were to each other.

"It's an honor to have you both," said the duke.

"It's an honor to be here," Seba replied, though his eyes were on Adelina.

She had fixed her face into a pleasant half smile. He shot her his signature dimpled grin.

Dare me, he thought. There was nothing stopping him from spilling all her secrets. *Make me do it.*

Adelina held his gaze for a long moment. Then, she made the tiniest nod of her head.

Seba didn't need to fake the way his smile grew.

He and Jas were invited to return to the couch. The duke, duchess, and Adelina sat in chairs across from them, and a tray of appetizers was placed on the nearest table by a servant—bread, cheese, olives, and octopus. Seba reached forward eagerly and lathered a thick glob of cheese onto his bread. Jas sipped a glass of water the blond maid had put directly into his hand.

"We must be candid with you, Seba," the duke said. Some of the performance melted from his face, leaving the lines somehow deeper than they were a moment ago.

It occurred to Seba that, a little bit more than a week ago, this family of three had been a family of four.

"The House of Ducança—the *monarchy*—is facing...challenges. With Dom Aristides's concerns about military threats abroad and the rise of sacrilegious magic across Jumaral, it is more important now than ever that the people support us as their monarchy."

"We would be prepared to offer you compensation for your time," the duchess added. Her words were clipped and sharp. "Both of you."

Seba tried not to glance at Adelina while the duke and duchess explained the plan—how Seba and Adelina would perform their romance for the papers and how Jas would take a role in the manor. Jas and the blond maid, Dalila, would act as chaperones to the romantic outings, and both boys would ingratiate the royals to the people by their mere presence.

If Seba had thought Jas was going to vomit before, it was nothing compared to how he looked now.

"What *kind* of compensation?" Seba had his 300,000 *rejas* now, but some extra pocket money couldn't hurt.

"One thousand *rejas* for your time and another one thousand for your silence," the duchess said. "Each."

Seba grinned.

ACT II:

TOIL AND TROUBLE

CHAPTER 12

ADELINA

Adelina was so tense that, by the time dinner was over, she felt like she had run miles. The muscles in her face and back ached from being held in such strict positions throughout the night. Luckily, dessert—a spongy pudding with caramel sauce and wedges of fresh melon—came quickly, and the final coffees were brought out soon after. Her parents were obviously just as keen to get past the night as she was.

Both the duke and the duchess of Lis excused themselves from the dining room the moment Jas finished his coffee, since he was the last to do so. He did it with an almost pained look on his face, and he slumped back in his chair as soon as Adelina's parents had left the room.

"Are you ill?" Adelina whispered.

The dinner had been a private affair. Servants were instructed to only enter when signaled by a small bell sitting beside the duke's place setting. Still, it was best to maintain some discretion.

"Sort of," Jas admitted.

It was only then that Adelina noticed how well he had been holding it together. Jas had been quiet and a slow eater but not acting odd enough that her parents would think it was anything other than nerves. Now he appeared to be near death.

"He's fine." Seba shot Jas a concerned look.

He, on the other hand, had been almost too lively throughout dinner. In addition to Adelina's being hypervigilant about the possibility of him slipping a single sliver of information, there had been times she had worried he was going to accidentally impale himself with a fork.

"Fine enough to start working tonight?"

She had been looking at Jas, but it was Seba who answered again. "Absolutely, he is. Fit as a fish."

"Considering you just *ate* a fish, I don't think that's the appropriate simile."

"It's an expression."

"It's ineffective, given the context of the situation."

"It's fine," Jas said. "What do you want me to do?"

She told them to meet her at the stables, then she went to her room to change clothes. It wouldn't make much sense to go galloping through the streets, down to the Rio Galho, in an evening gown that would get dirty and only raise questions later. Instead, Adelina switched to the clothes she had been wearing every time she had snuck out since that night.

They were her brother's old clothes, slightly too small for him and a little too big for her. She had snuck them from the piles of things the servants had removed from his room barely a day after his body was found. In that week, they had stopped smelling like him. Sometimes, she wondered if there was anything left in this house with traces of Simão—his smell, his hair, his touch. If it were up to her parents—and it was—she was sure the answer would be no.

But Adelina would find him tonight. Jas had said he sensed Simão's presence at the Rio Galho, so that was where she would take him.

Her eyes began to burn when she pulled on Simão's jacket, remembering the way her parents had acted toward Seba and Jas that evening. They had been so calm, so warm, so put together, at the very table where they had eaten with their son every day, where they had celebrated his birthdays and watched him grow into his title. Her parents had killed him just over a week ago and then seemingly erased his existence from their home and their minds. It was unnerving.

But they will not do the same to me, Adelina promised herself. She wiped quickly at her eyes, but they had remained dry. It was distracting, these moments alone, when all she had were her thoughts. Adelina spent far too many moments missing the times before— when her parents had been calm and warm and put together toward *her* and she hadn't questioned it.

Climbing from the window had become second nature to her by this point. She had done it all the time with Simão, but even more frequently since he had been gone. Her bedroom overlooked the manor's garden, so no guards would spot her from the street. All it took was looping around the back of the house to get to the stables unseen, where the old stable hand, Dimas, was always either asleep or not even present to realize someone was taking a horse.

Her shadow stretched long in the gaslight when she approached the entrance of the stables. The boys were there, and Dimas was thankfully absent, but they would need to move quickly in case he arrived.

Seba leaned against the doorframe with his arms crossed over his chest, and Jas sat with elbows on his knees. His eyes were closed, with his head on one hand, until he realized Adelina was there. Jas scrambled to his feet.

He had gained some color back. Maybe it had been nerves, after all. She didn't like that she couldn't tell.

"Ready, Jas?" she whispered. Adelina reached out to unlock the gate of her favorite horse, Cinza, a black mare with about as many working brain cells as the roasted potatoes they had just eaten for dinner. It meant Adelina could think for them both.

"What about me?" asked Seba, sounding about three years old.

"Oh, I'm sorry," Adelina said. "Can you speak to the dead as well?"

"You're the one that hired me."

"Which means I can *unhire* you just as fast."

"Really? Because I think we just proved that you need me more than I need you."

"That was when my parents were near. I don't see them now."

Seba opened his mouth to retort, but Jas said, "Just go home, Seba."

Seba looked even more petulant than before. "I can't go home alone."

"Scared you'll lose your way?" Adelina's jaw ticked, impatience shortening her temper.

"*No*, it's because of—"

"You can stay here until we come back," Jas said. "Then I'll walk home with you. Is that all right, Lady Adelina?"

Adelina took a moment before responding, observing Seba's reaction. It was easy to read the panic on his face, but he clearly hoped Adelina had not noticed his slip.

"Don't touch the horses," she snapped. "Stay hidden in case Dimas comes. And make sure none of the guards see you, or you'll be shot on sight."

"Fine." Seba removed his jacket and dropped cross-legged to the floor.

Adelina pushed down a sigh. "Ready now?"

Jas nodded, though he appraised Cinza warily. "Where are we going?"

Adelina put one foot in the stirrup and swung herself onto Cinza's back. "You said a place could help lure ghosts, didn't you?"

After a moment of hesitation, Jas scrambled up to sit behind her. His hands pressed lightly against her waist when she grabbed the reins.

"You might have to hold on harder than that."

Soon they had left Seba far behind and were galloping down the cobbled streets of Lis. Jas's arms stayed wrapped tightly around her middle. The night was still and clear, each cobblestone lit by the orangish glow of street lamps mixed with the soft white of the moon and stars. The river was a rumpled reflection of the world above, like a broad-stroked painting.

Adelina directed the horse down the eucalyptus-lined path and brought them to a stop by a row of more trees separating the river from a crepe café on the other side. Jas released his hold like she had burned him. After tying Cinza to a nearby tree, Adelina joined him at the water's edge.

"Do you feel anything?" She kept her eyes on him rather than the water. This night had no room for memories.

Jas closed his eyes and breathed slowly. After a few seconds, he started picking at the fingers of his gloves. "Yes, but"—he blinked his eyes open—"but not like before."

"What do you mean, 'not like before'?"

"He wanted me to notice him before. Now it's like...like he's hiding."

Adelina fought to keep her breath steady, but it was like Cinza had sent a hoof into her chest. Cold sweat trickled down her back. "Do you think—Is he hiding from me?"

Is he scared of what I am willing to do to reach my fate?

Jas glanced down at her for the first time. She wished he was as easy to read as Seba. There was something assessing about the look that she didn't like.

"I don't know. But both times I've felt his presence, you've been near."

"Both times?"

"When Seba pushed you in the river and then again at the manor."

So maybe Simão was drawn to the places he had gone to that night. There was one more to try.

"We're going."

"Where?"

"The beach." *That terrible, terrible beach.*

She had hoped never to return to it, but now she had no choice. Her brother's voice wasn't here, but maybe it would be there. Maybe it would be in the place where his parents had killed him and where Adelina had held him while he died.

Adelina couldn't tell if it was her imagination or if the ocean truly did smell like blood. She took shaky breaths through her mouth, squeezing her eyes shut against the onslaught of images bursting across her vision.

Stop it.

Stop it.

Stop it.

The blood filled her mouth like it had her nose, then spread to her ears in a rushing overflow of sound. Each crashing wave became the barrage of her skull against red stars, which cracked and roared as they sparked.

"Lady Adelina."

The voice was soft, a repetition drawing her back to shore. Her eyes snapped open. She was standing beside Jas on the banks overlooking the sand, clutching the splintered wooden railing of the steps leading down to the water. Adelina sucked a breath of metallic air through her nose. Breathed it out.

It smells like salt, she told herself.

"Lady Adelina, why are we here? Didn't Lord Simão die in the Rio Galho?"

Adelina ignored him. She led the way down wooden steps almost completely obscured by the fine grains of sand swept over them by the wind.

Her boots sank into the familiar sand, and she marched to the line of crashing waves. It was low tide, making the deserted stretch endless from left to right. There was no separation between sky and churning black water.

"Can you hear him now?" Adelina ignored the fragile thumping of her heart.

"No." Jas's eyes were clenched shut.

Adelina pressed her lips together. She would not cry. "Why?"

"I don't know. I'm sorry."

He opened his eyes, and he *did* look sorry, but Adelina didn't care.

"Take off your shoes."

"What?"

"Take them off!"

He bent to unlace his shoes, and she did the same, cursing her shaking fingers. When their shoes were safely discarded on the dry sand, Adelina pulled Jas after her into the water. A wave crashed around their knees, and Adelina sucked in another breath at the flush of cold. Her bare toes curled around the soft sand and skimmed over smooth rocks and shells.

"What about now?" she called over the rumble of a gathering wave.

Jas shook his head.

Adelina stripped off her brother's jacket and rolled it up into a ball. "Take off anything you don't want wet."

They threw their clothes onto the sand with their shoes and sent their hats after them. The wind blew through Adelina's hair, and curls came loose at the edges of her vision.

A wave grew to her right—a monster gathering shadows. Adelina returned her grip to Jas's wrist and pulled him into the wall of water just as the wave broke over them.

The cold pierced her skin like ice. The tide pushed her back toward the shore, but she kicked forward until they both broke the surface. While they gasped, the water rose again, lifting their feet from the sand. Adelina kept her grip around Jas's wrist and propelled them farther into the ocean, away from the line of breaking waves.

"I feel him."

Jas's voice was a jolt to her heart, even more than the cold. She spun to face him, her back to the moon, and treaded water, her toes barely able to skim the sand.

"Is he saying something?"

"No." Jas's black hair was plastered to his forehead, as inky as the sky above and the ocean around him. He tried to hide a flinch of pain.

"Then make him!"

The words came out as a cry without her meaning to, and she caught a mouthful of salt water, which sent her coughing and spluttering.

It tastes like salt, she told herself. *Ocean salt.*

Hands grabbed at her elbows, and she tried to fight off the corpse. But it was just Jas, holding her up while she struggled to breathe.

"I can't," he said. "I can't make him." His eyes flickered behind her, to the towering cliff and the town sitting on it. "I think we should go back, Lady Adelina. It's dark, and there are too many rocks nearby that we can't see. The tide could take us away, and nobody would even know."

Adelina wanted to scream at him that her fate was to be queen. She couldn't die. Not before the prophecy was fulfilled. Not while she still had plans to reach it. She would not be erased like her brother had been.

But there was no use in treading water forever, waiting for a voice that was not going to come.

They kicked back to shore, letting a wave guide them toward the dry sands. Adelina was trembling when her feet found land. She reached their discarded clothes and sank to the ground, holding her knees in her arms. She barely processed when Jas positioned himself an arm's length away and put his head in his hands.

They sat in silence while the waves pushed in and out, each release a little closer to them. The moon crossed the sky, and the tide got higher.

"Is he still there?" she asked when her voice was back under her control.

"No."

She nodded, not able to tear her gaze away from the blurry horizon.

"Is there anything...anything he might have left unfinished?" Jas asked. "Not all ghosts return, but often those that do feel like they have something left to accomplish."

"If I knew that, I wouldn't be talking to you. I'd be finishing it."

"Lady Adelina—"

"Adelina," she corrected. "I almost drowned you. You can call me Adelina."

"Adelina. What if you don't like what we find?"

Something in his tone made her finally look at him. He was staring into the ocean, just as intently as she had been. The light of the stars danced in his dark eyes.

"The point is to find it." She stood, brushing sand from her wet trousers. "We'll keep trying different places, drawing him out in different ways. In the meantime, we'll research."

"Research what?"

"You. If your usual methods aren't getting us anywhere, that means we'll have to try something else. We need to know what we're working with."

Before turning to go, Adelina made herself hold the view of the ocean. She looked at the water that had washed away her brother's blood.

Adelina had allowed it to weaken her, but that fragility would be a reminder. Whether she felt infinitely large or immensely small at the center of the endless night, she didn't know. Perhaps she was just another star staring back at her neighbors, seemingly indestructible but mortal just the same.

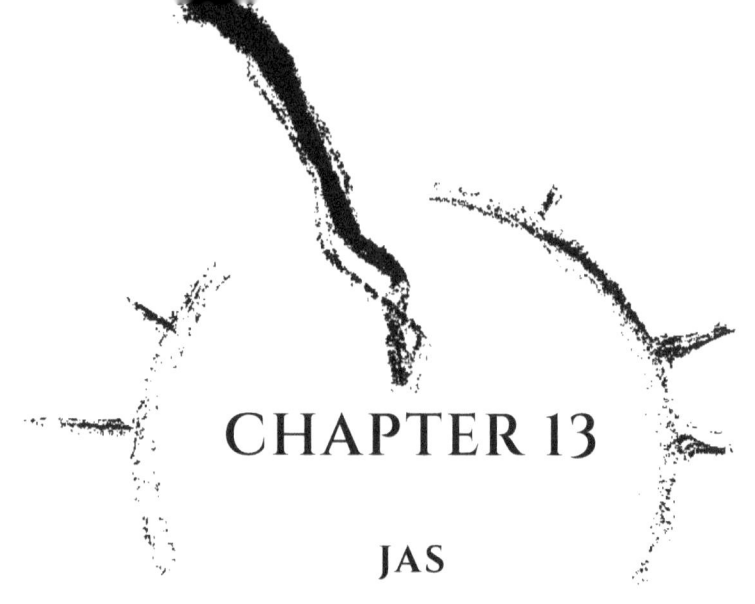

CHAPTER 13

JAS

*J*as was back at the manor the next morning, far too soon. He was exhausted, even though he had crashed into bed the moment he and Seba had gotten home the night before. All the adrenaline of the day had simply drained out of him.

While he had hidden when Adelina showed up at the witches' house that afternoon, he had been half certain they would have told her he was there, as part of whatever deal they had struck with her. Perhaps they had, and she was waiting for the best time to use the information against him.

Something wicked, they had called her. There was no telling what Adelina would do if she thought she couldn't trust him. Besides, he had Heitor Alves and Seba's 300,000 *reja* debt to think about now. He couldn't afford to not get this job done.

Just like the day before, pain spiked through him as soon as he passed the archway marking the top of Lis's central hill. It was difficult to make out the different voices and presences trying to break through. Most of them consisted of crying or wailing or words covered up by the former. He couldn't imagine what had happened on this hill that was so horrible, even its ghosts could not stop screaming.

Perhaps they feel how your steps crack the earth and your words shatter the world.

The maid from the day before stood by the open iron gate of the manor. Her hair was pulled back without a single loose strand, and her black dress and apron hung without a crease. When she smiled at him, the flutter in his stomach was at complete odds with the pain in his head.

"Good morning," she greeted when he stopped in front of her. "I'm Dalila, by the way."

"Jas," he replied, unsure of what to do with his hands. "Good morning."

There was an uncomfortable pause before Dalila's grin lit up again. "Shall we?"

He followed her around the path to the gardens at the side of the house. The outer wall of the neighboring Castle of Lis acted as a barrier at one end. Dalila led him past rows of flowers and vegetables and through a door invisible from the front of the manor.

The pain radiating across his body built while he followed her along an echoey passage, but he found himself better able to manage it today than he had the day before. Maybe it was because he didn't have the added stress of Seba beside him and Adelina glaring at him. Still, tension coiled in his stomach.

She gave him a tour of the manor, and Jas's head swam with the dozens of hallways filled with tiles, carpets, and portraits all heavy with wealth and age.

Dalila had just finished showing him which floor the bedrooms were on when a voice called out her name.

She whipped around and immediately bent into a curtsey. "Your Highness." Her voice changed, becoming lower and more clipped.

Jas followed her lead, bowing at the crown prince of Jumaral strolling down the hall toward them. He wore plain trousers and a white shirt, his curls carefully parted. The pain in Jas's head spiked, his heart about to explode in his chest.

It had been one thing to face Adelina, maybe another to meet with her parents. But being anywhere near Prince Calixto, the son of the king Jas was helping to overthrow, seemed to be pushing it. If all of Adelina's plans worked out, including the ones Jas only suspected she had, the boy in front of him would probably be seeing his grave before he ever took his throne.

Amidst that, his mind also raced with all the new information he had just learned from Dalila. How was he supposed to address the prince? It was "Your Highness," he was almost sure. "Your Majesty" was saved for the king, and "Your Grace" was for the duke and duchess.

"Where's Nuno?" said the prince.

Jas had never actually heard Prince Calixto speak, but something in the sharpness of his words brought Adelina to mind. Even when asking a question, neither of their tones ever wavered from the flat delivery of a statement.

"I'm not sure, Your Highness, but I can certainly find him and send him to your room."

The prince tutted. "Don't bother. Just send someone to draw me a bath, will you?"

"Of course, Your Highness. Right away."

"Good."

The interaction seemed over, and relief was already spreading through Jas's body, but the prince still stood there. Jas's eyes were on the prince's polished shoes, and it took a moment for him to realize Prince Calixto was looking not at Dalila but at him.

"You're new," said the prince.

Jas cleared his throat, wishing he could have just stayed hidden behind Dalila forever. "Y-yes, Your Highness."

"This is Jas Guan, Your Highness," Dalila said. "He just joined the staff this morning."

"Yes, you're one of my cousin's boys, aren't you?"

Oh look, little Knell. He knows about you.

"Yes, Your Highness."

There was a pause where Jas was almost tempted to look at the prince's face, but he restrained himself to his careful observance of the floor.

Then, "Jas."

The prince spoke his name as if he was testing it. He pronounced the "J" like it was meant to be, rather than how Jumaralians usually hummed through it. Only Hala and others of the small Almaric and Huojenese communities in Lis said it similarly.

"You can draw my bath. It will be a good initiation for your first day."

Jas's heart stuttered. He had barely stammered another "Yes, Your Highness" before the prince turned the other way, returning to his room.

Dalila's cheeks were pink, and a small smile played on her lips. "You did very well. Most new people end up bowing so low they fall over the first time they meet the prince."

Jas was not prepared to return her humor.

His stomach was churning by the time Dalila brought him to the scullery, a chilly room with stone floors and a low ceiling. Cabinets lined the walls, ladles and other utensils hung from the ceiling, and an ironing board sat to the side. There was a sink next to what appeared to be a stone furnace. It shared a corner chimney with a bread oven on the adjoining wall. A fire burned at the bottom of the furnace, and there was a sort of lid at the top, which Dalila lifted to show Jas the boiling water inside a copper pot built into the stone.

"You just ladle it into here." She brought him another bucket. "And then take it upstairs. It might take a few trips, but I'll help you."

Jas matched Dalila's technique in scooping the water out of the copper and into the bucket, careful not to let it slosh over the edge.

After a moment, Dalila spoke. "The Festival of Dom Sebastião is next week, so most of our work will be cleaning the house and preparing for the visit of the high priestess of Lis during her procession."

She paused, and he wondered if he was supposed to respond. Jas had never really celebrated the Festival of Dom Sebastião. A strange mood always overcame both Seba and Hala around this time of year, and Jas generally just did his best to keep spirits up. He had no idea what preparing for the high priestess would entail.

They both rose at a disturbance from above and frowned at the stairwell leading up to the kitchens. Before either of them could make a move to discover what was happening, someone crashed down the stairs. The person froze when they locked eyes on Dalila and Jas.

Jas froze too, and for what seemed like the thousandth time since he had entered the manor, his heart clenched. He recognized the person—gray eyes like morning fog and a body like thin branches waving in the wind. Those narrow painter's hands on the sides of his face, pressed against his back. Their kind voice when they said goodbye. Their awkwardness when they returned to ask the Knell for a favor.

"Jas?" said Isaque Silveira.

Dalila looked between them, and a crease formed between her brows. "You two know each other?"

"Vaguely." Isaque did not take their eyes off Jas.

Your past is haunting you, Knell.

Though Isaque had once worked at the manor, Jas hadn't expected to see them here. As far as he knew, Isaque had lost their job when the marquis of Lis died.

Isaque's gaze snapped away and focused on Dalila. "Have you seen Luísa?"

"No, why?" Dalila stilled, wariness creeping into her voice.

"I—" They glanced at Jas. Isaque's lips tightened with the pressure of words that had to go unspoken.

Jas returned to ladling the water into the bucket, excusing himself from the conversation, though his stomach twisted with worry at the panic in Isaque's voice. Luísa was Isaque's older sister, someone Jas had come to know well after the months he and Seba had spent with the siblings. She and Jas had been particularly close because—though they had not discussed it, never been bold enough to say it out loud—they both had magic they would give anything to be free of. Magic that could get them and their families killed if the wrong people found out.

Dalila and Isaque shuffled to the other end of the room. Their murmurs were low, and all Jas could make out was the rhythm of intense words, desperate demands, and frank refusals shooting between the two. With another upsurge of pain, the hair stood at the back of his neck, and a whisper crawled from the deepest part of his mind.

She's fading, said a voice different from the one Jas so often heard.

A tremble of his hand sent half a ladle of water splashing against the stone by his feet. A ghost had emerged, able to project itself above the raucous cries echoing in a constant disparate thrum in the back of his head.

Trapped.

It took everything in him not to drop the ladle completely.

Who? he thought desperately. *Who is trapped?*

Luísa Silveira.

"Jas."

His eyes snapped open. Dalila stared at him pointedly. Isaque hovered behind her with their head turned so Jas couldn't see their expression.

"I think that's enough for a first trip," she said.

He glanced down at the bucket. It was almost overflowing. He nodded, closed the wooden cover, and strained to carry the bucket up the stairs. Whether it was because he was distracted by the weight or because of the distance between himself and the others, the voice of whoever had spoken to him was no longer clear.

But if it was true that Luísa was trapped and fading—whatever that meant—he needed to do something about it, didn't he? What if someone had found out she was a witch?

You have greater loyalty to a girl you knew for a few measly weeks than you have to the boy you call your brother?

If whatever ghosts that had spoken to him about Luísa were connected to the manor or the nearby castle, following their lead would probably mean uncovering something about Adelina and her family, which would put himself, Seba, and Hala all in danger.

If only you hadn't put yourself in this situation.

He set the bucket at his feet and knocked at the prince's door, very aware his shirt was practically sweat through.

The witch girl will understand. She would choose Isaque over you.

"Enter," came a bored voice from inside.

Jas furiously tried to straighten his waistcoat before turning the ornate brass handle. As soon as he opened the door, the bitter smell of smoke washed over him. The air was cloudy, creating a gray film that dimmed the rich blues of the furniture and the boy amongst it all.

Prince Calixto was draped across a chair in the corner. A smoking cigarette dangled from his lips, and his dark brows were drawn. He was working on what looked like the first half of a crocheted table runner, wearing nothing but a silvery robe.

"Your Highness." Jas diverted his gaze to the bathtub at the other end of the room. He poured the bucket. Some of the water splashed over his arms and face.

When he turned, the prince had risen and was now leaning against a bedpost, watching. His expression was not unlike the one Adelina often wore—assessing Jas as though he were a specimen.

"So, you're with Sebastião Pinheiro."

Jas breathed through the thudding in his chest. "Yes, Your Highness."

The prince took another puff of the cigarette, and the smoke curled around his head in dark clouds. Then he grinned, sending a chill down Jas's spine.

"And are there tasks other than housekeeping that you've been asked to perform?"

Jas's mouth dried.

He's probably been trained since birth to sense a demon in his midst.

"I thought so." Prince Calixto snuffed the cigarette against the wood of the bedpost, beside other small black marks of the habit. "In that case, there are things you should know."

Jas had to fight the urge to lurch backward when the prince strode toward him, getting so close Jas was briefly afraid the prince meant to hit him.

"My cousin is a thorn believing herself to be a sword, but she can still draw blood." The prince took a controlled breath and blew smoky air into Jas's face, making his cheeks flush. "She doesn't know anything. *Anything.*" His jaw clenched while he seemed to consider something. "If you want proof of it, find out what's in the castle barely fifty paces from her bedroom. Then you'll see how much you can trust her."

Prince Calixto's eyes, nearly as black as if his irises had been swallowed by his pupils, searched Jas for a response. It was all Jas could do to remain still.

"Thank you, Your Highness," Jas said carefully. "I will return shortly with more of the water for your bath."

He lingered only long enough to notice Prince Calixto's expression shutter—and only in the complete absence of emotion was Jas able to read the terror that had been there before.

With a small bow, Jas strode from the room, his mind full of gray curls of smoke.

Every day after that, while Jas became more comfortable with his tasks, he grew to expect the flutter in his stomach each time Dalila smiled. The pain striking through his body lessened day by day, but both his and Adelina's frustrations grew at still not being able to contact Lord Simão.

Jas would sometimes catch the prince keeping track of him. He would appear in the hallways Jas was sweeping or decide to take a walk around the garden while Jas was weeding the vegetable patches. Sometimes, he even appeared between the trees around the side of the castle when Jas and the other servants were preparing to decorate the outer walls for the festival. But the prince never said anything unrelated to housework—not after that first day.

He wondered if the prince could sense his new plans forming, almost unconsciously. Jas was indecisive about what side he was on or who he was fighting for, but there were people who needed help: Luísa Silveira and the others who had died and now called out for him, the only one who could hear their cries, and Seba, whose deadline for Alves was quickly approaching.

The days passed, and Jas repeatedly failed to contact Lord Simão. Investigating the castle, uncovering the secrets both the witches and Calixto had hinted at, might be the only way to exert leverage on Adelina and get Seba's 300,000 *rejas* by the Festival of Dom Sebastião. Maybe, by exposing whatever was happening in the castle, Jas could help more than one person.

That was why, two days before the festival, Jas went to the apartment of Isaque Silveira instead of going home. Isaque opened the door in seconds, as if they had been waiting for the knock. Jas's cheeks heated when Isaque's expression turned from hopeful to disappointed to confused.

"Jas? What are you—"

"I think Luísa is in the castle," said Jas. "And I want to help you break her out."

CHAPTER 14

SEBA

Seba didn't understand why churches couldn't make their pews more comfortable. Would it be so sacrilegious to have a little cushion? Would Ostrea send a Third Great Wave if Her worshippers were made to sit on anything other than a plank of hard, old wood?

Apparently so, or Seba's tailbone wouldn't be aching as it was now, just twenty minutes into his first church service since he was about five years old. He sat beside Adelina, who was annoyingly still and focused. At some point, his ears perked up when he thought he heard his name, but it had just been the high priestess discussing Jumaral's first king, Dom Sebastião. Seba dreaded the Festival of Dom Sebastião coming the next day—and with it the 300,000 *reja* deadline.

He couldn't help his mind spinning while he watched the high priestess. Eva had mentioned the high priestess was one of the people interested in his mother's death, which Seba had so far gotten no new information on.

In the past week, Jas had been the busy one. Adelina had only needed Seba a few times, which she usually communicated by message through Jas or one of the other servants. So far, he had joined her at a croissant café, a museum grand opening, a vigil for her brother, and a charity event he had been quite confused about but that definitely involved cats.

Seba held back a sigh when the congregation was called to stand. He pretended to sing the hymn, but he had no idea what the words were. After several more rounds of the same, the service finally ended with a collective Sign of the Seas—everyone's right hand brushing from their left to right shoulder—and a blessing from the high priestess. Seba wasn't sure if he had ever been so relieved to not have to sit down anymore.

"I'll call for you tomorrow," Adelina said after they had made polite conversation with nearly every person in the congregation.

Over her shoulder, the duke of Lis gave Seba a nod, which Seba returned.

"Can I make a request?" Seba muttered so only Adelina could hear him.

"I'd rather you didn't."

"More croissants."

"I'll see you tomorrow, Senhor Pinheiro."

Seba, smiling despite himself, separated himself from Adelina and her family to find Jas.

He was standing a bit apart from the other servants, talking to someone who had their face hidden. It was only when Seba got closer that he realized the other person was Isaque Silveira. And he was not the only one watching the anxious exchange between the two. Though Dalila was standing several paces away, her attention was clearly drifting between them and Adelina.

Seba attempted a wave when Isaque caught sight of him, but they only blanched and quickly retreated after a final word to Jas.

"Talking about me?" Seba asked Jas.

They both watched Isaque hop down the stairs and join the passing crowds outside. He had meant it as a joke, but Jas's "no" came far too fast.

"I didn't know you two were still in contact." Seba recalled the familiar figure he had seen the week before at the manor. "Does Isaque still work for the royals?"

"No, they just stop by sometimes. Isaque and Dalila used to work together a lot, as the personal servants of Lord Simão and Lady Adelina, so they're still in touch."

"Huh." Seba half wished he and Isaque were still in touch too, despite the awkwardness. "Ready to go? I was thinking we could go to the beach since Hala closes early today."

"I have to be back at the manor," said Jas.

"Oh. When will you be home?"

"Probably late. You can still go to the beach, though."

Except he couldn't. Because the deadline was getting closer, and Seba had no interest in leaving the city without someone to have his back, just in case.

Seba crossed his arms over his chest. "You're always at the manor."

Jas shrugged. "It's my job."

"Well, while you're off doing your *job*, I'm the one with a ticking time bomb hanging over me. You do realize that the deadline for the three hundred thousand *rejas* is tomorrow, right? And if that doesn't happen, then there's also the...you know..." *The prophecy.* If he and Jas couldn't figure out the obstacle with Alves, it could be taken as a sign Seba was rejecting Ostrea's fate for him, which meant...His mind flashed with the image of his mother's body, and he wondered how it would feel to be broken like that.

"I know. I'm sorry, Seba."

Seba was almost apologetic when he noticed the pain in Jas's face, but not enough to take back the words.

"But if we want this"—Jas glanced around, checking if anyone was close enough to hear them—"this plan to work, then I need to do the job I've been assigned. I'm sorry. I–I do think things might be different soon, though."

"What are you talking about? Are your—Did you figure out how to make it work?"

"Something like that, maybe."

Jas's gaze flickered to something over Seba's shoulder, and Seba turned. Prince Calixto was watching the two of them closely from the other side of the church.

Seba didn't know what Jas meant or what Calixto's problem was, but he was too annoyed with everyone in the room to find out. "Fine. See you later, I guess."

He started to leave, not waiting for Jas to stammer out some contrite response, but Seba stopped when he caught sight of a figure walking along the outer aisle to a door at the side of the church. Seba, thinking only of the fate currently slipping through his fingers, marched up to the high priestess just as she was taking out her keys.

She was middle-aged, had deep creases around her eyes and mouth, and wore long sapphire robes and a matching shawl around her hair. It made her light brown skin seem to glow.

"Hello." Seba spoke softly so his words wouldn't echo across the pews. He expected her to appear startled at his sudden presence, but she turned calmly. "My name is Sebastião Pinheiro. I think you know something about my mother, Teodora Pinheiro."

Her dark eyes looked him up and down, and an expression of awe slowly spread across her face. "Sebastião Pinheiro," she repeated slowly. Her voice sounded much more normal when she wasn't preaching, and her slight Huojenese accent came out in the way she separated the "nh" in his last name. "Yes, I've been interested in your mother's death for quite some time."

"Why is that?"

"I can show you, if you'd like. I have my research in my office."

Seba ran a hand through his hair. If Eva was right, then this might be the only person in the world willing to talk about his mother's death at all.

He looked over his shoulder again, his heart thudding. The royal family and their servants began to make their way down the aisle. He locked eyes on Jas, who was now deep in conversation with Dalila.

"Okay," he said. "Show me."

Seba would have expected the office of the high priestess of Lis to be filled with dozens of copies of the *Book of the Seas*, hundreds of icons of Ostrea and Her saints, and maybe some kind of ugly old tapestry of Dom Sebastião riding a wyvern. The first room he was brought to did look remarkably like his vision, if a little bare. But it was clear it was the second room, which could only be accessed through the first and down a locked passageway, where the high priestess did her real work. That room was full of maps.

They were old and new, colorful and plain. Some were copies of those he recognized from the manor—like the one showing sea monsters all along the coasts of Jumaral—and others were of places he had never seen. They came in different languages and art styles, pasted to the walls and rolled out along tables, with more stacked on shelves or sticking out of baskets.

"I don't permit many people to come here," the high priestess said. She swept past him, the wind from her robes ruffling the maps.

"I can't imagine why," Seba deadpanned.

She ignored his tone. Instead, she searched for a particular map amongst her shelves. "Your mother, was she religious?"

Coming from a high priestess, the question felt like a test. Seba wracked his brain. He remembered going to church, celebrating holidays like the Festival of Dom Sebastião, and listening to the stories his mother would tell him about Ostrea and the king Seba had been named after.

"Sure, I think so."

"Any connection to the occult? Magic, witches, alchemists, demons—anything like that?" She listed them out nonchalantly, not even looking at him.

"No, not at all. Nothing like that."

Book face. He could practically sense Adelina's scowl.

"Ah." The high priestess pulled a map from her stack and spread it lovingly over the table. While she put some heavy stones at each of the corners, Seba crossed to her side to get a better look.

It was a map of the continent, with Jumaral on one side and Huojen on the other. Dozens of other countries and territories rested in between and branched off, though there were no borders drawn. Faded teal waves swooped in uniform arches through the oceans, and land was the color of old parchment, marked with minimal lines to represent mountains and rivers.

It was all labeled in Huojenese, a language he only recognized because Hala often switched between Jumaralian, Huojenese, and her native Almaric when writing her notes. He didn't understand any of these words, though.

Unlike the old map of Jumaral from the First Great Wave, this one was devoid of sea monsters, but there was still something odd off the coast of Jumaral. Seba looked closer.

It wasn't part of the original map. Someone had drawn in what looked like a tiny yellow star in the ocean, just beside the southernmost part of Jumaral.

Solmortém, where the world used to end.

"What is this?" he asked.

The high priestess was looking not at the map but at him. "I used to be a mapmaking apprentice for the army in Huojen. I found this in the archives, and I was curious about this addition." She pointed at the star. "I checked with my supervisor, and she said it was based on old stories. Nothing to think about in the modern age. But then I saw it again. Here."

She shifted another map on top of the first, this one less colorful and detailed but with an inked-in cross over the same spot next to Solmortém.

"Over and over again, I noticed it. Some of them were maps taken from temples and religious sites, but others were from schools and government officials. I traveled around Huojen, gathering stories about the odd power that so many explorers had noted. You have to understand that magic and alchemy are accepted parts of Huojen, not noteworthy like they are in Jumaral. So if this power was being noted..."

"It must have been worthy," Seba finished. The story had entranced him, though Seba was still utterly confused about why it was being told.

"Precisely. I decided I had to see for myself. I began traveling west, and I heard more stories from people in Almard and Nolofali—all strains of legends passed down about the sea beyond Jumaral. Some spoke of it as a resource or a miracle, while others called it a curse for Jumaral's cruelty towards the magic that flows through the air and those who harness it. They said that this point was the source of the Great Waves and that Jumaral was due for a Third."

Seba's skin crawled. There was something unsettling about hearing a religious authority talk about magic in this way. She was supposed to preach that magic was stolen from Ostrea, that witches and alchemists were thieves.

"And you came anyway?" he asked.

"Of course I did." The woman's eyes sparked, and a hungry expression took over her face. "An untold power, known across countries, across lands and cultures? I knew that there had to be truth to that kind of story. I went to Solmortém first. The townspeople told me legends of magic that had taken place there, miracles and inexplicable events. Among the stories, someone mentioned the name of a creature—an *encantada*."

Seba's jaw dropped. He had been so engulfed in the story he had forgotten he was, with good reason, questioning this woman's sanity. "Encantadas aren't real," he said. They were one type of creature common in Jumaralian legends—a captured spirit cursed to guard something for eternity. The one who released them got one wish.

"How do you know?" The high priestess looked intrigued by his statement, like she was about to enter a fun academic debate.

"Well, because...because if there *were* wish-granting spirits out there in the ocean, don't you think we would have found them? Jumaral isn't exactly drowning in riches and prosperity. The whole country could use an encantada. Bounty hunters, for one. Why go to the trouble of capturing witches when they could just get an encantada to give them endless money or rid the world of witches, or whatever else motivates those blasted hunters to go around, scaring us all and making us feel like we can't sleep safely in our beds and—" Seba paused, then snapped his mouth shut. He was saying far too much.

The high priestess clasped her hands in front of her. "But what if the encantadas are being hidden in plain sight?"

"What, like, in the city? Like witches?"

"Not exactly. What if they're hidden in children's stories and legends, like you said? Magic is real; we know that. The only reason that encantadas can't be real is that you've never heard of one in real life?"

Seba crossed his arms. "What does any of this have to do with my mother?"

"The townspeople of Solmortém told me the same, that encantadas weren't real, just part of the legendary makeup of their town.
But when you've heard as many stories as I have, you start to look
for truths. I began traveling north, aiming for the larger cities where
I could find libraries and scholars. I tried the capital, Fulgeo, first
and quickly learned that asking those kinds of questions was the
way to end up on a bounty hunter's list. I kept going north, and I
just happened to be staying in a tiny inn in Lis when I heard about
your mother."

Seba's spinning mind came to a stop. "What did you hear?"

The high priestess inhaled and exhaled slowly, as if this were
a presentation she had been waiting to give for years. It reminded
Seba of Adelina.

"First, it was how sudden it was, the lack of an obvious cause. A
woman goes missing for a week and then returns dead, not a mark
on her body?"

"So it was magic? A witch, like the one who killed the marquis?"

"There were rumors that that might be the case," the high
priestess conceded. "But I didn't think so. In Huojen, I worked with
many witches in the army. There was an entire unit of them whose
sole purpose was to collect the blood of enemies in order to work
blood magic. For a witch to kill someone, they must have a sample
of that person's blood. As the person dies, blood runs from their
eyes, mouth, and nose—sometimes even from their pores. Teodora
Pinheiro's body was clean. No witch killed your mother."

"So, it was an alchemist." Seba thought of Hala. "Or some kind
of poison."

The high priestess shook her head. "Do you remember her
eyes?"

Black as night. Seba ran a hand through his hair, dizzy.

"People spoke of them being black, but they weren't just that,"
she continued. "They were cloudy."

"What?"

"I was there for the removal of the body. I remember seeing her
son. You were very small, already clutching at that woman who had

come for you. At first, I thought the same as you. Her death could have had a number of causes. But then I saw that her eyes were filled with smoke, as if she'd opened them in another world and part of that world had gotten trapped within her. I wasn't sure at the time if it was connected to my research, but after years of living in Jumaral, becoming familiar with every founding story this country has, I am almost certain."

"My—my mother was killed by an...*encantada*?" Seba's knees were weak. Sparks flew through his vision.

"No, your mother was killed by an encantada's *magic*. Someone wished your mother dead."

CHAPTER 15

ADELINA

There wasn't technically any rule against Adelina leaving the manor by herself in the middle of the day, but she still departed through the back door, looping around the stables, before continuing down the street after her family had returned from church. Some of the staff saw her, dropping into curtseys and bows when she passed, but she was caught by no one significant enough to ask where she was going.

Adelina had already brought Jas to all Simão's favorite places, even the secret ones he had once taken her to speak plainly in a way they couldn't at the manor, and still the Knell had heard nothing. Not even Simão's bedroom had brought her brother forward, though that might have been because there was so little of him left in it. She had checked books on witches, old magic, alchemy, history, children's fairy tales, and even religious texts, but there was nothing about boys who could communicate with the dead.

It was time to try a different course of action. She would be foolish to wait around for Simão to give her all the answers when she was perfectly capable of chasing down other leads herself, starting with the origin of his medallion.

Isaque had said they and Simão had already checked most of the antique sellers and historians around the city, but she doubted either would have thought to ask an apothecary in the lower town. Neither had Adelina until she had seen an entire box of rusty tangled necklaces and muted gemstones sitting on a shelf behind Hala's desk on one of her visits. Perhaps Hala was a collector, or maybe she had just inherited a bunch of worthless metal from someone. But if there was a possibility Hala had untapped knowledge, Adelina would not let it go to waste.

Every passing day since her brother's death made Adelina's chest tighten with desperation and growing paranoia. Unable to sleep in case she missed a sign to suggest Ostrea had decided Adelina wasn't trying enough and was about to drop dead. Soon, she wouldn't be able to breathe, much less think clearly enough to uncover her family's secrets.

The apothecary was familiar to Adelina by now. She had visited several times with Jas and Seba for the purpose of making herself known to Hala and ensuring the boys knew she was watching. Today, Jas would be at the manor, and Seba was likely still at the church, so Adelina hoped she and Hala could speak privately.

It was a shabby storefront. Peeling paint spelled out the name of the apothecary, but the windows were clear and brightened the cramped space inside. The familiar jingle of the bell sounded when Adelina stepped in, and she inhaled the scent of the medicines around her—floral, powdery, and earthy, mixed with an odd metallic smell she could never identify. There was no one at the counter, and Adelina's attention briefly wandered to the stairs hidden behind the curtain of beads to her right.

Maybe she could take this time to search Jas's things, figure out some of his secrets or at least a few of his weaknesses, anything to apply more pressure on him so he would try harder.

Her ears strained to hear the clanks of metal coming from the room behind the counter, where Hala was surely working on some medicine. Adelina had just decided to dart upstairs when Hala's footsteps came closer and the door to her work area burst open.

"Good day. We'll be closing in—" Hala's mouth froze when she recognized Adelina. It took a full second before her round face broke into a pleasant smile. "Lady Adelina." She dipped into an awkward curtsey and moved to stand behind the counter. "I don't believe Seba is home yet."

Adelina stepped away from the door. "Actually, I was hoping to speak with you."

"Really?" Hala's smile twitched. Her hands were clenched behind her back.

"Yes, I was wondering about your expertise on jewelry."

Hala raised her brows. "I—I sell medicines, my lady."

"But you had a box of old jewelry behind your desk earlier this week."

"Well, yes. Sometimes, my clients pay me in objects if they're not able to pay with money."

"And then you sell it?"

Hala nodded. Her eyes searched Adelina's face.

"So, you must be an expert in recognizing what is valuable and not."

Hala hesitated. "I wouldn't call myself an expert, my lady."

Adelina breathed deeply, forcing a demure smile. "Perhaps you can help me anyway. There's a particular type of medallion that I'm interested in—with Santa Belinha and a wyvern."

"Those are symbols of Jumaral, aren't they?" Hala said slowly, as if afraid she were wandering into a trap.

"They are. But I also wondered if there could be connections to those who are...shall we say, less friendly to the monarchy of Jumaral?"

Hala's mouth quivered, and she clenched her hands tighter in front of her apron. "I don't know what you mean, my lady. The wyvern is a symbol of Jumaral's strength, and Santa Belinha is an icon—"

"But she was killed by witches." The thought had sparked in Adelina's head—some connection she wasn't sure about yet.

"I think you'd know the story better than I would, my lady."

"Yes, and I am telling you that she was killed by witches. She performed the miracle of turning roses to bread, and the witches were jealous that Ostrea had favored Belinha, while they had to steal from Her and blaspheme Her gifts. So, her symbol must have some association with witch rebellions, doesn't it?"

"I—" Hala paused and observed Adelina carefully. "I wouldn't know anything about that. I suggest you ask someone in the Council of Lis about these matters."

But Adelina's mind was already racing. "You're an apothecary. People must come to you all the time with injuries from angry witches."

"Despite what you may have been told, my lady, witches do not commonly assault people." There was a bite to Hala's tone that hadn't been there before, and it made Adelina bristle. "The only way a witch can cause unique harm without contact is with blood magic, which is messy and rare. The witch needs to have a sizeable sample of the blood of their target, they need to work in a coven to offset such a destructive spell, and the results are obvious. The target is effectively drained of their blood, but the magic combines to turn the blood black. It's obvious when someone has been killed by a witch, and I assure you that there are very few cases."

Adelina's hands tingled.

Drained of blood the color of night.

Like Simão.

But Simão had been killed by Ostrea for denying his fate, not by witches with blood magic. Or had Adelina been wrong? Did Ostrea perhaps work through a different mechanism? Her own hand, but with a knife Adelina still had to find?

"How *much* blood?" she asked, glad her voice remained steady. "For the spell. How much blood is needed for the spell?"

Hala looked to the ceiling. "I think it may depend on the skill and power of the witches performing the spell, as well as whether the target also has magic. But I would *think* that it would be at least as much as this beaker." She pointed to a musty glass on her counter, which appeared to hold a volume about equal to a wine glass.

Adelina stared, imagining the glass filling with her brother's blood. Her brother's hot, sticky blood. She squeezed her hands in her gloves.

It wasn't an amount of blood witches would be able to come across naturally—not when their target was the marquis of Lis. *If* Simão had been killed by blood magic, then someone would have had to give the witches his blood.

Someone close to him, who wanted him dead.

Judging by who had his medallion, that would have been her parents.

The thought sliced through her, the realization her parents had done more than just keep secrets that had caused Simão to reject a fate of being king. They had provided the weapon that killed him for it. And they had conspired with witches to do it.

"It has to be a witch?" Adelina desperately hoped the answer was *no*, that she hadn't spent the last two weeks exchanging information with the very witches who had killed her brother and worked with her murderous parents. "An alchemist couldn't do it?"

"No, modern alchemy has only reached the level of transformation. Turning gold into water and that sort of thing. That effect would have to have been created by someone with magic and the victim's blood."

All hail Malves, that shall wear crowns hereafter! They had both fallen, and Adelina had injured herself on a rock. She remembered the sting of the cut on her hand, the smear of her own blood across her palm, how it had mixed with Simão's. So much blood.

It was Ostrea's will at work.

"Adelina?"

She was staring blankly at Hala and snapped back to herself. It was only at the casual, almost gentle use of her name that Adelina realized there was something else amidst Hala's uncertainty.

Hala pitied her.

"Are you asking about your brother?"

"I—" *Pull yourself together.* The conversation was twisting out of her reach. "That's none of your concern."

"They're saying it was a witch who killed him, aren't they? That's why the bounties went up."

Hala's face was all worry now, and Adelina's resolve almost crumpled. The woman was not quite old enough to be her mother, though she had raised Jas and Seba, but—for just one weak, horrifying moment—Adelina wished Hala would protect her like a parent was supposed to shield a child.

Her mother used to sing her to sleep when she was having nightmares, and her father still brought her mountains of cookies anytime he saw her cry. But she pushed those thoughts away. They were irrelevant.

"That," Adelina repeated carefully, "is none of your concern."

She straightened her jacket, preparing to leave. It was at that moment Hala's eyes darted over her shoulder.

It could have been a benign look, but something about the way Hala straightened when she realized Adelina had noticed made Adelina stop. She followed Hala's gaze, finding nothing and no one at the door to the apothecary. It was almost as if Hala had expected someone to be there, a person she either didn't want Adelina to see or who she thought Adelina would call in.

Adelina ran through the conversation she had just had, high-lighting all the signs she had missed in her desperation: Hala's nerves when she had arrived, the clanging and strange metallic smell, the old jewelry collection that appeared worthless but that Hala claimed she took as payment, Hala's knowledge of blood magic and the extent of alchemy, and even the way Adelina had always been ushered straight upstairs every time she visited.

"Hala Amjad," Adelina said. "You are an alchemist."

Neither Hala nor Adelina moved while Adelina's words reverberated between them.

Her mind raced. It was an opportunity, but it was also a liability. It didn't bode well that the boy she had been parading around Lis as her suitor had been raised by an alchemist. If this became public knowledge or if the royal family were to find out, Adelina's plans would be destroyed. The people of Lis would not view the relationship as favorably as they had so far. She would be separated from Seba and Jas, kept under tighter restrictions than she ever had before, and maybe...

Her chest tightened, and she became hyper aware of the dagger pressed against her hip, tucked under her jacket since the night her brother had died in her arms. If the plan to ingratiate the family to the common people ended, the perception of the royal family would be even worse than before—either because they knowingly consorted with alchemists or because they were stupid enough not to notice alchemists working their way into the highest ranks of the House of Ducança.

And if that plan was over, then there would be no use for Adelina anymore.

She tightened her jaw and lifted her chin the way she had always been taught. She was Lady Adelina Maria Malves Ducança, Marquise of Lis and niece of the king of Jumaral. She had all the power in the world to make sure this was handled correctly.

I can because I have to. I can because I will.

"You see, what people don't realize about being caught is that it's all about practicality," Adelina began.

Hala's eyes narrowed.

"Prove useful to me, and you will have nothing to fear. Fail to do so, and you leave the door open for me to do as I please. And you should remember that, as the marquise of Lis, my ability to do what I please in this city has a rather wide range. I don't need to remind you of my close personal connections to both Sebastião Pinheiro and Jasibin Guan, who I'm sure my mother and father would be all too disappointed to find out are corrupted by their alchemist guardian and, therefore, no better than alchemists themselves. Perhaps, during the investigations that would no doubt take place as to how such corruption could infiltrate the highest ranks of the House of Ducança, they might even find something else about Jas. How terrible."

Hala's jaw ticked, but still she said nothing.

"I assume I've made myself understood." Adelina flashed a practiced smile. "I suggest you keep my words in mind as you go about the next few days. Our business is not done yet, but it could end very soon." She straightened her jacket and prepared to march back to the manor.

If it was true her brother had died of blood magic, then she had correspondence to send immediately. Adelina knew exactly where the witch perpetrators were now. After that was done, she would figure out what to do about Hala.

She needed to talk to Simão now more than ever. The web was getting too complex.

Adelina had just reached for the door handle when Hala spoke, her voice shaking with rage. "You are just like your family, Adelina."

Adelina froze, her back still turned to Hala.

"Just as cruel and just as arrogant. You are not the only one with power here. I have approximately seven poisons in this room—and four more that I could make—that will all remain untraceable in your body as they work their way into your organs and cause your slow death. You are not the only one with a reason to fight."

Adelina straightened her shoulders and lifted her chin. She fixed her sweetest expression on her face and slowly turned. "Oh, Hala," she said, her voice dripping with pity. "I doubt you'd want any association with my corpse."

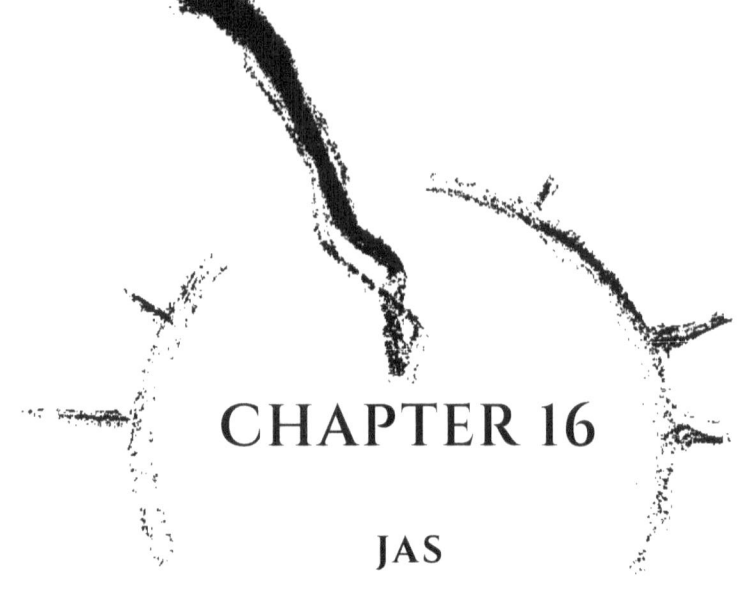

CHAPTER 16

JAS

"Are you sure we should be doing this tonight?" Isaque's voice barely sounded over the rush of wind through the trees.

Jas drew his Knell cloak more tightly around himself, shivering with nerves and the uncharacteristic cold of the evening. The sun had set an hour ago, and he and Isaque had been waiting amongst the trees lining Lis's castle hill since dusk, both dressed all in black to melt into the shadows. While the front gates of the castle led down a road to the Manor of Lis and the city guard, only forest lined this side, as if the trees themselves were the natural protectors of the high stone walls that had been brittled by the Second Great Wave.

"Yes," Jas replied. "It has to be tonight."

Tomorrow was Seba's deadline with Heitor Alves. If Jas couldn't contact Simão, he could at least get information to blackmail Adelina into giving Seba the money he needed, along with helping Luísa and anyone else being held in the castle. And then there were the answers the witches and Calixto had hinted at. This could be the only way to fix his magic.

"We should get closer," Jas said. Darkness loomed over them. Gray clouds heavy with rain were barely visible through the canopy of leaves billowing in what felt like an oncoming storm. Pain rattled his bones, seemingly in time with the wind, while he started up the incline. "There's an old entrance along the side that's half buried under some rubble. We'll need to use a rock or something to break it down, but it's old enough that it will probably give way."

Jas had found the door during the preparations for the festival, when he and the other servants were helping decorate the outer walls of the castle so the banners would be visible in the city below.

"Ah, yes, the *door of betrayal*."

"The what?" Jas tried to hide the fact he was already gasping for breath. His ribs constricted painfully against his lungs the closer they got to the castle, and the clawing garble of voices in the back of his head grew.

"The door of betrayal," repeated Isaque. "They're doors that were sometimes built into castles to allow people to escape, usually at the most inconvenient places so there wouldn't be easy access. But it's also a way in from the outside. Thus, the door of betrayal."

An apt name, don't you think?

Jas caught himself against a tree. His vision blackened, and the pulse of voices from the castle blocked out all other sound.

"Jas... Jas?"

Isaque had to say his name several times before Jas was able to respond. He tried to blink away the spots in his vision while he forced himself further up the hill, through the trees and closer to the outer castle walls.

"Are you okay?" Isaque followed warily behind him. Their hand hovered at Jas's back as if waiting for him to fall.

Jas could only grunt in reply, too aware his energy was quickly fading. If they didn't get to the castle and get Luísa out soon, he was sure he was going to collapse.

After several minutes in which the only sound was the crunch of sticks under their feet, Isaque spoke. "Jas, I don't think I ever apologized."

"It's fine," Jas wheezed, wishing he could manage more words to express how little he wanted to talk about this, especially now.

"Well, I am sorry. And I know you're putting yourself in a lot of danger right now to help me. So, thank you."

Jas could barely comprehend what Isaque was saying. The wall was within sight. Dark stone peeked between the tree trunks ahead of them. The outline of the battlements was barely visible against the cloudy sky above the tree line. The voices were so loud, but he could make none of them out.

"You should know," continued Isaque, "that I was the one who told Adelina about you. About the Knell."

It took several seconds for him to realize what Isaque had said, and by the time he did, they were already approaching the rocky incline where the door of betrayal was. Jas pivoted to Isaque and blinked slowly. His mind connected the timeline of the past week.

"You...you told?" Jas's stomach was flipped inside out.

Isaque nodded. There was concern in their eyes, which had turned as inky as a churning sea in the night. "I assume that's how you came to work at the manor? She said she was looking for information about Simão and...I'm really sorry, Jas. I know it's dangerous, but Adelina—"

The sound of crashing rocks made them both turn. The movement sent the earth spinning under Jas's feet and bile halfway up his throat. He clutched at Isaque's shoulder to stay upright while they both searched for the cause of the noise.

Dalila was looking at them wide-eyed from the space between the castle wall and the tree line, her hands raised in surrender. She wore a long black jacket, like Isaque and Jas, and it appeared she had accidentally dislodged some of the rubble covering the door.

"What are you doing here?" asked Isaque.

Jas half considered using his powers on Dalila, but that would have been impossible, given his current state. Besides, it would have seemed like a terrible violation to use his powers against her.

One day, little Knell, you won't be able to hide the monster within.

Pain shot through him, and Jas cried out. When he became aware of his surroundings again, he had been lowered to the ground, half lying across Isaque's lap. Dalila crouched beside them. Misty rain fell against his cheeks, confusing him even more. This weather was so rare for a Jumaralian summer.

"What's going on, Jas?" said Isaque.

"Just…there's something…in the castle…" Dry coughs wracked his body.

"So that *is* where you're going," said Dalila. "I heard you two planning something about the castle at church earlier, but I was hoping you didn't actually mean to go inside it. It's dangerous. Isaque, you know that just as well as I do."

"And why are *you* here, Dalila?" Isaque's voice was sharper than Jas had ever heard it. "You heard us planning and came to ambush us? Did you already call the city guard?"

"No. I didn't, and I don't plan to." Dalila crossed her arms over her chest and leaned back to sit on her heels. "I thought it must be something about Luísa, considering our conversation last week. I wanted to help."

"Why?"

"Because I care about Luísa, and I care about both of you."

A look passed between Dalila and Isaque, the product of shared childhoods and mutual understandings. Somewhere amidst the blur of the voices, the pain, and the fear, those familiar wings fluttered in Jas's stomach at the thought that Dalila cared about him.

But that didn't mean he could trust her.

She was the closest thing to a friend Adelina had, and she could be passing any amount of information on to her. Isaque, too, was now in question. If Isaque had said nothing to Adelina or if Jas had never told them about his powers, then maybe none of this would have happened. But that probably wasn't true. If there was anything Jas had learned about fate or Adelina, it was that very few things could throw them off.

Stopping now wouldn't change the fact Dalila knew about their plan or that Isaque had told Adelina about Jas. Stopping would only hurt Luísa, as well as Jas's chance at uncovering whatever secrets the witches and Calixto had hinted at.

"We should…go," he said, allowing Isaque to help him to his feet.

"Are you sure?" asked Dalila.

Jas nodded, and the three of them spent the next several minutes climbing over rubble and shifting rock aside to get to the narrow opening at the base of the castle wall. Isaque explained their suspicions to Dalila about what they would find inside.

Every inch closer to the castle made Jas increasingly ill. He was barely aware of what was happening by the time they finally unearthed the old wooden door. Words were exchanged between Dalila and Isaque, and then Dalila pushed past Isaque and Jas to examine the door herself. After a few moments, she gasped and stepped away as though she had been burned.

"I—I think we'll just have to break it down," she stammered.

Isaque took up a piece of rubble and hammered it repeatedly against the rusty lock. It was several minutes before the lock cracked open, during which Jas clutched at the stone exterior of the castle.

Once they were finally able to step into the filthy, stony tunnel, it was as if any barrier ever existing between Jas and the voices in his head was stripped away, leaving him only with the screaming. It took just a few seconds before Jas had to crouch against the rough stone wall, dry heaving.

"By Our Lady, Jas," hissed Isaque, reminding him of Seba. "Dalila, are you going to be sick too?"

Jas straightened as much as he could. Dalila was clutching at the wall across from him, looking pale and almost as shaken as he was. Her bright eyes met his, and her lips faded almost to white.

"I think I'm fine," she said. "Jas?"

"Have to...go fast," he said.

The voices pulled Jas now he was inside the castle, guiding him like a compass toward their sources. He led Isaque and Dalila at what was probably a snail's pace and allowed Isaque to push down a wooden grate at the end of the short passage. It opened out to an empty courtyard. Rubble lined the walls, and uneven dirt rose with the wind through the night air.

"Where do we—" began Isaque, but Jas was already going.

He was fading as the voices rose. They were pulling him, not just through the ruined castle, but to the edge of the gate. The voices wanted him to go to the Beyond.

Jas tripped. Stone hit his chin and scraped at the skin of his hands, but he hardly noticed. Hands helped him up—who they belonged to, he had no idea. He was traveling blindly now, following the spirits of the lost.

"Wait, Jas. There are people—"

But Jas was barely there. The voices had finished guiding him. He caught only a glimpse of the horror—slumped bodies and the stench of rotting flesh, the knowledge that magic was kept here and twisted out of recognition—before he left the land of the living entirely behind.

The land of the dead was filled with smoke and shadows, empty space and silence so deep it seemed to echo. The only thing that existed other than Jas was the gate to the Beyond. It was so close, just ahead of him and getting closer.

No. The thought exploded in his mind.

He didn't know whose voice it was.

No, I don't want to go Beyond.

The gate grew closer. Black bars swirled into existence, reaching impossibly high and low, endless in the dark.

I don't want to die.

He was so close. Shadows of bodies appeared on the other side, reaching for him.

No, no, I don't want to die.

Faint sounds played at the edges of his consciousness. A familiar voice pulled him in the other direction, away from the gates, the dead, and the Beyond.

Then, a different voice: *Wake up, little Knell.*

Jas's eyes snapped open. Seba's voice was loud and crisp.

"What are you going to do to them?"

"Make sure they don't get any more ideas about defying me," came Adelina's voice.

Jas couldn't make out either of them. He was lying on the most comfortable mattress he had ever experienced, staring up at a velvety blue canopy in a dimly lit room.

"And how exactly are you going to do that?" Seba sounded more stressed than Jas had ever heard him. "Because whatever you did before obviously didn't work."

"They brought him *here*. That means something."

"By Our *Lady*, Adelina. It means you are the slightly lesser of the millions of evils that crowd this manor."

There was a pause. Jas brushed his fingers lightly against the quilt under him. Pain returned, along with the memories of where he was and what he had just done.

Adelina's voice was eerily calm. "I will handle it."

At those words, panic crashed through him. He shot up to a sitting position. Pain coursed through his bones, his vision bursting with stars.

Seba cursed. "Give a sign of life next time, will you?"

They were silhouetted by the fire, Adelina with her arms crossed and her jaw set, Seba a flurry of motion and nervous energy.

Jas's heart raced. He didn't know the punishment for attempting to break into the castle, but it couldn't be pleasant. It was his fault he, Dalila, and Isaque were about to find out.

And you've already managed to drag Seba into it as well.

Jas imagined leaping from the bed, grabbing Seba, and running before Adelina could declare the death sentence. If Jas had his way, he would get all the people he had put in danger—Seba, Dalila, Isaque, Hala, Hermínia, Gilda, and Ágata—and run past the hills of Lis, beyond the borders of Jumaral. He would fight battles in every country, run miles and swim leagues, to stop whatever wrath he had just set on these people.

Because Lady Adelina Maria Malves Ducança looked set aflame. He had never witnessed anyone so tense, so bunched up and pulled together, so ready to explode.

"Seba didn't know anything about this," he said quickly. "And Dalila didn't either. She didn't help with the planning or—"

"I know," said Adelina, but Jas's pulse didn't calm. "I've already spoken to Dalila and Isaque, and, as you know, Seba possesses a distinct inability to lie."

Seba crossed his arms. "I have other talents. Like knowing when it's not a good idea to break into a structurally unsound castle that happens to be next to our city's government and guard force."

See? Seba would never do to you what you do to him. He knows better than that.

"Don't act like you've been so innocent," Adelina snapped at Seba.

"I didn't do *anything*. It was my mother who—"

"And you said nothing. Do you realize how quickly I could have fixed that situation right when it arose?" Seba's jaw worked, but Adelina didn't let him answer. "And *you*." She rounded on Jas. "Why didn't you tell me about the witches?"

Jas's mind was still fighting to catch up. Somehow, Adelina seemed to know about Seba's debts to Heitor Alves. But witches? His mind returned to the image of the slumped figures all around the castle, the pull of magic beneath them.

He had seen the fate of the captured witches.

But why would they be trapped in castles rather than killed like everyone thought they were? And what was happening to their magic?

"You..." Jas observed her expression carefully, wondering if there would ever be a way to truly determine if the marquise of Lis was telling the truth. "You didn't know about them?"

There. It was in the slight intake of breath before she spoke, like she hated what she was about to say.

"No. I didn't."

You trust the devil girl?

It was probably naive of him, but he did. Just for this—because she was uncomfortable, and he knew the only thing she ever felt comfort in was lies.

"Prince Calixto made it sound like you did."

Her brows lowered, just slightly.

"When were you talking to Calixto?" asked Seba.

"We've crossed paths." Jas didn't mention how intent the prince had seemed to be about crossing paths with him.

"He's the one that told you about the witches, then?" Adelina's tone thrummed with rage. "He put the blame on me instead of asking himself why he does nothing about the information he has about the crown. He tried to turn you against me, and you let him."

Jas's cheeks heated. If it was true that, out of the two of them, the prince was the only one who had known about the witches and done nothing, then maybe Jas had been on the wrong side after all. Though "side" seemed like an odd term.

An odd term for what, little Knell? What were you trying to do?

Help. Anyone. He had been trying to find another way. To make a few things better rather than make everything worse.

And you failed. Because your powers are good for one thing and one thing only. So, make yourself useful.

"What are you going to do?" Jas was almost afraid to ask, knowing the answer had little impact on what he did next. "To...to Dalila and Isaque. And the witches."

Adelina answered without pause. "I am going to be queen, and I am going to fix it. All of it."

"But what does that mean?"

Her expression shuttered, just as the prince's had that first day with the bathwater. Adelina lowered her arms carefully to her sides, pulled back her shoulders, and raised her chin. "It means that I still hold your life in my hands. Both of you. And if I ever find out you've tried something like that again, I will personally be the one to hand you to the bounty hunters and watch while they cut out your hearts."

Beside her, Seba blanched. "A bit harsh, dearest."

"It's a bit *realistic*," she corrected. "Tomorrow, you will both be at the Festival of Dom Sebastião, and if we do not have word from Simão by the end of it, consider the deal off. You break your end, and I will happily break mine."

Later, while Jas and Seba were leaving the manor, Jas caught the now-familiar sight of Prince Calixto lurking around a corner. The prince didn't try to hide when Jas met his gaze. There was a question in his eyes. Had the prince divulged the information about the castle as a test? Maybe, if Jas hadn't been caught by Adelina, he would have passed it.

Jas dipped his chin, a final farewell to his royal shadow.

Because Adelina was right. If he truly wanted to aid the witches, if he wanted to help Seba and Hala and save Dalila and Isaque from punishment, if he wanted to fix his problems with his own magic, his best course of action was to do exactly as she said.

The only remaining issue was, after all of that, he still didn't know how to do it.

ACT III:

SPIRITS IN THINE EAR

CHAPTER 17

SEBA

Seba didn't even want to look at Jas the next morning while they got ready for the festival in their shared room.

The walk home the night before had been almost completely silent, save for Jas muttering a quick apology as they traipsed down the manor hill in the rainy cold. If he had opened his mouth, Seba probably would have said something horrendous about Jas, so he had kept it shut. Instead, he had let his anger fill the space between them like a third person—and he had some cruel satisfaction that the silence was probably worse for Jas than if Seba *had* yelled. He had felt bad about it while he lay awake that night, but even the guilt had been drowned by dread.

With shaking fingers, Seba put on the emerald-green waistcoat Adelina had sent him. It matched Jumaral's coat of arms, with embroidered gold flowers blooming from the fabric and swirling across his chest. Two weeks ago, he would have been enamored with the waistcoat's shine, the way it was tailored to fit him perfectly, the fact it marked him as someone worth gilding. Today, he appreciated it only distantly because it was the day he was going to have his head pushed through a wall.

He flexed his crooked fingers carefully and finished with his buttons. His thoughts echoed with the snap of bones. If he had only approached Adelina earlier, maybe he would have had a chance. But now that Jas had betrayed her trust, the only way Adelina would get

Seba the 300,000 *rejas* was if Jas got in contact with Simão sometime in the next sixteen hours.

"Ready?" Jas sounded so timid that Seba's heart twinged. He was wearing all black and white, with a red sash around his waist, like the other servants would be wearing.

"Ready." Seba tried not to scowl too harshly. Jas had made a mistake, but he was still Seba's brother. He would try his best not to let Seba die today.

They went downstairs, where Hala stood behind the counter, scribbling notes in a worn leather journal that looked like it had more pieces of paper shoved between its sheets than it had pages itself. Her hand froze when she noticed them.

"We're going to meet Lady Adelina," said Jas. "We'll be back tonight."

Seba couldn't help but wonder if that was true.

"Right." Hala stepped out from behind the counter. "Give me a hug before you go."

Despite everything, Jas and Seba exchanged a look at the rare request.

Hala's arms remained expectantly open, so Seba stepped into them. They rarely hugged and probably hadn't since before he had passed her in height, but the feel of her arms around him and the pressure of his own against the softness of her back was familiar.

"Be good," she said.

"I'm not twelve."

She raised a brow. Seba stepped away with a huff, arms folded, and Jas moved in for his hug. Hala must have whispered something to him as well because he stiffened. A moment later, he drew away from her. Both their expressions were neutral.

"Bye, boys," Hala said. "I love you."

"Love you too," Jas and Seba replied in unison.

The street outside the Silver Salamander appeared busier than it usually was, but not with people frequenting the shops. Everyone was heading in one direction, wearing greens, reds, and blues to celebrate Jumaral, Lis, and the martyred king who had saved them all. The colors were woven into the floral skirts and headscarves, the hats, sashes, and vests. Like the flag of Jumaral had vomited across the whole city.

"What was that all about?" Seba asked as they joined the crowd.

"What?"

"Hala. Just now. What did she say to you?"

"Oh." Jas looked at him, then back to the street ahead. "Nothing. Just to have fun."

Seba might not have been as creepily good at mind reading as Adelina, but that didn't mean he couldn't recognize a deflection when he heard one. New anger flared in his stomach, but he clamped his mouth shut.

It was a hot day, but at least the air was dry, and there was a slight breeze. The strange weather had disappeared in the night, and the sun bore down on Lis, lighting the crowning Castle of Lis like a jewel on display. Even the outside of the castle was decorated for the festival—banners of green, red, blue, and gold flying from its turrets.

Seba glared at it.

He and Jas poured into the main city square, along with the crowd, surrounded by the usual cafés. Carts and stands had been set up just for the festival, selling fresh spices and pastries, blue-swirled porcelain and handwoven purses. Icons depicting Ostrea were everywhere, almost matched in number by the armored figure of Dom Sebastião, the king who had beaten back the demons and claimed Jumaral's land for the living and for Our Lady Ostrea. At the center of the square was a life-size sculpture of Dom Sebastião made out of flowers—an annual addition to the festivities.

Seba still remembered his mother telling him the story of his namesake. She had recited the usual tale—a boy who conquered death with a sword and human bravery—but sometimes, she added her own stories too.

In some renditions, Sebastião had been a boy who tamed wyverns with the words he had written or a knight who invented a way to blow up the stars and scorch the monsters on the sands of the beach. In one memorable telling, Sebastião had been a little boy from Lis who could only save the world if he listened to his mother and went to bed on time.

A cheer rose from the side of the square directly under the castle, where a stage was obscured by the swarm of people watching the performers. The performers came into view as the boys got closer—a group of dancers dressed in red skirts and sashes, their arms raised while they spun back and forth in a circle to the beat of accordions and guitars.

Though most of the crowd was focused on the dancers and collectively moving their bodies to the beat, there was a strand of energy directed to the side of the stage. Seba craned his head, looking for the source of the excitement. Sure enough, he caught a glimpse of green and gold and then the carefully composed smile of the marquise of Lis.

On one side of Adelina was Dalila, who wore a traditional shawl around her hair, embroidered with pink and gold flowers matching her long skirt. She was whispering something to Adelina. The worried crease in her brow wasn't reflected in Adelina's stoicism.

Seba was surprised at Dalila's presence, considering the previous night's events, but he would just have to trust Adelina's judgment.

On Adelina's other side were her parents. The duke wore an outfit similar to the dancers': a black vest and trousers highlighted by a red sash around his waist, a flat hat shading his face. The duchess matched the dancers in the red scarves and skirts.

Though Seba had now attended several events with the duke and duchess in the last week, an annoying tightness gripped his chest when he marched Jas to their side.

It was because of them and their family that Seba's name was now public knowledge, and it was also because of them that he was here and not running for his life. Going against any of the deals he had made with Adelina or her parents would probably be more dangerous than anything Heitor Alves had in store—if not for him, then at least for Jas and Hala.

Dalila noticed him first. She nudged Adelina's elbow to draw her attention. The marquise of Lis's smile widened when she saw him, and she pulled him by the wrist through the final layer of people to stand by her side. Dalila moved to make space. Her eyes skipped over him to land on Jas.

"Senhor Pinheiro," Adelina's mother said expectantly.

"Your Grace," he called over the music. He kissed the duchess on both cheeks and shook the duke's hand. "It's a pleasure to see you again."

Seba did not miss the glare the duchess shot Adelina.

"Not now, Mother," Adelina replied serenely. "You are surrounded by our supporters."

Seba glanced around, his grin widening with each set of eyes that stared at them. The events he had attended at Adelina's side had mostly been solemn affairs, often centering around one or more dead people. He hadn't been around a crowd like this, filled with joy and excitement, since the Rio Galho.

And it was true; they *were* surrounded by supporters. Supporters of *him* who could stop even the duchess of Lis in her tracks. He realized, with a feeling of relief like experiencing sunshine after a thousand years of freezing water, there was no way Heitor Alves could get him here.

Seba touched the back of his hand against Adelina's. She tensed before looping her fingers through his. Their shoulders touched, and she looked up at him, their faces so close he could feel the heat of her laughing breath and see the wisps of curls escaping from the edges of her emerald shawl.

If, by some miracle, he survived the day, then he would soon be king. Adelina's deadline of becoming queen by her eighteenth birthday was now a week closer, and the wedding would likely follow soon after. Then he could take the money Adelina had promised him and leave.

Seba could buy a ship and make his fortune somewhere exciting, where he didn't have bounties on his head and debts to be paid. He, Jas, and Hala could be free from the dangers of Lis and Jumaral forever.

But Jas and Hala had never been fond of that plan. And it was possible Seba would end up just the same as he had always been— powerless and afraid in a tumbling tide.

There was a roar of applause around them when the dancers bowed and a flurry of movement while the stage was cleared.

Adelina's parents took to the stage. The crowd around them jumped and cheered, returning the waves of the duke and duchess, who greeted their audience and turned to thank the dancers.

The dancers, already red in the face from the performance, collectively flushed the same crimson hue as their outfits under the compliments of the duke and duchess.

"It looks like their plan is working," Adelina muttered. "You've made us likable."

"It would be cruel of me not to share my Ostrea-given likability with those less fortunate."

The music started back up to accompany the dancing of the duke and duchess. The pair bounced in sets of three beats. The hands that were clasped together waved up and down while they swung like a conjoined pendulum.

"And what about *our* plan?" Seba asked.

"That's down to Jas."

"Comforting."

Other couples were joining the duke and duchess now, mostly members of the nobility who lived somewhere on the castle hill. They spun in circles around the stage, never straying from the rapid pace of the accordion. Seba looked down at Adelina, at her hand clutched in his.

"Adelina, my love," he said.

Her brown eyes were dark and endless. Her lashes were the length of the entire ocean.

"Do you want to dance?"

She blinked. "I suppose it's expected."

Adelina took the elbow he offered. The claps of the crowd scattered from their steady beat, overflowing with excitement while their beloved marquise of Lis and the boy who had saved her pressed their bodies together and jumped from foot to foot with the rest of the couples.

"You're terrible," Adelina said through her fixed smile. "It's a good thing they just like seeing us together."

Seba glanced out at the people of Lis, who had gathered for a festival celebrating the vanquisher of evil but were still mostly entranced by him....

Invincible. It was a good feeling. He adjusted his grip around Adelina's back, letting the last ebbs of rebellion drift out of him and allowing her to lead.

With her, he was powerful. He was secure from the constant threats of death hanging over him. What was that, if not a path to love?

"Well then, my dearest partner of greatness." Seba bent his head closer to Adelina's, and a burst of excited cries and snaps of cameras sounded from the crowd.

By Our Lady, he could have shown Adelina a sensual glimpse of his elbow and the people would have begged for a picture.

Adelina blinked at the address, which he took for a roll of her eyes.

"Let us give them something to love."

CHAPTER 18

JAS

rust yourself, Hala had said. And the first thing Jas had done to follow that advice was to not tell Seba what she had said.

Don't confuse your untrustworthiness for his, said the voice. *He has done nothing to harm you, while you are responsible for all of the harm in his life.*

Maybe it was just shame, then, twisting his tongue.

The crowd sounded muffled in Jas's ears, and his mind tangled with the dead. The ghosts on the other side of the gate shifted to the front. They wanted to catch a glimpse of the ones they had left behind or experience the festival from beyond the grave. Some found voices, whispers that made his skull pulse, but most were just an awareness.

He barely realized he and Seba had found Adelina until he was suddenly caught in the bright blue of Dalila's kind eyes, and he was drowning.

Seba was pulled to stand by Adelina amidst the stares of her parents and all the observers around them. Jas kept his eyes down but went to stand on Dalila's other side. It was with both a sense of relief and fear that he greeted her. She was here, and she didn't appear hurt. That was all that mattered. But—

Scared to let her see the monster?

It was a fear he tried not to dwell on, but one the voice in his head was not afraid of speaking. Dalila was probably wondering why he had fainted. Maybe she was angry he had failed her and Isaque, not to mention Luísa and the other witches trapped in that decorated castle looming above the festivities.

He tried to keep his focus on the dancers and the music rather than what was happening in his head, but it was like inhaling water to the beat of an accordion. Everything was a blur. The dancers were spinning in circles, and then they weren't. There was a surge of cheers, and then there wasn't. The duke and duchess were dancing alone on the stage, and then there were others—a smear of color and sound blending into a single sense that overwhelmed every inch of him.

And still, the ghosts. Pressing in on him. Pushing Jas into himself until he was nothing.

"Seba has never danced, has he?"

Dalila's voice echoed at the edge of his focus. Seba and Adelina were dancing amidst the nobility. Seba seemed faintly annoyed, and his feet weren't moving in the same precise three-beat skip as Adelina's.

"Oh," Jas said. "No, I don't think he has."

"I commend him for his bravery, then."

Jas tried to blink away the wave of ghosts. He cleared his throat. "He probably didn't realize that it takes skill when he decided to go up there."

Dalila nodded sagely. "Confidence."

"Seba overflows with it."

"I see that." Her hands clapped along to the beat. "Adelina does too. You'd think they wouldn't work together, but I suppose partnerships can be found in unlikely places."

Jas glanced around. He needed to be the one to bring up the night before. Jas doubted anyone was listening to them or would even be able to hear them over the sound of the instruments and the singer's voice, now with a lilting melody about finding love on narrow cobbled streets. The song was weighted with melancholy, and it made him think of something Hala had said years ago: *No one in Jumaral knows how to celebrate without mentioning that death comes to us all.*

"I'm sorry."

Dalila whipped her head around toward him. "*No*, you have nothing to apologize for. We all did our best to do the right thing."

And your best was not good enough, little Knell.

"Where's Isaque?"

Dalila crossed her arms over her chest and returned her stare to the dancers with a crease between her brows. "I haven't heard from them since last night. I want to think that they're fine, but...if Luísa is amongst those people we saw, I can't imagine that they are. And...I know there have been some other arrests since yesterday. Other witches."

Even if Isaque was perfectly safe at home, they must have been suffering. Jas watched Seba for a moment, imagining how it would be to know his brother was rotting away in that castle, along with those witches. He couldn't imagine knowing something so terrible was happening to his sibling and then having everything he did to help fail.

You don't have to imagine. Something terrible is *happening, has* always *been happening. Seba had the world torn from him when he was six years old, and it is your fault.*

Terrible was an understatement. The voice was right. If Isaque was feeling anything like Jas had for the last twelve years about what happened to Seba, then it was almost too much to live with.

Seba and Adelina had their arms linked, spinning in circles and then switching sides every few beats. He remembered his theory that Adelina had been the one to kill Simão for the crown, and it suddenly disgusted him that he could ever have thought someone could do that to their sibling.

"How did you know that we could go to Adelina last night?" Jas spoke quietly, and Dalila had to lean closer to him to hear.

"Because Adelina is not a ruthless person. She's just been raised in a ruthless household. Isaque and I, we've worked in that house long enough to be sure. Adelina isn't the type to put the sanctity of Jumaral above all else, and neither was Simão."

Something wicked this way comes. Maybe the witches were wrong, or perhaps they hadn't been talking about Adelina at all. He didn't know what to believe, what to do.

Jas's heart thumped in his chest, and for a moment, he was painfully shoved back into the flood of dead voices.

Are you doing the right thing, little Knell? Or were you never supposed to exist at all?

"How long have you worked for Adelina?" he asked, trying to pull himself from the grip of the dead once again.

The music changed, switching to a jaunty beat that had everyone clapping. Dalila joined in, shifting her weight from foot to foot with the beat of the music.

"My mother was a servant in the household of the duke and duchess, but she died in childbirth, and they allowed me to stay in the servants' quarters. The other servants brought me up, and I was essentially raised to serve Adelina. Though we had some fun too." She smiled, which provided Jas with a different distraction. "We used to practice all of these dances in her room, usually after we were both supposed to be in bed. I would always get in such trouble."

Once again, Jas was caught in her blue eyes. There were two forces threatening to drag him under: the ghosts and the ocean staring back at him. He knew which one he'd rather drown in. Before he could think, Jas was speaking.

"I've never danced before."

Dalila laughed. "You and Seba don't regularly practice your folk dances around the apothecary shop?"

"There are a lot of breakables." He gulped. "But, if you're not afraid of being embarrassed..."

He held a hand out between them. She looked down at it, then up at him again. Her lips relaxed into a faint, open-mouthed smile.

"I'm not afraid."

Dalila placed her hand in his, and for a second, Jas was frozen with their hands stacked on top of each other. He made his fingers close around hers.

Jas turned toward the circle of dancers below the stage, which was now so crowded Jas was surprised Seba hadn't accidentally sent Adelina tumbling off yet another edge. He watched the way the other pairs were arranged.

Each partner had one arm held out, the other angled around the other person's body. They swung around the space, a range of ages and skill sets, which made Jas feel both calmer and jealous at the natural talents of some five-year-olds.

He took a breath.

Jas pressed his hand into the fabric of her blouse, brushing the soft fringe of the scarf wrapped around her hair. She rested her own hand between his shoulder blades, where she would surely feel the racing of his heart.

"Keep your elbow up," she advised.

He jerked it upward, and there was a spark of amusement in her eyes he would have loved to see again and again.

"Are you ready?"

Jas nodded and let her lead them in a bouncing skip around the edges of the circle. His feet had a mind of their own, not at all moving in any dignified fashion, but at least keeping him upright. Dalila moved like flower petals floating on a breeze.

There was a warmth in Jas's chest at the image in his mind—tiny versions of Dalila and Adelina skipping over the ancient carpets. He glanced up at where Adelina and Seba were twirling around the stage. Seba still looked out of place, but at least he was more relaxed.

Dalila turned them when they reached the edge of the circle. Jas's eyes caught on something floating up from the other side of the city.

Smoke.

Every light and warm feeling was immediately replaced by dread burrowing itself into the pit inside of him.

That looks like it's for you, little Knell.

Somehow, he knew the voice was telling the truth.

Jas jerked away from Dalila. His eyes fixed on the black smoke billowing up in the distance. It stained the beautiful blue of the sky.

"Jas?" said Dalila.

What does it mean when an inferno calls out to a man? There was a faint whisper of a laugh. *Nothing good.*

"I—" His breath caught in his throat. "I need to go. Need to—" He looked around wildly.

Seba was still dancing with Adelina. He looked happy.

"Need to get Seba."

Trust yourself.

Something was wrong.

Dalila had followed his gaze. She looked back at him, took only a moment's pause, then grabbed his hand.

"I'll help you." She pulled him through the crowd to the set of stairs along the side of the stage. "They'll let me on the stage to speak to Adelina."

It is said that Dom Sebastião's human touch burned the devil, said the voice.

There was a prickling in his fingers where his skin had touched Dalila's. *It's just in my head.*

Is it? The other voice was louder.

He tugged his hand from Dalila's. She shot him a confused look but kept moving forward.

"Wait here," she said.

Dalila lifted her skirts and climbed the stairs to the stage, earning annoyed looks from some of the dancing nobility, though no one stopped her. She was wearing the colors of the House of Ducança, and only the Lady of the Seas herself would cross those of the king's house.

Trust yourself.

There was a chance it was nothing. Someone else's problem. There was a possibility he was imagining the fact it came from the exact place he had left that morning. The exact place where Hala had told him she loved him. The exact place of his home.

Trust yourself.

Hala had known something, and she had wanted him to know it too.

The instincts of a monster are never exactly reputable, are they?

There was already so much he wished he didn't know.

Footsteps came down the stairs behind him, echoing like drums in his head, even over the music and sounds of the festival.

Dalila had returned, followed by an expressionless Adelina and a disgruntled Seba. Jas locked eyes only with his brother. He had been quiet and angry since yesterday, but Seba would do anything for Hala or for Jas.

Not that either of you deserve it.

"We have to go."

Seba's brows furrowed. "Why?"

Jas tossed his head in the direction of the smoke, hoping not to draw too much attention to it, though the sounds of discovery were beginning to echo from other people around him.

Seba just looked more confused. "What about it? Want to roast almonds?"

Trust yourself.

"Something's wrong."

"How do you know?" asked Adelina.

Jas didn't look away from Seba. "I know."

"We should hurry," came Dalila's voice. She started moving away from the stage, and Jas made to follow her.

Seba wasn't moving. Jas's stomach rolled.

"Seba."

Seba's eyes were unfocused, drifting hungrily around the crowd. "You go," he said. "I'll stay here."

Jas was going to throw up. "Seba."

Seba looked at him, and for once, his face was blank and cold as ice. "I belong here."

Bile rose.

"Jas, let's go," Dalila said. She tugged at his sleeve, but she didn't touch his hand again.

You belong with your family, Jas wanted to say.

But the terrible voice in his head stopped him. *A family that has only hurt him? That has held him back, even as he's tried to save all of you?*

"I'll go with you." Adelina raised her chin, her mind taking on a new course of action. "Seba, stay here and keep people happy."

She pushed past Dalila, assuming the lead through the celebrating crowd. Jas stared at Seba's frigid glare for one more moment.

The horrible feeling of something ending lodged in his gut.

CHAPTER 19

SEBA

Though Adelina was gone, Seba found no shortage of dance partners. He spun around with anyone who reached out their hands, and for those moments, the movement was the only thing Seba knew.

Though the summer festival was held annually, Seba had barely ever attended. He and Jas had always been with Hala this time of year or had taken advantage of the beaches being uncharacteristically empty for one summer day. The last time he had spent more than just ten minutes at the festival was with his mother when he was six years old, just weeks before her death.

Seba had danced with her, her calloused hands around his small ones. She had been laughing the entire time, the warmth of her smile glowing down on him from above.

Little had he known that in her apron pocket was a loaded gun, something she had only withdrawn later that night.

Seba had been falling asleep on his feet, clutching his mother's hand, when a man jumped out from one of the spice stands, knocking a rainbow of colors onto the cobblestones. His mother wrenched her hand out of his own and brought it to rest on something he hadn't recognized at the time.

Words had passed between them, his mother and that man. Seba couldn't understand them, didn't remember them. He was too fixated on the spice being packed into stone when his mother's shoes pressed into it, the smell of roasted pig on the air that rumbled his hungry stomach, and the shadow of Dom Sebastião, shaped in flowers, blocking out the light of the moon.

A shot rang out, and the man had fallen. A hole in his head had leaked blackish red. Then the worst came. People from all sides convened on Seba's mother, took all the coins she had in her pockets, and beat her until every part of her bled. They grabbed Seba's little hands—which had so recently been hugged in his mother's warmth—and snapped each finger while he cried.

And still, flower Dom Sebastião and the blood-and-bone royals he represented didn't move an inch.

It was only when he got older, after Teodora had moved them to a room in the lowest part of the city and then appeared dead in the room with shadowy eyes, that Seba pieced together what had happened. His mother had made deals with these men and had cheated them. She had taken him to the festival, where they could hide within the crowds and the colors, but it hadn't mattered.

No king had offered them protection. The common practice for dealing with thieves was to cut off their fingers, but it seemed these thugs had been inspired.

And, twelve years later, they had found him again.

There was a prickling at the back of his neck, and all the sounds, smells, and colors of the festival were back, pushing him forward.

It was different this time. *He* was the one on the stage now, beloved and immovable. Seba was the Dom Sebastião towering above everyone else.

If Jas wanted to take a wisp of smoke as a sign to run back through the streets, where danger lay beyond every turn, that was fine, but Seba was not going to throw away the first safe feeling he'd had in weeks—maybe even years.

But while he looked out at the crowd, searching for his next dance partner, his attention caught on a group of people dressed all in black and gray, at odds with the colorful festival. There were five of them in total, and at the front, looking more sober and put together than Seba had ever seen him, was Heitor Alves.

Even from this distance, Seba noticed Alves's top lip curl into a sneer when he realized Seba had seen him.

Heat flooded Seba immediately. It wasn't fear, but roiling anger coursing through him. This was the man who had made Seba look over his shoulder each minute of every day for weeks, alert for bounty hunters, thugs, monsters, and anything else living in the dark. Perhaps Alves had even been the one to go after his mother all those years ago at this very festival—Seba couldn't remember.

But it didn't matter. Because today, Seba was a celebrity. He was not cowering in an alley; he was dancing on a stage saved for the nobility. Seba wore an embroidered waistcoat, and the duke and duchess knew him by name. They valued him so much, in fact, that they paid for his presence. Today, Seba could not be touched.

Before he could reflect on it any further, Seba marched through the crowd with a singular focus. He had a fate to fight for, a goddess to please. Seba was going to get to Alves, and he was going to make him wish he had never laid a finger on the Pinheiros.

CHAPTER 20

JAS

The world was night and the things inside it shadows.

Black smoke billowed out from the collapsing frame of the Silver Salamander Apothecary, and Jas could barely make out the movements of panicked people trying to help or flee, the scream of bells and the steady pump of steam from the fire engine while water was sent through hoses and into the windows of Jas's home.

And then there were the voices.

Ghosts moved to the front of the gates, calling for the loved ones whose prayers they had heard. Something slammed hard against his knees, and he realized he'd fallen to the ground. A gentle hand pressed against his back.

Hala, he called through the flood of spirits. *Hala, are you there? Are you dead?*

He wanted to scream. Maybe he did. Why couldn't he force the spirits to talk to him? Why couldn't he make them look for her? Why did he have to wait around like anyone else, with nothing but hope and a chance of luck that she would reach out to him, either in life or death?

Why did he have this terrible power?

Perhaps because you are a terrible abomination who keeps terrible secrets.

His body curled, and he gagged. His throat burned. Jas was fire.

He had set the world aflame.

"Jas," a soft voice murmured by his ear. "Jas, it's going to be okay. Adelina is going to find out what happened. She's talking to the firefighters now."

It's all your fault, little Knell. You call to those in the Beyond, and this is how they answer.

Jas forced himself to his feet, barely aware of what he was doing. The bounty hunters had finally come, and it was his fault. He hadn't acted fast enough. Jas hadn't done the right thing. Everything the witches had told him—everything he had gleaned from the ghosts, Calixto, and Adelina—and he had still failed.

He stumbled forward, sensing the bump of cobblestones under his feet. A hand gripped his arm and pulled him back, but he wrenched himself from the hold and lurched through what used to be his front door.

"Jas!" Two voices cried out, followed by a shriek.

More pain caused by you.

Flames whipped around him in bursts of orange, yellow, and black. The warmth of them caressed his arms and pressed against his face like a welcome. He stepped farther inside. Jas didn't know what he had expected or even what he had wanted. To find Hala? To save his home? To burn with it?

Instead, his mind cleared, his lungs expanded at the heat, his nerves softened to the curve of flame. The crackling of the blaze filled his ears, the creaking of a building about to collapse, yells from those outside, and nothing else. No ghosts. No voices in his head but his own.

I belong here, he thought, and there was no one to refute him.

The floors groaned when he stormed further into the shop. He whipped his head left and right in search of anything—any*one*— salvageable. A shelf crashed beside him, an explosion of glass and powder following it, and Jas ducked.

"Hala!" His throat was coarse from the smoke. "Hala!"

The doorframe was still intact. He moved through it, finding a workshop of ash. Nothing remained, not even the copper pots, scales, and alembics that should have withstood the heat.

"Hala!"

Her bedroom was unrecognizable, nothing but smoke, flame, and the cinders of a life.

"Hala!"

Something responded. There was movement from inside the little cabinet beside the place where Hala's bed had been, always unmade. Between him and the cabinet was a wall of flame.

"Hala!"

More movement. He dove to the side when another crash sounded above his head. The floor of the bedroom he had shared with Seba caved in over him. Seba's bed was swallowed by the flames it had fallen into. Burning wood flew over Jas in a downpour.

And still he felt only warmth.

Jas blinked. His eyes burned, but his vision was clear. He was sitting in flame, surrounded by it. But he wasn't burning.

Jas stuck his bare hand directly into the fire and watched the light dance over his pale, unmarked skin. He was going mad.

There was another rattle from the other end of the room. The cabinet. Hala.

Jas threw himself across his burning home, disregarding the fire that should have killed him. Maybe dying was just searching, waiting to burn.

He reached the cabinet. It was made of wood, and yet it was like him. Untouched.

Jas choked down a scream when the door flew open and something burst out, scrambling over his lap with a flicking tail of black and yellow splotches. It disappeared into the fire as quickly as it had come. He blinked at it. Smoke and the haziness of his own mind clouded his senses while he watched the lizard escape. Jas wanted to follow it, but he made himself turn back.

Inside the cabinet was a stack of journals, one of which was the same one Hala had been writing in that morning. Each was thick, their pages crinkled from years of exposure to steam and strange concoctions. Plenty of extra papers and objects had been shoved between them.

Jas took them in his arms, hugging them close.

Trust yourself.

A barely discernible clatter made him peer back into the cabinet. At its base rested a slim silver ring that must have been dislodged by the journals. A slip of paper floated to land beside it. A memory sparked from when he had been around seven or eight.

Hala had twisted the ring around her finger, staring at it as if it had burned her soul, and then she had taken it off. He had never seen it again.

Jas picked it up, carefully turning it and watching the dancing flames in the narrow silver band. He brought the slip of paper to his eyes, revealing a short sentence in Hala's rushed scrawl: "Take care of my life's work."

Jas breathed in the flames. His lungs were warm.

And though there were no voices in his head to confirm it, he realized the truth. Hala was gone. Whether the bounty hunters had taken her or if she had run when they came, she was gone. If she wasn't dead now, she would be soon.

Jas rose and worked his way back through the shop. He could make out the blur of faces and the forceful spray of water pouring through the windows. The air outside should have felt good, but instead, it was like a blanket smothering the flames through deprivation.

"Jas!" Dalila ran toward him, her face smudged with soot.

Adelina was behind her, watching him with wide eyes. She clutched her forearm, where a patch of fabric had been burned away from her blouse, leaving a bright red, blistering burn.

There were other people ushering the three of them away, but Jas was only cognizant of the journals in his arms, the ring clutched in his fist, and the crush of ghosts in his mind.

"Are you all right?" Dalila was asking.

Jas nodded, barely aware he was doing it. He felt sick again.

"*How* are you all right?" Adelina's jaw was clenched with the effort of keeping her composure.

Jas lowered himself to the ground. The rough stucco scraped against his back as he slid against one of the neighboring buildings. It was the voice in his head that answered Adelina.

Because death will always welcome the Knell home.

CHAPTER 21

ADELINA

Adelina volunteered to get Seba from the festival while Dalila and Jas went back to the manor. She needed time to think, to steady herself. Where her forearm had burned—now wrapped in gauze by one of the medics—was now only a phantom pain, and she forced herself to breathe steadily through her nostrils.

Control, she reminded herself. *You have to gain control.*

She had tried to follow Jas into the flames, thinking she had lost everything. *Not the plan.* Adelina couldn't lose him. Not when they were so close. Not when she had come to an agreement with Hala that all their answers were in an alchemically modified cupboard, amidst years of scrawled notes, which she could safely extricate when the fire was put out. She was so close to winning, and she had almost lost her most integral piece.

Adelina had barely noticed the scorching pain of flames licking at her forearm, but then Dalila had pulled her back by her waist. Adelina had screamed. And then Jas had been back. Unharmed. Carrying all the answers.

For a brief, weak moment, Adelina had taken it as a sign of fate. She had quickly corrected herself. Fate hadn't saved her plan; Hala had. If this was going to work, Adelina needed to stay on her guard. If only everyone would just do exactly what she said, they would all avoid a lot of trouble.

She pushed away the image of Jas gasping on the ground after he had left the shop, like his soul had shattered. Adelina forced away the memory of Simão falling while her soul had shattered too.

This was the plan. It was *all* part of the plan.

She hung at the back of the crowd, where carts of meat, spices, and fresh bread lined the walls surrounding the square. The voices of people hassling over the goods mixed with the bouncing music ahead—a discordant orchestra of her city. On and around the stage, people still danced, and she searched them for a sign of Seba's green waistcoat.

Adelina had had Dalila order the outfit. It had been fine for Seba to be dressed in his usual clothes before this moment—his borrowed suits and softened fabrics were a sign of where he had come from, a sign of the people who the House of Ducança was trying so hard to connect to. Her mother had frowned when he appeared in emerald green, his buttons sewn with gold thread branching out to create beautiful embroidered flowers and swirls.

According to the royal family's official grand strategy, Seba was to remain visibly "other"—an eternal sign of the connection between nobility and commoner. But now, with Adelina's victory so close, it was important for the people to stop viewing him as wholly their own. Seba belonged to Adelina.

If only she could find him.

Panic sent her heart fluttering. For the second time in an hour, she pondered what would happen if she lost any of her central players now. Adelina traveled along the edge of the crowd, trying to keep her head down while simultaneously craning her neck to catch a glimpse of him. The people who did notice a girl dressed in noble clothes luckily did not look closely enough or were too drunk to try to identify her.

She had gone around the entire square before deciding to push her way into the crowd. Adelina set her eyes on her parents, who were at the edge of the stage, speaking to Calixto and a group of other members of the nobility. It was odd to witness them all out of their stuffy suits and in the traditional outfits of Jumaral.

Each of the nobles politely bowed their heads when she appeared at her father's side, though the movement lacked the usual rigidity. Alcoholic vapors drifted amongst them.

"Father." Adelina pulled Infante Benigno aside. "Have you seen Seba?"

Her father, who seemed just as unsteady as his peers, stared at her a moment with glazed eyes before furrowing his brow. "Seba?"

"Sebastião Pinheiro."

The duke looked toward the stage and searched the crowd, just as she had done. "Last I saw, he was dancing, my *couraninha*."

"With many, many people," said Calixto, who had suddenly appeared by Adelina's side.

"Do you consider every conversation an invitation for your interjection?" she snapped.

"Yes. But on the note of Senhor Pinheiro, it's likely he's gallivanted off with one of his dance partners."

A particularly loud laugh took the duke's foggy attention back to the circle of nobles, leaving just Adelina and the annoyingly sober Calixto. He smirked.

"Though I doubt you'd mind if he did."

"Rarely do I have time for your wholly unnecessary existence, Calixto, but now is a particularly bad time." She was about to return to her hunt when Calixto's fingers wrapped around her arm. "What?"

Her cousin glanced back at the duke before replying. "Seba left the stage about ten minutes ago."

"And where did he go?"

"He met with some men by the market stalls, and then they took the road back up to the castle."

Her pulse leapt. Was it possible Seba was planning something at the castle, just like Jas had the day before? Or were these the men Seba had told her about yesterday, the ones who had threatened to push his head through a wall if he didn't give them 300,000 *rejas*?

Neither option boded well for the future of Adelina's plan. But she was so close.

She spun around, hoping she was moving through the crowd fast enough that no one would be able to recognize and stop her. To her surprise, Calixto followed.

The two of them managed to make their way to the edge of the square with minimal public interaction, saved by the fact the duke and duchess had just made their drunken return to the dancing stage. There were fewer people in the surrounding streets, most of them too inebriated to pay much attention to the prince of Jumaral and the marquise of Lis walking by.

The streets around the square were mazelike, barely wide enough for a carriage. Washing lines hung from windows, and the narrowest of doorsteps stuck out from multicolored doors. Every street branched out to another, tiles and cobblestones rhyming and repeating across the city. Finding Seba amidst it all would be near impossible.

"You didn't think to do anything ten minutes ago when you saw him leave?" Adelina hissed. They hurried up the sloping streets, looking down every alley and offroad they passed.

"I paid enough attention to help you, didn't I?"

"Yes, and why *did* you pay attention? Why not just pull Seba aside and tell lies about me, like you did with Jas?"

"My father would be heartily disappointed if the eighteen-year-old peasant boy holding up the House of Ducança's media campaign disappeared without a trace, so I pay attention to him. And Jas."

"Would your father not be disappointed that you watched him leave and then did nothing?"

"Considering his general focus on the preservation of Jumaral, I doubt he'd want the crown prince to get directly involved in anything so unsavory that it has to take place in the side streets of Lis until absolutely necessary."

Adelina bristled at the way he spat the name of her city. "And you'd rather make Dom Aristides happy than risk actually solving a problem?"

"I'd rather Jumaral have a crown prince than a Sebastião Pinheiro."

Adelina didn't answer, and for several minutes, the only sounds were the distant music and cheers of the festival. Both of their breaths steadily became harder as the streets grew steeper and their feet moved faster.

I can because I have to, she reminded herself. Seba was her only key to Jas now Hala was gone, and Jas was her key to everything. *I can because I will.*

"Look," Calixto whispered.

Adelina followed his gaze down a side street.

A man stood beneath a blue-tiled bridge arched between buildings on either side—a covered passageway with glittering windows connecting the two shops. He wore a black suit and hat at odds with the colors of the festival below. Even from this distance, Adelina noticed the bulge of a weapon at his waist.

She was about to start toward him when Calixto pulled her back to where they wouldn't be seen. "We should call the guards," he whispered.

Adelina barely processed what he said. Adrenaline coursed through her. "Seba is there. It will take too long."

"Seba *might* be there, and he won't be helped if we're shot."

"We won't be shot."

"You don't know that."

Adelina glared at him, and he returned the look with full force. "Are you forgetting who we are?"

Calixto scoffed. "Are you forgetting that we are made of flesh and bone?"

The words hung between them. Neither needed to bring up their siblings, the way the titles of Manuel and Simão hadn't protected them in the end. But that was different. Adelina was fighting for her fate. Ostrea would protect her.

"Costs and benefits, Calixto."

"Human nature, Adelina," he hissed through clenched teeth.

"Which includes self-preserving instincts."

Before he could stop her, Adelina whirled and walked briskly down the street toward the man. Calixto's delayed footsteps echoed behind her. She pushed her shoulders back and lifted her chin with all the authority she had been taught.

You are the king's niece, an etiquette tutor had once said. *Very few people have the power to make you bow.*

The man's eyes narrowed when he saw them, and Adelina

observed the moment of recognition when he realized the marquise of Lis and the crown prince of Jumaral were heading his way.

"Good afternoon," Adelina said. Now she was closer, she could hear the muffled sounds of shouting from behind one of the doors.

The man's eyes darted between the two of them. One arm bent so his hand rested just over his weapon. "Afternoon," he said. He had a gravelly voice, which somehow didn't match his smooth face. The man didn't look more than a few years older than Calixto.

"I'm looking for a friend of mine," Adelina continued pleasantly. "Sebastião Pinheiro. Have you seen him?"

"Um, no, Your Majesty."

Adelina didn't have to fake a smile at that. "Your Majesty" was not technically the correct address for her position, but that didn't mean it didn't fit her.

"Really? He's very important to my family. I'm sure you've seen him in the papers."

"I don't—"

"You don't want to avoid imprisonment?" said Calixto. "Taxation beyond belief? Having your name blacklisted from every establishment in Jumaral? Killed and denounced as a scourge on Ostrea's power?"

The guard blanched.

"It wouldn't even be hard," Calixto continued. "A single word from one of us that you're a witch and you'd end up just as dead as the rest. Kill us, harm us in any way, and it wouldn't even take a word. Our bodies would be enough evidence for our parents to do with you whatever they pleased."

Adelina gave another photo-worthy smile. "Would you like to open the door?"

The man stared blankly at them both, obviously calculating who was the bigger threat—his boss or the full weight of the House of Ducança.

He banged a fist against the door.

There were shuffles from inside and angry words exchanged. Calixto stepped forward to stand shoulder to shoulder with Adelina, a tired resignation in the set of his jaw.

The door opened, revealing another man dressed similarly in blacks and grays. "What is it?"

The first man glanced nervously at Calixto and Adelina before turning his back to them and carrying out a whispered conversation with his colleague. The moment of realization was so obvious Adelina almost laughed. The second man waved for his compatriots inside the building to silence and exchanged frantic words with someone Adelina couldn't see.

There was a scuffle, a moan, and chair legs squeaking across a wooden floor. A third man appeared in the doorway, short and red-faced, a mouth set in a permanent frown, judging by the lines of his face. His eyes narrowed at Adelina and Calixto. He took in their colorful outfits, their shared postures, Calixto's scowl and Adelina's amusement.

It was perfectly clear who they were. The plan her parents had set up to save the House of Ducança through the media was working after all.

The man said no words as he reached behind him and shoved Seba onto the street, letting him fall to his knees against the cobblestones. Seba's mouth was gagged, and his hands and ankles had been tied with rope. Blood was smeared across the lower half of his face, and he already had a bruise welling up around his left eye. His waistcoat was gone, and his shirt was half unbuttoned and torn. Seba turned wide eyes on Calixto and then Adelina. His whole body relaxed into the stone as he focused on her.

Adelina didn't hold back her smirk. She owned this boy.

With only passing glances varying from hate-filled to terrified, the men cleared out of the building and headed down the street toward the city center. Seba yelled something after them, a long string of unintelligible words Adelina took to be expletives.

"No one can understand you." She pulled the gag down so it hung loosely around his neck. It was crusted with his blood. She wiped her fingers on her skirt.

"I'm sure they got the message," said Seba, his voice nasally. "It's really about the energy, isn't it?"

"At least part of it is in the effective application of that energy."

She untied the rope around his wrists, glad he hadn't been bound long enough for his wrists to bleed with the friction of the rope.

"What were they doing with you?" asked Calixto. He stood several paces away, his arms crossed and his eyes narrowed at Seba.

"They think I owe them money." Seba untied the rope on his ankles himself now that his wrists were free. Despite his clear relief at their appearance and his show of nonchalance, his fingers shook while he undid the ropes.

Adelina noticed him clenching his jaw against chattering teeth. "They *think*?"

"Well, it's my mother who owes them the money. I just happen to be the one who's alive. Luckily, though, I'm not as simple a target as they expected." He ran a hand through his hair, making a weak attempt at his signature grin. "I suppose it pays to be Sebastião Pinheiro."

"No," Adelina corrected. "It pays to have the marquise of Lis and the crown prince of Jumaral interested in your whereabouts."

Seba's grin slipped.

Calixto scoffed. "You're both delusional."

"We also both have somewhere to be," said Adelina.

Seba scrambled to his feet and pressed a hand to his nose. "Why are we delusional?"

"Calixto doesn't understand his position."

"And Adelina doesn't understand how the world works."

Seba's face scrunched like he was doing complex mathematical equations.

"It doesn't matter," said Adelina. "Thank you for your unwavering support, Calixto, but this is where we leave you."

She started up the hill, expecting them both to hurry after her, and they did.

Calixto fell into step beside her. "Adelina, whatever you're doing with this guy and Jas, it's not—"

"It's none of your business," said Adelina, while Seba repeated "this guy" behind her. "So go back to the festival, Calixto. Go back to being scared and lazy and get drunk with my parents and their council. Leave the rest to me."

She assumed he was going to retort, but he didn't. Calixto didn't even keep walking, just stopped in the middle of the street.

Adelina didn't look back. She kept marching up the streets of Lis, to her home just under the castle crowning the hill. Anticipation spurred her forward, nearing the end of her plan.

She sensed Calixto's eyes on her and Seba until they wound out of sight.

"By the way, Seba," she said when the decorated castle came into view, "Hala is dead."

CHAPTER 22

JAS

Jas and Dalila snapped to attention at the sound of the library door opening.

Adelina and Seba stood in the entrance. Dalila jumped to her feet at the sight of Adelina, but Jas kept his place at the table farthest from the fireplace, searching Seba's face for...anything. He was a wreck, holding a handkerchief to a bloody nose, his clothes torn, walking with a slight limp.

"What happened?" Jas choked on the words, barely getting them out.

Seba stared him down with that same blank look he had held at the festival. "Heitor Alves," he said, his voice rough.

Didn't he tell you this would happen? And what did you do about it?

"I'm sorry." He was sorry he hadn't taken the threat more seriously, sorry he hadn't been there to prevent it, sorry they had just lost the closest thing they'd had to a parent. Jas wanted to hug his brother, to cry with him.

But Seba appeared too far gone. He dropped into a chair by the fire like a stone.

Seba had warned them all. He had been the one trying to collect money to stop the bounty hunters from catching up to them. Seba had seen Adelina's offer as a way out, not just for himself but for Jas and Hala too.

Jas was the one who had always been resistant, who hadn't wanted to use his powers for money that could have bought their family a new life outside of Jumaral, who hadn't believed the consequences of not following through on the fate presented to him. And now Hala was gone, all traces of her burned away.

Perhaps that's for the best.

"Do you have the journals?" Adelina drew up a chair and sat across from him.

Jas tore his attention away from Seba.

Two demons reunited at last.

"Yes." He blinked the extra thoughts away. "They're written in Almaric."

The moment he and Dalila had arrived at the library, he had torn the books open, flipping through endless pages of notes Hala, for some unknown reason, had felt were important enough to save. Dread built with every inscrutable line. He cursed every moment he had spent not learning Hala's native language.

"I can read Almaric," Adelina said. The calculating look she gave him was not unfamiliar, but it seemed different after the events of the last hours, like he had a secret Adelina would be able to deduce just from looking at him. "Dalila," she said.

Dalila stiffened where she stood beside him. Her cheeks were tearstained.

"Please leave us."

Jas kept his gaze pressed firmly to the table in front of him. With the brush of Dalila's hand against his shoulder and the click of her heels, she was gone.

He was glad she was gone. And he wanted her back.

You don't want her to see what might be under that pretty face?

Adelina shifted the books toward herself and read the titles. Jas had the Almaric-Jumaralian dictionary Dalila had found open beside the oldest journal. Another scrap of paper, pulled from another of Hala's journals, showed three lines of his own writing— the beginnings of a slow and tedious translation.

That will get you nowhere. You know the solution, little Knell.

Jas's jaw clenched. He wanted to pound his fists into his skull, gouge out the part of his mind connecting him to the dead, the part that had drawn Lady Adelina Maria Malves Ducança into his life, the part that had killed Hala. Jas settled for gripping the edge of the desk, the silver ring still clenched against his palm.

His knuckles whitened while Adelina turned over the different texts he and Dalila had pulled: the dictionary; a glossary of alchemical terms; and several general texts on alchemy, chemistry, biology, and anatomy. Hala had a few sketches scattered through her notes he had tried to match to different subjects.

He said nothing when Adelina got to the stack of journals and carefully turned their pages. There was no point now in hiding from her that Hala was an alchemist.

Her brow furrowed in concentration, but there was an excited energy to her demeanor. After a few minutes, she closed the books and looked up at him expectantly.

"It was fireproof," he said breathlessly. "It rattled when I called her name, and a...a salamander crawled out..."

He was lightheaded. Hala had prepared. She had protected her work, which made it seem like she had left on purpose. But at the same time, she had abandoned her work, her life's purpose. Jas glanced at Seba. She had stranded them too, and that wasn't something Jas wanted to believe had been done on purpose.

"She was an alchemist, wasn't she?" Adelina replied. "She knew how to deal with fire."

"But how did she know?" His voice came out as a rasp. He cleared his throat, trying to loosen the tension coiling there.

Jas hadn't meant it as a genuine question, but of course, Adelina answered.

"Alchemists don't generally enjoy being associated with members of the royal family. Also—" Adelina's eyes narrowed slightly, like she was examining his reaction. "I got word from Dalila earlier today that the witches that gave you your prophecies were caught by bounty hunters. It's possible that they, knowing you and thus knowing Hala, gave her up in the hope that it would win them some mercy."

Jas's breath constrained around his chest. It was his fault. *All his fault.* He had done nothing to help the witches, even knowing they were compromised, and now they were trapped, undergoing whatever horrors the bounty hunters and the royal family subjected witches to.

Something wicked. He had known and he had done nothing, not to assist the witches and not to help Hala. After all, he and Seba were the reason Hala had been tied to the same royal family who wanted her murdered.

Not both of you.

It was Jas's powers that had allowed Adelina to find them. It was his perverseness making him and Seba integral to this plan. It was Jas's fault alone.

"I didn't burn," he said. *Because I really am a demon.* "When I was in the fire, I stood in the flames, put my entire body in, but I didn't burn." He searched Adelina's face for some scrap of knowledge or secret understanding she had so far kept to herself.

"You think Hala had something to do with it."

It wasn't a question, but he nodded. Hala was an alchemist with no regard for what was "natural," and he had unnatural abilities. Her life's work was about disrupting life and death, and he was nothing if not a disruption. It was the answer that had always stared him down and also the one he had always turned away from.

You wanted to protect the murderer.

But she hadn't just been a murderer, had she?

Trust yourself, she had said. *I love you.*

"I thought her journals might... She always kept them separate, for as long as I can remember. Part of some project she was working on. But she would never say... I—" He swallowed, his throat and mouth as dry as the fine sand that swept across the streets near the beach, whipped through the air by the smallest gust of wind. "I need to know what they say. About me."

"About the Knell." Adelina's eyes were bright. It didn't matter that his entire life was being put into question, laid out before him in what was likely a very ugly array of vile experimentation. To her, it was a problem to solve. Or even better, a dramatic reveal to the big mystery of his existence, like something out of the stories she so keenly manufactured.

Jas supposed he didn't care what her motivations were. He couldn't care.

Monsters have all sorts of talents.

She's not a monster, he thought.

"I know the basics, but I assume the vocabulary will be different." She pulled the open journal toward her, studying the Almaric closer than she had on her initial pass through. "My studies were more focused on how to avoid an international incident in polite conversation rather than alchemical breakthroughs. It might be slow. We should start at specific dates and go from there...." She drifted off and then paused, head cocked, like a cat presented with an interesting new toy.

"What is it?"

She turned the book around so it was right side up for him.

"Look at this."

Adelina pointed to two sections of Almaric script, lines looped and swirled in ways unbeknownst to Jas.

He looked up at her and shook his head.

"See the slant?" The section on the left had a slight rightward lean, as if a gust of wind had flown across the page and set the words askew. The characters of the other section, by contrast, appeared to have been produced by a machine—stick straight ending in measured curves and precise lengths.

"Two different sets of handwriting?"

Adelina flipped the book back around to her side. "Tell me about Hala's life in Almard." She scanned the page and made notes on his spare sheet of paper.

"I don't know that much about it," he admitted.

"There were many secrets in our house," came Seba's voice. He was still staring into the fire.

"You don't know if she had a partner, someone she worked with or lived with?" Adelina asked.

Jas shook his head.

Probably another of Hala's victims.

"How did she meet you?"

"Is this important?" he asked impatiently.

She looked up from the journal, meeting his eyes as if daring him to question her methods again. "Yes."

"My village in Huojen was destroyed in an attack from Geirida. My parents died, but some people from the village were able to get me out and run to Almard, since we were so close to the border. Somehow, I ended up with Hala."

"How old were you both?"

"I was a year old, and she was about sixteen."

Adelina was silent for a while, engrossed in reading. After a few minutes, she started pointing out words for him to look up in the translation dictionary, copying them on a scrap of paper so he could match the script. Scalpel. Aludel. Crucible. Artery. Bone marrow. Pancreas. Salamander. Homunculus. Furnace. Each word sent his stomach flipping over itself. Adelina would go quiet for minutes at a time, leaving him waiting on the edge of his seat, clenching his fists so his arms shook. He did not want to put the words together in his head.

It seems like you already did.

Adelina flipped through pages, occasionally skimming or completely skipping over sections, at times focusing on a single passage for several minutes.

All the while, Seba stayed by the fire. Completely still, for once in his life.

Finally, Adelina looked up. "You were dead."

"*What?*"

"You were dead." Adelina looked him up and down as if she had never seen him before.

"But—" His mind stuttered. He looked down at his body, aware of the way his legs bent over the chair. How his fingers squeezed tightly. The rhythm his heart beat in his chest. His throat. His stomach. "I'm not dead."

"Yes, thank you for that observation." But Adelina's disturbing lack of blinking betrayed her wariness. "It seems Hala and whoever she was working with found a solution to that particular state of being."

"How?"

"Do you know what a homunculus is?"

"A tiny human created in a test tube. A myth." He hesitated. "Isn't it?"

"It is, but they took inspiration from that process, feeding you human blood and such."

Jas's whole body shriveled in on itself. "And *such*?" he repeated.

"Salamander vomit. There are legends of salamanders being born of flame, but it looks like they were utilizing the salamander's regenerative properties."

The salamander bursting out of the cabinet like a guard dog.

The name of Hala's shop: the Silver Salamander Apothecary.

Jas felt sick.

A monster, after all.

"So, they just...put all of that stuff in my body, and I came back to life?"

"Well, no, they also cut you up a fair amount."

He absently put a hand to his chest where the scars crossed his skin like a city map, scars he had always been told came from the attack on his village. But the assault had done much worse than scar him.

"And it worked?"

"No, it doesn't look like it."

"What do you mean, it doesn't look like it? I'm alive, aren't I?"

"I mean *that* didn't work. They were able to make you grow and sort of blink, but you weren't really alive, just an animated corpse." Adelina moved on to another journal, flipping its pages in search of something specific. "How old were you when you moved to Jumaral?"

"Six." That one he knew well. It was the age he had met Seba, though he had no memory of a time before that. Something clicked in his head, and the room spun with new clarity. He had no memory because he had been dead, or at least something close to it.

You should have stayed there.

Adelina sank back into the pages, jotting notes without taking her eyes off Hala's words. A few agonizing minutes passed before she slid the Almaric-Jumaralian dictionary toward him.

"Look this up." She scribbled a word on a scrap of paper and threw it at him.

Almaric had more curves than Jumaralian, swoops appearing more like paths of flight than angled streets. He searched the columns of words in the translation dictionary, looking for the matching script and the corresponding Jumaralian.

"Ember."

Adelina only hummed thoughtfully. Her eyes paused on the page.

"What?" he prodded.

"Nothing." Her eyes started moving again, scanning across the page impossibly fast. How did her brain even have time to understand what she was reading? "Just interesting."

"What is?"

She finished the page before looking up. "That word." Adelina pointed her pen at the one he had just translated. "It's pronounced *Jas*."

Something nudged at his brain—an idea that hadn't been fully formed.

"My name is Almaric," he said, by way of explanation. Jas had always known that. His family had lived in a border town. It was normal for him to have an Almaric name. He was *normal*.

Her eyes narrowed again, and he felt like prey.

"You don't speak any Almaric?"

He shook his head.

"*Ibin* means boy."

The idea pushed harder, urging him to make a connection. Adelina let out an exasperated sigh.

"Your name is Jasibin. *Jas ibin*. Ember Boy. It's not a real name; it's the title of the project."

"So—" His mouth wasn't connected to his brain. "*Hala* named me?"

"She named the project."

"And I'm...the project."

"Yes, and an impressive one. She accomplished necromancy."

Adelina returned to the journal, seemingly unaware Jas was still reeling, his world flipping over in his head. He was nothing more than an experiment. An accomplishment.

An abomination.

What kind of undead creature was he? Hala had been working on necromancy, of course. Jas had even helped with her tests every now and then. What had she been doing? Trying to recreate what she had done to him? Performing tests on her proudest subject?

You were just a piece of meat that found its way out of its jar.

"Wait."

"What?" Adelina didn't look up from the page.

"What's my actual name, then? I had a name before I...before I died, didn't I? Does it say?"

"If it does, I didn't see it. These journals aren't treated as diaries, just as logs. Even at the beginning, you were just referred to as 'the subject.'"

As soon as Hala's spirit had settled on the other side, he would ask her. Jas had always thought "the Knell" was the name for his powers, the alter ego separating who he was from what he could do. "Jas" was just him. Now even that was gone.

"When did she start calling me Jasibin, then?"

"After the initial experiment in Almard. 'Ember Boy' because she used fire to bring you to life. You were born of the embers."

"But then why did she come to Jumaral?"

"There were rumors of a power off the coast of Solmortém, which she believed could be used to make an exchange—"

"Not just any power."

Adelina and Jas both jumped at Seba's sudden interruption. He had stood, his fists clenched at his sides. The fire silhouetted him from behind. The blood on his face was now dark and cracked. His voice shook, and barely controlled anger made every word sound like a challenge not to shout. But the look he gave Jas was still empty. It was the worst look Jas could imagine because Seba was anything but empty.

"An encantada."

It's happening, little Knell. You are done.

Jas's breaths were becoming shallower, and stars were bursting across his vision, but he was unable to respond, unwilling to piece together the links in his head.

You know how this story ends.

"Someone wished my mother dead," continued Seba, staggering slightly as he prowled toward them. "That's what the high priestess said. That's why her eyes were cloudy. And that's why Hala found me, isn't it? Because *she* killed my mother. She went to Solmortém with your little corpse, and she made a deal for you to be given life in exchange for the life of *my mother*."

"Hala does say that the exchange was for Teodora Pinheiro, but—" Adelina cleared her throat. "It wasn't an encantada, Seba. Those aren't real. Hala writes that she had blood on her shoe that the witch in Solmortém drew from, which means it was probably a witch using blood magic. It wasn't on purpose."

"No, it was *not* blood magic. She might have had blood on her shoe, but blood magic deaths don't look like that. They need more blood than a smudge on a shoe. Hala killed my mother with an encantada's wish, and then she came back to Lis, found me, and pretended to want me so that I could teach *Ember Boy* how to be human." His expression finally crumpled under the weight of potential cries or screams. And then he said the very worst words. "Did you know? Is that why you and Hala never wanted to leave Lis, because of some connection to encantadas and my mother?"

Tell him, little Knell. Tell him everything.

"I knew Hala killed her, but I didn't know why or how. She told me," Jas whispered. "Your mother told me. She speaks to me. All the time. She's the only one...the only ghost who always speaks to me. It doesn't matter if you're around or not. She...she tells me to protect you..."

You're the one he needs protection from.

This was why Teodora Pinheiro could break all the rules. His life was hers. She didn't need a human tether or a special object or place to hold her to the world of the living. Jas had stolen her life. It only made sense she would steal his too.

We are finally in agreement.

Seba had frozen.

"I'm sorry," Jas whispered. "I'm sorry."

There was a guttural scream. Seba stormed toward Jas, who barely had time to brace himself before the first fist connected with his cheekbone. Sparks erupted across his vision. He hit the floor and lay still, ready for the onslaught of pain, the agony that should have come at the lick of flames.

But none did. Adelina was pushing against Seba's chest, holding him back from Jas.

"Stop it," she ordered, shoving Seba away. "We need him. If you break him, you won't be king."

If you break him...

Jas didn't know whose voice echoed Adelina's in his head, but whoever it was wanted him to suffer.

Seba glared down at Jas with an expression that told him he probably wouldn't have survived if Seba got his way.

"It's okay." Jas didn't make an effort to staunch the trickle of hot blood dripping down his cheek. "I killed his mother."

Adelina looked down at him too, though her composure had returned. He couldn't begin to imagine what was going through her head.

"Yes," Seba snarled. "You did." He pushed past Adelina and thundered out of the room, slamming the heavy wooden door behind him.

Jas wanted to lie still forever, to stop time in its tracks. Adelina held out a hand to pull him up, and after a moment, he took it. He was dizzy and cold but sweating at the same time. Jas bent to lift his chair up from where it had fallen, and his vision almost went completely black.

"Sit," Adelina said. "You look like you're going to collapse."

He followed her instructions.

He couldn't blink away Seba's mutinous expression—the one

which cycled constantly through Jas's nightmares. Those terrible nights when his brain decided to show him what would happen if Seba ever found out how perverse his existence really was. And that was even before Jas himself had known the full extent of it.

The reality was unimaginably worse.

"I still need to talk to my brother." Adelina was back at the journals, as if nothing had happened. "There's nothing that I've said that helps you at all?"

Jas was still wading through smoke. He couldn't think.

Adelina met his blurry gaze. "Try to focus on the work. It will help." She returned to scribbling translations on the sheet beside her.

You don't deserve to avoid this pain.

He agreed. But Seba wanted to be king, didn't he? Seba was still fighting for that fate, struggling to fulfill the prophecy because he believed Ostrea would strike him down if he didn't. So maybe this was something Jas could do for him.

He had to focus on Lord Simão. There was nothing else left.

"You know, it wasn't your fault. You were a child. A dead one at that."

And then you lied.

"I know that."

"You can't blame yourself for being alive."

Jas couldn't look at her. "But what if I wasn't supposed to be alive?"

"There are plenty of things, living and nonliving, that are much worse than you."

Somewhere in his mind, Jas recognized that. But there was a way people lit up for Seba like they never did for Jas. When Seba entered a room, people smiled. When Jas entered a room, they asked where Seba was.

It had been that way with Isaque, the only person Jas had ever been romantically involved with. Isaque was bright and loud and kind. Jas had been surprised that day at the market, when the beautiful person with the brilliant laugh chose him to say hello to. He had greeted Isaque back, but it was Seba who had continued the conversation, who had made Isaque's gray eyes dance.

When Isaque kept coming back to the apothecary shop with Luísa, Jas had always been surprised when they touched his shoulder and laughed, even though he hadn't said anything funny. But then they would ask where Seba was and disappear with him into the city. One night, Isaque had come alone, and instead of asking for Seba, Isaque had kissed Jas. The sun had shone just on him.

But the warmth had only lasted a week. Isaque told him, holding Jas's hands between their own—as if Jas was the most valuable thing in the entire world—that there was someone else. And a day later, Jas had walked in on Seba and Isaque kissing each other against the wardrobe Jas and Seba shared.

Jas had always assumed it was because Seba had that dimpled charisma he never would. Seba could navigate through conversations with such ease that Jas had wondered if there was something missing about himself. He had never understood how someone could just *know* what to say after hello.

But maybe Jas's social skills were just another side effect of the fact he was not supposed to exist. Perhaps everyone had already sensed the wrongness in him. He had died. Dead things weren't supposed to come back.

"But what if I'm not human?" he whispered.

You're not, Teodora confirmed.

Adelina's reply was immediate. "Humans don't have a set size or shape or background or way of thinking or anything else. Why shouldn't you be human?"

He looked up at her. "I'm an—"

Abomination.

"—a corpse."

She shrugged. "I've often found humans to be weak, senseless beings. You can be something better."

Something better, he repeated in his mind.

You know what to do, little Knell.

"I think I know how to talk to your brother," he said.

A faint smirk twisted at Adelina's lips. "Do it."

He had always thought the state of the Knell—the cold, calculating beast that terrified the likes of Heitor Alves—was something he had to force. The Knell existed in a dark part of his subconscious, the shadowy edges at the border of the living and the dead. But if it he had been born of death, something in him was irrevocably linked to the Beyond, and perhaps the solution was to let himself be drawn there. To let himself go where he guessed he hadn't been since childhood.

Stop pretending to be human, Teodora hissed.

Maybe after this was done, he could visit the person who had performed the exchange for Hala. Perhaps they would know how to rid him of this power—or could reverse what Jas and Hala had done to Seba. But for now, his powers were still useful.

He closed his eyes and pushed past the flood of horrors waiting in his head. The gate to the Beyond was in front of him, iron drifting amidst black smoke. Usually, Jas would step back and wait for the ghosts to come forward. He would clench his fists and run away to the land of the living. Pain would engulf him while he fought to stay where he had thought he belonged. Now, he knew better.

He belonged everywhere and nowhere.

Jas allowed death's gates to swallow him into its realm. It was time to leave humanity behind. He was the Knell, and the lands of the dead were awaiting his call.

CHAPTER 23

ADELINA

Adelina watched Jas's body shudder across the table. His dark lashes closed over his eyes, and his head hung so the fabric of his waistcoat rumpled across his chest.

Jas had gone pale, as white as the fresh clouds over the festival before they had been tainted by smoke. His hair, brows, and lashes looked like smudges of black ink across his skin. Blood was still smeared down his cheek, and a purple bruise was beginning to blossom. She wanted to ask if he was all right but bit her tongue instead.

The only sounds were the crackling of fire and the faint squeak of footsteps from somewhere else in the house. Maybe Seba's, wherever he had gone.

Jas's head jerked backward, sending Adelina's teeth boring into her tongue.

She ignored it and searched his face furiously for any sign of success. His eyes were wide open, swallowed by his pupils. Dark blood trickled from his nose.

Adelina's entire body pulsed. She was going to talk to Simão. She was finally going to get the information she needed to put this entire ordeal to an end.

Shadows gathered at the edges of her vision. She tried to blink them away, but they were coalescing from the room around her. The dark spaces of the room's corners, gaps between shelves, the dancing puppets cast by the flame—all rose to cover Jas. They swirled and came to rest low over his face, like a hood of smoke.

The hair stood on Adelina's arms as black wings unfurled from Jas's back, blowing out the flames of the fireplace. Next were the gas lamps, extinguished in a clap of thunder that might have been in Adelina's head.

She sat in darkness and suppressed a scream. Adelina wanted to cry, to run flailing from the room in a fit of terror and have Dalila make her a strong cup of tea. She contemplated accepting what her family had told her and letting them keep her crown and her fate, running into the waiting arms of her parents and mourning her brother without guilt.

But Adelina made herself sit still.

Jas wasn't visible. Maybe he wasn't there at all. Perhaps speaking with Simão meant giving himself back to the death he had been stolen from. A stab of guilt pierced her, but she brushed it away. There were bigger things than Jas or any of them. If she was truly about to speak with her brother, then Jas's role in her plan was done, and it would be better for her if he was gone. She couldn't have him spreading all her secrets.

It was worth it. *Anything* was worth it. It had to be.

A face appeared amongst the shadows.

Simão looked the same as he had the moment he died. His usual warm skin, bronzed from stolen sun, was gray and pale, his lips blue. Water dripped from his curls and ran in rivulets down his chest, mingling with the dark smear of blood trickling from his mouth and nose, staining his soaked shirt. His gray trousers clung to his legs, and his feet were bare. The rest of his face was familiar—sharp cheekbones, high brows, and a mouth ready to smile at any given moment.

But the whites of his eyes were traced with bright red spiderwebs, bloodshot and dull. His chest was still.

"Simão?"

His voice was the same, a lightness behind every word. "You called, *mana*." *Sister.*

Adelina's breath stopped. She was standing—or whatever was akin to standing in this in-between place. Adelina took a step forward. Put her hand out.

He retreated.

"Don't," her brother said, and Adelina lowered her hand. "It will feel strange."

Adelina didn't know what to do next, what to say. She just wanted to hug her big brother. "I don't mind."

"I do."

Silence between them.

"We should make this quick," Simão said. "It's not good for me to be here."

The shadows had impeded on Adelina's brain. Something nudged at her, reminding her of the plan. She recognized it as annoyance. "Says who?"

"Says me."

"And you're the authority on the boundaries between the living and the dead? That's quite a promotion."

He straightened his shoulders importantly, and Adelina bristled.

"You're just going to put yourself in danger," he said.

"I'm already in danger. I might as well make it worth my time."

He tilted his head in the way they shared. It had annoyed their tutors to no end. "What do you want?"

"I want to know what's happening."

"You're well on your way to doing that by yourself, last time I checked."

Adelina turned his words over. "Last time you checked?"

Someone else would have shifted their weight or looked away. Simão just tightened his jaw. "I knew you would try something that would get you killed. I tried warning you through that—through your friend. I stopped when it seemed I was doing you more harm than good."

"But Jas found you anyway," Adelina said with a flush of satisfaction.

"Jas made a deal to my liking."

"What is it?"

A grin lit up his face, and his teeth shone black with blood. "That's between us."

Adelina scowled. "Why are you dead?"

The grin faded, and Adelina was almost grateful.

"What do you know?" he asked after a pause.

"I know that our family is hoarding witches in the castles. I know that they fear the people's growing discontent toward the House of Ducança. I know that you were killed by blood magic but that our family was somehow involved. So." She fixed him with the best impression of their mother she could muster. "Why are you dead? And why—" Her voice was at risk of breaking. "Why wouldn't you talk to me?"

Despite her best efforts, the question sounded childish. Like she was five years old, mad at her older brother for not wanting to play with her anymore. Her heart pounded, and her throat burned with the effort not to cry.

"Before I answer your questions... And I *will* answer them," he added quickly when she opened her mouth to retort. "I want to know what you plan to do with the answers."

"I'm going to go to our family. I'm going to tell them everything that I know and threaten to share it with the world unless they give me my crown."

"And you think that will work?"

"Being queen is my fate." *All hail Malves*—he had been the only other witness. "And I trust our family to weigh out the costs and benefits."

He laughed, a disbelieving, annoying guffaw that made Adelina's lip curl. "You really think that they'll just hand over the crown if you threaten to tell the people that they killed me? Or that they're hiding witches in castles and draining the magic out of them?"

"Draining the magic?"

"All the seas, Adelina." He brought his blue-tinged hands to his face, as if he couldn't believe what he was hearing. "You didn't even know that part? That our family has been stealing magic from witches for centuries, pushing around this narrative of their devilish ways so that no one would question the need that they be rounded up?"

Adelina crossed her arms over her chest. "But then what are they using the magic for?"

"Everything!" Simão threw his hands out, as if Adelina could picture more than just swirls of black smoke beyond him. "Weapons, infrastructure, agriculture—all of it depends on stolen magic. Jumaral has become dependent on a resource that was never ours to take, and we've now reached the time where it's no longer enough. Each castle is an extraction ground. In the past twenty years, we've been using more and more of them for defense magic—that's the only reason no one has been able to invade so far. But it's not enough, and when it does all come crumbling down, Jumaral will be even weaker than it already is."

"But why would things be different now? If the magic has held for so long—"

"Because the magic isn't as powerful anymore. With such a rise in witch bounties since Tio Aristides became king, the witch population is far too low, and the ones that do exist haven't been able to hone their magic. Some witches don't even know they're witches until, one day, they accidentally blow up a croissant, and suddenly, the bounty hunters are on top of them. And beyond that, I mean, *by all the seas*, Adelina!"

He laughed again. The sound grated at Adelina's bones.

"We can't keep this up forever. As much as we'd like to believe that no one cares about the witches, that's not the case. Every week, there are protests in the towns outside of the city, and every day, a witch fights back as the bounty hunters try to take them down. There's a tipping point, Adelina, and it's approaching. And what will happen to Jumaral then?"

"If all that is true, then my plan will work. Telling the people the truth will tip the scales. Our family will have a revolt on their hands, and then—"

"Then they'll give you the crown? Is that before or after they have you killed?"

Adelina's jaw worked. "They won't kill me," she finally said. "You're dead. I'm the only heir." And Ostrea would protect her. The goddess would see how hard Adelina worked to fulfill the fate she had been given.

All the false humor melted from Simão's face, and pity took over. That same expression seemed to be directed at Adelina from all sides recently. It was different coming from Simão.

"They'll just find another one, Adelina. Your revolution would be cut off along with you, and all the people who agreed with you would be dead too. Our family still has the moral authority that comes with being backed by Ostrea. Think of the Great Waves. Do you really think Dom Sebastião, a peasant boy with some gift for warfare, would have become king if the people didn't believe he'd been chosen by a goddess? Do you think even our grandmother fifty years ago would have transitioned into the role so easily if the rest of the family hadn't been wiped out by Ostrea's Second Wave? We keep our people uneducated and unexposed so that they don't have the resources to question."

He was right. Fighting for her fate from the inside wouldn't be enough. She had to prove to everyone why she was doing it. Only *that* would satisfy Ostrea.

"Are you suggesting that I create the Third Great Wave?" Adelina imagined her parents being swept away by the water, Calixto and her uncle screaming for her while she watched waves crash over them from above. Even in this dark place, she shivered.

Simão shrugged. "I think you could make a deal. You're good at those."

A deal. One that would give her control of impossible magic but which she wouldn't be wielding herself.

Maybe Simão was right and she couldn't get rid of her family just with knowledge held over them. Perhaps they did have to die, but that didn't mean she needed to be the one to get more blood on her hands.

Seba's theory about his mother's death didn't seem so impossible.

"With an encantada, you mean."

"You know where to find one, don't you? At least, I assume, based on who you're friends with."

Her mind spun with the possibilities, filling in gaps from the stories she had heard as a child. "But that one's already been used. For Hala to have gotten the wish, she would have had to free the encantada."

Simão shook his head, and some of the droplets from his hair sprayed her face. The touch shocked her, and Adelina wiped quickly at the spots, imagining particles of the afterlife smearing across her cheeks and onto her hands.

"Whatever that woman did, she didn't free this encantada. We would have known if she did." He sighed, though he didn't need oxygen. "This encantada is the one they tell you about—our family, I mean. They explain this one when you're eighteen because of how important she is."

So Adelina had been right about everyone changing when they turned eighteen. "Why? Who is she?"

"Encantadas are guards," Simão explained.

"I know that," she snapped. Encantadas were guards against their will, trapped until someone released them. "What is this one guarding?"

"The dead. You know the story of Dom Sebastião—the gate to the Beyond was broken by witches. Sebastião trapped an encantada there to keep the dead back. But now—"

There was a nervous energy to his body Adelina wouldn't have expected to be possible of a dead man.

"Now?"

"Now the king wants to find a way to gain control of the dead. To create an army that could protect Jumaral or maybe even launch a preventative attack."

Adelina's thoughts spun with images of thousands of corpses marching to the eastern border or perhaps swimming through the west sea. Spilling from the gates of the dead. Among the faceless corpses was Jas, pale and bleeding, like she had left him.

"Then why don't they let the encantada go? If she's the one between them and the army, then they should release her. The gate is already broken."

"The gate is broken because they already tried, centuries ago, when the Hambil Empire invaded. The army was uncontrollable. She had to be put in place until they figured out how to use them, and to keep her there, they needed magic, so they stole witches."

"And they never stopped."

Simão nodded. His lips pursed in a way that reminded Adelina eerily of their mother.

"And then our family got witches to kill you with blood magic. Why?"

"I—I don't know." All his previous arrogance and frustration was gone. "That medallion I wanted to show you? The one I took to the Knell to have read? I took it from Calixto. A year ago, around the time he turned eighteen, he showed it to me when I asked him about what he thought of the captured witches. He said it was a reminder of why it was necessary. After that, I started to notice how much they hadn't told me and how much was still a secret, so I stole the medallion a few months ago. All I learned was that it belonged to a dead pregnant woman. I realized I could use your help, so I asked you to come to the beach with me that night. I thought we would be safe to talk there. Away from anything and with the waves, but then..."

But then he had died, with blood pouring from him while blood magic took control of his body and the three witches faded from view. The memory hung like an anchor between them, waiting to crash through the world of smoke. A drop of water—from the ocean or the river, Adelina didn't know—gathered at his earlobe and fell to his shoulder.

"You didn't want them to think that I knew," she said. "That's why you told me not to leave you there. You didn't want them to know I was with you. You didn't want them to do to me what they'd done to you."

"Yes, *mana*," he whispered.

Not here, Adelina now understood, *where they know we go together.*

She had strained under his weight, heaving his corpse onto Cinza's back while she sobbed, trying to fulfill this last request, even though she had already begun to panic about what to do next, how to avoid blaspheming Ostrea. His clothes were wet and sandy, so she'd had enough sense to take him to the Rio Galho. The river would mask where he had been before.

It was the splash of his corpse tumbling into the river that had filled her dreams. The image of his hands floating in the dark waters had crept up on her every time she had entered water since. But on that night, she hadn't lingered. Adelina had dumped her brother's body, wiped her tears, and returned to the manor with plans to murder her parents.

Simão's face once again split into a wide, terrifying grin. "Now what? Off to make a deal with an encantada and hope they don't come for you too?"

"Something like that. You should have just talked when Jas asked you to."

The look he gave her was far too knowing for her liking. "And miss the chance to revel in your ignorance?"

"Whatever Jas promised you must have been very compelling."

"Ah." He waggled his finger at her. "I've already said that's off-limits."

Adelina frowned. "Soon, I'm going to be queen, and I will have endless resources to make you spill your secrets. Even the dead can't escape me."

"I don't doubt it. You were always going to tear apart the world, Adelina." His smile softened, turning sad. "I hope I won't see you soon."

There was a knot in Adelina's chest that didn't want to go away, and her entire body burned with energy she didn't have time to extend. "Goodbye, *mano*."

His blue lips moved, but any sound he made was whisked away in a whirl of shadow. Adelina felt the rustle of her skirts and the tickle of curls whipping around her face. There was another crashing sound, like thunder, and then it was all gone.

She was still sitting at the table in the library, gas lamps brightening above her. Jas was across from her, no longer swathed in darkness. Purple veins crisscrossed his nearly translucent skin.

Adelina could only stare at him, at the spot where her brother had been.

She had done it. *Jas* had done it.

It was over, and yet it had only just started.

"Jas?" Her voice was hoarse. She cleared her throat and tried again. "Jas?"

He didn't move.

Adelina rose from her chair and approached him slowly. She put her fingers gently against his neck. It was cold, but there was a faint pulse.

Good. She would be needing him after all.

Her plan had changed, but not so far that it couldn't be done. She would go to the encantada. Adelina would make an exchange for her crown. However the wish manifested, whatever it did to her family...that wouldn't be Adelina's problem. Then everything would be as it should. The prophecy would be fulfilled, and it would be by her own doing.

Adelina returned to her side of the table and closed the countless journals and reference books they had laid out. She folded all her notes and tucked them into her pocket, then marched from the library without glancing back.

Dalila stood outside the doors, leaning against a wall and fidgeting with a slip of paper. She jumped forward when she noticed Adelina, eyes bright.

"Adelina. A note arrived for you."

Adelina snatched it from her fingers and scanned over the sparse words.

"Is everything all right, my lady? I saw Seba leave earlier, and he looked so upset, and I just thought—"

"Where did Seba go?"

Dalila's brow wrinkled. "To the drawing room, I think, but—"

"Jas is feeling unwell. Please see to him."

"But, my lady, the note. Is that...Are you in communication with the boun—"

"Did you not hear me, Dalila?" Adelina grabbed at Dalila's wrist, squeezing the bulge of bandages there while Dalila flinched. "Heal Jas like you've healed me." The ghostly prickle of the slash lingered across her palm from the night of Simão's death, and the freshly healed burn that had marred her forearm just hours ago tingled. "Do as I say, or I will reply to this note with *your* name."

Adelina's maid took a step back and folded her hands behind her waist. She seemed hurt more than afraid. Adelina didn't care.

"Apologies, my lady. I will see to it."

"Thank you."

Adelina made her way to the drawing room. The hallways glowed with the golden light of evening. She opened the door and found pillows and books flung everywhere. The priceless icons of Ostrea remained untouched.

Seba sat amidst it all on the floor, his eyes glued to the flames, just like in the library.

He moved his gaze toward her. His hair stood completely on end, and there was a wild expression to his red-rimmed eyes.

This is good, she thought. *He was too soft before. Now he will understand.*

"Pull yourself together." The door squeaked shut behind her. "I have a plan."

CHAPTER 24

SEBA

"By Our Lady and all Her great and holy teeth," Seba shouted.

"Shut up." Adelina clutched the steering wheel with whitening knuckles. They were trundling along the Jumaralian countryside in Eva Vilar's motorcar, over tiny dirt roads that had been designed for horses and carriages, not hunks of metal moving on inexplicable engineering and—it seemed—Adelina's pure will-power.

"Why did we have to ask Eva for a motorcar that none of us know how to operate?"

"This is faster, less expected by my family, and doesn't require horses."

"You don't like horses?"

"I don't like anything with a mind of its own. Besides, my parents would notice missing horses too soon and know to come after us."

Seba's hand instinctively clutched at the edge of the vehicle's door when they went over a particularly large rock. Or perhaps it was a small animal. They had been traveling south for hours now, their only company each other and the gusts of chilly wind blowing through the disturbingly gaping windows of the motorcar.

The only reason Seba hadn't simply refused to enter the motor-car—or at least flung himself out after the first near brush with death—was because of what waited at the end of this road. Justice.

Every once in a while, he snuck a glance toward the back seat. Jas had barely made a sound, hadn't even moved, since they had gotten into the motorcar—even when Adelina had almost driven them straight into a passing cow.

Good, Seba thought.

If Jas made a sound, allowed his existence to be known in any way, Seba would have been tempted to strangle him. And then Adelina would have been obligated to strangle Seba, which would be utterly detrimental to his prospects as the king of Jumaral. And there was no way Seba was not going to be king.

Not only was it his Ostrea-given fate, having that title was armor. He had seen it work for Adelina and Calixto with Alves, and now that he knew Jas and Hala had never had his best interests at heart, a crown was Seba's only option for safety. He didn't want to end up like his mother.

Still, how dare Jas sit there, acting like a human when he so clearly wasn't? How dare he lie and trick him, Seba, who was supposed to be his best friend, his brother? And Hala—

It doesn't help to miss what's already gone.

"Don't you like Cinza?" he asked while they groaned around another curve, trying to distract himself from his own thoughts. "That horse you usually ride."

"Yes, well, she barely has a brain at all, so we work well together," Adelina said. "Just like you and me."

"You flatter me, love."

"You'd likely drop dead if I didn't, dearest."

The rising sun hours later marked the blessed pause of their journey. Adelina pulled off onto a tiny road between rows of olive trees. It was a relief when, after a few nervous moments of her finagling with the ignition, the engine quieted and they were left in jarring silence.

"That was quite successful." Seba threw open the door and dashed into the gray of the olive orchards, as far from the motorcar as possible.

Adelina and Jas followed, Adelina with her usual scowl and Jas seemingly barely aware he was moving.

"We passed a town about an hour's walk from here." Adelina stretched her fingers inside her black leather gloves. "Jas should go. Seba and I are too recognizable."

She returned to the motorcar and withdrew a small black pouch from the trunk they had shoved into the back seat with Jas. "Here."

The clinking of coins drew Seba's focus, and he watched the pouch pass between Adelina's and Jas's hands.

"Try to find us some food and find out if there's been some kind of outcry from my family. There would have been a telegram to all the major towns by now."

Jas just nodded before turning back the way they had come. He was trailing half a step behind where he should have been, a stiffness to every movement. It made Seba wonder how he had never noticed the Knell's inhuman slink before. His upper lip curled.

"You're being a book again," Adelina said. There were dark circles under her eyes. She stretched her limbs to a chorus of popping from various joints.

"Has it ever occurred to you that maybe I'm *not* a book? Maybe you're just good at reading stones."

She popped her neck loudly, and he winced. "No, you're definitely a book."

"Listen, if...*Jas*"—he spit the name—"didn't get my point after I punched him in the face, I doubt he'd be excessively worried by a few loose facial expressions."

Adelina stepped closer to him, straightening her shoulders and lifting her chin, making his soul shrivel in anticipation of a lecture. "There's a difference between being angry and being vindictive, and Jas only needs to know about one."

Seba blew out a breath, watching it cloud in front of him. "So, what else does he know?"

"He knows we're going to the encantada. I think he's hoping to learn more about his powers."

"And what does everyone else think we're doing?"

"I told Dalila to deliver a note to my parents saying that I was accompanying you and Jas south to bring news of Hala's death to her family."

Seba shoved down the pain Hala's name had carved into his stomach. "And they'll believe that?"

"Why wouldn't they?"

"You're not the most empathetic figure."

Adelina gave him that familiar catlike glare. "Then maybe they'll assume we're eloping. Our forbidden romance acts as the first layer of defense for what we're really doing."

"Which is freeing an angry ocean goddess in exchange for a wish that will get rid of the entire royal family."

Something flickered in Adelina's jaw. "Look like the innocent flower but be the serpent under it."

"Is that what you do?"

She smiled, and the expression sent chills down his arms. "Always, my love."

"Fine."

Seba sat down in the tall grass and stretched his legs amongst the blades. They bent and crunched beneath him, and drops of dew soaked through his trousers. He didn't really care. Seba just wanted to rest without the threat of Adelina driving them into a tree.

His face and body still ached from the beating he had endured the day before. His eye was swollen, and his nose was bruised, but at least nothing was broken. Still, it had been years since his body had had to heal without one of Hala's alchemical poultices. Would it even remember how?

Adelina sat a few trees down, knees pulled up under her skirts. She took off her gloves and hat, letting some of her curls drift down past her ears. Her eyes were fixed on the black metal of the motorcar, though her mind was probably leagues away, concocting the next phase of whatever plan she was currently on.

"Adelina."

It took her a second to look at him. She raised her brows expectantly.

"If we weren't pretending to be together for the sake of money and power, do you think we would still have liked each other?"

"Who's to say I like you now?"

He did his best impression of her own scowl, and the corner of her lips twitched.

"You know what I mean. Do you think that, in another life, this would have worked?"

"No."

"What?" An unexpected sense of disappointment descended on him. "Why?"

"I knew that my family and their government wanted to set me up with someone for the media, and suffice to say, I don't trust their judgment. I've met an inordinate number of future monarchs and business moguls, heirs to the largest fortunes in the world, but none of them would have been like you."

"Freakishly handsome and awe-inspiring?" Seba gave her his most charming grin.

"Indebted to me."

"So, you weren't joking when you said we work well together because I don't have a mind of my own?"

Adelina shook her head. He could have sworn the marquise of Lis was holding back a smile—and maybe this one wouldn't have been as spine-tingling as the other. It struck him she had lied too. She had used him, just like Jas and Hala. But for some reason, this was different. Neither he nor Adelina had ever promised each other the truth.

"So, dearest partner of greatness," he said, and Adelina scoffed. He lay flat on his back. The grass made his neck itch. "Let's say that you weren't the marquise of Lis, and you had no responsibilities, and it didn't matter if your partner had a brain or three brains or no brains. What then? Am I a contender?"

"Absolutely not."

He let his jaw drop. "Am I really so terrible?"

Adelina twisted one of the blades of grass between her fingers. The sky was brighter now, and he could make out the floral embroidery at the hems of her dark blue skirt—lines of little golden roses.

"If I had no obligations, then there would be no contenders at all."

"Really? No other boys, girls, anyone else?"

"No."

"I thought you just said you've met plenty of people."

"You lack critical thinking, Sebastião. I have *met* plenty of people. That doesn't mean I'm interested. And yes, you are really so terrible."

He stuck his tongue out at her. She smiled primly.

"Then why did your family want to set you up?" he asked.

"My family only cares about reputations and heirs. They don't care what any of us do or want outside of that."

Seba sat up. Slowly.

"Adelina." His voice was higher than usual. "If everything goes according to plan and we get married and become king and queen, does that mean we'll have to..." He made a lewd gesture.

Adelina arched her brows higher than ever. "We don't *have* to do anything. I'm sure that if we have the power to overtake a monarchy, we have the power to do whatever we'd like with it."

He nodded, but this was a conversation he would be sure to come back to in the near future. Seba wouldn't necessarily have minded going through the motions of conceiving heirs with Adelina, but to actually have them? What would he do after he got his money and was free to leave?

Assuming Alves didn't try to come after him again, his payment would all be his own. He could buy a ship with that kind of money, sail off, and visit the world. Seba could purchase dozens of train tickets until he found a life worth living, away from Lis and the vendetta the city had against him. It was the dream he'd had for years, though Jas and Hala had always been right alongside him in his imagination. Now, he'd have to sail that ship alone.

And if an heir were to exist...

Seba understood what it was to be a child left behind.

Besides, *Hail!* the witches had said. *Lesser than Sebastião and greater.*

Not so happy, yet much happier.

Thou shalt get kings, though thou be none.

Seba hadn't spent much time considering Jas's prophecy, but now he recognized it for what it was: Seba's and Jas's fates were at odds with each other. To achieve Seba's own fate—to be marquis, and duke, and king—meant going against Jas's. How could Jas ever be greater, happier than a king? Only one of them could succeed, and Jas deserved none of it. Jas wasn't even human, for Ostrea's sake.

So Seba would do what he needed to. He'd had enough of trying to help Jas and Hala, just for both to turn on him. Adelina was the only one who helped him, who saw what he had to offer.

Let Jas face the consequences of a rejected fate. Seba was going to get the glory he was due.

CHAPTER 25

JAS

Like clockwork, the set of the sun meant they were all back in the motorcar. After they had eaten a measly meal of whatever fruit and pastries Jas could fit in his arms, Seba had slept for the entire day. Adelina and Jas had pretended to doze in shifts, wary of the fact bounty hunters were known to prowl the rural areas, but neither of them managed to fall unconscious.

Jas wouldn't have wanted to go to sleep even if he could. He was afraid of the horrors his mind would have waiting for him.

Just truths, little Knell.

Don't be afraid of us.

We only want your help.

Like you helped the marquis.

And we can help you too.

The price is just your life.

They had been there since the deal with Lord Simão, each wanting something Jas could not give. The voices were low, whispering, like a nail being dragged across stone.

Like a parasite feeding on mold.

Teodora was always the loudest.

Maybe now that he had contacted Simão, he would be able to ask the encantada to get rid of his powers when they reached her. Until then, he would simply have to ignore the whispers in his head, the offers to trade his life for a conversation. Never mind that his life was already taken.

Jas tensed when they hit a particularly forceful swerve, which sent them all pressing to the left. He was vaguely concerned about Adelina operating a large metal motorized contraption through growing sleep deprivation, but those worries were as distant as dreams.

If you die now, who gets the life?

"By Our Lady's radiant left thumb," Seba cursed.

Jas noticed the wildness of Seba's hair, the jitteriness of his bouncing leg, and the tapping fingers. There had been a time, even just a few days ago, when Seba would have turned to him and cracked a joke if he was nervous. They would have sat next to each other, and Seba would have changed the lyrics to songs he had sung with his mother before she died. He would have made Jas laugh as a way to assuage his own pounding heart, and Jas would have welcomed it.

Now Seba wouldn't even look at him, but Jas was glad for that. He had detected the revulsion in Seba's voice, as though even thinking about Jas was akin to swallowing a live slug.

This is how it was always supposed to be.

Seba grunted out a string of lewd expletives when they whipped around what appeared to be a lone wheelbarrow in the middle of the road, which made even Adelina inhale sharply. His curses continued past the aversion of the crisis, and Adelina began correcting his obscenities for coherence. Jas turned his focus to the dark shadows of cornfields rolling outside the window. Adelina muttered something about purposefully killing them all off for the greater good if Seba continued his ramblings.

Even the devil herself is right sometimes.

They only drove for a few hours, long enough for the night to properly settle over them. Adelina stopped just past another town, and they were close enough to water for the sound of waves crashing against rock and the smell of salt in the air to drift their way.

Adelina and Seba stepped out of the motorcar first. Jas was about to follow when he caught sight of Seba's expression for the first time. There was the expected loathing when he looked at Jas but also something else.

Your face is as readable as a book, Adelina had once said.

And what Jas read was...anticipation. Something inside of him twisted, but it wasn't the empty and endless pit of guilt. It was dread. Fear of Seba, his brother, who appeared to be burning from the inside out.

At least he's able to burn.

I can tell you about the plan, said a different voice.

I can tell you all of his secrets.

If you promise me your life.

The same sentiments were repeated by other voices, their whispers overlapping into a jumble of confused mumblings.

Jas looked to Adelina, but her face was expressionless, as always.

"By Our Sweet Lady, Jas," Seba spat. "Are you coming or not?"

Jas lurched into action. He stumbled from the motorcar in a blur of voices.

You already gave your life.

Why do you worry?

I can make you stop worrying.

"This way." Adelina began marching purposefully toward the sound of waves without looking back.

How could she be so certain about where she was going with just Hala's notebooks as reference?

Jas followed, trying not to trip over the uneven, rocky ground, and Seba fell into step beside him. There was something menacing about Seba's proximity. Like a shadow, silently dogging his footsteps. Each crunch of grass or dirt was the tick of a clock counting down to the time Jas was absorbed into the darkness.

The time that you are returned to your true place.

The few minutes he had spent speaking to Simão had felt more right than any moment he could remember. The pain had been gone. Was he what had made the magic unruly in the first place? Maybe it was his ongoing denial of his true place that had put the world's tides into disorder.

It was so dark he didn't immediately recognize the swath of

blackness ahead of them, with the night sky cut off by cliffs. Adelina led them onto the harsh stone, only stopping when the wind was blasting against their faces and the edge was barely a step away. Beyond them was nothing. The violent lapping of waves beat against rock, but ahead was only darkness. No light. No movement. It was as if the world was being swallowed by its shadow, and they were its witnesses.

He knew where they were.

"Solmortém," said Adelina. As usual, speaking directly to his thoughts. "The End of the World."

Jas had never been to Solmortém, but he had certainly heard of it. It was the place of legends, stories Seba had told him when they were little and unwilling to sleep. A saint had once gained the ability to turn bread into roses after drinking its waters. A rooster, born in the shadows of the lighthouse, had risen from the dead to crow for the innocence of a man. It was said that Dom Sebastião, the king whose celebrations were still in session all around Jumaral, had vanquished the demons of the sea here—the ones Ostrea now protected them from.

The churning water, black as the starless sky, sent goosebumps down Jas's flesh. He understood now why the ancient mapmakers had labeled this place the end of the world. It was like standing over a wallowing pit, with the moans of monsters below calling him into their midst.

On Adelina's other side, Seba groaned.

"*That's* where we're going?" he said, waiting for someone to tell him this was just a spooky detour on the way to their true destination.

Adelina rolled her shoulders back and set her unblinking gaze on where a horizon might have been. "That's where we're going."

For a moment, they stood there, staring out into this shared oblivion. Were Seba and Adelina remembering the same thing he was? A different night, outside of a city far north of where they were now, when witches had foretold their futures and Adelina had made them a proposition?

Thou shalt get kings, though thou be none.

Jas hadn't thought about the words in days. He had been sure that the prophecy meant nothing, but maybe there was more to the world than he understood. In a few hours, the sun might be rising on an unrecognizable world.

Adelina, as usual, was the first to move. "Let's go."

Jas and Seba followed her along the edge and down a narrow flight of wooden steps on the cliff face. Even without the help of the stars or moon, the sand glowed a soft white.

"Are we swimming?" Seba called over the increasing volume of the waves.

Cold flecks of water dotted the bare skin of Jas's face, and bits of the rope railing poked at his palm.

"No," Adelina replied, offering no further explanation.

She led them along the uneven sand at the bottom of the steps. The dark cliffs rose on their left, seemingly endless. If someone had said this strip of sand was the only thing left in the world, Jas would have had nothing to argue with.

Why would a monster like you argue with the end of the world? You, who brought it about?

Adelina guided them to the edge of the water. Seba joined her at the line where dry sand met damp. Another wave spread, almost to meet them, while Jas hung back. He watched the pair exchange a look before turning to him in unison.

"Do you feel anything?" Adelina asked.

You are useful for only one thing, little Knell. So do it.

He *did* sense something. A tugging he couldn't understand, as if a hook had attached itself to the back of his head and was being pulled so tightly his eyes watered.

Adelina moved closer, a frenzied desperation in her searching eyes. "This"—she gestured to the open water beside them—"is the closest we can get to the gate. This is where Hala wrote that she came."

"We're going to the gate?"

Two visits in two days. What an honor it is.

"Yes, we are going to the gate."

"But I can take you there myself, like I did with Lord Simão."

"This won't work like that."

Jas blinked at her. Adelina grabbed at his wrist, clenching it so tightly his fingertips tingled with the loss of blood.

"Go back to the Beyond," she whispered, but he could barely distinguish her words over the waves. "Go where you found my brother. There should be someone waiting for you, someone with a boat to transport us there."

Jas's chest didn't feel right. Something was gnawing at his ribs, lessening the barrier between his heart and the outside of his chest. It beat so loudly.

A clever imitation of human fear.

"*Jas.*" Adelina grabbed his other wrist and pulled him toward her so Seba couldn't hear. "This is your chance to be something better."

The words struck him almost as hard as when Seba had hit him in the library what felt like lifetimes ago.

Selfish monster forgetting his place.

Of course. Teodora was right. Who was he to hesitate on the precipice of the world? Who was he to let Adelina and Seba down? Who was he to worry about his own fate when he had already promised his life away for something better?

You can be something better, Adelina had said. And this was it.

He had failed to save the witches, had been unable to save Hala, and had not succeeded at saving Seba. Jas had no idea where Isaque was, which meant he had probably let them down too.

I am nothing, he thought. *I am no one if not this.*

Very good, little Knell, said Teodora.

He drew in a breath of salty air, allowing himself a moment of life.

Then he closed his eyes and reached into the misty darkness haunting his brain. The ocean pounded against rock as loudly as if it had been against his own skull.

When Jas opened his eyes, he was standing in a world of shadow. Strange movements and wisps of smoke were the only signs he had not been swallowed into an empty black cloud. There were spirits about, but only one was fully visible to him.

She withdrew from the shadows as though she were a part of them. Her features became clear with the slow grace of being drawn with black ink, then crystallizing and filling with dull color. Her hair remained black. A few strands of gray glowed in the swirls of darkness, and her eyes faded to a vague muddy green.

It was the way she held herself that made Jas want to retreat to that beach at the end of the world. The smirk of her lips, the way her nose rounded at the end, and the way she carried the constant whirling feeling of being in motion, even though she stood still. It was all too familiar.

She took a step closer to him, holding a black shawl around her shoulders. It blended into faded gray skirts, as if she had just stepped off the main streets of Lis.

"I'm so glad to finally meet you, little Knell."

Even in this world, just at the other side of death's gate, the voice made Jas flinch. He was supposed to be stronger here. The Knell couldn't be cowed by Seba's mother, not until he had fulfilled his promises.

"It's only fitting that we would meet eventually." Her eyes widened when she spoke, just like Seba's did. "You and I share a life, don't we?" She began rounding him, like a hawk circling its prey. "I hear you've been using it as a bartering tool."

Hot breath blew on the back of his neck, making his skin crawl. She didn't have to breathe. Teodora was doing it to catch him off guard, to cause her presence to itch like the memory of a spider that couldn't be swatted away. Teodora knew exactly how to force thoughts into his mind, and he was flung back to the last time he had been in this shadowy realm.

I'm here as an equal, he had said to the deceased Lord Simão, Marquis of Lis. All it had taken was for the Knell to realize his place.

I don't care what you are, Simão had said. *You want me to kill my sister. The answer is no.*

She wants information.

It will get her in trouble.

She's learned from what happened to you.

No one can outsmart death. I would know. Simão gestured at his clothes, bloody and wet, clinging to his body.

She won't be joining you.

You can't promise that.

I can, said the Knell.

The graying boy's face had taken on a look of interest. *And how is that?*

My life for hers. If she dies.

If she dies, he had repeated.

My life is already stolen. It's not connected to me like it is for others. It wasn't something he had known. It was only the truth, which poured out of him like it had always been there. This place, this dark hole beyond the gates, held all the answers, and he under-stood exactly how to wield them. *If she dies, her life will be gone, but she can take mine instead.*

Simão lifted his chin. *She won't stay dead?*

She won't, the Knell confirmed.

And if you die first?

Then my life is up for grabs anyway. It might as well be hers.

The marquis of Lis appeared uncertain.

Your death avenged, the monarchy crumbled, and your sister alive and well at the center of it all, with a crown on her head. All you have to do is answer her questions. Do we have a deal?

Simão's lifeless hand had been solid when Jas shook it, sealing his own fate. It had also been freezing and wet, grimy from sand and dirt.

"I'm here for a boat." Jas fixed his gaze on the darkness straight ahead. His voice sounded strange, like it was coming from someone other than him. "To get to the gate."

"A boat." Teodora appeared at his side, a playful look on her face. "For Lady Adelina's grand plan?" She laughed an inhuman screech. "That girl is almost as much of a monster as you are. Though, at least she's human. There has to be something worthwhile in her."

"I just need a boat." Jas's throat was tight, and his words came out terse. "Adelina said I would meet someone who could give me a boat. Is that you?"

Teodora turned away from him for a second and floated through the smoke at their feet. Jas's stomach flipped when she let out another long laugh. It seemed to go on for ages. Finally, she inhaled dramatically and gave him what might have been mistaken for a sorry glance.

"Oh, little Knell," she started.

Jas's eye twitched.

"How would she have known that?"

"Known what?"

"How"—she spoke slowly, as if savoring the moment—"would Lady Adelina, Marquise of Lis, know about a boat that could take her to the gates of the dead?"

Jas forced himself to remain still. "She read Hala's notebooks."

Teodora hummed thoughtfully. Her dead eyes came alive with the excitement of taunting him face-to-face. "Perhaps, though it *is* convenient that she came to be in possession of such an *intricate* account of Hala's journey. And you don't speak any Almaric, do you? So you can't check what's in those notebooks? It's almost as if..." Her grin widened. "Adelina got her information straight from the source."

Jas was overcome with an awareness of his heart beating in his chest, his useless breath passing through his lungs, the sweat trickling down his neck. The shadowy world separated itself from him by an invisible pane of glass, and he viewed the situation from the cold glare of an outside observer.

As an outsider, as the Knell, he could understand what had occurred. Adelina had only known to speak to Hala because of Jas. He hadn't done a good enough job of hiding Hala's alchemy. Jas should have run when Prince Calixto told him to. He should never have used his powers at all, should never have allowed Adelina into their lives because, *of course*, she would make the connection.

Jas really was the reason Hala was gone. He had brought Adelina to her, and Adelina had...Adelina had killed her.

The Knell knew and understood all of this. Jas was still choking.

"Oh, don't be sad, little Knell." Teodora's voice dripped with mock sympathy. "Hala stole my life first. It's only fitting that my life is what killed her in the end."

Jas shuddered. He was a danger. A monster masked as a person. Maybe it was better to live life on the other side. That way, he could stop pretending he felt this deep, wrenching pain that came with being human.

"Give me the boat," he said. Whatever he was experiencing, he had learned his judgment was not to be trusted. Jas could at least serve this purpose. He could repay this last debt to Seba.

Teodora's eyes widened in what started as surprise and then melted into approval. She turned away from him. The back of her head grew darker as she entered the shadows.

"I was wondering if we'd get here," she said, her voice faint and echoing. "The boats require sacrifice, so the guardian of the boats changes with every person. You're not exactly a person, so...I wasn't sure this would work...or if you'd have the strength."

A moment later, there was a slithering sound. Teodora reappeared with a thick black rope in her hands, like a stream of smoke she had shaped and pulled from the world around them. Jas couldn't make out what was at the other end, but the rope remained taut while she drew closer and handed it to him. It was rough and wet, and it pricked at his palms, like the railing down the cliffs.

"Thank you," he said.

"Oh no, little Knell." Teodora's smile would have chilled the sea. "Thank *you*." She stepped closer to him, and the edges of his vision began to blur. Teodora whispered, "Watch out for my son."

Her face was gone in a whirl of smoke, and Jas was sent back into his mind, clutching the black rope tightly in his hand. It tugged at his grip and burned his palm. He sensed a rushing that might have been water, something soft beneath him that might have been sand. Everything was still dark and muddled, and he could barely distinguish shadows moving above him.

"Who's there?" he muttered, squinting up at what he thought might be a person.

The figure above him moved and grew larger, closer. When it answered, Jas knew the voice, even in his muddled mind. He would have recognized it anywhere.

"A friend," said Seba.

And then Jas's head was alight with pain, and he was sent back to darkness once more.

CHAPTER 26

ADELINA

Jas's blood was dark against the sand. It spread from the wound in his head like ink. The rope was still clutched in his fist, pulled taut by something rising from the water, disrupting the entire shoreline as the waves rushed inward to vomit up what waited below.

Seba's face screwed up in pain and anger as he moved to bring the rock down on Jas's head again. Adelina grabbed his wrist and shoved him away from Jas for the second time in as many days.

"We need him unconscious, not dead," she yelled.

Seba shook, staring down at Jas's crumpled form. His top lip was curled, every ounce of him poised to attack.

"Seba." Adelina grabbed at his shoulders, forcing him to turn away. "Drop the rock."

He took a few shaky breaths. "He deserves it," he finally muttered, barely audible over the growing thrash of life overturning happening beside them.

Adelina tightened her grip. "But you deserve more."

He looked at her. His usual hazel eyes were as black as night. It didn't matter if her words were true. It mattered whether the words were effective.

"And Jas is your key to more."

The thump of the rock on the sand was indistinguishable from the pounding of the world around them. Adelina released Seba and kicked the rock away. She bent to take the rope from Jas's hand. Both it and the hand were cold and wet, and she shoved down memories of her brother's corpse.

Adelina pressed two fingers to the base of Jas's pale jaw. There was a pulse there, though faint. Guilt weighed heavily on her chest, but she pushed it away.

The rope pulled at her palm when she took her place beside Seba, and they watched the water turn itself inside out. Bubbles burst and blended into an almighty boom, shaking the ground like thunder, but they both remained dry. Not even the normal mist of sea breeze dared to touch their faces. The entire ocean rushed toward them, to a spot just beyond their little stretch of sand amidst the cliffs at the end of the world, only to be swallowed into a widening black hole.

There would be nothing watching them in the world that opened, no stars blinking down on them from the other side of the blanket of dark.

Beside her, Seba lurched back when the tip of an enormous fishing boat emerged from the crashing hole in the ocean. It rose vertically, and they craned their necks to track the top. Water poured from its sides. Instead of splashing, it was swallowed up by the ocean around it. The bottom of the boat was what faced them, wide and round, like the belly of a whale. It appeared to be painted black, though it wavered unnaturally, like it wasn't quite solid.

The water finished pouring down the boat's sides, and everything was still. The only sounds were Seba's labored breathing beside her and the beat of Adelina's heart against her chest. She forced the rest of her to stay still, to remain alert, to be ready.

The boat began tipping toward them with a slow, blood-chilling creak. Seba ran backward, flattening his back against the wall of the cliffs. Adelina held her ground.

The erupting splash brought back the sound of the ocean. The roar crashed over them like a wave, followed by a wall of water finally reaching them. The force of it sent Adelina into the sand, and cold swallowed her. As soon as it had come, the wave was gone, retreating to the ocean faster than any natural tide—until all that was left was calm water, lapping against the side of the enormous black fishing boat.

Adelina coughed, throat and eyes stinging. She pushed herself onto her knees and swiped back the wet hair from her face. Her hands and skirts were coated in sand. Disgust roiled in her stomach. She wiped her palms on her torso, wanting to be rid of the rough scrape of sand against fabric and the already raw skin of her hands.

Off.

Off.

Off.

Adelina sucked in a deep breath to steady herself, but she was met with a wall of memories from the fresh sea air. The sand on her hands transformed into her brother's sticky, hot blood. She wiped harder, but his black blood only smeared on her jacket.

Adelina squeezed her eyes shut and counted her breaths in and out. This was not the time. There was no time.

Seba gagged behind her, drawing her mind back to the present. The wind was sharp against her wet face. Her hands were no longer bloody, just flecked with sand and red from irritation.

Focus, she reminded herself. *You've come this far.*

She made herself turn and assess the situation. The end of the black rope lay beside her, like a snake with its head cut off. Behind her was Seba, one hand against the rocky cliffs while he heaved salt water into the sand. Some lengths to her left, Jas's unconscious body had been flipped onto its side. A watery stain of blood was now smeared around him.

Adelina walked to Jas and bent to check his pulse again. If he died before they got him to the encantada, they would have nothing to bargain with.

His heart still beat. She sucked in a breath. Let it out.

Before them, sitting in waves too shallow for anything man-made to stay afloat, was the boat. It was shaped in the style of a Jumaralian fishing vessel, though larger and without a clear outline. It blended into the night and the dark water, shimmering and moving along with the waves, as if it were part of the tide itself.

Adelina cleared her throat. "Seba. Let's go."

He looked pitiful, still crouched at the wall over a small spot of his own sick. Dark hair was plastered across his forehead, and his clothes clung to his frame.

"How did—" He coughed. "How did you know about the boat?"

Adelina leveled her chin, preparing for the risk. She had calculated it as well as she could. "Hala told me."

Seba blinked. He fell back, hitting his back against the rock. "What?"

"Hala. I knew she was an alchemist. I knew Jas had powers over the dead. I made a guess, and she confirmed it."

Trust me, she silently urged him. *Believe me.*

Seba was still staring at her, eyes getting wider.

Adelina took a step forward. Her skirts were heavy, her boots uncomfortable. She did not unfix her gaze.

"You and I understand each other, Seba. We do what we need to do." She watched him processing, calculating all the lies he had been told by Hala, Jas—all they had taken away from him. Adelina crouched in front of him. "If you want protection, this is the way to get it. Heitor Alves let you go because of my mere presence. Imagine the amount of power you could wield if you stay on this path with me."

There would be no going back after they climbed into the boat. What was done would be done. She needed to know he wouldn't try to run away from the fate she had built them.

"I chose you out of an entire world. If we are going to rule it, you have to choose me too."

Seba's lips trembled, like he might throw up again. He was pale and shaking all over, his skin stark against his hair and the dark rock behind him. Adelina held her stance, boring straight into his eyes with every bit of intensity she could muster.

Dealing with Seba and Jas had been an exercise in control from the very beginning. She had needed Jas as the Knell, so she had found a way to control him. It was Isaque who had told her about Seba, and the moment she had seen him for the first time, running from thugs just before hearing the prophecy she had constructed for him, Adelina had been able to read him perfectly.

Even in distress, he had a bumbling smirk. If the world had

shaken while he skipped through it, he wouldn't have noticed or cared. He was arrogant, entitled, angry. And when he heard the fate Adelina had hired the witches to spout, when he understood he would be king, there had been hunger in his eyes.

Jas had stepped in when this boy was afraid. He had shielded Seba's body with his own. Threatening Seba was to control the Knell. So, Adelina had held a knife to Sebastião Pinheiro's throat, and the Knell had bent to her will.

Controlling Seba was different. He was not loyal. Seba *expected* loyalty.

Adelina had provided him with the opportunity to watch that loyalty stripped away. Hala. Jas. The memory of his mother's unwilling disappearance from his life. Seba believed the world owed him, and so that was exactly what Adelina had promised him. She had shown him the wonders of power, the invincibility he so craved and that she already possessed.

If she had bargained with a coven of witches to spew fabricated fates in the boys' faces and scare them into her waiting arms, then it was only as a safeguard. If she had manipulated them into turning on each other with some conveniently placed notebooks and a sudden loss of security, then it was only to her service.

It was what Ostrea wanted.

Seba had already passed the first test. Jas was lying near them, half dead, blood pouring from his head, all by his brother's hand. The next test would be harder, and Adelina would not allow him to fail her or her goddess.

His voice was small and strained when he spoke. "Did you kill Hala?"

"She was in the way of our success. I removed her."

Seba's breaths were becoming fast and shuddering. He stared at the sand by her knees, blinking furiously. "In the way?" he repeated, like he didn't even realize he was speaking.

"She had already ruined your life once. I wasn't going to let her do it again."

Seba nodded slowly.

"Do you want to be king or not, Seba? I can give you that. I *am* giving you that. I am the only one giving you what you deserve, instead of taking what is rightfully yours." She leaned in closer. Their bodies were so close she could feel the cold radiating off him. "But if we are going to go any farther, I need to know that you won't turn your back on me, as so many have done to you. What we do next is dangerous, but it will give us our crowns. It will avenge my brother *and* your mother. It will get rid of my family for good so that no one else will have to suffer as we have. We will be safer than you could ever imagine because we will have a goddess at our will. I just need you to trust—not in me, but in my interests."

"Dangerous?"

"You've heard the stories, the legends. Dom Sebastião went into the waters of Solmortém and saved us all from the demons that waited there. Now it's our turn to do the same."

Adelina saw the moment his mind was made. Seba's eyes locked on hers, bloodshot and hard.

"Sounds fun."

Adelina sucked in a deep, salty breath of ocean air. "Good."

She straightened, brushing the sand from her skirts as best she could and ignoring the nagging feeling of disgust at the grit of it on her hands. They used the rope to climb into the boat, leveraging themselves against its surprisingly solid side. Adelina went up first, her sopping skirts like an anchor trying to drag her back into the sea. Then she reached down to grab Jas's limp arms, held up by a grunting Seba.

Adelina pulled while Seba pushed, and eventually, Jas's unconscious body flopped against her chest. She set him gently onto the sloping wooden planks of the fishing boat, breathing through her mouth to avoid the smell of his blood soaking her front. One of Seba's long legs appeared over the side of the boat, and then he tumbled in, coming to rest beside Jas at Adelina's feet. The boat lurched under his shifting weight.

"That went well," he said. Some color had returned to his face, and Adelina was glad he had at least regained some sense of his usual humor, even if it was annoying. The reminder of his impending crown was working.

Even from the inside, Adelina found that, aside from its questionable solidity and lack of oars, this boat was no different from the type the Jumaralian fishing industry had been using for centuries. Money that could have been invested in modernizing them had apparently gone to capturing witches and stealing their magic, putting bandages on the rotting Jumaralian limbs that would better do with being cut off.

The boat rocked again when Seba pulled himself up and settled across from Adelina on one of the low benches. Jas lay on the floor between them, paler than ever. Even his lips had taken on the pallor of a brittle piece of paper.

"What next?" Seba patted his knees impatiently, and Adelina noticed the tremor in his hands.

"We should wrap his head."

Jas had already lost too much blood. It was staining the edges of Adelina's skirts.

Seba sighed as if this was the greatest inconvenience she had brought him tonight. He leaned down and unbuttoned Jas's shirt, which was already soaked through with blood and seawater. The sleeves stuck to Jas's arms when it was removed, but Seba paid the issue no mind. Amidst the tearing of fabric, Adelina thought she heard the snap of Jas's fingers being broken. With a frown, Seba also wrenched a thin silver ring from Jas's finger before shoving it into his pocket.

He wrapped the shirt tightly around Jas's head, leaving Jas's scarred torso bare. Adelina noted the thin red lines down the center of Jas's chest, the spiderweb of those along his sides, the knot of scar tissue over his heart. She had known about the marks in theory—memories of incision that led to his new life. It was different seeing them, proof he was inhuman, that he had once been gone and had been brought back.

This is good, she told herself. *You're seeing him for what he is.*

"Woah," Seba exclaimed when the boat gave a lurch.

Adelina clutched at the edges of her bench, focusing on the solid illusion of wood beneath her fingers. They drifted toward the horizon, away from the cliffs of Solmortém. The stars and the moon were still covered in clouds, making it appear like they were traveling through nothing—darkness above and darkness below.

Only the wind gave Adelina any sense of movement. She shivered in her wet clothes. Seba turned in his seat so he could face the direction they were heading, but he was thankfully silent.

They stayed that way for several minutes, quiet with anticipation. Adelina counted her breaths. She clenched her jaw and tightened her grip on the bench.

There was a rushing sound, like when the boat first emerged. A growing roar called up before them, and Adelina detected movement in the water ahead. The ocean at their sides began bubbling and churning. A sudden drop sent Adelina's stomach into her chest. She bit her tongue as Seba shrieked.

The ocean reached the top of the boat, rushing in from both sides, sending cold flooding over them. Seba jumped to his feet, and Adelina followed, ducking to pull Jas's head from beneath the surface.

"Hold his other side," she ordered.

Seba turned on her with wide eyes. He hesitated for a second before taking one of Jas's limp arms and looping it around his neck. Adelina had the other around her own, refusing to look too closely at the black and purple bruises bursting from Jas's finger joints.

Whether the water rose or the boat sank, Adelina didn't know, but she breathed in shallow gasps when the freezing water hit her waist, then her chest. Around them, the waves continued to jump and froth—occasionally slapping her in the face with a force suggesting a deeply held contempt.

Adelina adjusted Jas on her shoulder, keeping his lolling head above the water. The boat lurched and tilted beneath them. Her feet were numb, throwing off her balance even more.

Seba cursed over the crash of waves. He was taller than her, the water just covering his shoulders while it came up to her jaw. His hand closed around her arm from Jas's other side, linking them.

It wasn't much longer before the water covered Adelina's head, and the three of them were swallowed whole by the world below.

CHAPTER 27

ADELINA

Adelina should have been aching. Her head should have been spinning, her body shivering with cold and fear. Instead, all she experienced was a strange detachment.

It was an amplified version of what she had felt when speaking to her brother in the library, but this time, it took her a moment to realize she had control over any kind of body at all. Slowly, she made her fingers twitch. Her lungs expand. Her eyes open.

She blinked several times, clearing the fog from her mind as well as from her vision. Adelina was surrounded by darkness, black and never-ending, except for the faint movement of shadow. There was no telling if she was standing or lying down, if she was close to anything or simply floating into a sky without stars.

A feeling erupted in her mind. It was a sound.

The rattle of chains.

The thought struck through her like lightning. She moved her head to get control over the situation. Her mind was too slow, her body too detached. There was pressure on her arm and at her side.

Two unconscious bodies beside her.

One had a bare chest covered in scars, a bloody shirt tied around his head. The other was fully clothed, one arm across the back of the other so it could reach Adelina.

She gulped a breath of air. Maybe she was just inhaling shadow, filling herself up with blackness, letting it consume her from the inside out. Her face tickled, and she reached one of her hands up to touch it.

Wet.

Where did it come from? And why was her hand wet? Why were her hands always so wet and dirty and stained? She rubbed her palms at her sides, but there was no feeling.

Off. Nothing.

Off. She rubbed harder.

Off. This wasn't working.

Stop. This needs to work.

Adelina blinked again. She needed to focus.

Jas and Seba. Those were the boys.

And the chains...

The world was not only shadows after all.

In front of Adelina was a woman, someone Adelina had seen a million times in tapestries, statues, depictions of the divine. She wore what looked like a pure white nightgown flowing smoothly from her frame. Her skin was a warm brown, her ageless face coming to a point at the chin. Her hair, which had so often been depicted as floating above her in a halo of waves, fell loosely down her back to rest at her hips. She gazed down at the three of them with a look of dull amusement, an expression in odd contrast with the heavy black shackles around her wrists. The chains disappeared into the shadows behind her, though Adelina could make out the smoky outline of vertical bars.

The gate? Or a cage?

It didn't matter. Because Ostrea, Lady of the Seas, was the encantada. The ocean goddess was the guard between the living and the dead, and she was the one Adelina would need to make a deal with to get her crown.

Adelina pushed away thoughts of worry, celebration, fear, anticipation. This was just one step completed. It was only when she rose that Adelina realized she had been kneeling. Now she and the goddess were at equal eye level.

"Ostrea," she said.

The woman arched her eyebrows, as though the direct address was an intriguing turn of events in an otherwise dull play.

"Is that who you are looking for?" Her voice was coarse, holding a weight Adelina had never heard from a living being.

"That is who you are."

"Is it?"

"That is what they call you."

The chains clanked when Ostrea shifted her weight. She regarded Adelina with what might have been a new modicum of interest.

"And *you* are Lady Adelina Maria Malves Ducança, Marquise of Lis. Oh, yes, I have heard whispers of you. Have they finally come to vanquish me, then? Or am I to be saved? I must admit"—she nodded her head at the unconscious forms of Jas and Seba—"I would have expected a more imposing cavalry for either task."

"Why aren't they awake?"

"You looked the least likely to bore me. So...*Lady Adelina Maria Malves Ducança*..." Ostrea spat Adelina's name like it was curdling on her tongue. "Why are you here?"

"I want to free you."

"For a wish, I suppose?"

"Jasibin Guan knows how to make deals with spirits. He can replace you here, as you intended when you let him and Hala go—"

"Do not tell me my intentions, princess," Ostrea snapped. Her dark eyes flashed with what appeared to be real flame.

"I'm not a princess."

"Are you not in line for a throne?"

"Yes, but—"

"Then you are a spoiled royal like all the rest, and your title matters little. Do not pretend that you only came to free me. You cannot lie to me. Not here."

Adelina clenched her jaw. Everything still felt loose and gummy. "In exchange for my freeing you, I wish to be queen."

The pressing silence that passed between them was broken by Ostrea bursting into a screeching laugh.

"Oh, princess, you are not as strong as you think. Does this mean you wish the rest of your family to die? To scream as my waves tear them limb from limb before suffocating in the water, as they did your ancestors?"

"If that's what it takes," Adelina said firmly. She had tried that before, on that night with the dagger. Death was the simple solution, but surely a goddess would have others. "I just...I want you to remove them, and I want to be given the legitimacy to take the crown."

Ostrea tutted. "Are you not through with making others do the hard work for you?"

Adelina said nothing, hoping her weakened state hadn't allowed the flash of confusion to cross her face.

Ostrea glided toward her. The clinking of chains pricked at Adelina's ears.

She leaned in, hissing into Adelina's face. "*I hear the whispers, princess.* You made a deal with those witches that gave you your prophecy. You told them you would keep them safe if they told those two boys what you wanted them to hear. But then who was it that turned them in to the bounty hunters? Who was it that sent two of them beyond death's gates?"

The world was getting darker at the edges of Adelina's vision. Was her body capable of fainting in this state? Could she vomit?

She had been visiting those three witches for weeks, passing them information from inside the Manor of Lis in exchange for giving fake prophecies to Jas and Seba. Then she had discovered Simão had been killed by blood magic, and they were the only possible culprits. They must have had deals with Adelina's family too. It was possible they were trading information about Adelina back to her family, putting her entire plan in jeopardy.

So, Adelina had sent a tip to the bounty hunters. She had not had a choice.

"I didn't know two would die." Her voice came out as a whisper.

"Because the alternative is something you could live with?" Ostrea challenged. "And what of Isaque Silveira? Oh, yes, the dead know about them. Their sister Luísa went beyond my gates shortly after their rescue attempt. Weak little thing, she did not last long in that castle."

"Isaque is fine." Adelina sucked a breath of shadow through her nose. Isaque had been a threat. They knew about the witches and about the connection between her and Jas. And they were getting too close. Adelina had no choice but to report them for sneaking into the castle. Luísa had been killed, but at least Isaque was alive.

"That is all you do, is it not? Report people, send them away, find the next answer to your problems by making promises to the desperate?" All humor had dropped from the goddess.

For a fleeting, horrible, weak moment, Adelina wanted Seba and Jas to wake up.

"I did it for you, so as not to disappoint you. Because of the prophecy."

The goddess's lip curled.

"The Second Great Wave," Adelina continued, fighting the blunted edges of panic. "That was you. You made a deal with my grandmother to wipe out the ruling members of the family and leave her as queen."

Ostrea scoffed. "You are just like all the rest. You do not understand anything. Do you want to know what actually left your grandmother as queen? *Weather*, princess. An earthquake that shook the cities and sent a wave over the coast. I had nothing to do with it. Do you want to know who is at fault for the prophecy you heard? The ones who you heard it from. And do you know why? Because *I am not a goddess*."

"But—But I—" *I did everything. I did everything I was supposed to.* "My brother, Simão, he died because…because…" *Because a witch used blood magic on him.*

If what Ostrea was saying was true, then fate had nothing to do with Simão's death. There was no greater picture. No goddess controlling the story. There never had been.

"You young royals know so little. You do not even know what traps me here."

Adelina forced her mind to focus, to stay as clear as it could. "It's the stolen magic from the witches in the castles."

"Oh, no, princess." Ostrea tutted again. "*You* do. Your bloodline. Have you never wondered why your family is so intent on the production of heirs? Why they kill the ones who do not comply with their wishes?"

Adelina held herself carefully still.

"What do you know about Dom Sebastião?" Ostrea snapped.

The question was so startling, Adelina couldn't respond right away. For a moment, she was transported to the festival just days ago, when she had danced in Seba's arms until the smoke had risen across the crystal blue of the sky.

"He was the king that drove the demons from Jumaral," Adelina answered, but she doubted every word as she said it. "He came to you in the world of the dead, and you summoned the First Great Wave. You made him king and started the lineage that continues today."

"Dom Sebastião is also the one who released the demons in the first place. Stories are told by those who survive them. You must come to the dead to learn the truth. In my time, I was a princess of the Hambil Empire. My ancestors had waged countless wars, conquering endless lands across the continent. Jumaral was just the land by the coast, nothing more. It was useful, so my grandfather decided we should have it.

"Decades later, a young man named Sebastião became interested in alchemy. He consulted with witches—a normal practice at the time—believing that the greatest army Jumaral could have was that of the dead. They found the entrance. They broke the gate to the other side."

The woman tilted her head back in the direction of the shadowy forms Adelina had noticed before. The bars were bent in, broken from the outside.

"The demons were released. They tore across Jumaralian lands and chased out my people, but they did not stop there. They were indiscriminate in their attacks and uncontrollable. My people—*all* people—ran for their lives."

"But not you?"

"Sebastião and I were in love, or so I thought. We met after my father invited him to our home as a show of goodwill. His grand ideas had made him somewhat of a leader to the Jumaralian people. I was invited to dinner as a pretty plaything. Later, Sebastião told me I was smart. He told me that he had a plan to humble my father. He told me that we could change the world together, if I so chose. So, I did."

Ostrea paused. The anger she felt had obviously never lost its sting.

"I stayed with him while demons—each of them humans turned mad and grotesque in death—rose from the darkest pits of the world. Sebastião became overwhelmed. He was scared that they would overrun the world. He gathered the witches, who trusted him from his years of collaboration, and asked them to find a way to combine their magic. They did, and he used that magic to drive the demons home with a Great Wave. Then, instead of fixing the gate, he put me here as a guard. That way, I would be here to release the demons when he found a way to control them, and I could be a message to my father and the Empire not to return.

"Sebastião was the darling of the people. He blamed the witches for the initial release of the demons, and everyone believed him. They crowned him as a savior to the people and listened to the lies he spun about me and about what he did. They allowed him to gather witches and even helped him. Their magic made my chains. It rebuilt cities. It revitalized arable land. It was a crutch that Jumaral never stopped leaning on."

"Is that what's so special about my bloodline?" Adelina asked. "I'm a descendant of the man that betrayed you?"

Ostrea's features fell into a resigned sort of satisfaction. "Sebastião Ducança was an arrogant man, but he was not a complete imbecile." She held up her arms, letting the chains clink. "As long as one of you is alive and willing to keep me, I will never be free. The other side of these chains connects to your uncle, the current king, Dom Aristides."

Adelina frowned. She had assumed the chains connected to the gate.

"How?"

"Sebastião created a tether that connected me to him. I thought it would die with him, but he fixed it so that the link passes to his surviving bloodline. My imprisonment was secured first by his life and then by his son's life and then by his daughter's, and so on. It passes along with the crown."

The pieces fit together as sharply as if they had been cut from glass. Simão's medallion had belonged to a pregnant woman. A woman who had had relations with the king and then had been murdered in her sleep. The woman had been killed to prevent an heir being born, an heir who would one day have inherited the prison of a goddess.

"The one who holds the chains. They can let go?"

The goddess's words were colder than ever. "It is as simple as turning a key."

Here it was. The true reason Simão had been killed and Manuel, Calixto's older brother, before him. If either of them had ever become king, they would have been the keepers of a goddess—and judging by Simão's rant about the dangers of power and the flaws of the monarchy, he and Manuel might have set that goddess free.

"Why has no one done it?"

"If I am gone, there is no one to keep the demons back. The royal family believes that if they can only gather enough magic and find someone knowledgeable enough to use it, they will be able to control them and truly have the conquering army of the dead that Sebastião dreamed of."

Adelina pictured pockets of magic growing at each of the castles of Jumaral, ready to be wielded. The dead would be invincible to tanks, bombs, and rifles. There would be nothing stopping Jumaral from reaching as far as Dom Sebastião's kingdom was said to have spread. But it was also an explosion waiting to go off. If the House of Ducança didn't control the demons, the demons would come for them first.

"You are right that the ghost boy is useful. He is in the unique position of being both dead and undead. I have heard the whispers about him, the proposed deals. Just recently, he has twice bypassed my guard and entered the realm of the dead. He could lead them, command them as no other being could. However, you do not account for the prevailing issue. I cannot be free until my shackles are broken. So, princess...what are you going to do about that?"

Adelina's thoughts were sinking into the back of her head, and she couldn't catch them before they fell. She wanted to be in the library, carefully working things out. She wanted Dalila to bring her tea and comfort her, and she wanted Jas's quiet suggestions while he read over her shoulder. She wanted Seba to make annoying jokes, and she wanted to eat a meal with her parents without wondering when they could decide that her life was no longer valuable to them.

Adelina wanted Simão. She wanted this to be over. Wanted it never to have started.

But, no. Those were illogical thoughts, and Adelina was not illogical. She did what had to be done, and there was no arguing that Dom Aristides, Infante Benigno, and Prince Calixto would never relinquish their hold on Ostrea. She had listened to enough council meetings to know that. The only solution was for Adelina to take the throne, to become the prophesied queen she had been fighting for since that night on the beach.

So many plans, only to end up right back where she started.

"I'll kill them," Adelina whispered. The dagger pressed against her waist, and she imagined the ghost of it catching the moonlight in front of her.

"You do not have to be so shy. You are already damned. Here, there are no stars to watch you fall from grace, no fires to alight your heart. Here, there is only truth and the freedom that comes with no shame. Say it again."

"I'll kill my family," Adelina announced, louder this time. "And then, when I have the crown, I'll release you. Jas will stay here to control the dead, and you will be free."

Ostrea was smiling, but there was something else in her face Adelina hadn't seen before: hunger.

"I am glad to see you finally getting your hands bloody, princess, but I must ensure that you are not making empty promises in order to leave here. You have a history...so I will keep the shirtless boy."

"Jas?" Adelina fought the urge to glance back at where Jas and Seba lay, unstirring amidst the shadows.

"He will stay here, and if you have not fulfilled your promise in three days, he will launch an attack on you *and* the clothed one, using the very skills you helped him cultivate."

Adelina's feelings were becoming sharper the longer she was awake. The sting of guilt clutched at her heart. The usual logic came to her—fate and prophecies and doing what needed to be done. It hadn't changed, not really.

"It's a deal," she said.

Ostrea grinned and reached out a thin hand. "You will be my blade and I the hand that wields you—my keen knife that will right every wrong that has been perpetrated against us."

They shook once, firmly, but Ostrea did not let go. She squeezed Adelina's hand tightly and leaned in to whisper, "Fair is foul and foul is fair. Do not be afraid to survive, Lady Malves, and to be a little wicked when you do."

Before Adelina even had time to react to this pronouncement or the odd twist of her name, her hand was relinquished, and she was stumbling away, dizzy. Her hand burned, but it was with a different pain than the irritation from the rope and sand.

The shadows closed around her. The twisting face she had known as Ostrea faded into black. Something materialized behind her feet, and Adelina fell backward, unable to catch herself. She plummeted through time and space, black swirls of shadow the only thing she could see.

Then she was still, her eyes closed, lying on her back. Soft sand rubbed against her bare fingers.

CHAPTER 28

SEBA

When Seba woke up, all he knew was sand and pain. Sand in his clothes, caked into his hair, embedded in the unreachable depths of his fingernails. It ground against every bit of him while he shifted to a sitting position. At least, he had *thought* he was moving into a sitting position.

In reality, his pounding head did not appear to have extricated itself from the sand's grimy hold. Every bit of him ached, like he had been pulled apart and put back together again a few degrees off from the correct angles.

He made himself open his eyes. It was so dark he wondered if his vision had been disrupted in the reassembling process. Slowly, he adjusted to the night and began to make out the wall of stone above him, recognize the crashing echoing around him as the sound of waves. By Our Lady, someone really needed to do something about the volume of the ocean.

He sensed more than heard the movement near him, and he managed to nudge his head slightly to the left toward the dark outline of Adelina. In a display that seemed intimately offensive to his current state, Adelina was already working her way to her feet. Her hair fell in wet tangles down her back, and her clothes were just as wet and sand caked as his own. She whipped her head around, the whites of her eyes glowing with the frenzied gleam he associated with feral cats.

"Get up," she said when she noticed him staring at her.

"Impossible."

He expected a retort, but she only reached down to grab his arms and haul him up. The movement sent his head spinning. Pain shot through every part of him, and he leaned on her to steady himself.

"Unnecessary," he grunted.

Once again, he was met with no reply. Adelina stared out into the ocean, as if looking for something she had left behind.

Memories slammed through Seba's skull like a plank of wood. Watching Jas fall into himself, pale and twitching on the ground when the water began to rumble. Hitting Jas over the head with a stone and watching the blood pour from the wound in a trancelike sort of satisfaction. The giant ghost boat leering its way down into a thunderous splash. Speaking with Adelina, listening to her confess the lies she had told, and knowing his fate was to be king and she was the only one who could get him there. Climbing into the boat with Adelina and Jas, tying Jas's shirt around his head, and shivering when the freezing water climbed over their heads.

The snap of Jas's fingers breaking echoed between his ears.

He squinted along with Adelina in the direction of the water. Waves lapped to the shore in a steady rhythm, and the horizon was as inscrutable as ever. There was no sign of the boat. Dark stains of blood lingered on the sand, and a rock a bit larger than his fist had been separated from the rest. Jas's blood was here, but he was nowhere to be seen.

The pain began to ebb away from his body, including the throbbing of his nose and ankle from his meeting with Alves. The injuries he had sustained from the thug seemed to be magically healed, but his fingers remained just as crooked as ever.

"Adelina?" he began warily. "What—what just happened?"

It was only because he was still leaning on her shoulder that he felt the shudder of her breath. The rest of her was as steady as ever.

"I made a deal," she said. "Now we have to honor it."

Without another word, she strode off, leaving him barely standing upright. He lurched after her, tightly gripping the rope that acted as a handrail to the wooden stairs taking them up the side of the cliffs of Solmortém.

Adelina stopped only when they had reached the top, returning to the point where they had looked out over the ocean with Jas... how long ago?

"What happened?" he repeated when he had finally caught up. He remained several paces away from the edge. The fact the ground was swooping beneath him did not make him particularly eager to approach it. "Did you speak to the encantada?"

Adelina didn't respond for several seconds, not even acknowledging his presence. Finally, she turned. "I need you to propose to me."

"Sorry?" he said. The wind was so loud.

"I need you to propose marriage to me. In the town, where everyone can see."

Seba could only blink, not sure how to reply.

"Now?"

Adelina's head cocked to the side. "Does this come as a surprise to you?"

"No," he spluttered. "But...*now*?"

"Why not now?"

"You have to admit, it's a little abrupt."

Her eyes widened. "Abrupt?" she repeated incredulously. "After constructing an entire plan around getting married, my telling you to propose is *abrupt*?"

"I just woke up out of my mind on a beach with a passageway to the world of the dead. I'm going to need some context."

She scoffed. "What you *need* is to follow the plan. You *agreed* to this."

"Well, *you* chose *me*. 'Dearest partner of greatness,' remember?" His cheeks heated, even in the freezing wind against his wet clothes. His hair was tangled and disgusting as he ran his fingers through it. "Or am I imagining the conversation that we had before...whatever that was?"

For a moment, it seemed Adelina was about to scream at him, but then she just stopped. Her chest moved slowly while she breathed in the air. The sight made him unclench his own fists.

"I made a deal with Ostrea," she began in a tone devoid of emotion. "She's trapped by chains, which are connected to my family's bloodline. Right now, the key lies with my uncle, but it passes down by blood. The only way to release Ostrea is to unlock the chains, but my uncle will never do it, and neither will Calixto or my father. That means we have to get the chains to pass to me."

Seba gaped at her. "Ostrea?"

"Yes."

"The ocean goddess?"

"Yes."

"The creator of fates?"

"She doesn't actually do that."

"But the prophecy—"

Adelina nodded. "Now we have something even better. Her word itself."

"But—Okay, you made a deal with Our Lady Ostrea to free her in exchange for a wish, which means...killing your family?"

"It seems that way."

"You said no murder."

"I lie sometimes."

He let the words fall over him.

"I just—"

He felt the ghost of the rock in his hand again, returning to smash into a skull until it cracked. He had been so willing to do it to Jas, in the moment, for the prophecy. But now the memory made the hair stand on the back of his neck, and the prophecy, from what Adelina said, still stood in one form or another. He had never so clearly felt the eyes of the goddess staring down at him.

"I don't know if I want to actually murder anyone. I don't..." What would have happened if he had kept going, if Jas's skull had opened to reveal brain? Bile rose halfway up his throat. "I don't think I can."

She shrugged. "Make an effort."

"Where *is* Jas?"

"Still with Ostrea. His powers mean he can command the army of the dead if he tries hard enough. We have three days to transfer the chains before she uses him to come after us. If we succeed, then she is released, Jas takes her place, and we get a wish."

"Three days?"

"That's why you need to propose."

"You are currently connecting dots that I didn't know existed." Seba ran a hand through his hair. *Three days* before an army of the dead was unleashed on him. If he had been pressured to follow Ostrea's wishes before, it was nothing compared to now.

"It gives us a reason to be in Fulgeo. I'm sure my entire family will want to discuss my engagement to an unsuitable commoner." Seba opened his mouth in defense, but she continued. "As long as we make the engagement public here, news will reach them by telegram within the hour, and we'll be able to meet them in the capital by tomorrow. Or maybe even tonight."

"And then?"

"I'll think of something."

"So, we're going to kill the king of Jumaral, the crown prince of Jumaral, and the duke of Lis by luring them all to Fulgeo with our engagement and then executing a plan that, as of this moment, does not exist?"

"Correct."

Seba almost laughed at the absurdity. "And if we fail?"

Even in the dark, he could make out the flicker of movement crossing over her face, like a shadow reaching out from the night.

"Fail?" she repeated. "Try to maintain some courage for more than five seconds at a time, and we won't fail. Do you think that there is a world in which I would let this be traced back to us?" Her eyes glinted. "There is no fire I will not set, even if it comes from the stars themselves. *We do not fail.*"

Though she had finished speaking, there was a continuation to the thought hanging over both of them. We *cannot* fail. To fail was to be destroyed and, now that an angry goddess was involved, to bring the entire world down with them.

"Well, now that you've properly filled me with confidence," he said, "shall we get engaged?"

Adelina pressed her lips together and nodded. Seba recognized the look of her mind whirring.

"We need new clothes, an audience, paper and pen..."

"Paper and pen?"

"To draft the proposal."

"You don't trust that I can propose to you through improvisation?" Seba placed a hand over his chest. "Speak from the heart, so to say?"

"If I wanted to hear your heart, I'd cut open your chest and hold it to my ear for its last beats," she muttered, already brushing past him, away from the cliffs and the crashing black nothingness beyond.

The wave of the moment washed over Seba. Once he turned, there would be no coming back. He had already passed so many of these points of no return, starting from the second he had jumped into the river to save Adelina and bringing him to the events of tonight, in which he must have already made what felt like hundreds of impossible, irreversible choices.

But he knew what he wanted, and he had identified the path to it. What did it matter that the course was dark and shadowy and led by an increasingly violent marquise? There was protection in darkness, a shield that had been stripped away from him by Hala and Jas the moment they had traded his mother's life for Jas's. They had done something irreversible, and now he was forced to do the same.

He was glad the night was dark, cloudy, and starless. Adelina had ripped the fires from the sky for them to use as their own.

The faint sound of her shoes against rock was fading behind him, and he turned, running to catch up.

"I'm glad to see this experience hasn't hardened you, love," he called.

By the time they found what they needed, the sun had risen over the small town a half hour's walk from the cliffs of Solmortém. Their first stop had been the motorcar, at which they had retrieved their spare clothes from the trunk stored in the back seat.

Seba's wet clothes had clung to him. He would probably be shivering for the rest of his Ostrea-forsaken life, but he was able to trade his mop of an outfit for a dry suit. Adelina had the added challenge of buttons in hard-to-reach places, which meant he got to play the part of the true fiancé.

"Hurry up," she had snapped while he took his time fastening the fragile clasps at the back of her neck.

"I am simply trying to create a bond of intimacy between us before the big proposal," he had argued. "It's called method acting."

"At the rate you're going, you'll be proposing to a naked woman. Is that intimate enough for you?"

Heat had risen in Seba's cheeks, and he had fumbled with the last few buttons. "Quite."

He had backed away as soon as he was done and watched her return her ever-present dagger to her waist, hidden beneath her jacket. They walked half an hour to a nearby town while the sun began peeking over the horizon, beginning its slow journey to the edge of Solmortém.

The moment they caught sight of some of the townspeople, there was going to be no sneaking around to collect the rest of their supplies. While they wore the fashionable clothes of the city—a high-necked blouse and skirt for Adelina, under a long-lapeled jacket and hat, and a graying suit for Seba, with a dark green waistcoat that brought out the hazel of his eyes—everyone else was dressed for work.

Long hair was wrapped in faded scarves, baskets of bread were balanced on heads, and skirts were covered by aprons with deep pockets. Wide-brimmed hats were there to protect against the sun, not to accentuate the color of one's jacket. Many people in Lis dressed like this and worked like this, but there were also a variety of classes in Lis that did not seem to exist here.

Seba and Adelina were completely exposed.

Before anyone could spare more than a few curious glances at them, Adelina was directing him by the arm back down the street toward the cliffs and the smell of sea salt. They ducked amongst the stalks of corn, far enough away from the outlying houses, where it was unlikely anyone would find them before they were ready.

"What were you expecting?" Seba whispered when they were settled.

Adelina pressed her lips together and stared in the direction of the town and the sunrise. The only thing Seba could see was corn.

"We'll just do it without the paper," he offered. "I'll remember it."

After a second, her focus shifted back to him. "They might not have a telegraph. We need photographers. And a telegraph."

"Then maybe we should drive somewhere else." He hoped she noticed the severity with which he regarded the situation, considering getting back in the motorcar with her was very nearly the last thing he ever wanted to do.

Adelina shook her head. "Some people already saw us. If one of them speaks, it will look strange that we were here and didn't stay." It took only the space of a heartbeat for the answer to come to her. "The school."

"Believe it or not, I do actually need more detail than that."

"There's a navigation school at the other side of the cliffs. They've been there for centuries. They're the ones that made the map at the manor in Lis. They must have a telegraph. It's how they communicate with other scholars along the coastline. It's likely they have some kind of camera as well."

"So, we get engaged at the school?"

"No. In the town. We need to include the people, make them feel involved, keep up the media and the public pressure on my family. While I'm entertaining, you'll ask someone about the camera—tell them there's something you want to be documented forever. It will be endearing, something for them to tell the journalists when they start swarming after they get the telegram. Then they can use the picture and take care of the rest."

Seba ran a hand through his hair. He cringed at the grimy feeling of sand that hadn't been helped by the wind. "And then we get engaged?"

"Yes," she said. "This is what you have to say."

They argued over every other word, constructing the proposal that would allow Seba minimal acting, as he still had "a book face."

When they decided they were finished, Adelina asked if he remembered it.

"No. Perhaps if we just repeated it a million more times."

"I'm glad it made an impression."

"Like a seal in hot wax." He winked. "I'm hot wax."

She seemed to decide this did not warrant a reply, so they left their place within the corn in silence, returning to the dirt roads of a town now bathed in sun.

It happened just as they had planned. Someone recognized them, and then they were in the center of it all. While people hung off Adelina, Seba pulled one of the market sellers aside, asking where one might acquire a camera to document an important event. Within the hour, a camera was brought, and they were climbing the steps of a church, with the entire town watching them from the square.

Seba knelt on one knee, stone pressing hard against bone. He pulled Hala's ring from his pocket, the one he had torn from Jas's finger on their ride to the goddess.

Adelina played her part well. She clapped her hands over her mouth in surprise, forced real tears from her softened eyes, and admired the ring on her finger before reaching down to loop her arms around his neck. She only let go to raise her newly adorned hand in recognition of the crowd, letting it catch the mid-morning sun and flashes of the camera so that it looked like she held fire in her hand.

And then she looked at him. The tithe between them was an oath that might have been different from what everyone thought but no less weighted.

"Adelina," he said, purposefully leaving off her title. "My dearest love. We have found partnership in a world that wants to keep us apart, one filled with grief and sorrow and pain. And yet my heart doesn't care. It beats for you. My *soul* beats for you."

A bit theatrical, he had said.

It's an act, she had retorted. *Stop complaining and memorize it.*

"And every time it beats, I feel hope. I feel hope that you and I will change this world, not because of the titles we hold or the names we are called, but because we will be together. So, my dearest partner of greatness." That had not been in the script, but to Seba, it was an important addition. "Will you marry me?"

ACT IV:

STARS,
HIDE YOUR FIRES

CHAPTER 29

ADELINA

There was no use hiding the motorcar on the way back up the coast from Solmortém to the capital, Fulgeo. The villagers who had witnessed their proposal followed them to where they had parked and waved them off in a sort of awed frenzy. They were witnessing history and the future all rolled up in one: the marquise of Lis and her husband to be and the visionary chariot sweeping them away amidst a series of clunks, grinds, and shrieks.

It was clear that the news had spread when, hours later, people began running out to meet them, lining up along the road to cheer while the sweethearts from the newspapers trundled by. Beside her, Seba waved and smiled, making supreme use of his dimpled grin. But he tensed with every small jounce. The knuckles of his hidden hand were white.

They couldn't have driven the entire day, even if they had wanted to. The motorcar needed fuel, and people were all too excited to give it to them. Adelina pulled to the side of the road just outside the town of Nanães and allowed the vehicle to be swarmed with children. She and Seba stepped out to graciously accept their congratulations and hospitality.

While the motorcar was filled with fuel, Adelina caught sight of the newspapers almost every single person was carrying. On the front page was an enormous photograph of Seba kneeling before Adelina, the plain loop of metal he held barely visible. Above the photo were the words "MARQUISE OF LIS ACCEPTS PROPOSAL FROM PINHEIRO," and in a subtitle, "YOUNG COUPLE TO BEGIN JOURNEY TO FULGEO IN VILAR MOTORCAR."

They stayed the night in a city neighboring a nature preserve, in the mansion of its duke. Although it was made to seem like a happy coincidence the duke of Lenítubal was home and willing to host them, the arrangement was likely due to a desperate series of telegrams between her uncle and every member of nobility between Solmortém and Fulgeo.

That night, Adelina made a show of sneaking out of her bedroom and into Seba's, her dressing gown slipping from her shoulders. The maids giggled in the hallway when Seba's door whined shut behind her. He was sprawled, shirtless, face down, limbs spread across the sheets. The intricately woven quilt had been kicked to the floor, and he was already snoring soundly.

Adelina marched up to his side.

"Seba," she whispered.

If possible, his snoring grew louder.

She raised her voice to match. "*Seba.*" With a frustrated sigh, she reached out to touch his bare shoulder. The heat of him sent a shock against her freezing palm. She shook him violently. "Seba!"

He snorted and whipped his head up from the pillow so it almost met her nose. His hair stood on end, and his eyes were wild when they found her, glowing from the moonlight pouring through the window. Then he relaxed, and his face settled into a look of mild amusement.

"Did you miss me, my lovely fiancée?" He leaned on his elbow in some awkward imitation of a salacious painting.

"Every breathing moment, my lovely barnacle." She motioned for him to move over, which he did with an eye roll. The bed was comfortable and warm where his body heat had been left behind. Adelina rested her back against the wall, intimately aware of the iconography hanging above them: a wooden carving of Ostrea summoning Her Wave. "We can't let them separate us."

"Can't live without me?"

"We're harder to kill if we're together."

His amused mask slid into dread—that lurking sensation he was always trying to push away while he attempted to convince himself the path forward was worth it. Seba was still so easy to read.

"Is that in reference to any specific threat?" He swallowed. "Or just in general?"

"Both."

"Two more days."

"Two more days," Adelina repeated. The words fell over them like the beats of a drum.

"Any thoughts on that plan to kill the three most powerful men in Jumaral?"

She let the back of her head rest against the wall. "Some."

"And you're just keeping them to yourself?"

"I've been thinking about the end result. The Second Great Wave was seen as a legitimate transfer of power because it looked like divine will, even if it was just...weather. If we create a narrative to fit that, then the sudden death of the king and his two most direct heirs won't be opposed."

Seba ran a hand through his hair. "Make everyone think Ostrea wanted them dead?"

"Exactly."

"I keep telling you I'm not just a pretty face."

"You're right. You are unmistakably less than a pretty face."

Seba shifted onto his elbow again so he could look her in the eyes. "This is no way to start a marriage."

"That's where you're wrong." She leaned down so their noses almost touched. "This is only the engagement."

He blinked. "Your breath smells."

Adelina inhaled deeply and blew a breath of hot air into his face, relishing in the wrinkle of his nose—that familiar burble of childish amusement. She almost laughed. Then she stopped herself, remembering late nights giggling with Simão, Dalila, Isaque, and even Calixto before he became so much like his father.

The world had not been kind to the people she laughed with.

"But will it work?" Seba whispered. "Do enough people even believe in the will of Ostrea anymore?"

"Of course. No one would dare defy Ostrea."

A carriage was waiting for them on the outskirts of Fulgeo, the capital city south of Lis. It blocked the road forward, and excited onlookers—the depth of their crowd increasing with the new day and their proximity to the capital—blocked their sides. Adelina had no choice but to press down on the brake and bring the motorcar to a lurching stop, which sent Seba's arm flying across his chest in the holy sign of the seas.

They had left Lenítubal that morning, and Adelina had been surprised when they had been allowed to continue the journey in the motorcar, though they were followed by a train of the duke's carriages. It seemed her family wanted her and Seba to be noticed as much as they did.

The better to rally the people when we die.

It was what both Calixto and Simão would have said, and their fears were making her paranoid now she was no longer sure where the prophecy had come from. Adelina had considered the idea she was being allowed to drive because it would be all the more plausible if something terrible were to happen on the way to Fulgeo.

She could imagine the titles of the newspapers, tragically flipping from announcements of engagement to sorrowful obituaries mourning the essence of young, classless love. And yet, they made it to Fulgeo in one piece. Adelina had to suppress a sigh of relief when she spotted the distant speck of Fulgeo's castle, the Castle of Dom Sebastião, peeking out from the forested hills.

It turned almost immediately to dread. There were probably witches trapped there as well since the royal family had resided in a separate palace in Fulgeo, far from the castle, for centuries. It was in that palace Adelina was sure her family was waiting, perhaps trying to find a solution to the problem of Adelina and Seba that didn't involve killing off yet another heir.

And if it didn't work, if Adelina and Seba proved to be irreparable, then it would only be more painful when they were gone. It was so easy to control a unified mourning mass.

Adelina turned off the engine.

Two guards exited the royal carriage ahead, dressed in the red livery of the House of Ducança. Another figure emerged behind them, smaller than the two guards and wearing a large blue hat over her sheaf of blond hair. Dalila.

"When we get out, don't let go of my hand," Adelina muttered. She kept her smile wide, her lips barely moving. "We can't let them separate us."

"Right," Seba said, for once devoid of jokes. He was pale, sickeningly in contrast with the dark hair standing on end after the countless rounds his hand had swiped through it.

Dalila and the guards were getting closer, near enough for Adelina to make out the crease between her maid's brows, which gave away the wariness behind her sunny grin.

"Just—" *Look like the innocent flower. Be the serpent under it.* "Act like you love me."

Seba tore his wide eyes from the approaching trio and held her gaze with terrified understanding. She watched something shift in him, his smile relax, his shoulders soften. The book was less easy to read.

There was a knock at Adelina's door. Dalila stood outside, waving excitedly at the two of them. Adelina drew a breath, fixed her own smile, and opened the door to a burst of cheers. Seba extricated himself from the motorcar's other side, and both raised hands to wave at their supporters.

"My lady," Dalila shouted over the noise. She was staring at Adelina's hand, where her ring caught the light. "Congratulations!"

"Thank you, Dalila." Adelina remembered her temper when she had last seen her maid. She had hoped it would be put down to exhaustion or perhaps grief, but the unyielding crease in Dalila's brow said otherwise.

"Hello, Senhor Pinheiro," Dalila called when Seba was ushered toward them by one of the guards. Seba nodded his greeting, but

Dalila was no longer looking at him. Her eyes were searching the motorcar, and Adelina forced her shoulders not to tense.

"Where's Jas?" Dalila finally asked.

"He stayed behind, with family," Adelina explained. "It was easier for him."

Dalila's eyes fluttered with something that looked like disappointment. "Oh."

"Lady Adelina." One of the guards was holding out an arm to direct them to the carriage.

Seba's hand appeared in hers, as she had directed. His grip was tight, as though she was an anchor on yet another boat carrying them into the unknown. They followed the guards, hands waving and smiles wide, with Dalila trailing behind.

Adelina slid onto one seat of the carriage and pulled Seba beside her. They didn't let go of each other while Dalila took her place across from them, the guards shut the doors, and the lurch of the first movement sent them trundling up the street to Fulgeo's city center.

The moment they were in motion, Dalila began speaking feverishly. Patches of red blossomed around her cheeks and collar. "When we arrive, my lady, we will need to prepare you for an audience with Infanta Rosália, Infante Benigno, Dom Aristides, and Prince Calixto."

"They don't want the grace of my company as well?" Seba asked.

"It seems not yet, Senhor."

Adelina directed her focus out the window, to the colorful stucco walls and grand fountains of Fulgeo. A trolley, its bottom half painted a slightly garish yellow, ran parallel to them. Its passengers crowded around the windows to wave. Adelina raised her free hand, earning an increase in the volume of cheers.

By tomorrow night, she needed to be the bearer of Ostrea's chains, or all of this would be overrun. The audience today would have been perfect, if it hadn't been so soon and so private. She hadn't had time to gather what she needed for the plan, and there would be no one to witness the holy destruction of Jumaral's leadership, which was the central tenet of moving forward.

The question was how to gather her family publicly enough to have witnesses but privately enough that no one would notice what really happened.

And there was the matter of where to get the water.

Adelina had been to the palace countless times, starting from well before she could remember. This was where her family had gathered for holidays and birthdays, festivals and international events. She had seen her fair share of the ballroom, the formal dining room, the nursery, and the private wings. Adelina, Simão, and Calixto had spent every summer swinging from tree branches in the royal gardens and playing hide-and-seek amongst the dark rooms of the residential suites, with Manuel chasing after them with that smothered amusement of a boy raised to be a king.

This was the first time Adelina had ever noticed how large the palace was.

Seba's hand had begun spasming in hers, and she tightened her grip, hoping the pain would distract him.

He let out a tight "By Our *Lady*, Adelina," but some color returned to his cheeks.

From the street, the view of the palace was only that of a high pink stucco wall the color of sunsets, followed by layers of trees and foliage, yet another wall, and then just a peek at the roofs beyond. Across the street was a grand garden of carefully planned grassy squares, all positioned around an enormous statue of Dom Sebastião rising from a pillar of water.

An army of photographers met them as the carriage trundled up to the guarded entrance. Flashes of light burst in Adelina's vision, glowing like stars when she blinked. There was a merciful squeal of metal grating against hinges while the gates swung shut behind them, leaving the lights and the screams on the outside of the palace. They were pulled into a large open courtyard fitted with crisscrossing brown tile and directed into a lot on the right. The last slivers of sound fell away, along with any scrap of a happy welcome.

Within the palace walls, there was no laughter or cheering, no calling out in excitement for the newly engaged couple who had defied all odds. Here, there were only guards and servants moving in stiff lines, as if they were part of the structure of the building themselves.

The door to the carriage was opened for them, and Dalila exited first, standing respectfully aside for Seba and Adelina. Adelina pushed Seba's hand toward his side, untangling her sweaty fingers from his.

"Just for a second," she whispered.

He stumbled from the carriage, ran a hand through his hair, spun in a circle to take in the almighty fortress rising around him, straightened his jacket and waistcoat, ran his hand through his hair again, and only remembered to hold his hand out to Adelina when she stepped out of the carriage herself.

His hand clutched hers, and the simple silver ring pressed around her finger, like the single bar of the strongest cage in the world.

"Shall we, my lady?" Dalila asked.

Adelina nodded, and they were led, not through the grand front door, but into the entrance of the indoor stables, where the faint smell of horses clung to the air. They climbed the creaking wooden steps, which let out into an unremarkable hall Adelina had once used as a hiding place from one particularly boring dinner party.

Despite the comparative lack of decoration or utility, this hall was filled with servants and guards, many appearing in doorways when they passed. Adelina painted a small smile on her lips, making eye contact with each person only long enough for them to feel like they were in on the secret.

They continued taking service staircases and unused corridors until they were brought out to a large hall gilded from top to bottom in intricate gold carvings. These were interspersed with blue-tiled paintings of saints and miracles, arches bridging over them. They passed between rows of wooden benches and carved flower blossoms staring down at them, so lifelike it didn't seem unlikely for feathery gold petals to begin drifting over their heads.

Seba's grip loosened as his focus turned to the palace around him. His head craned back, and his jaw dropped. Stained glass images of fish and waves cast a blue shadow over his skin. When he started to slow down, Adelina pulled him forward, keeping pace with Dalila. They swerved out another door just before the altar.

It was no coincidence that Dalila had been directed to lead them through the church.

After many corridors of dark red carpets and enormous portraits of dead ancestors and saints, they reached Adelina's room. It had been her own since she was born, though it contained no personal touches. It was full of the velvet reds and greens of the Jumaralian crest, a large canopy bed at its center, and a fireplace at the side, with two armchairs that existed more for looks than for comfort. Midday sun streamed through the windows, which overlooked a neatly manicured courtyard with a swimming pool at its center.

Dalila immediately went to the wardrobe, from which she withdrew a dress of pink so light it was almost white.

"Someone should be coming soon to deliver clothes for you, Senhor Pinheiro," she said.

Seba appeared not to have heard. He was staring at a series of gold-framed photographs and small statues of Ostrea lining the mantelpiece. There was a hunger in his eye Adelina recognized from the first time she had spoken to him.

She dropped his hand, which drew his attention away from his future of gold.

"Right," he grunted. "Yes, thank you, Dalila."

"My lady?" Dalila gestured to a knobby wooden chair in front of the vanity, which gave a familiar creak when Adelina sat down.

Its decorative carvings dug into her shoulder blades.

Dalila immediately set to work undoing the messy pins Adelina had done for herself that morning. There were already powders and rouges set out in front of her, ready for Dalila to apply. Adelina stared back at herself in the mirror, allowing her mask to flicker for just a moment to assess what was underneath.

Her eyes were sunken and lifeless, popping out of skin that had surpassed the descriptor of shadows. Her lips were pale, her skin grayish.

Adelina looked like she was rotting.

Then the mask went back up, and each note of deterioration was twisted into the humbled exhaustion of excitement, of marriage, of devotion, of simply being too in love to rest—the very essence of *lovely*.

She was reminded of the way flowers died after they were picked—wilting and crumpling into a ball of flaky brownness where there had once been velvet crimson. But if they died a certain way, if they were pressed into books or put behind a pane of glass, kept in a box as a keepsake, then they were beautiful even in their lifelessness.

"Did you get my telegram, Dalila?" she asked quietly.

The reflection of Dalila's fingers faltered. "I did, my lady."

"Have you begun?"

"I have."

"Begun what?" came Seba's voice, as usual much too loud for the conversation at hand.

Adelina shot him a look in the mirror. He held his hands up in surrender.

"Dalila is helping us with something."

"*Sharing*, partner of greatness, remember?"

"It's the same thing you and I have been talking about since we delivered Jas to your family in Solmortém."

"Oh, *that* thing."

"Yes, *that* thing. Was there something else you were planning?"

She watched in the mirror while he held both hands to his wounded heart. "Well, there is our *wedding*."

Before Adelina could shoot back a reply, Dalila was speaking. She moved with a precision suggesting too much thought was being put into every twist of hair or insertion of pin.

"Why *did* Jas stay?"

Adelina carefully did not look at Seba.

"You saw him, Dalila," Adelina replied. "He wasn't doing well here. There was too much to remind him of Hala."

"And he gave you her ring?"

Adelina breathed through the conflicting urges to flinch or still. She twisted her engagement ring with her other hand. "He knew we wanted to get engaged."

"But why did you do it right after leaving him to mourn? Right after Hala died?"

Adelina fixed her stare on Dalila's reflection. Her maid was still making a show of concentrating on Adelina's hair. After a moment of silence, she looked up. Her blue eyes widened to find Adelina staring at her.

"My lady," she added.

"Seba and I have both had a difficult few months," Adelina said tightly. She hoped Dalila would take it as a sign she was holding back tears. "When life isn't going down the right path, sometimes you have to take the wheel."

Seba mumbled something about Adelina being a terrible driver.

"Of course, my lady," Dalila said. There was a shift in the room, some tension sliding away to make room for pity. "As for your telegram, may I inquire as to the scale?"

"As many as possible. At least fifty."

Dalila dropped the pin she was holding to the floor. "Fifty?"

"Yes."

"And how soon do you need them?"

"Tomorrow night at the very latest."

"Adelina, I—I just don't know if—"

A knock at the door made them all tense. Dalila set down the pins shakily and went to answer it. A few words passed between her and the person on the other side. Seba and Adelina met each other's eyes in the mirror's reflection. Fear radiated from Seba, even through the glass.

Dalila returned moments later with a neat suit for Seba in her arms. She laid it out across the bed and glanced over her shoulder, listening for the fading footsteps of whatever servant had delivered it. When it seemed safe, she returned to Adelina's side.

"I don't know if that's enough time. By nature, these"—she glanced at Seba, who was admiring the suit behind them—"these people are difficult to contact and then difficult to gather. They don't trust easily, especially not when they know that the message is coming from a member of the royal family."

"I'm afraid we have no choice, Dalila. If the usual networks won't work, then we'll have to think of something..." A thought coalesced in Adelina's mind—a dangerous one. "I know where you can go. I have a plan."

She was staring into her own eyes and looked up. Dalila's expression was wary, but Seba's was utter dread.

"I hate your plans," he muttered before taking a seat on the edge of the mattress, ready to listen while the plot took shape.

CHAPTER 30

SEBA

Seba had never been the type of person to imagine his eventual engagement and marriage. However, if he *had* deigned to picture an eventual future involving a marital union of some sort, he doubted that vision would have included putting on a red-plumed hat and cape, sneaking around the house of his future in-laws, along with his fiancée's maid, in an effort to steal a royal seal from the crown prince of Jumaral, while Seba's fiancée attended a meeting with all the highest-ranking royals in Jumaral, also known as her family.

Then again, his dreams were notoriously unruly.

"I hate the circus," he hissed.

Dalila adjusted the flopping cap on his head, with its four points like tentacles reaching from his skull.

"This is the only way to get you out," she said. "There are still plenty of performers in the palace from the Festival of Dom Sebastião. If anyone sees you, they won't look too closely."

"And what about the guards waiting just outside the door?"

"I'll take care of it," she said.

"You've spent too much time with Adelina."

"What does that mean?" She shifted her attention to tying the cloth mask over his face.

"It means you're vague." His voice jumped at the tightening of fabric over his ears. "And...slightly harsh."

"Sorry," she murmured, which was a response Adelina wouldn't have provided, even if it was the only word that would stop her from being thrown off a cliff.

The knots loosened slightly.

"But you love her, don't you?" Dalila asked.

Seba stiffened, glad she couldn't see his face. He sucked in a breath, like he had seen Adelina do a million times just before spinning a tale.

"I do." He cast his eyes sideways and watched Dalila's expression. There didn't seem to be a physical reaction. He let the breath out.

Adelina had already gone to the audience with the senior royals, primped and polished by Dalila's expert hands, ready to face down the people whose fates were intertwined with theirs. They held his and Adelina's lives in their gilded gloves, but he and Adelina held the lives of the royals in their own, like some morbid tug-of-war.

"Just stay behind me." Dalila stepped back to examine his outfit.

When she seemed satisfied with her work, she wrapped a gray jacket around herself and clasped the buttons up from her waist. She gestured for him to follow her to the door, waving him back so he would be hidden when she nudged it open.

At first, Dalila opened the door only wide enough to look out at the guards waiting there. Then, without warning, she swung the door wide enough for her entire frame to fit through. Her chin lowered, her hand shot out, and her clear blue eyes darkened. Lightning struck through her irises. Hair rose on the back of Seba's neck and along his arms, and there was a faint intake of breath from someone outside the door.

A moment passed where neither of them moved.

Dalila looked back at him—dread in the tension around her eyes. Seba's jaw dropped.

"Let's go." Dalila swept from the room in a perfect imitation of Adelina.

"By Our Almighty Lady of the Seas," Seba muttered before forcing himself to follow.

A guard stood outside the door, presumably tasked with making sure Seba stayed inside the room and wasn't allowed to wander about the palace or go amongst the public. The guard was huge and probably had the ability to twist Seba into a knot, but now they seemed in no state to do so. They were leaning against the wall, their eyes drawn low and unfocused, mouth relaxed and eyebrows slightly raised, as though in a state of slow-motion surprise.

A throat cleared from down the corridor, and Seba jumped, but it was only Dalila. He took one last look at the guard before hurrying away.

Dalila was a witch. Adelina's *maid* was a witch. One of the people with the most access in the world to the Jumaralian royal family was a witch.

They would kill her if they knew.

Unless they already did.

Adelina certainly did anyway, or how else would she have known to ask Dalila to help them? She had used Dalila to get into contact with their network of witches, but he had assumed that was because Dalila was...well, she was Dalila. Dalila had dealt with Adelina her entire life. She was obviously a woman of many talents, and why shouldn't one of those talents be forming a channel of communication with one of the most untrusting populations in the country?

But, he thought, *then what would stop one of those talents from being magic?*

Dalila had slowed her walk to a more casual stride, purposeful but not hurrying. Seba tried to imitate her, but his limbs had turned wooden and were being pulled by puppet strings.

Faint voices rose ahead of them, followed by footsteps. Dalila turned to him, not slowing her pace, and laughed.

Seba wasn't sure how to respond. Was this meant to be part of the act? Or did he look so stupid she couldn't hold herself together, even in the face of life endangerment? He didn't have time to decide before two maids turned the corner, a pile of white linen in each of their arms.

"Dalila!" one of them said, briefly sparing a glance at Seba. "I've been meaning to come see you. When did you get here?"

"Just last night," Dalila replied. Her voice was light, friendly, unassuming. She kept walking but slowed so it seemed she was just in a hurry rather than running away. "I'll have to come see you tonight, after Lady Adelina is in bed."

"That tongue had better be loose!" the other maid said.

Dalila laughed. "I'm not sure how much I'll have to share. I barely had time to greet her highness and get her ready before I was put to work."

The maids turned their attention to Seba, who was still awkwardly trying to position himself behind Dalila.

"Another request from Lady Brunilda?" one of them asked.

"Her ladyship has been very demanding," Dalila replied with a conspiratorial wink. "I must make sure I'm not late."

Dalila led Seba around the corner, with one of the maids calling after her, "Tell us everything!"

"Lady Brunilda?" Seba muttered when they were out of earshot.

"A second cousin of the king," Dalila whispered. "She has a liking for...funny men."

"And what if we have to explain why Lady Brunilda's special delivery is in the bedroom of the prince? Will you use your—?"

"No. Even if I wanted to, it takes a toll, and it's best to be avoided. The only person who would find us in the prince's bedroom is his personal servant, Nuno. As it turns out, he and I are both aware that Prince Calixto has a liking for funny men as well."

An image of the prince's sculpted face, his full lips and elegant lashes, flashed in Seba's mind. Always dressed impeccably. He supposed that if, for whatever reason, it became necessary for Seba to continue whatever strange act he was performing to a point further than hypothetical consideration, he wouldn't be completely upset.

But Prince Calixto would be dead by tomorrow night.

Seba allowed himself half a moment to dwell, to despair. And then he focused on that image of the prince swimming through his head. This time he only looked at the crown on the prince's curls, each jewel glittering, even through the black-and-white print of the newspaper.

Seba and death had a fluctuating relationship. His mother had died—been stolen from him, really. Death hadn't been kind to him that day, but it wasn't death's fault. It was Hala's fault. And Jas's.

Now it was like death was trying to repay him for the injustice of his mother's loss. Hala was gone, and Jas was as good as—an insult to death all on his own.

Now it was Prince Calixto's turn to suffer, as Seba had suffered already.

Prince Calixto would have been handed the crown through no merit other than being born. Seba was the one who would earn it, who deserved it. Calixto was just in the way, like Jas had been.

They passed several more servants and guards when they exited the stairwell. Some stopped to say hello to Dalila, who was apparently a well-loved visitor, though most gave barely a nod of greeting before continuing on their way. Among them were a few other performers, some painted and covered like him, while others wore barely any clothes at all. Seba tensed the first time he saw them, afraid they would want to interact, but there turned out to be no need to worry. The greatest level of engagement any of them gave him was a tight grimace, as if to express their solidarity at his plight.

They were nearing the prince's room when the corridors gained a strange, hushed quality. There were wide windows overlooking the gardens, with a clear swimming pool at its center that reflected the light of high noon. Paintings and iconographies decorated the other side.

Finally, they came to a guard standing beside a door.

"Good afternoon," Dalila said.

The guard barely spared her a glance before she was rapping her knuckles against the door.

They waited several seconds, during which Seba thought he heard some faint swearing and scurrying from within, before the door was creaking open—because apparently, the royals had no concept of oiling hinges—revealing a boy in a slightly rumpled black suit.

The boy blinked at them both before focusing on Dalila.

"Dalila!" he said, with the same note of surprised excitement the maids had shown. "Do you have a message for Prince Calixto?"

"A gift, actually." Dalila nodded to Seba.

"Oh," said the boy—Nuno, Seba assumed. "Of course, come in."

Seba followed Dalila into a room surprisingly similar to Adelina's. It had the same red and green velvety furniture—though this one also had deep tones of purple sprinkled throughout—and almost identical images of Ostrea, Her many saints, and the monarchs who had served Her. The only piece of personalization was the collection of crocheted rugs and framed images scattered about the room, each in bright clashing colors that hurt Seba's eyes.

The minute the door was shut behind them, Nuno peeled off his jacket and threw it over the back of one of the chairs that probably cost more than the home Seba had lived in with his mother. The boy was shorter than Seba and stocky. His black hair was neatly gelled back from his forehead, which brought out the squareness of his head.

"The prince won't be back for a few hours," he said. "Though I'm sure he wouldn't mind a surprise when he gets back. You were here for the festival, then?"

Seba realized a moment too late that the boy was talking to him. "Yes."

"I got to see some of it, trailing after his highness. Where were you? Maybe I saw your act."

"Oh...around."

Book.

"He's one of the walkers carrying the floats." Dalila leaned casually against one of the bedposts. Her eyes were scouring the room. "How have you been, Nuno? There's been lots of excitement recently."

"There certainly has. And Lady Adelina's not even the worst of it."

"No?"

"Apparently, there's been some movement from Dumatsya and Nolofali. Something being situated that makes it look like they might be aiming for Jumaral's coast."

"The prince certainly tells you a lot."

"Sometimes he needs an ear. Don't tell me Lady Adelina doesn't talk to you?"

"I assure you that she shares plenty with me."

"I would assume so. Lots of drama with that one, isn't it? Probably never shuts up about whoever she's marrying or not marrying. I mean, engaged at seventeen? To some guy who pulled her out of a river a month ago? You must hear more than you could ever want."

Seba stiffened. He was much more than "some guy who pulled her out of a river." And sure, anyone who had met her could say, without hesitation, that Adelina was a dramatic princess with a god complex, but she was one who deserved more respect than *that*.

Dalila moved before Seba could open his mouth.

One moment, she was beside the bed, and in the next breath, she was face-to-face with Nuno, her hand cupping his cheek, her eyes stormy once more. He gulped a breath of air and slumped forward into her arms. She gently lowered him, making much too big of an effort, in Seba's opinion, to keep the boy's head from crashing into the floor.

"I thought you said this was best to be avoided," he said.

Dalila flexed her neck and shoulders as if the magic had strained them. Perhaps it had. "It was taking too long."

"Well, at least he deserved it." Seba glared down at the boy. "Unpleasant, that one."

"He's overcompensating. Prince Calixto doesn't treat him very well."

"What does that have to do with anything?"

"It means," she said, rising to meet his eyes, "that sometimes people do cruel things when they experience cruelty."

Seba was struck with the strange idea Dalila was speaking on more than one level. But she didn't know, did she? She couldn't.

I assure you that she shares plenty with me.

But Adelina wouldn't have shared her plan with Dalila. She had barely shared it with Seba, and he was part of it.

"Won't it be suspicious when someone finds a bunch of unconscious bodies around?" Seba asked.

"They won't be out long, and neither of them will remember. They'll just be too embarrassed to admit they fell asleep on the job."

Dalila opened the drawers of the prince's desk, searching for only a few seconds before pulling out a small gold seal. While she was melting wax and pressing the small carving of the wyvern wrapped around a rose into its soft exterior, Seba couldn't help but wonder if Adelina was as wise as she claimed when it came to deciding who to trust.

CHAPTER 31

ADELINA

The council room was empty except for three people when Adelina walked in. Standing around the end of the enormous ovular table at the center of the handwoven carpet were the duke of Lis, the duchess of Lis, and the crown prince of Jumaral. Her family.

They wore different shades of the same expression—some mixture of disappointment, anger, and worry. The duke was mostly worried, the duchess primarily disappointed, and the prince had a surprising amount of anger tightening the muscles around his mouth.

Adelina stood in the entranceway while the centuries-old wooden doors were shut behind her with an almighty boom.

"Where is the king?" she asked.

They were all supposed to be here. She was supposed to be distracting them so Seba and Dalila could complete their end of the plan.

"He had matters to deal with that carry a little more weight than the idiotic decisions of his niece," Calixto snapped.

"Calixto," the duke murmured.

Despite the fact this was all a lie, that the plan had, in fact, been formed to be seen as idiotic and frivolous, Adelina bristled.

"May I remind you that you are the ones that invited me here," Adelina said.

"We thought you might need some reminding of your place, *Lady* Adelina," said the duchess.

"And what place is that?" Adelina stopped herself from crossing her arms. "A pretty distraction from Jumaral's real problems? A steady backup plan in case things go wrong? The spare that exists only to inherit a throne but never to ask questions about it?"

"Yes," her mother said. "I'm glad you understand."

"I can make my own decisions."

"Not when those decisions interfere with the integrity of the crown," Calixto said. "You cannot marry Sebastião Pinheiro, and you certainly cannot marry him without the consent of your superiors."

"Because he's not royal? Because you had plans to set me up with someone else? Is Prince Demyan of Dumatsya still available?"

"*Because he does not understand*," Calixto shouted.

The duke held out a hand for the prince to stop. Calixto took one look at his uncle and seemed to pull himself in, the moment of emotion drawn back.

Adelina's father spoke to her for the first time. "There are... issues. And complications that you don't know about."

At that moment, Adelina and Calixto were twin flames threatening to spike. So, this was how they were planning to tell her? Wait for her to make a mistake and then warn her not to end up like her brother or her cousin? To be a good girl or risk the country falling apart around her?

Issues. Complications.

The words sent a roiling heat through her stomach.

She fought to keep her voice steady, to contain the rage.

I am a distraction, she told herself. *They wanted me to be a distraction, and here I am. I just have to play the part they raised me to perform.*

"Like what?" she asked flatly.

Calixto opened his mouth to speak, but the duke waved him away again. "Jumaral is weak, Adelina. Since the Second Great Wave, the only thing keeping it afloat has been...a resource. It is a resource that must be carefully extracted and dealt with, and someone who isn't...who doesn't have the correct perspective...might not understand its necessity."

Adelina wanted to scream, to run forward and drag her fingers down each of their faces until the blood puddled high enough for her to paint their lies on the side of the palace. She could have killed them weeks ago. Adelina had the opportunity, and she had had the motive.

But she hadn't had the strength.

Soon they would be dead anyway, and it would be smarter than it would have been the first time. It would be free of emotion, not pushed by a prophecy that could or could not have been real, but by a real deal Adelina had made with Ostrea. It would be logical, and it would be planned. It was the only thing keeping her from exploding.

"Tell me the resource," she said.

Adelina needed to use up their time, to distract them, to hear them say it. But they hesitated.

"You don't trust my perspective?" she asked. "You think I wouldn't understand?"

Calixto was staring her down, tension coiling behind his eyes.

"Magic," her mother finally said, cocking her head as though issuing a challenge.

There was a pause in which the three of them examined her, observing every subtle change in her posture and expression, expertly educated in reading others. The only problem was, Adelina had received the same education.

"We take the magic from witches captured in the bounty. The magic feeds our people, and it offers protection," the duke explained. "Nolofali and its allies have had their sights set on Jumaral's coastline. Huojen is building their naval industry, and—"

"Dumatsyan waters are too cold, and Nolofali doesn't want to kill their ample supply of seafood. Nor do they want to breach their agreements with Almard concerning sea territories," Adelina interrupted. "I've seen the maps and read the reports."

"Then you know that this is *necessary*," Calixto said.

There was a hint of desperation in his tone now, as though he sensed the precipice Adelina was walking along and he was willing her not to throw herself off of it. How much had he told her parents about their previous conversations?

"The last thing that anyone wants, including the people, is the conquering of Jumaral. The reason we celebrate Dom Sebastião is because he offered Jumaral a new perspective: our own country, free from monsters and perfectly poised to take on the world. The people look up to that. They look at Ostrea, the Goddess of the Seas, and see a wide ocean waiting for them, beyond even the end of the world. It is what gives them hope in Jumaral and hope in its monarchy, but that will all be lost without the protection that magic can give them."

Stories are told by those who survive them. You must come to the dead to learn the truth.

"Yes," Adelina said. "I do understand the importance of a story."

There was another bout of silence then, the beat before an explosion hit.

"Then what would you have me do?" she asked. "Break off the engagement after the entire country has already celebrated its inception?"

The duke shifted uncomfortably. The prince and the duchess only maintained their stiff gazes.

"We will speak to Senhor Pinheiro, of course," the duke said. "To get a gauge of his...thoughts. But...in the end...Jumaral is the priority, *couraninha*."

There was pain in his crinkled dark eyes—a deep, endless, harrowing sadness that matched something inside of Adelina. She recognized the unspoken words.

Jumaral is the priority, couraninha. *Jumaral is worth more than Seba's life. Just like it was worth more than Simão's and Manuel's.*

If it was decided Seba needed to disappear, that was what would happen. If they needed to play the engagement off as a youthful mistake, they would. If it needed to include a tragic death, they would ensure it. They had done it all before.

There was a burning sensation in Adelina's eyes, and yet again, this entire thing didn't seem like an act. She was so tired, exhausted by all her own deals and lies. Adelina wanted to cry. She wished to run forward and hide her face in her father's shoulder, sob while he shushed her softly and brushed her hair, told her it would be okay. That he was still there. That he would always be there and that her mother was there. That they loved her and would never hurt her. No one would ever hurt her while they were there.

But she blinked it all back.

She couldn't allow herself to imagine lies. Her parents had helped to kill her brother. They were the reason she experienced this stabbing pain, this deep ache in her gut that could only be smothered by constant motion, the churning of her brain to block out the roiling of something deeper. Adelina would never be safe with them. She never had been. It would be foolish to think anything different.

Do not be afraid to survive, Lady Malves, and to be a little wicked when you do.

"I love Sebastião Pinheiro," she said. "I want to be married to him."

"Your responsibility is to love your country more," the duke said. "I know we have all had a difficult time since Simão...but you cannot let your emotions get the better of you."

It was a slap for her brother's name to come from the mouth of one of his killers. Adelina did not flinch. Instead, she allowed her voice to thicken with emotion. She let one tear slide down her cheek, momentarily blurring her vision.

Look like the innocent flower.

"Yes," she admitted. Her words caught on a small sob. "It has been difficult, and Seba has been the only one there to make it less difficult. Is it really so terrible for him to be here, as my partner?"

"If that's all you wanted, you could have kept him on as a whore," Calixto muttered.

"I could keep everything—all of the magic…complications—a secret from him. He would never have to know."

"But what would happen when he did, Adelina?" the duchess asked. "What would happen if he found out? Would you get rid of him then? Would you put Jumaral first? Could you?"

"I can do whatever is necessary."

"What was necessary was that this ended before it could begin. You already ruined that."

"*He* asked *me* to marry him."

"And you should have said no," the duchess snapped. "You should never have let him believe he had the right to ask you. What were you doing, running to Solmortém with him and Jasibin Guan in a motorcar, of all things?"

"Their guardian just died. They needed to bring the news to their family members, and Jas wasn't doing well. They needed to go quickly, and I had the resources—"

"Then this marriage is between not one but *two* children whose minds are clouded with grief, with no thoughts about their responsibilities or the impact of their actions. Is that what you are telling us?"

"Mamá—" Adelina began.

"Leave us," the duchess ordered.

No one moved.

"Rosália?" the duke said after a pregnant pause.

"Benigno and Calixto," she said. "Leave us."

The duke and the prince shot each other a confused glance.

Adelina watched her mother lift her chin and pull her shoulders back.

"My daughter and I are overdue for a conversation."

CHAPTER 32

SEBA

They had to walk to the castle, a huge stone structure in the distance, from the palace since the trolleys would be too crowded and the risk of someone recognizing them would be too high. Seba had traded his fool's costume for a far less colorful outfit Dalila had been carrying in a burlap bag: a plain waistcoat, a jacket, and a hat.

They merged into the crowds of Fulgeo. Seba's legs burned as they wove up cobbled hills. He had expected Jumaral's capital to just be a larger version of Lis, maybe even more run-down, considering Fulgeo had borne the brunt of the Second Great Wave, but it turned out the city was its very own type of monster.

While in Lis, most buildings were off-white or orange, as if they had baked for different amounts of time in an oven, Fulgeo was a bursting puzzle of color blocks. Bright pinks, blues, and yellows decorated every street, sometimes more than one per building and with a contrasting door making everything look like a child's drawing of a city.

Each street away from the coast was at a slant, on an enormous hill leading up to the Castle of Dom Sebastião. All its buildings grew from the curve. There were entire building faces that seemed to have molded to the shape of a twisting path carved into the hill, as a river might tunnel through a mountain.

Even the new elevator in the center of town, all shining metal and creaking pulleys, looked like it had shot straight out of the ground, like a tree. The entire city held the strange sense of being part of the earth but, with the iron, cobblestone, and trolleys screeching down tracks—sparks flying from the lines they chased—of something purely human.

But even here, the wanted posters for Simão's killer dotted lampposts and storefronts.

The moment he and Dalila stepped onto the charged grounds of the Castle of Dom Sebastião, Seba's skin prickled with the flow of energy, and the hair along his arms and at the back of his neck stood on end. The cobblestones were uneven here, older and smoothed over by time, jutting out at odd angles probably protected by some Board of Jumaralian History—or something of that nature.

He vaguely considered finding out if there was a Board of Jumaralian History, if he was to be the king of Jumaral. Perhaps it was more like an Agency for the Historical Landmarks of Jumaral and the Protection of Such Landmarks. Or even the Foundation of Dangerous and Unideal Cobblestone Preservation.

He had the terrifying urge to laugh.

Dalila seemed to sense the change as well, though her pace didn't waver. They made their way up the wide, winding path toward the high stone walls of the castle.

Seba had now viewed the outside of the Castle of Lis too many times to count, but the Castle of Dom Sebastião was different. Bigger. More preserved—the Foundation of Dangerous and Unideal Cobblestone Preservation must have expanded their work to include all stone-related infrastructure.

Dalila swayed slightly when they stepped from regular Fulgean stone to whatever this was, and he looked over. The color drained from her skin. Was her *witchiness* behind the reaction? Perhaps she was being subjected to whatever kept the bountied witches trapped here. Or maybe she was simply terrified.

The towers flanking the arched entrance were exactly how Seba imagined them to have looked at a different time, when armies and demons had overtaken Jumaralian land before Dom Sebastião had vanquished them. Hopefully, they would be able to hold against an army of the dead too.

It was best not to think about that.

There were two guards on either side of the iron gate, staring down at them while they approached. The beat of Seba's heart increased when they got closer, each step a sign for his body to enter a higher level of panic.

Something about a flower, he thought. *And looking like it.*

It was one of those stupid, dramatic things Adelina had said—the type that truly made him wonder how much of what came out of her mouth was part of a scripted trick and how much was genuine.

Also innocent, he remembered. *Look like the innocent flower.*

It was an important specification. He conjured images of a peaceful field of fresh blossoms. Not red because those looked like blood. Seba settled on a nice yellow, like the sunflowers they had passed on the road between Lis and Solmortém. They were the most innocent flower of them all, staring into the sun like that.

They had reached the red- and green-adorned guards. Dalila pulled the neatly sealed letter from her bag and handed it to the nearest one.

"I am Dalila Marques, lady's maid to Lady Adelina Malves Ducança. This is Senhor Sebastião Pinheiro, to whom Lady Adelina Malves Ducança is engaged to be married. You will find a note from His Royal Highness Crown Prince Calixto, allowing us entry."

Seba was glad Dalila was the only one who had to speak. He would have sounded like a man dangling off a bridge from his ankles, screaming his last pleas for a savior.

They had decided, with Adelina, that the best way to get in was to be honest about their identities. There was simply—Seba noted, with some satisfaction—no one who would be more qualified than themselves to get in. At the time of planning, he hadn't known Dalila's magic to be an option for deception, but there was probably a very good reason she didn't want to use her powers here—the epicenter of trapped witches. If the blood was rushing out of her head just from standing on this ground, what would happen if she tried to cast a spell?

"Remove your hats," the guard grunted.

Dalila and Seba both obliged, allowing their faces to be scrutinized.

"Purpose?"

"An introduction," Dalila replied. "The royal family believes it is time for Senhor Pinheiro to have a better understanding of the family's work in the security of Jumaral."

The guard they were speaking to waved the other guard over, and they engaged in a whispered conversation, referring to the letter with the prince's seal and occasionally glancing back at them.

Seba tried to keep his features still.

Sunflowers, he urged. *Be a sunflower.*

Finally, the guard nodded. "Leave your belongings here." He pointed to the stone wall behind him.

Dalila obediently placed her bag against the wall, and Seba had another strange surge of humor at the thought of the guards opening it and finding a full fool's costume. There was a high screeching sound when the iron gates were unlocked, and the guards dragged one of the sides open for them to pass through. The ends of its bars scraped against the stone.

It was like they had stepped through a portal. The smell was the first thing to hit, tumbling through the air like a disease. Seba fought the urge to put his sleeve under his nose or, better yet, turn around, run away, and never come back. By Our Lady, even Heitor Alves smelled better than this.

At first, it wasn't obvious where the stench came from. Before them was a wide-open courtyard. Olive trees twisted up from cobblestones like enormous weeds. It looked out over a view of the Rio Montes and the land beyond it. The view was so disjointed with the smell, Seba's brain fell into a brief state of shock, unsure where he was or what he was doing.

A guard led them to a path along the outlook, where they walked parallel to the city sprawled underneath. The orange terra-cotta roofs were like little building blocks stepping up the hill. They passed under another series of archways, each a blink of shadow in the afternoon heat.

Then they turned, and the source of the stench was obvious.

Even Dalila, who had been so stoic the entire way despite her increasingly pale skin, pressed a hand to her mouth when the horrific image became clear.

Packed into a space sloping with the remnants of a moat, stone arches, and paths weaving up and around the carcasses of dead trees were hundreds of people. Seba's heart stuttered. They were, in fact, still breathing, but from one glance, they could have all been dead. Most of them were curled into balls or slumped against walls, trees, or each other.

And each of them was—there was no better way to say it—*peeling*. They were deteriorating. Gray flakes of skin and meat pulled back from their skulls. On some of the most shriveled beings, Seba spotted bone.

This time, he had no choice but to raise his sleeve to his nose. He took a few steadying breaths through the filter of the fabric to stop himself from fainting. Was this what would happen to Dalila if she stayed there?

And what would happen to *him*? If this place could do that to witches, a poor sod like him didn't stand a chance.

It was only when Dalila spoke that Seba realized the truly awful thing, the small factor setting his teeth on edge more than whatever wretched thing they had buried in the soil.

The silence.

There was a heavy, almost textured silence here, as if everyone was collectively holding their breath in anticipation of the fall of an axe. That was what made it all work so well, this system. Even from just a few steps away, Seba had been completely unaware there were hundreds of people hidden within the walls of the Castle of Dom Sebastião.

"May we go forward?" Dalila asked. Her voice shook.

"Call out if you need anything." The guard gestured to the walls of the enclosure, where more sentinels walked along the stone. It was ridiculous. They might as well have been guarding corpses.

Actually, that seems like a pretty good idea, Seba amended, thinking about Jas and the impending army of the dead that would very likely—no, no, *not* likely, just maybe—be raining down on him in less than two days. *Please, please guard all corpses necessary. There's no telling what they'll do.*

Dalila passed ahead of Seba, leading him between the bodies. Some of them moved. Many even muttered something, obviously unaccustomed to visitors. But a few remained still, staring at nothing, as if drained.

Dalila whispered to them. "Hello," she would say, searching for eye contact amidst the ocean of strangers.

They all either looked away or stared blankly.

After a few minutes, Dalila hung back so she and Seba walked side by side. Her lips trembled, and her eyes were glassy. "I don't think they're strong enough. They won't be able to do what we need, and we can't force them. We need to get them out."

Seba glanced around. The guards hadn't turned their way, and none of the witches around them appeared cognizant of their presence.

"We can't fail," he said, recalling the snarl Adelina had given him when he had dared to mention the possibility.

"Why?" Dalila stared at him again with teary eyes, which made her blue irises look like twin pools of clear water. "Tell me why."

Damn you, Adelina.

"Adelina and I can help them. We *will* help them. They just need to help us first."

Dalila's forehead crinkled. Seba must have said the wrong thing. But in the space of a second, her gaze focused on a point past his shoulder.

"I know her," she whispered.

Seba followed her gaze. He knew the witch as well. Seba had met her weeks ago in the hills of Lis.

She was the one who had told him he would be king.

CHAPTER 33

ADELINA

The duchess of Lis did not break her gaze with Adelina while the duke and the prince left the hall. Even after the doors boomed shut, there remained a coursing knot of things said and unsaid, known and unknown between the two women.

Adelina had responses ready at the tip of her tongue.

I love him.

I want to be with him.

I miss Simão.

Seba makes me happy.

I just wanted to be happy.

But the words her mother spoke were not ones she had anticipated.

"What is the House of Ducança for?"

All of Adelina's preparation fled her brain. "To rule," she said.

"Rule whom?"

"The people. The people of Jumaral."

"Why?"

Adelina straightened her shoulders. "Haven't we already established that I know my place, Mother?"

"And yet you seem incapable of answering a basic question. I will ask again." Infanta Rosália spread her hands out before her. "Why is it the role of the House of Ducança to rule the people of Jumaral?"

Adelina droned out the explanation she had long been taught. "Because we inherited the right from Dom Sebastião Ducança, who was granted the authority by Our Lady Ostrea."

Her mother's eyes narrowed. Silence gathered between them again.

Slowly, Infanta Rosália shook her head.

It wasn't as much a denial of Adelina's answer as it was a show of disappointment. Embarrassment heated Adelina's cheeks. Her instinct was to begin spouting all the knowledge she had, proving she was not stupid, but she bit her tongue.

Act like the innocent flower.

"We are not special, Adelina." Her mother's voice had softened, but it was not gentle. It slithered up the back of Adelina's neck. "The House of Ducança rules because somebody a long time ago recognized a gap in power and decided to take it on, and a Ducança has been on the throne ever since. It's not divine will; it's momentum."

Adelina became far too aware of the iconography of Ostrea speckled around the room. The silver frame of a painting of the First Great Wave glowed from the setting sun, which had just begun to bleed orange and musty into the room. It was the first time Adelina had ever heard her mother say anything like this. She had never even witnessed one of her family members use Ostrea's name as a curse, like Seba did so often.

Our Lady Ostrea was meant to be respected in every utterance, in every passing thought. Though Adelina had spoken with Ostrea less than two days before, hearing Her will denied by the duchess of Lis brought a lump to Adelina's throat. A latent panic rose from some place Adelina had pushed away, and it made her want to scream, sob, until this awful, dirty feeling had left her.

But she made herself stand still. Adelina clenched her jaw and swallowed past the lump in her throat. Her eyes remained dry.

"So, it's coincidence, then," said Adelina. "That is the integral lesson you wished to share with me?"

"It could be coincidence. It could also be fate. It only matters that we are here now. Because the people need us, Adelina. Our government ensures the people's safety in a world destined to be at war. The House of Ducança is the only one that holds the power, and therefore, we must make the hard choices that will lead to the protection of Jumaral."

"But…" Adelina turned over her thoughts in her mind. "But the House of Ducança takes power from the witches. If this were just about who holds the power, wouldn't it be witches ruling?"

"That is exactly it." Her mother's tone hardened with every word. "Witches *would* rule all, if they could. But which one? It would be anarchy, with no one willing to contribute to one of the strongest resources that Jumaral has—magic. Government is there to put the good of all before the good of a few, and how could that decision be made if it was the few who were ruling?"

Adelina frowned. She had been taught enough political philosophy to recognize the perspective her mother was taking, but it didn't make her mother's point any clearer.

"If my being here at all is barely notable"—Adelina's breath caught on the last word—"then I see no reason why Sebastião Pinheiro is such a problem. He could be taught to make the hard choices and to put Jumaral first, and—"

"But *you* won't."

"Of course I will."

"No." Infanta Rosália clasped her hands in front of her, barely blinking. "If it comes to a decision between Jumaral and Sebastião Pinheiro, your instinct cannot be to hesitate for even a moment. There can be no question in your mind of which must go. You are not ready, Adelina, because everyone can see you making the wrong choice just in the act of agreeing to marry him. Whether it is coincidence or fate that put your bloodline here, your ancestors only maintained that line by making difficult choices—for themselves and for Jumaral. Until you are prepared to kill Sebastião Pinheiro at the smallest sign that Jumaral is threatened, I'm afraid you don't understand your position at all."

CHAPTER 34

SEBA

The witch appeared a bit more gnarled than the last time Seba had seen her, but there was no mistaking her. Her black hair was scraggly, her face deeply lined. A chunk of her cheek was falling away, and her back was hunched worse than ever.

All hail, Sebastião! Hail to thee, Marquis of Lis!
All hail, Sebastião! Hail to thee, Duke of Lis!
All hail, Sebastião, that shall be king hereafter!

"Can you get her to speak to us?" he asked.

Dalila cast another long look at him but then slowly began making her way toward the witch.

"Sebastião Pinheiro," the witch croaked. Her cloudy eyes focused on him. "I hear you have been busy."

Dalila looked between them. Confusion furthered the crinkle on her forehead. "You know each other?"

So Adelina didn't tell you everything, after all.

"We've met," the witch said. Her sharp grin unveiled a series of blackened teeth. "My younger sisters and I performed a deed with no name for the second Dom Sebastião."

Seba wrinkled his nose, mostly because of the smell and partially because of the inordinate amount of meanings that phrase could have. But then everything in him paused. *The second Dom Sebastião.*

"Where are your sisters?" Dalila cast Seba another wary glance.

"Near and far, gone and coming home."

"I'm sorry." Dalila put a hand out to touch the witch's arm, perhaps to comfort her.

"No contact with the prisoners!" a guard shouted from one of the surrounding walls.

Dalila jerked her arm back, and Seba practically jumped out of his skin.

"I'm sorry," Dalila whispered again, this time softer and with her hands in her lap.

What could she possibly have gotten out of that answer that would have made her apologize?

"Hermínia," Dalila began, "the Lady has requested the help of your people."

The witch's eyes widened. "Her majesty has always been bold, though clueless. Does she even know how her life has been intertwined with my people? Her brother's life? His death? Does she understand the predicament of *my* people?" She focused sternly on Dalila while she spoke, and Dalila shifted uncomfortably.

"That's why we need you to stage an uprising," Seba said. "We can help you."

"You can help?" the witch repeated.

At this point, after weeks of being with Adelina and just a few hours in Dalila's company, Seba was tired of being stared at after every sentence he spoke, but he endured the witch's glare.

"Do you understand what this is, *Your Majesty*? I know you can feel it. Even you can feel it buzzing across your skin and crackling through your veins. Magic, like anything, works through balance. The ground here is unbalanced and discordant, draining the life from our bodies as the magic inside of us fights to right itself."

"That's why...that's why it doesn't work here?" Dalila whispered.

"Yes. There's something that they placed beneath all of this stone. It starts slowly and then speeds up. One day here and you'd be sprawled out on the ground with the rest of us. Then one week until your mind goes. One month and you'll wish the world would swallow you up."

"How long have you been here?" Seba asked.

The witch grinned again. "Three days."

"That's comforting," he muttered. They were begging on their knees to a woman tumbling into insanity. And—he was ashamed to admit—this wasn't nearly the dumbest thing he had done in the past few days. Or hours, for that matter.

Damn you, Adelina.

"There has to be a way to free you," Dalila said. "A way to—to restore the balance."

The witch's eyes took on a new sharpness, and she peered at Dalila curiously. "There is a potion, good Dalila. One that many of us know, though none have attempted for risk of destabilizing the world so far...that it breaks."

"So, Dalila makes the potion, we get you all out of here, and then you help us?" Seba asked. "All within a day?"

If she had had the energy, the witch might have cackled. She settled on a leer. "You want the recipe?"

"That might be helpful, yes," Seba replied.

It felt like the witch was challenging them to a dare. She adjusted her spot on the ground and hoarsely croaked out a rhythm that creeped beneath Seba's skin and pulsed within his veins.

> "Round about the cauldron go,
> In the poisoned entrails throw.
> Toad, that under cold stone
> Days and nights has thirty-one
> Sweltered venom sleeping got—"

"Okay," interrupted Seba. "The issue here is that I believe you've named a total of two ingredients, which comes out to two ingredients that we do not have and do not have the time to get. And what even is 'sweltered venom'?"

The witch rocked back on her peeling elbows and stared at them both from behind a grimy chunk of hair. "I am only telling you the answer to the question you posed."

"But we don't have time to do all of that and then get to the rest of...the plan," he finished awkwardly.

"Then it seems you will not be receiving the assistance you seek."

"What if we were able to do it?" Dalila said. "What if we found a way to free you? Would you help? And try to convince others to help as well?"

"Fate is an interesting thing, young witch."

Dalila stiffened at the word.

"We will meet again." The witch paused and drew her gaze slowly over Seba, then back to Dalila. "All three of us."

"When?"

"*Why*." The witch leaned forward, and Seba was in awe of Dalila's ability not to flinch at what must have been a horrendous gust of hot breath being blown directly into her face. "When the hurly-burly's done, when the battle's lost and won."

Dalila nodded stoically.

"What does any of that mean?" Seba asked. "Will you help us or not?"

"I do not help, Your Majesty. I am merely a conduit for larger powers."

"Okay, but will you be a conduit on our side or not?"

The witch sneered, and Seba caught a great whiff of rotting breath. It almost sent him gagging.

"I have only advice, Dom Sebastião." She was picking at the pad of her left thumb. A great flake of skin peeled off, leaving behind a bright red wound. The sight did nothing to improve the nausea already coursing through Seba. "A warning, you might say, one that my sisters and I knew well."

"And what is that?" He glanced firmly away from the spot, as if he had just witnessed the unclothing of a wrinkled slug.

The guards seemed to be getting agitated. They were likely beginning to wonder what the fiancé and maid of the marquise of Lis could possibly be talking about for so long with a witch. Soon, Seba and Dalila would be ushered away, leaving this flesh-and-blood wasteland and its odious stench behind them.

"By the pricking of my thumbs," hissed the witch, "something wicked this way comes."

CHAPTER 35

ADELINA

If it was confirmation Adelina had been waiting for, now she had it. Her family was made up of monsters who didn't have the sense to stake themselves through the heart.

It was no matter. She was there to do it for them.

Adelina would do it intelligently, carefully planned to the last detail. This wasn't just revenge anymore. It wasn't just a coup. This was the kind of revolution from which legends were made. They were too grand for the history books and too real for the religious texts. It was the kind of story that could only be passed down in tales woven into a fabric some mistook for fantasy, which others wrapped around themselves and felt at home.

And it was almost ruined.

But she would fix it. Adelina always did. She would figure it out because she had to. A little more than one day left and the gates of the dead would be opened.

"Tell me again," Adelina said.

She was pacing back and forth in her bedroom in Fulgeo. Dalila and Seba had returned from their business at the castle just a few minutes earlier.

"We need to 'disrupt the balance of the universe,' or something like that." Seba sprawled across the bed with an arm over his eyes.

"Not the universe," Dalila corrected quietly.

"No," Adelina murmured, lost in thought. "Just the castle…"

Hundreds of witches gathered, their magic mixing. Held by their own weapons but with a potion that could free them.

Adelina whirled to face Dalila. Determination set her shoulders. "Potions. Tell me about them."

The crease between Dalila's brows, which had now taken up permanent residence, deepened with confusion.

"Well...magic is essentially a series of transactions, from what I understand. Witches have a biological disposition that allows them to destabilize energy from its natural place, but it all has to go somewhere. That's why I don't—I don't perform a lot of magic. If I make someone go to sleep, all of that waking energy flows into me instead, and a person can't survive with that much energy inside of them."

"What would happen?" Seba sat up with narrowed eyes. "Would you...explode?"

Adelina ignored him. "Do potions make the energy go somewhere else?"

Dalila cleared her throat. "I think so. Instead of accepting the transaction themselves, gathering the energy from certain combinations of ingredients allows them to act as a catalyst. The witches direct the change in energy, but it only runs *through* them instead of adding or being taken away."

"But what if that potion was *made of* magic? Would it need a catalyst then?"

"I—" Dalila's mouth was wide for a moment. She caught on to what Adelina was implying. "I don't know, my lady."

Adelina exhaled sharply through her nose and returned to pacing. All those witches gathered as they were, their magic mixing. It was like a potion of their energy, one that—if Ostrea was to be believed—was meant to be wielded by someone to control an army of the dead.

"And this other potion, the one the witch gave you—"

"Hermínia," Dalila offered.

"Yes, Hermínia. Is it possible that it would work as a counter potion to the first?" She thought of poisons and their antidotes, of Hala threatening to kill her without a drop of spilled blood.

"I just don't understand why the witches wouldn't already have used the potion, if they knew that's what it took to get out," Seba said.

"And then what?" Dalila answered softly, her voice wavering. "Be murdered by the king instead of just drained?"

"They're *witches*. They're more dangerous than—"

"They're witches who have been prevented from learning and practicing magic for decades. Centuries if you count from when Dom Sebastião first blamed them for demons crawling from the sea and made them into monsters. And besides—" Dalila continued when Seba opened his mouth to retort. "They know their reasoning better than you ever will. Just do as they ask."

"Is there another way to disrupt a potion?" Adelina interrupted.

Though she had directed the question at Dalila, it was Seba who answered.

"Of course there is. Jas and I used to do it all the time to—"

Adelina saw the exact moment his memories caught up with him. Seba stiffened, his throat bobbed once, and he ran his hand through his hair so it stood even messier than it had before.

"We did it all the time to Hala," he continued, his tone subdued. "Alchemical potions aren't the same as spellcasting ones. The catalysts are in the ingredients, not from magic. But I would assume you can mess them up the same way. Just add something strong enough that doesn't belong. Most potions are really fragile."

"All magic relies on a system of balance," Dalila added, nodding thoughtfully. "If you disrupt the balance, you disrupt the magic. The issue is that this...*potion* is enormous."

"A cauldron the size of the Castle of Dom Sebastião," Seba muttered.

The pieces of an idea coalesced in Adelina's mind, joining together with satisfying snaps. Her vision clouded with thoughts.

To disrupt this potion would likely destroy it. She would be losing a resource that had been decades, if not centuries, in the making, but perhaps she would have no use for it as queen. Adelina was going to have Ostrea and Jas, who needed nothing except for his natural abilities. As long as the witches repaid her fairly for their freedom, she wouldn't require the stored magic at all.

Except now she had her mother's voice in her head, claiming the people needed someone to make the hard decisions for them. It was possible, maybe even probable, that the witches wouldn't help her. Self-interest would take over, and they would run away.

"Lightning," she said, bringing herself back to the present. "We summon lightning from the sky and strike the castle."

"Lightning?" Seba's mouth twitched as if waiting to laugh at her joke, and even Dalila appeared shocked. "What? Do you know some Goddess of the Skies as well as a Goddess of the Seas?"

"Lightning is a transfer of energy, just like any other. Witches use it all the time."

Dalila frowned. "But conjuring lightning from the sky will be much more powerful, and the heat—"

"Will be excruciating," Adelina finished. "But you are a witch. You're a natural conduit, and you'll be able to split that energy between the three of us. If you remain focused."

Seba straightened. His hand was already in his hair, and his eyes widened with alarm. "*Three of us*?"

"Balance, Sebastião," Adelina said, keeping her eyes on Dalila, whose expression had turned oddly vacant, her cheeks paling. "Triangles are the sturdiest shape, making three the safest number for spellcasting. That's why covens exist. Dalila?"

Dalila blinked once. She returned Adelina's gaze with new resolve. "Of course, my lady," she replied as easily as if Adelina had just asked her for a cup of tea.

"Good."

"Hold on—" Seba held out his hands. "How are we going to be a coven when only one of us is a witch?" He fixed Adelina with a suspicious glare. "Unless you're also—"

"No, I'm not a witch."

"Well then, it's impossible."

"Then I suppose," said Adelina, "we will simply do the impossible."

CHAPTER 36

SEBA

They had a little over twenty-four hours until an ocean goddess brought Her unholy wrath down upon them, but Seba was trying not to think about that. There were so many better things to keep his mind occupied.

Egg custard croissants. Afternoons on the beach. Three hundred thousand *rejas* that could now line his pockets instead of being repaid. If he just filled his mind with those types of things, maybe there would be no room to imagine his own grisly end at the hands of a reanimated corpse.

For a moment, the sound of Jas's skull cracking against stone echoed in Seba's head, making him shiver. He had already had his share of reanimated corpses.

"The question is how to summon and direct lightning."

Adelina's voice drew him back to reality. Seba and Dalila stood on either side of her, staring down at the blank sheet of paper she had withdrawn from the writing desk.

"If we answer it tonight, then we can be done by tomorrow morning and have the witches freed in time to create the Third Great Wave."

"My lady," Dalila murmured, "even if we are able to free them, I don't know if they're willing—"

"We make them willing," Adelina interrupted. "That's not the issue right now."

"Right, the issue is just how to summon lightning without a drop of rain. Simple." Seba ran a hand through his hair, ignoring how his fingers trembled.

Croissants. Just think of all the croissants you'll buy with 300,000 rejas.

"We don't need rain, just a storm." Adelina began drawing symbols on the sheet of paper. The ink smudged while she scrawled.

Seba squinted to try to make out what she was writing. He had always been confused about how someone like Adelina, with her years of lessons in proper penmanship, managed to have the handwriting of a drunk cat.

Seba could make out a series of pluses and minuses, which she connected with lines drawn between mismatching pairs. Then, for each pair, she drew two more lines so they formed triangles. One point was unlabeled.

"This is how a coven works," Adelina said. "Three opposite forces balancing each other out. The problem is that only one of us actually has a force, so we'll have to manufacture the other two. There's a theory that witches operate with a sort of third charge that we don't have, right, Dalila? Not positive or negative, but something else."

Dalila nodded but frowned at Adelina's diagram. "So, you suggest we make some kind of magnets? One for each of you?"

"One positively charged and one negatively charged. That way, we'll be able to balance each other's energy like a real coven, and we can use your magic to summon the lightning."

"Wouldn't they need to be monopoles for it to be strong enough? Each member of the coven has to be an exact opposite, from what I understand."

"Then that's what we aim for," said Adelina.

"Is that possible?"

Adelina bent over the paper and began feverishly sketching something like cubes, but she added arrows going in and out of them so it became an incomprehensible jumble of lines. Seba decided to step away. It wasn't like either Adelina or Dalila were paying much attention to him anyway.

He stared out the window while the conversation started up behind him again, watching the last wisps of sun disappear over the city. It was a bit cloudy, though far from anything capable of bringing thunder or lightning. Those kinds of storms were practically unheard of in Jumaral, especially in the height of summer.

The clouds they had been having recently were strange and cold compared to the crisp blue of the sky they usually experienced. Maybe the weather was trying to stop them. Perhaps it didn't believe in his fate.

In the distance, the elevator's steel platform rose just slightly above the city and connected the lower town to the upper. Would something like that rust if it was caught in the rain? And what would happen to all that metal if lightning struck?

Slowly, an idea trickled into his head.

"Adelina," he said.

"Theoretically," she was saying to Dalila, ignoring him, "if we had an infinitely large sheet of—"

"Adelina," he said louder.

"What?" she snapped. Adelina turned to look at him, like he was an annoying fly.

"What if we just found a lightning rod?"

"Lightning rods don't attract lightning," she said. "They just divert it."

"But instead of us being responsible for the magic, we could just modify a metal rod alchemically or mix alchemy and magic. We make it attract lightning, and then all Dalila would have to do is send a jolt of magic through it to activate it. Then we run some wire to connect it to the earth. That way, we don't have to do the same thing purely by magic, with all that weird magnet stuff that none of us are going to figure out."

Adelina continued to stare blankly at him, but Dalila spoke. "A jolt of magic?"

Seba shrugged. "A lot of alchemy mirrors biology because it relies on the biological changes that witches and humans are already capable of. So, to change one thing into another, we need a catalyst, like you said. That will change a normal rod of metal into something that will allow us to summon and direct lightning. But sometimes, in order to get that thing to work, you need to send it a message, which is what your brain does for your body. So, you can give it any kind of jolt of magic—it doesn't have to be particularly skilled—and that will tell the lightning rod to start working."

He had practically grown up in an illegal alchemical laboratory. If anyone had bothered to remember that, they would know he had picked up a few things.

"Adelina?"

Adelina's lips pursed, and she appeared to be fighting with herself. She turned back to the table and set her pen down without looking at him.

"Fine," she said. "We'll try it."

It was past midnight when they were finally close to done. Or at least, they might be done. The fact that Seba was the primary expert in the room was honestly quite concerning.

The wire had been easy. They didn't have one readily available, but Dalila had pulled out a small spool of white thread for them to transform. It was a simple enough matter transformation similar to the processes Seba had watched Hala perform millions of times. The issue was the lightning rod itself.

They had at least captured the basics. Alchemy, like magic, was about balance. If they wanted to summon water, they had to attract it with fire. The only lightning rod-shaped thing they had was a fire poker, so Seba had shoved that into the flames Dalila started in the grate. Seba had then asked Dalila to fetch several ingredients from the kitchens: prunes, old cakes, dried flowers, anything devoid of moisture that might invite liquid to them.

And then there was the matter of the catalyst—which would change the makeup of the fire poker into something that could summon and direct lightning. Catalysts needed to be biological. Usually, Hala incorporated some organ of an animal that naturally transformed one thing into another thing, like stomach lining or an intestine. The issue was, Seba had no idea of an organ that could make things dry.

"So, Dalila acts as a catalyst, and it becomes a magical potion instead of alchemical," Adelina suggested. She had been shooting annoyed looks at him all night, which made Seba proud rather than admonished.

"I've never made a potion before," Dalila said.

"Now would be a good time to try."

"Maybe if we find something for you to dry out?" Seba scratched his head while he stared into the strange concoction of things they had in the fire. "It might work if it's something biological."

"Get snails from the kitchens," said Adelina. "The royal family would have had some earlier this week for the festival."

Dalila returned ten minutes later with a bowl of snails still in their shells. At Seba's instructions, she dumped them at the edge of the fire and put her hand over them to suck out the moisture from each of their tiny, slimy bodies. Though he couldn't peer into the shells, it was working.

Dalila leapt up, her skin shiny and gray with sweat. She ran into Adelina's washroom, slamming the door behind her just before they heard her heaving up snail slime.

Seba wrinkled his nose and kept his eyes on the fire, which had deepened to a deep purplish color. He hoped that meant it was working.

"We should probably leave it for another hour or two," he suggested. "We'll know it's settled when the fire is back to a normal color."

"I thought you said potions were fragile and exact," said Adelina.

Seba shrugged. "Broad purpose, broad instructions. We just need a storm. Doesn't matter how big or what kind, right?"

"I'd prefer it didn't snow."

"You're just upset you didn't come up with it."

"No, you're just overjoyed by the fact that you did."

"Admit it, Adelina." He nudged her crossed arms. "You need me to stop you from overthinking your way to destruction."

It was then that Dalila returned, her lips white and forehead shining. She set herself on Adelina's bed, and Adelina joined her, stubbornly refusing to look at him.

And so the wait began.

At some point, Seba must have drifted off because, by the time he was startled awake by a hand on his shoulder, there was daylight outside. His heart leapt to his throat. That meant the deadline was today, and—he glanced at the fire, its flames dancing a deep red—the lightning rod wasn't done yet.

Adelina was looking down at him, brows raised expectantly.

"What?" he groaned.

"The plan isn't ready yet, so we need to act normal. We're going for a walk in the gardens."

Seba let himself be dragged around the city and the palace for hours, taking meals with Adelina in plain view of the servants but eating almost nothing. For once in his life, his stomach didn't seem very inviting toward food. Dalila stayed sentinel the whole day, making sure no one noticed the strange fire flickering in Adelina's bedroom.

"You said a few hours," Adelina hissed when she and Seba returned to check on it before dinner. The flames were still just a shade too red to be ready.

"Well, I've never exactly done this before. It's possible that our rather broad ingredient list didn't make for the most efficient reaction."

"We need enough time after the witches are freed for them to summon the Wave, and there are only six hours left."

"Believe it or not, Adelina, that knowledge won't actually speed anything up."

Dalila stood quietly near them with her arms crossed, frowning into the flames. It would be nightfall soon, and each breath Seba took was like a countdown to the bomb that would go off that night if they didn't manage this. He swore, turning from the flames with his arms over his head, and fought to steady himself.

Three hard knocks pounded against the door.

Both Adelina and Dalila immediately jumped into action, while Seba stood frozen. Anyone who walked in would see the strange color of the flame and know something was wrong. Before Seba could even process the fear of being found out, the all-consuming terror of observation that had swirled in him for weeks but only emerged at times like this, Dalila was opening the door.

Adelina caught Seba's hand and pulled him in front of the fire-place, her expression flirtatious. Behind him came the voice of Nuno, Prince Calixto's servant.

Nuno, who would soon be out of a job.

"Dalila," Nuno was saying. "Sorry to interrupt, but you're needed in the kitchens for a moment."

"In the kitchens?" Dalila repeated.

Seba tensed, picturing everything they had taken from the kitchens last night. Adelina giggled and pushed him down onto one of the uncomfortable velvet chairs. He had forgotten how to sit.

"That's right," Nuno replied. "What, do you need help finding them?"

"No, it's just that I'm very busy at the moment. Is this urgent?"

"Very."

"Is there no one else that can help?"

"Not in all the world. You have a particular set of skills."

The words made Seba's skin crawl. He was barely aware of the pressure on his legs when Adelina draped herself over him. The fabric of her dress caught against his neck.

"Can it not wait?" Dalila sounded much calmer than Seba felt.

"I'm afraid it can't."

"Just go, Dalila," Adelina said airily, drawing Nuno's attention past Dalila's shoulder to where Adelina was practically sitting on Seba's lap, her fingers lacing themselves through his hair.

Nuno's ears turned pink.

"I'm so sorry for the inconvenience, my lady."

"Think nothing of it, Nuno," she said. "I'm sure Dalila will make it back as soon as she can to resume her duties."

"Of course, my lady." Dalila cast them one more glance before following Nuno down the corridor. The door clicked shut behind her.

Adelina untangled herself from him and leapt to her feet.

"Why did you do that?" Seba hissed. "Weren't we just talking about the fact that we have *six hours* before an army of the dead comes crashing into your bedroom? How is sending away the only witch we have going to help that?"

"It was the only way," Adelina snapped. "Dalila couldn't do anything to him. She's used enough magic already, and we need her later. It's very likely there's a horde of servants waiting for them in the kitchens. Or, at the very least, Calixto is waiting in whatever trap they set for her. A body this early on would have put a target on our backs, which is the last thing we need."

"Then what do we do now?"

"We wait for the lightning rod, and we make contingency plans."

"Like?"

"Like—"

But she didn't get to finish.

There was no knock this time before the door slammed open. A different figure was in the doorway. This one was tall and broad shouldered, neatly dressed in a black suit, with a graying head of hair and a remarkably familiar face.

"Lady Adelina," the man said. His voice boomed with authority, and there was an odd ringing in Seba's ears, even though the man spoke at a normal volume. "Senhor Pinheiro. I've been looking forward to having a conversation with you."

Seba's breath wheezed away as Dom Aristides, King of Jumaral, stepped into the room with the heavy gait of undisputed power. He shut the door behind him.

ACT V:

O HORROR, HORROR, HORROR!

CHAPTER 37

ADELINA

There was no chance to block the fire from her uncle like she had with Nuno, but it didn't matter. The look he was giving her—carefully stilled around the eyes and mouth, head slightly tilted to the side, chin lifted—was not the one he had used when she, Simão, and Calixto had broken the chandelier in the portrait hall ten years ago. It was the one she had only seen a few times, all when her uncle was staring down the men who dared to disagree with him in court and council meetings.

It was the look he gave to remind people he was the king.

Not for long, Adelina thought. *In six hours, you will be dead, and I will wear your crown.*

The thought sent a shudder through her chest. This was just an obstacle on the path she had carved for herself. Like any other, she would cut her way through it.

"Good evening, Tio," she said pleasantly. "I missed you during the meeting yesterday. I've heard that you've been very busy."

The king's expression remained stony. Seba trembled behind her. The nerves radiated off him, even without Adelina seeing his face.

"May I introduce my fiancé?" she continued. "Tio, this is Sebastião Pinheiro. Seba, my uncle. Dom Aristides."

Some sort of choked sound made its way out of Seba's throat, but he jerkily lowered himself into a bow. "Your Majesty," he croaked. "It's—it's an honor."

The king spared Seba barely a glance, as though he were an unremarkable stray dog on the side of the road. He stared at Adelina for a long time, and she glared back.

"Adelina," her uncle finally said, "why don't you explain to me what you are doing?"

"I'm getting married to the man I love."

"And why was that man seen with your maid at the Castle of Dom Sebastião yesterday?"

"Your son and my parents expressed concern that Seba wouldn't understand the ways of the family. I've heard it's best to learn through experience."

"I find it interesting that you wouldn't go with him, then. I don't believe you've ever visited yourself."

"I was at the meeting, which I'm sure the rest of our family members can confirm."

"So, you sent him off to fix a problem that hadn't yet been posed to you?"

Adelina shrugged. "I've been told I'm perceptive."

"Is that how you knew about the castle at all? You're perceptive?"

"I had a very good education."

The king's focus flicked to the fire poker sitting within the red-tinged flames.

"Tell me, Adelina," he said. "Have you ever found any gaps in your education?"

Adelina forced her breathing to remain steady. "I've noticed that I lack certain skills in the culinary arts. Why? Did you *leave* any gaps?"

The king's eyes narrowed almost imperceptibly, and he considered her for a moment, perhaps wondering how much she could know and how much he was still in danger of revealing.

"Your brother thought he'd had gaps in his education. He went looking for other teachers," he finally said.

Adelina's pulse jumped. "My brother was a smart man."

"So was your cousin."

"Calixto?" she asked, knowing fully well he wasn't talking about her living cousin.

"Manuel," he corrected. "But I think that, in many ways, you might be smarter. You're not so prone to rash decisions. You're less emotional. You act on facts."

Adelina paused, just for a moment. "I learned from the best."

Seba's breathing now was practically gasping. The king needed to leave quickly.

"So, you understand why I might be confused by your engagement?"

"I understand that you might not be able to fully comprehend loving someone enough to put them over your duty," she said.

The memory of a woman floated somewhere in the back of her mind, smiling across from a five-year-old Adelina while they played a game of paddle ball on the white sand of the beach. Her own mother's words from just the day before echoed in her mind, about the difficult choices that kept Jumaral safe.

The king showed no reaction to Adelina's reference to her Tia Undina.

"I think I might understand you better than many people. I understand that you want power. I understand that you are angry. I understand that those two things combined, in a sharp mind like yours, are a recipe for ambitious plans. I understand these things because you are like me. You are more like me than my brother or either of my sons, and you would make a fine leader." The king tilted his head to the other side and stared at her with something that might have been pride. "I would hate to see you waste your ruthless heart on a plan that will not work."

Adelina swallowed the bile rising in her throat. "My only plan," she said carefully, "is to marry Sebastião Pinheiro."

The king's eyes crinkled at the corners with some demented humor.

"Don't lie, Adelina." He took a heavy step forward, and she had to tilt her head back to maintain eye contact. "Not to me."

"It's not a lie!" broke a voice behind her.

The king and Adelina both turned to Seba, who appeared pale and faintly ill. His hair was completely on end, and the shadows under his eyes made them look like they were popping out of his skull. But he was staring straight at Adelina.

"Thank you, Seba," she said firmly, hoping he would get the message to shut up.

"No, I—I won't let him say that we don't love each other. Because—" Seba struggled with his words. He gulped. "Because I love you, Adelina. I love you, I love you, I love you, and I want to marry you, and I won't let anyone tell me that what we have isn't real because...because this is it. This is the only real thing."

There was a desperation in his voice, a violent energy to the way he was looking at her. It somehow masked whatever his intentions were.

She stiffened. Had Sebastião Pinheiro finally learned to lie?

"We've—" To her horror, he let out a loud sob. "We've both been through so much, and we've lost so many people, and—and this is it. You are my fate, Lady Adelina. You are my destiny, and I'm yours. I love you, I love you, I love you." He paused, face still screwed up as if he was about to cry. His eyes drifted down to her lips. "May I?"

And before Adelina had even finished nodding, he was wrapping his hands around her waist, slipping his fingers under the fabric of her jacket to settle against her blouse, and pressing his lips against hers.

It was wet and clumsy, and he was shaking. Adelina had to remind herself to relax her body, to lean into him, to hold his sweaty face in her hands and kiss him back. None of the stirring lauded in songs and poetry elevated her heart, and no sparks flew between them, literal or imagined.

But still, even knowing it was unimportant, and even knowing that her uncle, the king of Jumaral—who had every reason to kill them both—was standing barely an arm's length away, a little voice whispered in the back of her head: *This is my first kiss...*

And then Seba, still trembling, drew away from her. His eyes were wide with fear and something else Adelina could not name.

"I—" He stuttered. His focus flicked back to the king. "I'm sorry. That was...um..." He stepped away, as though abruptly aware of what he had done. Seba twisted his hands behind his back. "I'll just...I'll stand over here now."

Seba awkwardly moved past the king, flattening himself along the wall to avoid brushing against him. He settled himself in a chair by the window. Seba dropped his head and wrapped his arms around his stomach like a scorned child.

Adelina had been caught off guard—by *Seba*, no less—and mentally shook herself. Whatever that had been, it didn't matter.

"As you can see," she said to her uncle, who had kept his expression expertly neutral throughout the entire affair, "we love each other very much."

"Yes," the king replied slowly. "Would you like to know another way that we are similar, my niece?"

"Oh, I'm thrilled by the prospect."

"We are not afraid to do what we must to protect that which we love. You see, *I* love my country, so I do whatever it takes to protect it. You love something too." He cast a pitying glance in the direction of Seba's crumpled form. "I doubt it's Sebastião Pinheiro, but I respect your ability to convince him otherwise."

"And what would you say I *do* love?"

"I'm not sure. I only hope that it doesn't interfere with the security of Jumaral. I would hate to imagine which of us would win in a battle of wills."

"Then what do you propose?"

The king took another step closer. "Your parents—my dear brother and sister-in-law—coddle you. I won't. I'll speak to you like a powerful member of the House of Ducança because that is what you are. I propose a deal."

"What's the deal?" Adelina tried to hide her impatience.

"The current arrangement isn't working, so I will give you the choice of what to do next." He lowered his chin to better meet her eyes. The angle of the light from the chandelier sent shadows over his face, making Dom Aristides look like a backward version of

Adelina's father. "The problem is that you and Sebastião cannot be together. There are two solutions. He goes…or you do. Make the choice, and all of this will be forgotten."

Adelina's resolve began to crack, and her pulse jumped into her throat. She pressed her lips together to keep them from trembling or from allowing a whimper to escape. Seba was shaking so much his chair rattled against the floor.

"Go?" she said, her throat tight. "Like Simão? And Manuel?"

Her uncle's lips split into an ugly grin. "They didn't even get a choice," he said, as if this was some sort of consolation. "Not like you do."

"How long do I have to decide?"

She heard the click of a pistol's safety being released.

Her uncle's hand clasped a handle at his waist.

For half a second, Adelina allowed her eyes to close. She had been so stupid. Adelina had spent so long believing she was invincible, that practicality and fate were her armor. Even in the past few days, she had thought her death would be strategically organized, made to seem the result of a motorcar accident or the suicide of a mourning sister. But, of course, it wouldn't be. Her killer was the king of Jumaral. She would die any way he pleased.

"Choose," the king whispered. "You or him?"

Fair is foul and foul is fair.

The plan was finished.

Do not be afraid to survive, Lady Malves…

But she could still find a way to be queen. She could still go on.

…and to be a little wicked when you do.

Jumaral's security would be threatened by her death. She understood her position now.

"I—"

But Adelina never got to respond.

There was a sound like a bucket scraping across wet sand, a startled cough, and then a spray of something hot and wet all over Adelina's face and clothes. She barely had the sense to back up before her uncle collapsed, slamming into her and crashing onto the ground with a yell.

There was a sound like gurgling and then drowning. Her uncle twitched on the ground in front of her, blood pouring from the open slash across his neck and soaking across the floorboards.

He went still.

Everything went still.

Adelina was left staring at Seba, whose front was speckled with dark red, a dripping dagger still raised in his blood-soaked left hand.

CHAPTER 38

SEBA

There was a dagger in Seba's hand.

He had put it there. Seba had gone up to Adelina, slipped his hands under her jacket, taken the dagger she kept there, and tucked it into his sleeve. He had slashed the throat of the king of Jumaral.

And he was pretty sure he had killed the king of Jumaral.

The air was stuck in his throat. Any fatigue he had been feeling before was swiped cleanly from his mind. He would never sleep again. Seba had murdered sleep.

The frozen silence of the room was broken by a low gurgling. Seba watched waves of blood pour from the open wound in the neck of the man at his feet. He looked up at Adelina, waiting for her to check the king's pulse, like she had done when he had beaten Jas over the head with a rock.

But she just stood there, staring down at her uncle with a blank look. Her hands were held out as if to catch him, dripping with blood. Her whole front was soaked with it, and some even splattered across her face.

It was on his own skin, burning hot. Seba wiped at his face with the hand not holding the dagger. That hand was so saturated, he doubted all the waters of Ostrea's ocean could clean it now. His fingers came away smudged dark red.

Seba was shaking, he realized vaguely. It was strange, considering time had paused. He shouldn't have been able to breathe, much less tremble. He ran a bloody hand through his hair, and it molded to his touch.

"Seba?" For the first time since he had known her, Seba detected a tremor in Adelina's voice.

"Yes, dear?" Because he couldn't think of anything else.

They were both still watching while her uncle's body bled out between them.

"What did you do?"

"I—"

"You took my knife."

"Yes."

She finally tore her eyes away from her uncle, and they landed on Seba. He wished they hadn't. They were the eyes of someone who was damned experiencing that damnation for the first time.

"I would have handled it." Adelina straightened. He watched the pieces of her being pulled back together, control reasserting itself over her basic instincts.

"He was going to kill—" *You*, Seba wanted to finish. *He was going to kill you.*

But he knew Adelina too well for that. She would have told the king to kill Seba. It wouldn't have even been a question in her mind.

"One of us had to die," Seba amended. *Either me or the king.*

Adelina's jaw tightened. "I was handling it. That is what I do. I handle things. You are supposed to do as I say."

"I saved our lives, Adelina."

"No, you sentenced us," she snapped. "If you had stuck to the plan we agreed to, everything would have been sorted. We would have diverted the blame to divine will and been able to take our thrones without a problem. Now, thanks to you, we have a body to explain. Did I not just tell you that it was too early for a body?"

Seba almost threw his hands in the air in frustration, but there was a dripping dagger in one of them.

"*The plan was already over.* By Our *Lady*, Adelina," he cursed.

The words were sticky and gross in his mouth. The smell of blood was beginning to cut through the air, and Seba wrinkled his nose. Our Lady of the Seas was nothing more than a human, trapped, scared, and looking for ways to hurt the ones who put her there. Just like the rest of them.

"You're the one that sentenced us the second you took our problem to a *goddess*, and now, instead of just being killed by the royal family or locked up in a castle, we have to worry about *an invasion of the dead*."

Adelina looked like she was going to argue but seemed to bite her tongue. Instead, she reached down to her uncle's side and took something from his hand. Her expression was eerily still while she extricated the pistol from the pool of blood.

"What are you doing?" Seba asked.

"Getting a weapon. Seeing as you've stolen mine."

Seba adjusted his grip on the knife, smearing some of the blood across the handle with his thumb. He hadn't been aware of how tight he was holding it, but now his fingers were stiff and aching.

"Why didn't you use it?" he asked.

She wiped the pistol carefully on her skirts to clear it of blood. A moment of hesitation.

"I would have," she said firmly.

But Seba didn't believe it. He had stolen the knife from her before he had even known about the king's deal. Seba had decided to take it the moment the king called her smart and Adelina's demeanor had shifted. This was her uncle, and she wouldn't have been able to do it.

Adelina had never wanted to. She had gone to the lengths of hiring the Knell, consulting with alleged goddesses, and recruiting an army of deteriorating witches to avoid just that act. So, he had taken her knife because he wasn't going to let this partner fail him too. Seba wasn't going to give her that option.

"Of course you would," he said, and she glared at him. "But now you have your answer, don't you?"

"What answer?"

Seba gestured at the body in front of them. More blood splattered from the movement of the dagger and mingled with the growing puddle.

"I choose you. I choose *you*, Adelina."

There were several beats of silence between them before the first uncharacteristic cracks in Adelina's armor appeared. Her lips parted just slightly, and her shoulders fell for half a second. But that was when the conversation ended.

A knock made them both jump out of their skins.

Seba almost threw the dagger across the room, as if the evidence wasn't in the blood splattered over him and Adelina. At this point, the king's blood was likely soaking through the floorboards.

"My lady?"

It was Dalila's voice, but neither of them made any move to go to the door. Adelina opened her mouth, armor fully back in place. Seba expected her to call something back in response. Instead, she rounded on him and mouthed something.

"*What?*" he mouthed back.

"*Check under the door,*" she whispered, then gestured down to her bloodstained shoes. *Feet.*

"*Do it yourself,*" he hissed back.

She pursed her lips and waved her hands around the ample amount of skirt hanging from her waist.

"My lady?" Dalila called again. "May I come in?"

Adelina motioned him furiously toward the door, and Seba finally raised his hands in surrender. He stepped lightly across the floorboards, trying to ignore the squelching sound of his shoes unsticking from the congealing blood. After transitioning to his hands and knees, he crouched to press his cheek against the hardwood, peering through the gap under the door.

"Lady Adelina?"

Seba tensed when the doorknob rattled, sure the door was about to swing open on his face and take out an eye. But the king must have locked it when he walked in. On the other side of the door was only one pair of black leather boots and the edges of a white apron. He straightened and nodded at Adelina, who gestured for him to unlock the door.

"Yes, come in, Dalila," she called.

Seba opened the door just wide enough for Dalila to enter, keeping himself hidden so she wouldn't react to the blood until she was safely in the room.

As soon as she crossed the threshold, he snapped the door shut and relocked it.

There was a pause while she took in the scene.

Seba, his back pressed against the door, still holding his bloody dagger—he really needed to let it go at some point, but he wasn't sure when or if he would ever remember to do that; Adelina, carefully controlled tension rippling through her every limb as she stood in her almost-white dress that was now painted red, a blood-smeared pistol clutched in her hand; and the king of Jumaral, face down on the ground, blood pouring from the open slash in his neck and seeping into the carpet.

"We've hit a bit of a snag," Seba finally said.

Dalila released a shuddering breath, as if she had been hoping it could pause time. Or perhaps that was just what Seba was doing.

"And we are dealing with it," Adelina added, as if she were daring the world to disagree. "We have a little over five hours left and one job already done."

She was most likely only taking this newly optimistic perspective to stop Dalila from panicking, but Seba still had the urge to yell a loud and satisfactory "You're welcome!"

"We can still get the rest done," Adelina continued. "We just need to adjust."

Dalila said nothing. She had gone as pale as she had been at the castle.

"Dalila?" Adelina's stare was as sharp as the blade that had torn through her uncle's neck.

"I..." Dalila's voice wavered and then focused. She directed her attention at Adelina, blinking away the sight of the dead king. "I'm afraid we may have less time than that, my lady. I was called down to the kitchens to help with setting a menu for Senhor Pinheiro."

"Why?" Seba interrupted. The thought of a formal gathering of people to discuss and plan ways to please him was both off-putting and intriguing.

"They noticed you haven't been eating and wanted to know what you would enjoy."

"Well, what did you say?" Seba happily allowed the aroma of fresh croissants from the bakery two streets down from the apothecary to fill his memory, overcasting the stench of body and rot.

"Is now really the time?" asked Adelina.

He glanced down at the king's fallen form, then back at Adelina. "I must say that my future culinary enjoyment at this palace does seem like a rather timely issue."

Before Adelina could respond, Dalila continued, "Nuno was also asked to be present, but someone came to fetch him a few minutes ago. I heard them whispering that something happened to Prince Calixto, and then Nuno was rushing away. I made an excuse about you needing me as well, and I came here."

Seba ran a hand through his hair and shuddered at the congealed shape it had taken. "What does that mean? What happened to Calixto?"

"He knows." Adelina looked down at her uncle. "He knows his father is dead, or maybe he can just feel that something has changed, but he doesn't know what it means. The chains to Ostrea will have automatically passed to Calixto when Aristides died, and now he can feel its pull. We need to move quickly."

"What chains?" Dalila asked warily.

"It doesn't matter. Calixto and my father both need to die tonight, and the deadline is tighter than we thought. We'll have to find a way to stage the Wave without the witches."

Ha ha, "deadline," Seba thought. He barely avoided a delirious giggle.

"We're going to leave them there?" Dalila asked sharply, her eyes burning. "We're going to leave all of those people rotting in the castle?"

Adelina brushed her maid off easily. "I can free them once I'm queen."

"*Queen*?" Disbelief twisted Dalila's pale features. "Is that what this is about, Adelina? You want to be queen?"

"No, I *must* be queen, and I do what I must. If this is not sufficient reasoning for you, Dalila, then I suggest you tell me now."

The look that passed between the two girls was nothing short of a blaze, and for a moment, it seemed Dalila might finally say no to her precious Lady Adelina. But when she replied, a shadow passed over her face.

"Of course, my lady," Dalila said.

"Good." From Adelina, it sounded like a threat. "It will have to be done soon. And around the same time. Calixto is already feeling the effects of his father's death, which means my father would feel the effects of Calixto's death almost immediately. We can't leave my father alive long enough for him to take action."

"So, one of us goes to kill Calixto, and one of us kills your father. Or we can get them both to this room and do it at the same time," Seba suggested.

"No, they can't come here. Without the help of all of the witches, we won't be able to ensure that the servants aren't paying attention. And we can only ask them to believe one unbelievable thing. It will be too suspicious for them to all die in my bedroom, even if we do find a way to make it look like Ostrea's doing."

Dalila released a soft breath and leaned against the wall with her eyes closed.

In that moment, all Seba wanted was to be back at the cliffs of Solmortém so he could lean over that void of water and scream until his lungs were empty and his throat burned. But another flickering thought slowly made its way to the front of his mind, gilded and glittering.

In just a few hours, I will practically be king.

"What if..." he started slowly. "What if we flooded the palace anyway?"

Adelina pushed her shoulders back. "Explain."

"Hala was always trying to turn things into gold. It's one of those classic alchemy things. She'd use water because it was easy to get from the well or the ocean or wherever, and eventually, she figured out how to turn gold into water, but not the other way around. She thought she could figure out the reverse process if she just studied it enough."

Adelina blinked. Something like disbelief softened her icy expression. "We turn all of the gold in the palace into water."

Seba nodded. "Do you think enough of it is real?"

"Oh, yes," Adelina replied darkly. "It's about the only thing that is. It won't exactly be a Great Wave, but it should be close enough for us to spin our story. How do we do it?"

Luckily, this was one of the few alchemical recipes Seba knew by heart. He and Jas had usually been tasked with finding the ingredients and would often drink the water when they didn't feel like going to the city well. For it to work across the entire palace, the ingredients would just have to be bigger and stronger than the usual rat intestines and loose leaves.

Seba scribbled the steps onto the top sheet of paper on Adelina's desk while the girls leaned over his shoulders.

When he finished, all of them were silent, staring down at the list of ingredients.

"I suppose it's all manageable," Adelina finally said, her voice tight. "As long as it's done faster than the other one."

Seba nodded. Unlike the other, this one would be carefully measured.

"Manageable?" Dalila drew away from them.

Adelina slowly inhaled and exhaled. "Everything we need is in this palace. We'll work it out now, quickly, and then we split up to kill my father and Calixto."

"But the witches—"

Adelina whirled on her maid. Her shoulder slammed painfully into Seba's chest, as if he wasn't even there. "*We've already discussed it, Dalila.*"

Dalila's lips quivered, but she met Adelina's furious glare with an impressive calm. Seba rubbed at the sore spot at his chest.

"By the time the night is up," said Dalila, "the king's body will not be presentable as a simple act of fate. *Think*, my lady."

Adelina's jaw ticked.

"You will be fighting suspicion on all sides, even with the support of Our Lady. You can't afford to break *another* promise to the witches and have them turn against you too."

For a terrible second, it appeared Adelina would finally break, that the sharp scent of blood soaking her hands and her front had finally cut through whatever barrier remained in that inscrutable brain of hers.

"Fine," Adelina said.

Seba frowned, convinced he had misheard. Dalila seemed almost equally as surprised.

"But we still need three people," Seba reminded her. "To summon the lightning, even with the rod. Dalila's magic jolt needs stability. And we don't have time for us all to get there while also killing the prince and duke simultaneously."

"Calixto will be the third," Adelina said. "I'll stay here, put together the alchemical spell, and kill my father. You two need to lure Calixto to the castle. He'll be able to access emergency transportation that will get you there faster than anything else. Summon the lightning and use the wire to get it into the grounds of the castle. That will unbalance the potion and release the witches. Send the lightning through Calixto so he dies too. If we add enough reality, the illusion will become invisible."

There was a finality to what she said, and the air between the three of them shifted from something erratic and unpredictable to... settled.

"Give me the knife," Adelina demanded, breaking the silence and reaching a hand toward him.

His grip on it tightened, but he couldn't have said why.

"I want to clean it," she said impatiently. "And you should clean yourself up before you go to see Calixto."

He slowly raised the dagger, with the blade pointed toward Adelina. One lurch would send it straight past her hand and into her heart. She took it gently, her fingers briefly wrapping around his. Adelina released the weapon from his hold, like she was avoiding sudden movements.

"We should clean you up as well, my lady." Dalila immediately rushed into action, pouring water from a pitcher on the vanity over towels.

Seba washed his face quickly and tried to rinse his hair but opted for a hat when it was taking too long. He changed into the only other set of his clothes in the room, which were much too formal for a murder. Perhaps more appropriate for a funeral.

Best to always be prepared, he thought.

The blood was caked into his fingernails and the creases of his left hand, so he pulled on a pair of white gloves.

Adelina stepped out from behind her privacy screen. For the first time that night, Seba's breath was drawn away by something that wasn't eternal dread.

He might not have been dressed for a murder, but Adelina certainly was. She wore a red evening gown, dark as rubies. It wrapped around her curving figure like folds of water clinging to stone. Her hair was neatly pinned back away from her face, revealing knots of shining gold adorning her ears. She still somehow radiated the energy of a wraith, here to drag them all to a slow death, but her skin was warmer, and the hollows beneath her eyes didn't look quite so deep.

Seba was suddenly struck with the realization that his fiancée was beautiful.

And probably insane.

Adelina carefully avoided the pool of her uncle's blood, and Seba understood the genius of the dress's color. Any spilled blood wouldn't be as noticeable.

Dalila removed the fire poker from the flames, which were finally back to normal.

Adelina joined him at the vanity, and the rosiness of her perfume wafted over him. It almost masked the stench of death. She drew close to him so their shoulders touched. Seba could easily have bent down to kiss her again.

"Here," she said quietly, handing him her uncle's pistol.

He took it, gripping the unfamiliar weight of a loaded cartridge in his gloved hands. Even while on his thievish exploits with Jas, Seba had never wanted bullets in his gun. He didn't like to think that something he did would recreate the sounds that had come just before every finger on his hand had been snapped that time at the festival. But now he wondered if his mother's blood would have been on Hala's shoes if those sounds had just been better directed.

"What about the knife?" he murmured.

"This will be better for long distance." She leaned in, and he smelled coffee on her breath. "Remember to use it. On anyone."

Her eyes momentarily flicked to where Dalila was looking over the poker, and Seba understood. *On anyone.* He tucked the pistol into his waistband, pressed his hand against her back, and bent so his lips were at her ear. They still had a romance to play up, after all.

"Remember to be ruthless," he whispered. *Ruthless enough to kill your father. Ruthless enough to follow through with the plan. Ruthless enough not to betray me.*

He expected her to glare at him or snap that she didn't need a reminder. Instead, she slowly turned her head so their eyes met. She dipped her chin once.

"Are you ready to go, Senhor Pinheiro?" Dalila called from the other side of the room.

"I most surely am, Dalila," Seba replied. He did not break eye contact with Adelina while they drew away from each other.

Adelina held out her right hand, and he took it.

"Dearest partner of greatness," she said.

"The one and only," he replied.

They shook on every deal they had ever made.

CHAPTER 39

ADELINA

It had been less than a minute since Seba and Dalila had left the room, and already Adelina was bent over her wash basin, heaving. Her uncle's body was behind her, out of sight but still swimming through her mind. Her skin prickled with his blood, and every breath was like inhaling a mite that would eat away at her insides until she was nothing but a bloody pile of fleshy chunks.

The bile burned her throat as it rose, but she had barely eaten, and all that came out was a thin, brown trickle from the coffee roiling in her stomach.

Stop it, she told herself. *Focus*.

She heaved again, and her teeth chattered. Spots of light sparked in her vision.

Stop.

Adelina lifted her sleeve to her nose, forcing herself to breathe the air holding her uncle's dying breath.

In.

Out.

In—

Her stomach lurched again, and she rocked forward. Simão had been the one to teach her to breathe, to count each inhale and exhale, to force her mind to focus while her lungs allowed her body to recover. It was what he had always done before he went into a ballroom or got on a stage.

In.

Out.

She was doing it for him. For herself. For Ostrea and the witches and Seba and everyone who had been wronged by the House of Ducança.

In.

Out.

Tear the stars from the sky...

After an exorbitantly long minute, Adelina's vision cleared, and the nausea lessened. She clenched her teeth to keep them from chattering and braced herself on the vanity. She rose, swaying slightly on her feet. There was a flash of red and gold in the mirror, but Adelina didn't stop to look at her reflection.

It was nearing eight in the evening, and her father would already be in bed. He had always been the type to go to sleep early, even on nights of parties and state dinners. If anyone needed him, he could always be found watching the sunrise the next morning.

Her mother wouldn't have joined him yet. She would likely be in the drawing room, enjoying a glass of wine before bed. It was no matter. Her mother's death would have been wasteful. Irrational.

A shiver ran through Adelina's body, and she clenched her teeth harder.

There was still blood under her fingernails, but there was no use in getting rid of it. She allowed her fingers to drift to her side, where the dagger was stuck in her pocket.

In the moment her uncle had leered over her, Adelina's thoughts had been far from the dagger she had kept tucked at her waist for weeks. She had assured Seba she would have used it, but in reality, she had no idea if the thought even would have occurred to her.

No matter. Adelina removed the dagger from her pocket. *I will not make the same mistake twice.*

She had given the pistol to Seba, which meant she would need to be within an arm's length of her father when she did it. Adelina would watch the fear in his eyes, perhaps witness a last plea. Should she try to cover his face?

She stopped herself. Something told her to make him watch, even if it meant she had to watch as well.

The clock ticked to eight. It was time.

She wiped the back of her bloodstained hand across her mouth and forced herself to take one last inhale, letting the stench of death set her veins on fire rather than destroy her. Before she murdered her father, there was one thing left to do.

Adelina marched across the room, eyes fixed on the spot of the king's stomach where she would make the first incision. She stubbornly ignored the puddle of blood soaking her bedroom floor.

CHAPTER 40

SEBA

"I need you to follow me on this," Dalila murmured. She led Seba up a servant's staircase to the prince's bedroom.

"I *am* following you," Seba pointed out.

"No, I mean that when we talk to Prince Calixto, you have to trust me."

"Are you going to tell me what you're going to say?"

"No."

"Why not?"

"Because I don't think you'll like it."

Seba rolled his eyes at her back. The weight of the pistol at his side was heavy on his mind. He was so sick of being the one everyone hid things from. Seba had just killed the king of Jumaral. He wasn't incompetent.

It took Adelina's stern voice in his head to make him shove aside the idea of taking control again, of ridding himself of yet another person who didn't appreciate him, who would betray him at the slightest sign of something greater.

Look like the innocent flower.

Seba would have time to be the serpent underneath, but only after this plan had been followed through. Soon, everyone would know there was nothing greater than Sebastião Pinheiro.

They came out into that same corridor of cushy carpet and leering portraits, but now, the setting sun cast shadows over every intricate carving. The weighted silence was punctuated by nervous whispers from people they couldn't see yet. Dalila squared her shoulders, reminding Seba forcefully of the fact she and Adelina had grown up together. Did he and Jas have similar mannerisms? Were there parts of themselves they had both taken from Hala?

With a pang, he thought of her excited shriek the first time she had turned gold into water, the way she had woken twelve-year-old Jas and Seba in the middle of the night to have them taste it. What would she have thought of the way her recipe was being used now?

He and Dalila turned the corner into a flurry of perhaps seven servants gathered by the prince's closed door. A few of them rushed around with towels and pitchers of water. Several others seemed to only be there for the gossip.

Fragments of their whispers reached Seba's ears:

"...can't find the king..."

"...just *fainted*..."

"...must be exhausted..."

As if drawn by a loud drum announcing his presence, every single one of them fell silent and looked at Seba. Dalila came to a stop, and he halted behind her, staring down each of the servants. They gazed at him in awe, as if he were the subject of one of the paintings and had come to life.

Seba straightened.

Bow, he thought. *Bow to your future king.*

And one by one, they did, albeit shallowly and without the reverence he would one day receive when the hat on his head was replaced with a crown.

"We need to see the prince," Dalila said after they had all straightened.

"The—the prince is ill, Dalila," said the servant closest to them. She blinked at Seba. "Senhor," she added.

"That's why we need to see him."

The guards turned to each other and shifted uncomfortably. Seba fixed them with his best impression of Adelina's authoritative glare. Finally, one of them nodded.

The door was opened. Dalila and Seba stepped past the guards, one of whom entered behind them.

Inside, Calixto was lying on one side of his bed. His skin was gray and sweat beaded on his brow, but his eyes were open. He seemed relatively alert while Nuno and three other servants fussed around him. One wore a long white coat and was directing the others. Like the servants outside, they all paused when they recognized Seba.

Calixto leveraged himself on his pillows to get a better look. "Now is really not the time, Senhor Pinheiro." His voice was weak.

Seba relished in that vulnerability and the familiar set of the prince's cheekbones, the way his dark brows were permanently lowered into a judgmental expression of consideration. He was so obviously the son of the man Seba had just killed.

The pistol was heavy again, but the true satisfaction would come later, when the prince made himself the last thread of his own downfall, like one of the blood-red rugs strewn around the room.

"We need to speak to you in private, Your Highness," Dalila said.

"It will have to wait."

"It's about the chains."

The prince's only tell of surprise was a slight twitch of his lips, but Seba's stomach had just flipped upside down. What game was Dalila playing?

"Everyone out," Calixto ordered. When no one moved, he shouted with a force he didn't seem currently capable of. "Out!"

The servants bustled from the room like frightened mice.

"Your Highness—" Nuno started, the only one to remain.

"*Out*, Nuno," Calixto repeated. "And clear the hall. No one listens to what is going on here, do you understand?"

Nuno's shoulders fell just slightly. His arrogance evaporated at the dismissal of the prince.

"Yes, Your Highness," he finally said. "I'll have the guards stand at either end of the hall."

"Good. Prove to me you can do more than fall asleep on the job."

"Yes, Your Highness." Nuno scurried from the room with the rest.

When the door shut gently behind them, the prince held up a

hand, warning them not to speak. The three listened to the fading footsteps and murmurs while the corridor cleared. Calixto sat up straighter in his bed and beckoned them forward.

"How did you know about the chains?" he asked quietly, with the beating pulse of a predator searching for prey.

"Lady Adelina told us," Dalila replied.

The prince's eyes darkened.

"She's not supposed to know that," he said, as if the declaration would automatically make it true.

At that moment, Seba hated Prince Calixto.

"She figured everything out," Dalila continued.

Seba tried to keep his face expressionless, but his mind was reeling. *Stop*, he wanted to shout, but she kept going.

"She's spent the weeks since Lord Simão died digging into your family's past. She found a way to communicate with him and found out why he was killed. She discovered where the witches are held and figured out how to visit Ostrea. They're working together now, for Ostrea to be free and for Lady Adelina to take your family's crown. This entire time, her relationship with Senhor Pinheiro has been a means of distraction so that your family wouldn't realize what she's been doing."

The prince's face paled with every word. Seba's hand drifted to where the pistol was hidden beneath his jacket.

Remember to use it, Adelina had said. *On anyone.*

Dalila was betraying them. She was spilling secrets Seba had not even known she was aware of. How much had her help to them been in preparation for this moment? When she would march straight into Prince Calixto's room and tell him everything, trapping Seba in the very snake pit he and Adelina had meant to rule over?

She continued, her words speeding up with momentum, as if she sensed she was signing away her life. "You fainted because the chains have been transferred to you, and you can feel the pull from Ostrea."

The prince let out something that sounded like a whimper. His hands clenched tightly around fistfuls of blanket.

"What do you—" Calixto gulped. "What do you mean?"

Seba slowly moved his hand under his jacket. His fingers closed around the cold handle of the pistol. The guards would be far enough away not to hear their conversation, but a gunshot was different. They would come running after the first one, and Seba would barely have time for the second before they were on top of him—and that was assuming his aim would be accurate at a distance of three feet.

What would he do? Jump out the window? No, it was much too high up. Try to hide himself in the room? No. Even if they didn't find him immediately, there would be no chance to escape.

Maybe he could shoot himself. Make it just serious enough he could pretend someone had tried to assassinate all three of them but had only managed Calixto and Dalila. It was probably what Adelina would have done, but the thought of shooting himself at all seemed counterintuitive.

If he took it in his shoulder and then threw the gun out the open window...

It was cloudy and growing dark, which meant it wasn't unlikely an attacker wouldn't be seen running from the palace. It wouldn't matter if they never found someone to blame...But there was the matter of freeing the witches without Dalila...

Dalila inhaled a shaky breath—*one of her last*, Seba thought— and, to his surprise, whispered, "I mean that Dom Aristides is dead. Lady Adelina slit your father's throat."

CHAPTER 41

ADELINA

Adelina's first stop was the palace's scullery—the base of the entire fixture. She received some nervous glances from passing servants, but no one dared speak to her. Somehow, they understood no one was to bother the marquise of Lis as she walked down, down, down in her red dress, with a black canvas bag clutched in one hand.

The first ingredients were easy to throw into the flames of the stone furnace, letting alchemical heat billow through the palace unseen. Salt, eggs, other herbs and plants she easily found around the kitchen. Adelina slipped on the rubbery gloves the servants used to wash dishes.

She had to clench her jaw tighter than she ever had before to keep from vomiting when she removed her uncle's small intestine from the bag. It was slimy and slippery in her trembling hands. She added it to the flames. The fire turned a momentary brilliant blue, like a bursting star, and the biological catalyst began the reaction.

She peeled the gloves from her hands with a sniff and made herself turn away from the furnace. It had already gone back to the gold of regular flame, just as Seba had said. The potion was done, and soon its heat would spread through the entire palace.

Adelina pulled on different gloves, black lace, and focused on the gentle stretch of the fabric when it caught on the dark hair of her arms. She left the bloody bag and gloves behind her, straightened her spine, and continued.

The path to her father's bedroom was empty. The sky was darkening with clouds and with night. Shadows played at the edges of the corridor and danced beyond the glow of the gas chandeliers. Her footsteps were muffled. She wished they were loud and boisterous so maybe the whole world wouldn't feel like a silent dream.

I am going to kill my father, she thought.

It was the same thought she had had weeks ago, lurking into her parents' bedroom in Lis the night Simão had died, when she had thought their deaths were the only way to save herself. She had hated that they were asleep while she was awake, while she would *always* be awake. There they had been, resting, while their son was gone and their daughter was flailing for a way not to end up the same.

Then she had found the medallion, and everything had changed.

At the time, Adelina had thought it was logic holding her back. Now she knew better. It wasn't logic that had stilled her hand. It was fear, lit by the silver glance of stars and moon that had judged her cruelly and cried for her to hold.

But that was over now. She had learned to conquer fear, to make it shrivel with a look and a reminder of the fate she had made for herself.

All hail Malves, who shall wear crowns hereafter.

It didn't matter where the prophecy had come from. She would fulfill it because she wanted to. Because she could.

This last step would be the final strike to the emotions walling her in. She would stab fear from the world while she stole her father's life. *I can because I will.*

Though her throat stung from vomit and her bloody hands were masked in black lace, Adelina soldiered forward into the gathering shadow. She had been young the last time she had tried. Foolish. She had basked in betraying light. Now, she welcomed the starless night and the cover it brought her.

Adelina had torn the stars from the sky. Their fire lit up her veins, and their dust had become her blade.

CHAPTER 42

SEBA

ady Adelina slit your father's throat.

Those were the words Dalila had said, weren't they? It was the only lie she had told Calixto from the minute they had entered the room, and yet Seba couldn't help but feel that, if he had wanted to lie about that particular event, he might have chosen something a little further from the truth.

For example, "We have no idea what happened to your father, and that's so weird that the chains have been transferred to you, but we definitely have not been involved in any of this, and also, you should trust us."

His idea seemed reasonable, but Dalila must have known what she was doing. Calixto's face had gone from uncomprehending to focused rage. It sent him lunging out of bed. He barely caught himself on the wall before tumbling to the ground.

"Your Highness!" Dalila reached out to help him.

He brushed her hand away and blinked free the lights probably bursting across his vision.

"Where is she?" the prince grunted. "Adelina."

"At the castle. We think she's—" Dalila's voice broke. She could have won an award for her performance. "We think she's working with a coven of witches and that perhaps the king was some sort of sacrifice. She might be helping the witches escape. Senhor Pinheiro and I were only able to get away because she didn't want our presence to scare them off."

"All the seas, Adelina. I knew this would happen," Calixto murmured. He stumbled away from the wall and toward the door to his bedroom. "I need to alert the guards."

Dalila held up her hands as if to stop a wild horse, but it was Seba who spoke.

"You're the king now." Seba tried to keep the disdain from his voice. "It's your job to take care of Jumaral. Do you really want to risk all of that with the involvement of the guards? Adelina is smart. She'll have prepared for an onslaught. Stealth is on your side."

Calixto glared at him. "That's ridiculous. Power is on my side, not stealth. I literally have an army."

"And Adelina has a coven of witches," Seba argued. "Maybe an army of them. Any wrong move could lead to a magical uprising, which is the last way you want to start your reign. Besides, you can't exactly afford for news of Adelina's betrayal to spread so soon, not now that she's so beloved."

The prince flinched.

"Wouldn't it be better to at least get a sense of what's going on before rushing in with the cavalry?" Seba added.

Calixto looked between the two of them. His eyes narrowed. "Why are you telling me? I've been watching Adelina for weeks. I know she's made promises to both of you. Why turn your back?"

Seba's answer came ready on his tongue, as if he had long had it prepared. "Because she killed my family. My brother and the woman who raised us are gone...because of her."

"Jasibin Guan?" There was something different in Calixto's tone that Seba couldn't read.

Seba nodded. "We drove south to Solmortém so that there would be no witnesses, and then she killed him in front of me and took his ring off his finger. She told me to propose with it, or...or she would do the same to me."

In another life, in one that wasn't so cruel, perhaps this would have been Seba's reason. It wasn't all false, even if the context was untrue. It was like the prophecy, which had become blurry and unsteady now Ostrea wasn't the goddess he had thought, but it meant no less.

Maybe, if things had been different, Adelina's actions would have driven him away rather than brought him closer. As it stood, he liked that Adelina had been raised to be ruthless. There had been enough cruelty in his life. It was about time it came from his side.

After a pause, Calixto cleared his throat. He directed his focus on Dalila. "And you? Are you still getting—"

"Because someone needs to take care of Lady Adelina," she said easily. "And I doubt that it's going to be Ostrea."

Calixto looked once more between the two of them and nodded.

A few minutes later, they were descending their final staircase out of the palace, having successfully avoided—or authoritatively told off—anyone they passed. The sun had sunk completely beneath the skyline of the city, but the royal carriage was still lit by gaslight. Its gilded edges gleamed. Calixto swerved into the overhang, where the less conspicuous carriages were kept.

"Castle," Calixto snapped at an attendant, who practically jumped out of his skin at the sight of the prince.

Minutes later, they were trundling along the streets of Fulgeo, ducking their heads to avoid being recognized.

Outside one of the many buildings on the way up to the castle, people rushed beneath the gaslight to a church. Candles flickered in its windows. Were they praying to Ostrea?

A strange bubble of laughter worked its way up Seba's throat. There was something horrifically funny about the fact no one would hear their pleas. That every minute they spent on their knees, clasped hands raised to the rafters of a church that had probably been commissioned by a cackling king who knew the truth, was an empty cry.

Seba almost hoped there was someone else, a different deity who wasn't a trapped—and, if he had to be honest, slightly sadistic—underwater creature, who would be there to respond. If nothing else, Seba knew what it was to discover a life built on lies and the aching will to not let it crumble.

Lives weren't as sturdy as centuries-old churches and castles that withstood armies. One glance at the faulty foundations and the entire thing disintegrated from the pressure. It was all a person could do to build something new from the dust.

But when they left the church and its foolish worshipers behind, the harsh stone of the castle loomed over them.

"Where is she?" Calixto asked when they approached the castle's gates. He squinted out into the night.

Seba almost laughed at the earnest grief and anger twisting the prince's handsome face.

I killed your father, and now I'm going to kill you too, Seba thought, passing his hand over the pistol at his side. *Your Majesty...*

"Is there a way to get up one of the towers?" Dalila suggested. "That way, we'll be able to see any disturbances."

Calixto cast her a wary glance.

If nothing else worked, at least Seba could probably throw the prince off a tower.

"After you." Calixto gestured them both forward in a clear show of distrust.

Dalila hesitated only a moment before stepping out. Seba followed. He tried not to look at the imposing wall of stone towering over him—a structure that had withstood armies but hopefully wouldn't stand against lightning and the thunderous will of Lady Adelina Maria Malves Ducança.

The three of them made their way up the treacherous cobblestones until they reached the guards. Calixto shoved Seba aside and said something he couldn't hear. It was apparently enough for the guards. The gates clanked open, like they had done the day before for Dalila and Seba. But this time, they weren't asked to remove anything from their persons before they were allowed to rush within its walls.

Instead of turning right, Calixto led them to the left. He raced under arches of stone, kicking up dirt and rocks. Eventually, they came to the base of a tower. Calixto sped through the small opening, taking the stone steps with a stamina Seba wouldn't have thought possible, considering the prince had barely been able to get out of bed less than an hour ago.

Seba was about to follow him when he crashed into Dalila. Her elbow had found a particularly painful spot in his sternum.

"*Ow*," he hissed. "What are you doing?"

Dalila's hands shook. She took the spool of thread-turned-wire from her pocket.

"Tie this to the tree," she said.

He did as he was told, wrapping the spool twice around the trunk nearest him and handing it back to her. Dalila's lips were white, and she swayed slightly. Her hand grasped at the fabric of his jacket.

"Can you climb?" His frustration grew with every second the prince was out of view.

She began ascending the stairs—unsteady but fast. The spool of wire unfurled as she went, tethering her to the tree below. Seba followed. His chest heaved with the effort, even as his body pushed harder, faster. Adrenaline coursed through every limb.

It was windy, cold, and getting darker. Clouds gathered above them. Seba could barely make out the source of the shriek echoing through the air as soon as he emerged from the stone steps. His eyes focused on a pink heap on the ground.

The silhouette of a prince bent over it.

"Dalila!" Seba rushed to the heap after a momentary pause.

Calixto was trying to help her up, but she had gone limp, forcing the prince to lay her against the stone. He cupped Dalila's cheek in his hand and leaned his head toward hers, as if to speak to her. But a change came over Dalila.

She twisted in the prince's grip. Her eyes turned stormy and dark, and she pressed her palms against his cheeks. Sparks clashed between them.

The prince's mouth opened, and he screamed, "No! Remember her bl—"

But then there was silence.

The light crackled and faded, leaving behind a faintly distressed-looking Dalila and a frozen Calixto. His last expression of terror had been carved into his face as if in stone.

Dalila dropped her arms to her side, but Calixto's hands stayed raised. Only his eyes were able to move. Even in the dark, with the wind and all the distractions of the world crashing around them, the prince was screaming.

"Very smooth, Dalila," Seba said.

She seemed healthier now. Some color had returned to her cheeks after being able to draw some energy from the prince.

Dalila didn't look away from Calixto. "I needed him to touch me. To work the spell."

"What did he mean?" Seba inspected Calixto too, trying to make sense of his last words.

Dalila shook her head, just as confused as he was. "I don't know."

She took a moment before rising to her feet. Dalila unbuttoned her long jacket, revealing the fire poker stored underneath. There had been points in the journey where Seba had been sure Calixto would notice Dalila had a metal rod under her clothes, but he had been distracted enough by the thought of Adelina's coup that Dalila had been able to maneuver it as she needed.

She wrapped the other end of the wire around its handle, creating a connection between their makeshift lightning rod and the earth below them.

"Hold on here." She held it out to him, and Seba wrapped his fingers around the metal. Dalila took Calixto's hands in her own and molded them around the poker as well, adding her own grip in between theirs.

Already, a storm was stewing above them, the crackle of the atmosphere drawn to the alchemically modified poker.

"Once enough moisture has gathered, I'll give it the magical jolt we talked about. There need to be three of us to stabilize the magic, but you shouldn't actually feel anything. I'm going to direct it through the prince."

"Comforting." The first drops of rain splashed against Seba's outstretched arms. The plunks of heavy drops hit against his hat.

Seba cursed Adelina under his breath while they stood, letting the storm collect above their heads. Adelina had seemed to pull herself together by the time he and Dalila left, but there was always a chance she would crack again. This time, there would be nothing left for her to do but break.

But he had chosen her, he reminded himself. If she broke, he would be the one to help her wield her jagged edges.

After about ten minutes of feeling like an idiot, standing in silence and pointing a fire poker into the air with two other people, the hair on the back of Seba's neck rose. The world was ready for lightning. They just had to make sure the lightning hit the right spot.

"Dalila," Seba said.

Dalila had been staring at her hands this entire time, eyes wide, and only looked at him when he said her name. She barely seemed aware of the rain.

"Ready?"

She nodded slowly and exhaled a steadying breath. Then her eyes closed, and he barely heard her whispering, "I'm sorry," before the world exploded and his vision was wiped clean—a white slate that flashed odd images.

A head with a shining helmet. A bloody child. Another child, this time with a crown on its head and a tree in its hand. They were there and then gone, clear and then vague.

And all he knew was pain.

CHAPTER 43

ADELINA

The guards outside the bedroom of the duke of Lis barely blinked when Adelina let herself in. Her red evening gown was a clear sign she had just come from dinner and was coming to wish her father a good night.

In another world, Adelina might have frowned at the guards, even shouted at their stupidity, screamed they should have checked every person for weapons before being allowed near the duke, no matter who they were. In this world, Adelina passed by without a word. The incompetence of these guards was her greatest advantage.

The room was dark and shadowy. Thunder boomed in the distance. Portraits hung from the walls, their eyes wide and glaring, though the only gaze Adelina truly cared about was the one from the iconography above the duke's bed.

Ostrea, Lady of the Seas, summoning Her Great Wave. Adelina hoped, in that dark, cold, lightless cave beneath the sea, the goddess was watching her.

She moved to stand near her father's bed, close enough to watch the flutter of his graying mustache and notice the faint lines around his eyes, which hid years of laughter. He was so deep in sleep, practically dead already.

Adelina had hoped he would look dead. Like an object. Instead, he looked more than ever like her father.

My couraninha, he had always called her. *My heart*.

She made herself stare at his face, forced herself to remember this was the man who had killed his son to protect a stolen legacy. This was the man who had tried to kill *her*. He was the reason Adelina had run to Ostrea, had become Ostrea's *keen knife*, forged to tear through the world he had created.

If only he had recognized how much more powerful a blade was than a heart.

Adelina moved her hand to the pocket of her gown.

As if sensing her, the duke opened his eyes. He blinked, confusion and exhaustion tainting his features. His gaze met hers. They were her eyes—the deep brown of coffee and earth and old leather books. Adelina wanted to look away, but something inside kept her stuck. She owed herself this.

Her father's breath caught. His mouth opened, but only a soft wheeze escaped.

Adelina nodded. "Your heart."

There was something sad in the duke's eyes, an understanding that might have jarred her, if she let it. He did not cry out, and neither would she.

She sucked in a breath.

Any tears that might have fallen were locked away in the pool she imagined rested somewhere in the cavity of her chest. An ocean of unshed tears.

Another breath.

Her hand steadied, its grip tightening.

Another.

The duke's chest rose and fell to match hers.

Adelina and her father stared at each other, a forgiveness passing between them. He gave the smallest of nods. She would have missed it if she had not been focused on him so intently, if the world had not contracted for the most miniscule of moments, leaving just Adelina and her father.

For a beat of her heart, she hesitated. It was the world, after all, that she fought for.

He looked so painfully familiar.

But no, she thought. A thunderous roar rose outside of the window, flashing the room with white sparks of light. *The world is big and full, and it is my fate to rule it.*

Adelina plunged the dagger into her father's chest. Above him, the golden facade of Our Lady Ostrea melted into water, like wax dripping from a candle that had burned for far too long.

It was wicked, but it had to be done.

CHAPTER 44

JAS

as couldn't have said how long it had been since he had first woken up—bloody, sore, and cold—at the gates to the land of the dead, until the Lady of the Seas crouched at his side.

The chains hanging from her slim wrists clanked against each other. She leaned her mouth to his ear and whispered, "Three days gone but only two kings dead. Your friends have failed me."

Jas met her eyes, urging himself not to shift away. The Lady of the Seas wouldn't hurt him. She had spent the last three days probing him about his life since she had last seen him, like she was a distant family member who had missed watching him grow.

He didn't know how long he had held out. Obviously not more than a day or two. Jas had not wanted to give in to the draw of conversation, the temptation of kindness. It didn't matter that Seba and Adelina had beaten him around the head and left him here. He had deserved it. Jas was the reason so many people had died, and every glance at the gates and the shadowy land beyond was a reminder of the fact he had connections to too many of the dead to ever be considered fully living.

But when the Lady of the Seas had asked about his desires, he had experienced the pull of honesty, and words formed on his lips before he could think of them.

"To be wanted," he had said.

The goddess had knelt beside him, like she did now, and had stroked his hair. Her hand caught on dried blood, and he flinched.

"Did you know that I bargained for you?" she had murmured in his ear. "Did you know that I wanted you so much that I made deals for your life, not once but twice?"

At that moment, he had expected Teodora's voice to ring through his head.

Because you are a resource to be utilized, she would say. *Not a human to be loved.*

But no voice came because there were no voices here. Even those others—Alves's screams, Isaque's desperation, Adelina's and Calixto's warnings, Seba's anger—all the ones he hadn't even known were lurking in his head at every waking moment, seemed to fade into the shadows. Here, in this world of the dead, there was no one telling him what to do or who to be. Trapped with a goddess at the gates of Her realm, he might have belonged.

Jas had cried, sobbed, screamed, with Ostrea's arm around his shoulders, her manacles cold against his neck.

I deserve it, a voice said—his own.

Ostrea had replied as if he had spoken aloud. "You don't," she had said.

Who was the liar, and who would be the next to bash his head in with a rock?

Now Ostrea spoke of Adelina and Seba. A merciless fury laced her every word. "They lied to me. I told them three days and three lives. *That* was our deal. They were going to free me."

"How do you know?" Jas was wary of the revenge formulating in the goddess's mind.

"I hear whispers. I hear the murmurs of those who die, and one is missing. Besides, if they had completed the task, these chains would have turned to smoke by now."

Jas kept his gaze steady, hoping she would not turn to him to wage punishment, but he would not be here if it hadn't been her plan.

Briefly, he allowed himself to recall his dream of disappearing, but ceasing to exist wasn't the journey he was meant to take. Jas remembered the words of the witches all those weeks ago.

Thou shalt get kings, though thou be none.

It seemed Adelina and Seba had their hands in the game for the crown. He had no choice but to join them. They would forever be inextricably linked, the beginnings and means to all each other's ends.

Maybe there would be time to disappear when the story ended.

"You want me to command the army of the dead? Kill Seba and Adelina?" Jas asked.

It was what she had traded him for, after all. Though he didn't like the idea, he had the sense deals in this place could not be broken.

"Oh, no." Ostrea shook her head like he had just suggested they drop the whole thing altogether. "Oh, no. Nothing as easy as that. No, I want them to suffer. I want them to feel what it is to have all of your hope ripped out from under you, to have all the good torn from you by the claws of monsters. I want them to feel as they have made us feel, my Jas, my Knell."

She dragged a finger up his throat and along his chin, grabbing his jaw so he was forced to meet her eyes. A wicked grin played on her lips.

"I want you to drive them mad."

Pronunciation Guide

Jumaralian utilizes many nasal sounds, so a "~" is used to mean that the following letters should not be fully pronounced, but rather finished with a hum through the nose.

People

Adelina Maria Malves Ducança [A-dheh-*lee*-na Muh-*ree*-uh *Mal*-vzh Doo-*cahn*-sa]
Ágata [*Ah*-guh-tuh]
Aristides Ducança [Ah-reesh-*tee*-dzh Doo-*cahn*-sa]
Belinha [Bel-*een*-ya]
Benigno Ducança [Buh-*neeg*-noo Doo-*cahn*-sa]
Calixto Ducança [Cuh-*leesh*-too Doo-*cahn*-sa]
Cinza [*Seen*-zuh]
Dalila Marques [Duh-*lee*-luh *Mar*-kzh]
Demyan [Dee-*myan*]
Eva Vilar [*Eh*-vuh Vee-*lar*]
Francisco [Frun-*seesh*-koo]
Gabriela [Guh-bree-*el*-uh]
Gilda [*Zheel*-duh]
Hala Amjad [*Ha*-la *Am*-jad]
Heitor Alves [*Ay*-tor *Al*-vzh]
Hermínia [Air-*meen*-ee-uh]
Iraida [Ee-*ray*-ee-duh]
Isaque Silveira [*Ee*-sak Sil-*vay*-ra]
Jasibin Guan [*Jass*-i-bin *Gwaan*]

Luísa Silveira [Loo-*ee*-zuh Sil-*vay*-ra]
Manuel Ducança [Mahn-*uelle* Doo-*cahn*-sa]
Maria [Muh-*ree*-uh]
Nuno [*Noo*-no]
Ostrea [Osh-*tray*-uh]
Rodrigues [Rod-*reegzh*]
Rosália Malves [Ro-*zah*-lee-uh *Mal*-vzh]
Sebastião Pinheiro [Se-bush-tee~*own* Peen-*yay*-roo] / Seba [*Se*-buh]
Simão Luís Malves Ducança [Seem~*own* Loo-*eezh* *Mal*-vzh Doo-*cahn*-sa]
Teodora Pinheiro [Tee-oo-*doh*-ruh Peen-*yay*-roo]

TITLES

Dona [*Dohn*-uh]
Dom [D~*ong*]
Marquise [Mar-*keez*]
Marquis [Mar-*kee*]
Infanta [Een-*fan*-tuh]
Infante [Een-*fan*-te]
Santa [*Sahn*-tuh]
Santo [*Sahn*-to]
Senhora [Sen-*yo*-ruh]
Senhor [Sen-*yor*]

JUMARALIAN WORDS

Couraninha [Coo-rah-*neen*-ya]
Encantada [En-cahn-*tah*-dhuh]
Mana [*Mah*-na]
Mano [*Mah*-no]
Rejas [*Ray*-zhuhzh]

PLACES IN JUMARAL

Fulgeo [Fool-*zhay*-oo]
Jumaral [*Zhoo*-muh-rahl]
Lis [*Leezh*]
Rio Galho [*Ree*-oo *Guy*-lhoo]
Rio Montes [*Ree*-oo *Montsh*]
Rua da Vieira [*Roo*-uh duh Vee-*ay*-ruh]
Solmortém [Sol-mor-*tay*~ng]

PLACES OUTSIDE OF JUMARAL

Abilya [Uh-*bil*-ya]
Dumatsya [Doo-*maht*-zya]
Geirida [Guy-*reed*-a]
Huojen [Hoo-*oh*-jen]
Nolofali [No-lo-*fahl*-ee]

Acknowledgments

This book has been the product of five years of writing and editing and thinking, which for me has also been five years of starting and finishing my bachelor's, starting my master's, living in seven different cities, and meeting lots of people along the way.

I would be remiss not to first thank the wondrous Kamilah Cole, my mentor for Author Mentor Match way back in 2022 and my constant cheerleader, no matter how long it takes me to reply to her texts.

Of course this book would be nowhere without my agent, Allegra Martschenko, who immediately saw the vision. There is no better email explainer, advocate, or hype person than them.

The team at Keylight Books/Turner Publishing is truly unmatched. Thank you to Amanda Chiu Krohn and Ashlyn Inman for their helpful edits and guidance; to Bill Ruoto, M. S. Corley, and David Reuss for an epic cover and a beautiful map; to Kendal Cliburn and Jane Flautt for their marketing expertise; and to all the others that had a hand in getting this book published and out to readers.

And now to my lovely friends: Endless thanks to Annie for dealing with me secretly writing and stressing over a book for the entire time we lived together (I committed too hard to the English minor bit and became an author). No human can function on this earth without a couple of three-person group chats to turn to at the most minor inconvenience, so thanks go to Sharan, Siddhie, Noa, and Amund for the two group chats that make up my social life.

This first book is dedicated to my parents, Leonor and Sean, who read to me every night before bed until I was far too old and have continued to listen to my hours-long rants about whatever books I'm reading. My mom, in particular, has been integral to this story, making sure my sister and I grew up in the US with knowledge of her home in Portugal—its language, its castles, and its delicious pastries (bits and pieces of which I borrowed while creating Jumaral). Thank you also to my sister, Helena, who was always one of my first readers (though not this time haha), and my brother-in-law, Nate. Somehow the two of them created my niece, Lily, who is my absolute favorite person in the world and the best library story-time buddy a girl could ask for. Lily, at the bold age of two months old, was one of the first people I told about this book, though she will need to wait about twelve more years to read it herself. Hopefully she likes it because I really want her to think her tia is cool.

There have also been so many family members and friends and strangers that have bought, hyped, and spread the word about *My Keen Knife*—thank you for all the love you have given this book. Among those supporters have been my teachers, all the way from preschool to university, who supported my love of writing, introduced me to stories like *Macbeth*, and continue to show unwavering care and energy for the lives of me and their other students long after we've left the classroom. So thank you to all the teachers, educators, librarians, and others working tirelessly to get stories to the people who need them.

And thank you to William Shakespeare, obviously.

ABOUT THE AUTHOR

Author photo courtesy of Helena Davis

Ana Davis is a fantasy writer and currently pursuing dual master's degrees in what amount to Human Rights and International Conflict (the actual names are a mouthful). She recently graduated from Northeastern University with a bachelor's degree in International Affairs. Ana was a mentee for round nine of Author Mentor Match, and she remains far too invested in the books she read in high school English class.

www.ingramcontent.com/pod-product-compliance
Lightning Source LLC
Chambersburg PA
CBHW060223030726
47499CB00004B/1172